always a
bridesmaid

always a bridesmaid

USA TODAY BESTSELLING AUTHOR
CINDI MADSEN

Entangled Publishing, LLC
10940 S Parker Road
Suite 327
Parker, CO 80134
Visit our website at www.entangledpublishing.com.

Amara is an imprint of Entangled Publishing, LLC.

Edited by Stacy Abrams
Cover design by Hang Le
Cover art by
LightFieldStudios/iStock
AJ_Watt/iStock
GlobalP/GettyImages
Pollyana Ventura/GettyImages
ozgurcankaya/iStock
Interior design by Toni Kerr

Print ISBN 978-1-64063-904-1
ebook ISBN 978-1-64063-905-8

Manufactured in the United States of America

First Edition June 2020

AMARA

for new adult readers

Getting Lucky Number Seven
Anatomy of a Player
Crazy Pucking Love
Confessions of a Former Puck Bunny
Until You're Mine
Until We're More

for teen readers

All the Broken Pieces
Losing Romeo
The Cipher series
Demons of the Sun
Operation Prom Date

To my sisters, Randa and April.
Sisters are our first and forever friends,
and I'm so glad that you two are mine.

CHAPTER ONE

The ironic thing about whenever Violet Abrams entered Uncertainty, Alabama, was how uncertain she felt about being there. It hardly helped matters that back home, in what *used* to be her favorite chapel, a grand ceremony was taking place without her.

Yep, the irony was strong today.

Maybe she was using *ironic* the wrong way—words had never been her strong point. She captured images that could say a thousand words without uttering a single one.

Or she used to, anyway.

Before a jerkface who'd promised *always and forever* had made a mockery of her best-laid plans. Obviously he hadn't meant it in the classic *every single occasion, without exception, without ending* definitions.

Which brought her to the annoying word *never*. As in how she'd sworn that she'd *never, ever* live in Uncertainty, Alabama, again. Not unless someone dragged her kicking and screaming.

And yet, there was the sign that welcomed her to town.

Memories from the last time she'd been in Alabama drifted to the surface, prompting her to eye the rearview mirror.

Violet jerked her chin level and gripped the steering wheel that much harder. She was trying to let the past go. Finding silver linings and redirecting her negative notions and emotions. "While my closest girlfriends are in Spanx, binding dresses, and pinchy high heels, I'm rocking the hell out of these comfy yoga pants."

The clerk at the 7-Eleven she'd stopped at earlier to refuel and re-caffeinate had definitely noticed. He'd checked her out quite thoroughly, and considering she had on yesterday's smudged makeup, she was slightly flattered.

Even if he had focused a bit too much on her butt.

Funny enough, the woman in the chip aisle had also examined Violet's backside. And she'd wondered if she was accidentally putting out the wrong vibe, thanks to recently swearing off men.

It wasn't until Violet had removed the nozzle from the gas tank and caught her reflection in her car's side mirror that everything clicked into place. Turned out her lilac yoga pants were light enough to display the bright pink hearts and scribbled *ciao for now* on her panties.

Suffice it to say, Victoria's Secret was out.

While it'd been super embarrassing, at least she'd worn her pretty underwear and not the granny kind.

Look at me, being all optimistic.

The brakes squealed as she pulled her car to a stop in front of Maisy's Bakery, and the binder Violet despised but couldn't quite bring herself to toss slid out from underneath the passenger seat.

So much work. So many beautiful images that'd once brought her joy. All contained in a bulging, glittery purple binder that made her want to cry. "I'm working on positive thinking right now, thank you very much. And you're not helping, Mr. Binder, so just go to your…room."

Violet stretched over the console and shoved the

cursed object back under the seat, along with the discarded soda bottle and empty candy wrappers from her four-hour road trip from Pensacola, Florida.

Ooh, what if I call this a sabbatical?

No, a journey of self-discovery. Like Eat, Pray, Love. *Or* Wild, *but with less walking and outdoor shit.*

The last page of her inspiring memoir formed shape in her mind: *And in the end, I discovered eating pastries in the middle of an air-conditioned room and boinking burly mountain men who showered on a regular basis was the true way to happiness.*

Ah, I feel enlightened already. Since she was an all-or-nothing girl, Violet brought her hands up in prayer position and added a "Namaste."

It worked like a charm, too. Her uncertainty, along with the other crap twisting at her insides, eased as she took in the gilded letters that spelled out MAISY'S BAKERY across the window.

Excitement fired through her, and she pulled on the sides of her messy bun until the elastic band hit the crown of her head. To ensure her butt got less attention this go-round, Violet snatched her hoodie off the box in the front seat.

Multicolored frames stuck up from the box, providing a striped peek of the pictures inside. Just enough to determine which wedding they'd been taken at. The jeweled magenta headband meant Leah, the first from their crew to tie the knot. The other picture was upside down, the mauve dresses Amanda had chosen for her bridesmaids on display, along with the strappy silver heels that'd cut off circulation to their toes.

Seven used to be Violet's lucky number. But Maisy's wedding marked her seventh time acting as a bridesmaid, and after how disastrously that turned out, Violet had given up all things wedding-related.

Problem was, it was hard not to think of weddings when a) your biggest jobs involved them and b) your favorite pictures were from your closest friends' weddings.

Think about Maisy and cupcakes and baby cheeks. She wouldn't even have to work on stifling her warring emotions once she got ahold of those three things.

Violet climbed out of her car and hit the auto lock button, even though Uncertainty was one of those idyllic places where the only crime was not waving.

All her belongings were inside, though, including the expensive Canon 5D Mark IV camera that'd once felt like another limb.

I'll get there again. Maisy and I have a plan, and everything will be better if I can just make it through the last few hours of the day.

The door to the bakery chimed as she stepped inside, and Maisy was waving to a customer as she said, "Bye. Have a sweet day!"

"Violet!" Maisy shouted, loud enough that the customer jumped. Her half sister rounded the counter at a sprint, and Violet took a few large strides herself.

A moment before they met in the middle, she hesitated, a pinch dubious about going all in, since they'd never done the squealing/huge-hug combo before.

But Maisy closed the last foot of space and gave her a hug worthy of a python, squeezing Violet's breath out over her shoulder, and it'd never felt so reassuring to be breathless.

Due to their complicated family dynamics, they

hadn't been close growing up, and the embraces they'd previously shared were quick and robotic. Their conversations had been about the same up until the past few months.

"I'm so happy you're here," Maisy said. "Obviously the bakery is in severe need of a sprucing—not that you have to get started right away. I've just been waiting all day, and you're actually here, and in case you can't tell, I'm super excited."

"I think the term is 'high on sugar.'"

Maisy laughed and leaned in, as if she were about to divulge trade secrets. "I also invested in an espresso machine. After too many nights with too little sleep, it went from a want to a need."

The chime over the door sounded, and Maisy glanced at the family of five walking in.

"Don't mind me," Violet said, stretching her neck from side to side to work out the kinks the long drive had left her with. "I'll have a look around and start making plans. We'll catch up once you close shop for the day."

Maisy bobbed her head and hustled over to assist the family studying the glass display of treats. Her chatter filled the air, and Violet wondered just how many espressos and cupcakes Maisy had downed today. And if she would hook her up with enough sugar and caffeine to counteract the bittersweet thickness coating her throat.

Being here was…surreal.

Speaking of surreal, let's focus on art! Violet propped her fists on her hips and studied the dingy walls of the bakery. They definitely needed freshening, and she was confident she could do better than bleak white walls and sparse, dusty decorations.

The wall underneath the front counter could use a duskier color that'd turn the glass display into more of a focal point. The wood floors were beautiful, and with a bit of buffing and perhaps a coat of varnish, they'd be perfection.

There's a lot of potential. As she watched Maisy place her sugary works of art in a pale-pink box while beaming at her customers, it was so obvious her sister was doing what she loved. Out of nowhere, a wave of affection slammed into Violet so strongly her knees wobbled.

It was so good to see Maisy in person again.

She'd thought the phone calls would fade, especially once Isla had been born—a whole month early. New babies were time-consuming, so Violet completely understood.

But if anything, she and Maisy talked even more.

And when Violet had broken down, spilled her guts, and added how much today was going to suck, Maisy insisted she come and stay with her for a while. At least until she got her feet back under her.

"I don't want to impose," Violet had said. Maisy had clucked her tongue and told her that with her husband deployed, she was desperate for company. Plus, she happened to have an extra room, no charge.

Not wanting to feel like a freeloader, she'd insisted they strike a deal: Violet would renovate the bakery while she was in town.

Which, if she had it her way, would only be a month. Two, tops.

"Have a sweet day," Maisy said, bidding farewell to the final customer. She flipped the sign on the door to closed and walked to where Violet stood, still staring at the wall.

Blank canvases used to give her happy tingly vibes. Sadly, the spark didn't magically ignite and spread.

"So?" Maisy asked. "What do you think?"

"The place has great bones, as they say. And the flooring is amazing." Violet stomped on it, as if that were a proper test. "Fresh paint, color accents, and well-placed artwork, and it'll reflect how people feel when they bite into one of your delicious desserts."

Maisy's smile was a lot like her mother's, but unlike the "smiles" Cheryl Hurst gave Violet, Maisy's was genuine. "I'm so glad you're here to help. When I first bought the place, I had to focus on updating the appliances. After that, I hardly had money for ingredients. Now I finally have the means to revamp the rest, but, thanks to my adorable baby, not the time. Plus, I'm no good at decor."

"Yeah, I remember your childhood bedroom. It was like a color-blind person had decorated it."

Maisy shoved Violet's shoulder. "*Hey*. It wasn't that bad."

Violet huffed a laugh. "As someone who's been trained in complementary colors, I can confidently say it was. You also had a poster of that caveman-esque dude with the big head, large nose, and oddly tiny mouth above your bed."

The gasp Maisy made echoed off the wall. "It was a *One Tree Hill* poster, and you must not've watched the show if you don't understand the allure of Nathan Scott."

"I *have*, and Lucas Scott was the better-looking brother by far."

"Seriously? He has a squishy face. And he never fully opens his eyes."

Violet started to argue but then slowly let her mouth close. "Fair point on that last part, but he had great hair. Besides, guys with the pale skin and dark hair combo aren't my type."

Maisy swept a chestnut strand that'd fallen out of her ponytail behind her ear. "You'd rule a guy out just because of that?"

While Violet had never accepted the Hurst last name, she didn't have a choice about sharing the same dark reddish-brown shade as her father, half sister, and half brother. Whenever she visited, it was the trait that left the locals saying "Oh, you've got so much Hurst in you."

As if that wasn't a disturbing way to put it.

During her teenage years, she'd highlighted her hair uber-blond to avoid blending in to the family she'd never belonged to.

Sure, staying away from anyone semi-resembling her father was a flawed theory at best—one that hadn't done a great job saving her from pain—but she clung to it anyway. Too many other things had changed in the last several months, and she craved the familiar. "I have a very precise system. Basically, I look at a guy, and if he's a hot douchebag who strings me along for years and years, I decide he's the one."

Thanks to being based in reality, the joke didn't quite land.

Before Maisy could send any pity her way, Violet swiped a hand through the air. She'd gotten good at pretending losing an entire decade of plans didn't get to her. "Anyway, that was my old system, before swearing off men in general. Who needs 'em?"

"I do." Maisy sighed, a dreamy lilt to her words when she added, "I just wish mine wasn't so far away."

Violet winced, and not only because the words pricked the spot over her heart. "I'm sorry. That was insensitive of me. I know how much you miss him, and Travis is one of the good ones."

This time, it was Maisy who waved a hand through the air. "Not a big deal. I get what you mean." She draped her arm around Violet's shoulders and rested her head against hers. "I do hope that someday, when you meet the right person, you'll change your mind."

A nice sentiment, but when it came to the "right" person, Violet had decided it wasn't in the cards for her, and most days, she was fine with that.

It wasn't like getting married was her main goal in life. And in spite of what her ex or anyone else who'd been around her this past decade might think, her near-obsession with planning her own nuptials truly hadn't been about the wedding.

Back when the photography muse was being kind, weddings had been her favorite jobs. They runneth over with emotion, and Violet had mastered the art of capturing unscripted moments: the father of the bride choking up as he no longer became the main man in his daughter's life; grandparents reminiscing on the day they'd wed as they shared a dance; kids sneaking cake in their fancy clothes; and the bridesmaids laughing together, working to ensure the bride had the perfect day.

Then there were the vows.

That was her very favorite part of weddings and what always made her cry. Declaring to everyone that you were *choosing* this person to spend your entire life with. Pledging to continue doing the little things that'd make them feel cherished.

Always and forever… The prick over her heart turned to a stab, one that reopened old wounds.

"Violet? You okay?"

Violet blinked, annoyed to find wetness clinging to her lashes. "Sorry. I'm so used to working in silence that I began mentally flipping through color schemes."

Skepticism flitted through the tight press of Maisy's mouth, but she was nice enough not to call her a liar, liar, wedding plans on fire.

"Does this mean my idea might work?" Maisy asked, a whole heap of hope in her voice.

During art school, Violet had dabbled in several mediums. The theory was that taking on a low-pressure job would get her creative juices flowing.

As the image of the renovated bakery took shape in Violet's mind, the tingles she'd searched in vain for earlier flickered.

"Stripes or large dots in cheery colors will go on that dividing wall." A familiar buzz skated across her skin and kickstarted her pulse. It wasn't as strong as when she used to peer through her camera lens, but it whispered that passion was still somewhere inside her. "We could also paint and re-cover the chairs to match."

"I trust you," Maisy said, and a string tugged in the center of Violet's chest.

Maisy's phone chimed. "Time to pick up Isla from day care. I used to be organized, but having her zapped my brain. I kept losing track of time, so I set an alarm. Occasionally I bring her back to finish up, and today is gonna be one of those days."

"Do you mind if I stay and brainstorm?" In addition to wanting to take advantage of the creative spark, Violet didn't want to see people in town. Namely, her father and his wife. With everything else messing with her head today, she couldn't handle an uncomfortable interaction with the rest of the Hursts.

"Not at all." Maisy slipped off her apron and tossed it on a nearby table. "But could you do me a favor? I poured batter for a couple batches of cupcakes but was waiting for the oven to preheat. Can you stick them in for me?"

"Just stick them in?" A simple request, but Violet's nerves stretched thin at the idea of anything involving baking. She'd told Maisy she would gladly assist with the selling and eating of goodies but not to expect help in the kitchen.

"Yep. And set the timer for fifteen minutes." Maisy swung open the door. "The place isn't far, so I'll be back soon."

Just put in the cupcakes and set a timer. Sounds simple enough.

"Before I forget, are there almonds in any of the pastries? Not that I'm going to eat everything, but I also might eat everything, and I'd rather not go into anaphylactic shock when I do."

Maisy laughed. "Steer clear of the poppy seed muffins and the bear claws. You can see the slivered almonds on the top of those, though. Other than that, chow down."

Violet rounded the wall that separated the front of the bakery from the kitchen. She found two giant cupcake tins, the batter pink, cream, and brown. Suddenly she was craving Neapolitan ice cream.

Heat blasted her face as she opened the enormous oven door. *Wow. I bet this fancy equipment practically bakes the cupcakes itself.*

Her phone chimed and then rang as she put in the second tin. Violet fished the vibrating thing out of her pocket and, when it was the college roommate responsible for her first time as a bridesmaid, answered. "Hello?"

"Oh, hon," Leah said. "How you holding up?"

Shit. Violet should've known better than to answer. All this conversation was going to do was remind her exactly what day it was. "I'm fine. I'm with my sister and—"

"Your wedding would've been so much classier. The bride's gown is totally making guests uncomfortable. Girl's one movement away from a nip slip, and I'm about to passive aggressively play 'Rock Your Body' so we can relive Justin Timberlake ripping off Janet Jackson's top and calling it a wardrobe malfunction. Amanda and I sent you pics through the group chat so you can see for yourself."

Violet shut the oven door with her hip and stared at the strange buttons and controls. And she'd thought the stove in her apartment was perplexing. She hit one, five, and searched for the timer button.

"Benjamin made his choice, and honestly I hope they're happy together." The words scraped on the way out, leaving her throat achy and raw. Okay, so while she was trying to be the bigger person, she wasn't quite there yet.

"I give the marriage less than a year," Leah said.

"Six months," Violet heard in the background, meaning Amanda was chiming in and they were seated next to each other.

"Just promise me if the bastard comes crawling back to you, you won't take him back."

The *beep, beep* sounded as Violet pushed more buttons. The digital readout didn't begin counting down, so she tried a few more. "I won't, I swear. Right now, I'm trying not to think about him or the wedding at all."

Or the fact that he popped the question at month two and got married within six months of meeting her.

"I know, I know. We just thought it'd make you feel better to know that Crystal went the tacky route. You're so much funnier and more down to earth…"

AKA, plainer, with a witty personality that made up for the plainness.

"But now I'm also thinking…" Leah shifted from gossip mode to weepy in two seconds flat, which meant she'd been enjoying the open bar. "It's my fault for introducing you two in the first place. I wasn't even going to come to this sham of a wedding on principle, but Ben is Casey's best friend"—*sniff*—"just know that I know the jackass never deserved you. You're going to find someone so much better."

Informing Leah she'd sworn off men would only make her cry more. Then she'd grab Amanda so they could FaceTime and lament how it was supposed to be Violet. Perhaps even suggest single friends, even though they'd been in the same group of friends forever and knew all the same people.

Violet assured Leah she was fine and suggested she go enjoy dancing with her husband, who was a great guy regardless of his taste in friends.

Since she wasn't sure if she'd set the timer right, she

noted the minutes on her phone, doing her best to ignore the group chat they'd titled "The Bridesmaid Crew." Since her friends from college had busy lives and were active at different times, they'd created it to stay connected no matter what.

Beads of sweat formed, the heat driving Violet toward the front of the bakery, where she snagged a frosted sugar cookie.

As she perched herself on the edge of a table, she pressed her phone screen against the worn fabric of her yoga pants. It began to burn her thigh, urging her to flip her cell over and study the pictures of her ex's wedding that she absolutely didn't want to see.

Why would she torture herself?

As if someone else were in charge of her wrist, it twisted. Without permission, her thumb tapped on Leah's message.

Then there they were. Her ex-basically-fiancé and his blushing bride.

I'd blush, too, if I were wearing that gown. The neckline of Crystal's dress plunged halfway to her belly button. On a slender, small-breasted woman, it might look classy, but Crystal's fake boobs were about to make their escape. The tapered waist showed off the fact that, unlike Violet, Crystal didn't need to lose twenty pounds, and the skirt and train were detailed with—what else?—crystals.

Maybe the gown was on the risqué side, but there was no denying how radiant the bride was.

Leah had added a GIF of Heidi Klum making a face, the word *wow* along the bottom, and Amanda had added a *yikes* one that showed Britney Spears pulling the kind of face you did when you'd just seen something bad.

With the torture already in full swing, Violet shoved the last of the cookie into her mouth and scrolled to the next picture—this one sent by Amanda.

Violet's heart ceased beating when she spotted the bride's bouquet and the color of the bridesmaids' dresses. The image blurred as her eyes filled with unshed tears.

There were only so many colors, but *purple*? Seriously? Benjamin couldn't tell Crystal, *Whoa, hold on there, Violet's favorite color is purple, and I've seen pictures in a dream wedding binder that are eerily similar to everything you've picked out*?

How dare they take that from me. My name freaking means purple!

No longer fully in control of her body, Violet stormed out of the bakery. She yanked open the passenger door to her car and dug around for the stupid binder she never wanted to see again.

Her bun snagged on one of the screws underneath the seat, prickling pain accompanying the tug that freed it. A mad sort of dizziness set in as she withdrew the binder.

As if to spite her, it glittered in the last rays of daylight.

Violet grabbed the lighter out of her glovebox and stormed into the alleyway beside the bakery.

"Someday, my curvy ass!" *Someday* had been Benjamin's favorite lie. The way he strung her along for an entire decade.

We'll get married after we graduate college.

After I land this job.

Once we have more money saved.

I'm so stressed right now, babe. Let's wait till after I get the promotion.

Someday soon, but I really need a new car, and it's the smarter investment.

After every single wedding they attended together—most of which she'd been a part of—Benjamin would lovingly peer into her eyes and say, *Babe, we're next.*

Ten years she'd waited.

Toward the end of Maisy's reception, where she'd once again been a bridesmaid, Violet had gone in search of her boyfriend. She'd resolved to tell him it was high time they set a date and do the damn thing already.

Only when she finally found him in an abandoned room of the reception hall, one of the female wedding guests had been straddling him, her skirt up around her waist and Benjamin's tongue down her throat.

"That *asshole.*" Violet chucked her wedding binder against the outside wall of the bakery. Satisfaction mixed with the anger coursing through her as she watched pages scatter across the dirty ground.

She squatted and ripped out more pages, which wasn't easy to do, since she'd slid everything into reinforced plastic sheet protectors. She shook loose the glossy magazine spreads with their beautiful tiered cakes and bridal dresses and bouquets, all in varying shades of purple.

That should be enough kindling to set the rest on fire, she thought as she rolled her thumb over the lighter.

A blue-and-orange flame flickered to life, and she couldn't wait until it grew and decimated her former hopes and dreams.

• • •

"For the bridesmaid dresses, I'm thinking super-low-cut tops with short skirts," Ford said as he flopped on his couch for the first wedding-planning meeting of what he'd been informed would be many. "Not short enough that I've gotta tuck my junk, but I want to show off the muscular thighs my firefighter training has given me."

Addie, one of his very best friends and the bride-to-be, giggled.

Lexi blushed.

The three German shepherd puppies that'd been delivered to him earlier this week ran amok.

A lot of life-changing events had happened within his tight-knit group of friends last fall. His buddy Shep—Will Shepherd to most everyone else—had married Lexi, the blond debutante currently tilting her head at Ford. Then, in the middle of all the pre-wedding activities, two of his other closest friends had gone and fallen in love.

At first, Ford had hated the idea of Tucker and Addie. But once he'd seen how hard Tucker worked to win over the girl beside him, how good they were together, and—most importantly—realized the group wasn't going to be split by their merger, he got on board.

Now they were soon to be hitched.

When Murph, known as Addison Murphy to the rest of the town, had asked him to be her bridesdude/man of honor, of course he'd said yes. He'd do most anything for his friends.

Lexi, one of the other bridesmaids—along with Addie's sister, Alexandria, who was lucky enough to get out of wedding planning on account of living the next state over — withdrew a giant binder and a few thick magazines from her bag. She tossed them on his coffee table next to the dog toys and the remotes, where they starkly contrasted the pile of *Alabama Outdoor News*.

"This should get us started," she said, notebook and a pen at the ready.

"Started?" Addie blinked at the stack. "Are we startin' a fire? 'Cause that's what that pile of nonsense makes me wanna do."

Lexi sighed and crossed one leg over another, the skirt of her red dress flaring with the motion.

Like he said, he'd do anything for Murph, who'd always been one of the guys, but wedding planning tiptoed mighty close to the line. Her brown eyes were as wide as he assumed his were, though, and they'd sworn long ago to never leave a man behind.

Since he was the best dude and Addie didn't know the first thing about being a girly girl, Lexi was the only one experienced in everything a wedding entailed, so here they were.

Staring at a color-coded binder.

Addie reached for the six-pack of Naked Pig Pale Ale beer. After taking a large glug from her bottle, she hesitantly lifted the binder off the table.

Give him a fire to fight, a lost hiker to find, or a destructive force of nature to contend with, and he'd jump right in, no fear. But wedding to-do lists filled with line upon line of gibberish? Well, he was about to cry for his mommy.

Time to nut up. Unfortunately, he needed to put the puppies through search and rescue training after this meeting, so he'd be getting through it sober.

Ford grabbed a non-alcoholic beer and cracked it open.

Murph flipped to the section marked TABLES and blinked at the contents. "Um, I guess we'll start with... table decorations?" She glanced at him, as if he had any idea what kind of decorations would go on tables. Wasn't that what plates and food were for? Everything else just got in the way of eating.

The leather of his couch creaked as he shifted closer and peered over Addie's shoulder. "Sure. Those tablecloths look nice," he said, gesturing to the rows of multicolored fabric.

Lexi frowned. "Those aren't for tables; they're for the chairs."

"Chairs need tablecloths?" he asked, and Lexi sighed.

Addie nudged him with her elbow. "Yeah, didn't you know that, Ford? That way, instead of using the tablecloth as a napkin, you've got one on your chair, too."

"Smart."

They laughed. Lexi pursed her lips.

Over the course of being one of Shep's "groomsmen," Addie had grown close to Lexi, but moments like this brought out how different they were. If it were up to Addie and Tucker, they'd keep the ceremony small. Around here, though, weddings were as much for family members and townsfolk as the couple, and it was easier to go with the flow than catch flack the rest of their lives.

The puppies barked as they began play fighting, yelps and growls filling the air. Pyro, Ford's trusty black

German shepherd, lifted his head from his bed by the fireplace. While his dog was over the extra company already, Pyro couldn't help but help. It was why he was the best rescue dog in all of Alabama.

That and because Ford, who trained K-9 units for search and rescue missions, had trained Pyro himself, from the time he was a bouncy puppy.

Lexi glanced at the dogs. "I'm not denying your new litter is ridiculously cute, but we can't plan a wedding like this. They're so noisy."

"Noisy" was a given in the beginning. "You'll be amazed at how much better they are in a week or so."

Ford hadn't named the puppies yet, but the biggest troublemaker lifted his leg and peed on Lexi's high-heeled shoe.

To her credit, she didn't shriek or even scold the puppy. The arched eyebrow she shot Ford, on the other hand, made it clear *he* was in the doghouse. "Can I please have an hors d'oeuvre to go with my odeur d'pee? Oh, that's right. You didn't make any."

To say Lexi was used to playing hostess was an understatement. Normally he'd let her have at it, but if he left the puppies alone too long, they'd destroy the house. "I brought out the tub of jerky and a six-pack of beer, didn't I?"

"I think we just picked out the wedding meal," Addie said. "Jerky and beer for all."

"Hear, hear." Ford tapped the end of his piece of jerky to Addie's, and then they both took giant bites.

Judging from the unamused expression on Lexi's face, they were *both* in the doghouse now.

"We'll have the next meeting at your place," he said in a placating tone.

"I know it's overwhelming, and I'm here to help." Lexi leaned over the coffee table and flipped to the tab marked COLOR SCHEME. "Once we pick your colors and pin down other major details, the rest will fall into place."

"All's I care about is that it's not crimson," Addie said. "No offense," she added because they'd given Shep shit about crimson being one of his wedding colors. "But I work for Auburn, and it'd be embarrassing to have the coaches at my wedding wonderin' if I'm a traitor."

Ford lifted his can of beer. "War Eagle!"

Lexi pinched the bridge of her nose. "Not this again. As I've explained, *I just like red*. And while I realize I said 'pick whatever you want,' an orange wedding would be hideous. I doubt you want your bridesmaids to look like they recently broke out of prison."

"Considerin' the guy next to me, it wouldn't be a total shock," Addie teased.

Pyro lifted his head and barked, and Ford's spine went stick straight. From the puppies, he wouldn't think twice, but Pyro didn't bark unless there was a reason.

"What is it?"

Pyro jumped out of his bed and barked again, his nose aimed toward the fireplace.

"McGuire," Addie said to him, plenty of scolding in that one word. "Didn't we talk about turning off the scanner and being present? About how you've got to keep yourself from getting burned out?"

His friends got on him about how he never took a break and answered every call, no matter how big or small. Sometimes they were the next town over and he'd show up about the time things were wrapping up.

He was attempting to regain more balance in his life, but so far, he'd mostly failed.

Problem was, he never wanted another "what if?" on his conscience.

When Ford heard the chirp of his beeper—not the scanner that he *had* turned off—he stood and retrieved it from the mantel. He hit the recall button and listened to the message.

Smoke reported at Maisy's Bakery.

"It's a fire." While there were several paramedics throughout the county, there weren't many volunteer firefighters in town. It was almost a relief he had a solid reason to take the call so he didn't have to wonder how it'd gone all night, and Lexi and Addie both nodded their understanding.

The radio crackled as Ford clicked it on and depressed the button. "I'm responding to the situation at Maisy's Bakery."

"Copy that," dispatch said. "The caller said there's not much smoke, but she wanted to err on the side of caution. Darius is near the station and is gonna bring the truck, just in case."

Ford's keys jingled as he scooped them off the mantel, and Pyro stood at his side, ready to leap into action. "I'll meet him there."

• • •

I realize now what we were missing. Why I could never set a wedding date.

The explanation Benjamin had given Violet after catching him *in flagrante* flayed her right open, but the javelin to her exposed heart came when he explained that with Crystal, it was love at first sight.

"And when you think about it," he had said, delivering the final, decimating blow, "it's a good thing she and I met before you and I made a huge mistake and got married."

"I'll show you mistake," Violet said now, the metal gears digging into the pad of her thumb as she reignited the flame that'd flickered out. She lowered the lighter to the crumpled bridal magazine pages, thinking how cathartic it would be to watch the blaze consume the entire pile.

Smiling brides shriveled in on themselves as the edges curled and turned black. Plastic sheet protectors melted to the papers Violet had reverently cut out to add to her collection.

Then a breeze kicked up, the mound she'd formed glowing bright orange. A couple of partially burned pages fluttered and blew off the top of the pile, one landing against a dried-out weed, which caught.

"No, no, no." She stomped it out, chased after the other sheet, and did the same to it. As her heart pounded from the adrenaline, she thought of how easily the fire could spread and burn out of control.

Just like that, Violet returned to her body, the possessed, jilted woman no longer in control.

This was stupid. Dangerous.

And in the end, nothing would change.

Violet peeled off her hoodie and used it to beat out the blaze, adding stomping to her efforts once the flames flickered and sputtered. As soon as she was sure the pile had been extinguished, she plopped on the hard ground.

Defeat weighing heavy on her shoulders, she slid

her melty binder from underneath the charred heap, gathered it to her chest, and let loose the tears she'd tried to hold back all day.

She sniffed and swore she smelled smoke—different than the scent that'd accompanied the burning of the magazine pages. Less…chemical, maybe?

She lowered her mangled binder and stared at it, double-checking that it wasn't aflame.

Her eyes stung, and acrid fumes burned her nose.

What the—? Violet sprang to her feet when she saw puffs of gray belching from the back door of the bakery. "The cupcakes!"

She sprinted over and tapped the handle with her fingertips before wrapping her hand around the metal. When it didn't scald her palm, she tugged.

Luckily, the door wasn't locked. As she rushed inside and took in the hazy air and the flames flickering around the edges of the oven door and crawling up the wall, she didn't feel so lucky.

A quick scan didn't reveal the location of a fire extinguisher, so Violet grabbed a potholder and tried to yank open the door.

It wouldn't budge, and intensifying heat seeped into her skin, making it impossible to hold on.

"Wait. Why are you at six hundred degrees?" she shouted at the oven when she caught the temperature on the display.

Since the appliance didn't answer and the smoke was growing thicker, Violet dialed 911, hoping it wouldn't take forever for someone to respond in this dinky town.

CHAPTER TWO

The engine of his Cummins Diesel Dodge Ram growled as Ford depressed the gas pedal and rocketed down the back streets of town before slowing and cutting across to Main.

He nosed his truck into the alleyway between Maisy's Bakery and Lottie's fabric store, and sure enough, there was smoke.

Ford did a quick assessment.

Color: white. Volume: little. Velocity: low. Density: thin.

Charging in alone was never a good idea, but waiting until the fire went from small to large wasn't a stellar idea, either.

He leaped out of the truck and grabbed his ax, along with his medic kit. Fires weren't very common this time of year, so his bunker gear was in the firetruck.

His pulse skyrocketed when he heard a female voice yell, "Why won't you open? I can't put out the fire if you won't let me in."

The hacking cough that followed had him rushing toward the open door, Pyro hot on his heels.

A woman who looked like Maisy, yet not quite, stood in front of the oven. She batted at the spitting flames with a potholder as she rambled about her sister trusting her and the "shittiest day ever."

Ford stepped between her and the oven, nudging her backward. The sweltering air seeped through his shirt and pressed heavy against his skin. Experience took the wheel, his focus narrowing to clearing the building. "Is anyone else inside?"

A cough burst from the brunette, followed by a wheeze. "No, it's just me. Which is why—"

"I've got it from here, ma'am. Please exit the building."

Pyro gently bit onto her pants and tugged, trying to coax her to safety.

Since she wasn't doing as instructed, Ford nearly used his surge of adrenaline to scoop her up and rush her outside. But his brain had already launched into analytical mode, spinning over the facts as fast as his heart hammered in his chest.

There wasn't anyone else in the bakery, and the fire was contained to the oven. *Cutting off the source of heat will be the safest, fastest course of action for everyone.*

Ford pulled his shirt up over his nose and mouth, focusing on inhaling and exhaling through his nostrils. "Stand back."

Pyro bumped the woman's legs with his snout, herding her toward the open doorway, and she seemed to notice his dog for the first time. She backed away, giving Ford much-needed space.

The damn plug didn't want to come free of the outlet, and a growing sense of urgency pounded away at the base of his skull. He gripped the handle of his ax and used the edge of the blade to pry the hard plastic free.

With the oxygen in the oven running short, a minor backdraft could turn into a big problem, so even if the door would open now, it wasn't a good idea. At the risk of the blaze spreading and the bakery going up in flames, he couldn't simply leave the oven be.

As soon as the temperature drops, I'll deal with the fire.

A siren blared, growing louder and louder, and Ford put his hand on the woman's back and rushed her outside.

Darius drove the firetruck up to the door, and he and Ford threw on their bunker gear. The thick gloves made it hard to get a solid grip but protected them from searing their skin. Getting the giant oven through the back door was like birthing an elephant, but eventually they managed to maneuver the appliance to the center of the alley, where they waited to see if it warranted dousing with the hose.

With the danger mostly dealt with, Ford went looking for the woman who'd been in the kitchen, attempting to put out the fire herself.

Pyro stood at her side, watching the commotion, ready to spring into action if needed. Sometimes Ford thought his dog was as big of an adrenaline junkie as he was, which wasn't always great and had left them in tight spots before. Rest or regret, it was a question that'd haunted him more than he liked.

"Good boy," Ford said, reaching through two layers of clothing, withdrawing a doggie treat, and giving it to Pyro.

"I'm so sorry," the woman said with a shake of her head. "I might've left the cupcakes in a little too long, but I don't understand how they caught fire. Or why the door wouldn't open."

Ford finished patting Pyro's head and straightened. "It was set to self-clean mode. It turns the temperature way up and torches anything inside so later you can just wipe away the ash."

The woman's smoke-streaked face paled. "And if there are two giant tins of cupcake batter inside?"

"They boil over and start a fire."

Her body sagged, and Ford lurched forward and gripped her shoulders, worried her knees might give out. Pyro pranced around her legs, glancing from Ford to the woman, awaiting orders on how to help.

"She'll be okay," he reassured his dog. "Just experiencing a bit of shock."

She threw a hand over her face. "More like mortification and wishing the ground would open and swallow me whole."

"Then Pyro and I would have to hack open the ground and come find you, and I think you'll agree we've all had more than enough excitement for today."

Her hand fell away as she tipped up her chin, and he got his first good look at her. Hair the same color he liked his coffee—one cream, two sugars; heart-shaped face streaked with gray and what he suspected were trails of mascara; and a slightly prominent nose that drew his attention to her irises, which were a deep shade of brown that almost melted into her dilated pupils.

He continued to gaze into the depths, searching for…he wasn't even sure, but whatever it was, he was relatively certain he'd found it.

Pyro barked, awakening him from her spell. People were beginning to gather at the mouth of the alley, a mob of moths to a literal flame.

The woman ducked her head, a hand going up to shield the side of her face. "Oh, great. Why is the entire town showing up?"

"Probably saw the smoke, and if not, they heard or saw the firetruck. Not only is it giant and red with flashing lights, it comes out rarely enough to attract attention. Plus, there's not a whole helluva lot to do in town. This here'll probably make the front page of the paper."

She groaned, and while he knew better than to say so, her disheveled appearance suggested she'd had as shitty of a day as she claimed. "I was trying to lay low."

"Little tip: Uncertainty isn't the place to hide out if you're on the run. We also don't do low-key very well."

Her snort-laugh was part sob, but at least he'd teased out a hint of a smile. She stepped back, patting the messy bun on the top of her head and then frowning when she touched the section that stuck up like the red comb of a rooster.

With a huff, she let her arms flop down. "Thank you for your help…"

He extended a hand. "Ford. Ford McGuire."

"How very James Bond of you with the introduction," she said, slipping her small hand into his. As if he'd touched the end of a wire, a jolt coursed through his arm, and he had to force himself not to hold on past polite range.

A wet nose nudged the hand he'd dropped, and Ford patted his furry companion's head. "And this is Pyro."

Amusement flickered through her features, softening her exasperation and making him want to come up with more witty things to say. "A firefighter with a dog named Pyro?"

"I like to think I'm clever," Ford said. "And you are…?"

"Violet!" Maisy pushed through the crowd, and the captivating firestarter in front of him dashed toward the woman who owned the bakery.

They collided in a hug, and the woman—*Violet*—began apologizing while Maisy asked if she was okay. There was also a comment about trying to do the safe thing and *not* start a fire before the conversation morphed into squeaky words he couldn't decipher.

Easton approached, dressed in his police uniform. They nodded at each other, and Ford gave him a quick rundown. Given the hijinks they had pulled growing up, their friends often gave them shit about somehow ending up on the right side of the law. Having his buddy to help out on emergency jobs came in handy, and whenever they regaled the rest of the gang with their tales, they did the fishermen thing, their adventures growing larger with each retelling.

With Easton updated, they both fell silent, and Violet's voice drifted above the din. "…not sure how I'll afford it, but I'll work on the nearest street corner to get you a new oven if this one is ruined."

No stranger to exaggeration, Ford recognized the statement for what it was. The idea of the curvy Violet standing on the corner, however… Despite being on the up-and-up nowadays, he might not be able to refrain from swinging by.

Not that he'd ever had to pay for it, but it had been a long time, and… *This just went down a weird path.*

"Don't be ridiculous," Maisy said, wrapping Violet in another hug. "I'm just glad you're all right."

"Yeah, but what if you'd been there? Or Isla?" Her

voice pitched higher, panic coating the words. "Is she okay? Where is she?"

"She's fine. Lottie, the woman who runs the craft store next door, is watching her while I get everything sorted out."

"Okay, okay." Violet wrung her hands together, and a fat tear tracked down her cheek.

Pressure grew underneath Ford's ribs, his instinct to help kicking in, even though he'd never been very adept at dealing with female tears.

Pyro whimpered and glanced at him, silently asking how to console her. His dog had a better chance than Ford did, and at his nod, Pyro padded over and nudged her hand with his nose.

She let him sniff her before giving him a nice rubdown. "I forgot to thank you, didn't I? You were trying to keep me safe, and I was too preoccupied to listen."

Guess I should put my nose against her palm. See if she'll run her fingers through my hair. He'd likely stick out his tongue and pant just like Pyro was doing. Later tonight, he and his dog were going to discuss how he'd done most of the work and Pyro still got the lion's share of the attention.

A purple flash hit Ford right in the eye, and he squatted next to the tire of the firetruck and retrieved the... *Yikes.* Lexi's wedding binder must've scared him more than he'd thought, because he swore this was similar to the one that'd been tossed on his coffee table. Only crumpled and speckled with fat flakes of black ash.

"*Noooo*," Violet shrieked, taking a leap at him and yanking whatever it was out of his hands. She flattened the bundle of papers and the glittery purple cover to her chest.

"Sorry. It's just…private." She bent and gathered several stray papers—a few of which had definitely been burned, not to mention the globs of plastic melted to them. "Anyway, sorry again for all the trouble, and thanks for your help. Again. Yeah, so…" She straightened with so much force the top of her head bumped his chin, rattling his teeth together.

"Ouch," she said, rubbing her head and backing away as if *he'd* been responsible. "I'm going to go put this up."

Earlier, he'd been hoping to coax a full smile out of her, but the one she flashed him had a manic edge to it. Talk about a whiplash in moods.

A big part of his recent dry spell came from his indifference to dating. He'd given up on serious relationships a handful of years ago. Yet after a search and rescue mission down south, casual dating had lost its appeal. Shallow interactions didn't seem worth the effort, and his life didn't allow time to pour into activities that left him unfulfilled.

But Violet… There was something undeniably intriguing about her.

Figures he'd go and experience his first spark in ages with a woman who appeared to be in the middle of planning a wedding.

Possibly even her own.

• • •

Violet stared into the charred depths of the oven along with Maisy, even though she had no idea how to tell if the damage was bad enough to require a new one.

Was that something you could determine by eyeballing it?

Guilt settled heavy in her gut, along with a righteous lump of unfairness that made her want to stomp her foot. She'd been trying to help and avoid a disaster, and, in what had become one of her classic moves, had only made things worse.

Much like the time she'd attempted to prove how fine she was and scheduled an engagement photoshoot two days after Benjamin moved out. Then she'd gone and had a breakdown that resulted in refunding the couple's session and referring them to another photographer.

No wonder she was no longer inspired.

Hell, no wonder Benjamin hadn't wanted to put a ring on it. On top of being the ditz he often teased her of being, she was a complete and utter mess. Something she was acutely aware of with the beefy firefighter standing a few yards away. He undoubtedly thought she was bonkers for ripping her binder out of his hands.

The idea of him flipping through her failed hopes and dreams, though?

Even now, it made her skin feel too tight.

Violet had taken her bedraggled binder and hidden it in one of the kitchen cupboards. Then she'd trudged back to the alley to face the disaster she'd caused.

And the sexy firefighter with a deep voice made for dirty words. Don't even get her started on the defined scruffy jaw and ripped arms that were on display now that he'd taken off his firefighter coat.

His fellow firefighter was handsome as well, a few inches shorter than Ford but on the bulkier side. He was also sporting a gold wedding band that contrasted his umber skin. The scene called to mind firefighter fantasy scenarios—only in real life, mortification dented her ability to fully appreciate the eye candy.

If Violet didn't think Ford and his dog would attempt to revive her, she'd pass out from embarrassment.

As if her half sister sensed she needed comforting, Maisy wrapped an arm around her. "It could've happened to anyone."

Violet sniffed loudly—it wasn't like the guy standing on Maisy's other side would look her way twice anyway, even on her best, most dolled-up day. "That's so nice of you to say, but I'm the girl who can't even put cupcakes in the oven."

"Maisy's right," Ford said. "It happens all the time."

There was that deep voice again. Her ears perked up, begging him to say more. The guy's only flaw was his dark hair, which was chin length, irresistibly disheveled, and stood out against his fair skin.

Not that the longer, I-woke-up-this-way style didn't suit him. It completed the whole hot country-boy look, adding to the notion that he caught fish with his bare hands and wrestled alligators for fun.

Yep, it was a good thing she didn't go for dark-haired guys with fair skin, because clearly *that* was the only thing standing in her way. *Ugh, could this day get any worse?*

At least the crowd at the mouth of the alley had thinned, most of the looky-loos deciding the exciting part had already come and gone. "Wait," she said, scrunching up her forehead. "You said the firetruck doesn't come out very often."

Ford gave her a curled-lip smile that had her

thinking of the old-school Elvis movies her bubbie used to watch. "Not very often. When there is a fire, it's either a controlled burn that got out of control or an electrical house fire caused by appliances. Toasters, blenders..." He patted the blackened machine next to them. "Ovens."

"While it looks a little worse for wear, I don't think the heating element is damaged," Maisy said. "And if it's done-zo, I have insurance for this very reason."

In an attempt to placate Maisy, Violet nodded, but she could hear her ex in her head. *Classic Violet. You've got a bullet-point wedding and life plan, but you go to the store and fail to get the* one thing *you went there for.*

Countless times she'd put dinner on to cook, only to forget about the food entirely. Benjamin would get so frustrated, calling the burned meals a waste and complaining about the townhouse perpetually smelling of smoke.

You're the most disorganized organized person I know, he'd told her on a regular basis.

Violet's lungs contracted. Part of the reason she insisted on organization was to help manage her ADHD. Scattered attention and the inability to focus were the better-known symptoms, but the other side of the coin was becoming so immersed in activities she enjoyed that she became oblivious to everything else.

As hard as she tried, she'd constantly get lost in photo editing or adding inspiration pictures to her wedding binder. What seemed like minutes turned into hours, and she'd emerge from the soothing world inside her head to one filled with chaos, confusion, and, worst of all—Benjamin's disappointment.

That'd fuel her anxiety, and from there, it was

almost impossible to do anything right.

Eventually the firefighters and cop dispersed, and Maisy locked up the bakery. She handed Violet the house keys and told her to go on ahead and make herself at home while she picked up Isla.

After dumping her bags in the spare room and hitting the shower, Violet felt halfway human again.

As soon as she walked into the living room, Maisy gestured to the two glasses of wine she'd poured. Instead of choosing one, Violet waved her fingers in the classic *gimme* motion. "First things first. I've been waiting to snuggle my niece all day."

Isla was warm, smelled of baby oil, and had on darling onesie pajamas with a star on the bum.

Violet settled on the couch, laying her niece on her lap before reaching for the wine and taking a sip. She returned the glass to its coaster and then ran a knuckle over Isla's chubby cheek. "One day, when you're older, Auntie Violet will tell you what not to do with your life—she happens to be an expert on the subject."

"Stop. People who have it all together are boring, not to mention annoying." Maisy raised her wineglass into the air. "And think about it this way. The rest of your stay can only go up from here."

"Are you still sure you can handle me for that long?"

Maisy cocked her head as if she'd asked a preposterous question. "Everyone makes mistakes, Vi. Do you know how many pastries I've maimed in my bakery? I've tried weird combinations that've made me wish I didn't have taste buds. After every disappointment, though, I dump the batter and try again. That's how I came up with my three-berry hazelnut torte, which is famous round these parts. And in case you don't re-member, *I* begged *you* to come visit."

It'd surprised Violet, how vehement her half sister had been about staying with her. In the past, she'd felt like Maisy—and the entire Hurst clan, really—was only going through the motions, doing the "proper" thing by her.

"Well, I'm going to do my best to avoid causing any more fiascos," Violet said. "And if I never see a firetruck again, it'll be too soon."

"Are you sure about that? You and Ford seemed to have some"—Maisy peered down her nose at Violet—"dare I say, *sparks*?"

Violet closed her eyes, as if that'd help her go back in time and undo being such a disaster in front of the guy. "The only thing sparking was the oven, but seriously, did he have to be so hot? And did I have to be so not?"

"You looked…" Maisy grimaced and patted Violet's knee. "Let's go with charmingly disheveled."

Violet groaned. "Guess it's a good thing I've given up men."

"That's what I say about chocolate every day, but you'll notice my hips aren't getting any smaller." The flicker of glee in Maisy's expression gave Violet more than a flicker of apprehension. "I *knew* you liked guys with dark hair."

Shower-damp strands tickled Violet's neck and cheeks as she shook her head. "I don't—and it's not just the hair, remember? Sure, I can recognize certain dark-haired, fair-skinned members of the male species aren't exactly difficult to look at. Doesn't change the fact that they're not my type."

"Mm-hmm."

Isla began to wiggle and fuss, and Violet sat her up and peered into her big blue eyes. Using two fingers, she formed a curl with the tuft of hair on top of her niece's head. "You, on the other hand, rock the dark hair and ivory skin. Yes you do." She kissed Isla's plump cheek. "*Mwah, mwah, mwah.* Are you ready for lots of cuddling and cheek pinching? Maybe a late-night party where we drink way too much milk and crash out on the couch?"

Isla opened her mouth as if she had a ready response. She cooed, and Violet's heart melted, along with the stress of the day. If she'd followed the first draft of her life plan, she'd have one, if not two kids by now. But every time she'd brought up the idea of a baby, Benjamin went with his famous "sure, someday" answer.

In this day and age, I don't need a man to have a baby. Just his sperm, and I can get that without dating, so ha!

Naturally she'd want a donor who was big and strong and brave. Sorta like Ford the Firefighter, who'd charged in, known what to do, and been kind to her, even when she'd acted so irrational.

She highly doubted those type of guys frequented sperm banks. But before she ended up with a bullet-point plan and binder filled with possible names, baby gear, and nurseries she loved, she supposed she should get her life—namely her career—in order.

First, I'll refill my creative well by helping Maisy decorate the bakery, and then I'll see where I'm at and make a plan from there.

Violet placed her niece on her shoulder and

snuggled her close, and in this moment, her life didn't seem like such a mess. She was guilty of piling one bad thing on top of another until every setback weighed her down and crushed her spirits.

Being arrested during her lowest point certainly hadn't helped, but that was another rearview-window item she hoped to leave in the dust.

Maisy propped her elbow on the back of the couch, and then tears brimmed her eyes. "I missed out, Vi. We could've had so much fun together when you stayed with us during the summers, but I was so pissed my dad had cheated on my mom and that we couldn't just move on because…"

"Because of me," Violet finished, her voice cracking.

"I'm afraid I was a selfish, horrible kid. I'd always wanted a sister, and then I had one, and instead of embracing you, I kept my distance."

As children, it'd been hard not to compare. Maisy had a pert little nose, gorgeous blue eyes, and delicate eyebrows that didn't need constant taming. She had Dad's love in spades, and Violet remembered wondering what it would be like to have a full-time father who bragged about her over dinner, the way Dad did about Maisy and his son, Mason. "It's okay."

"It's not. With Travis gone, our phone calls are the only reason I haven't lost my mind. I love Isla, but the rest of my family is always busy as usual, and I miss adult conversation. I can't tell you how glad I am to have you here." A tear rolled down her cheek, and she swiped it away. "I'd like to try to make up for the time we lost and take a second shot at being sisters in the more classic definition."

A lump formed in Violet's throat. "Honestly, I've

been lonely, too. I'd be happy to steal your Barbies and borrow your clothes without asking and...whatever else sisters do."

Maisy laughed and gently hugged Violet, bringing Isla into the group hug as well. "Thank you for being here."

Although Violet wanted to point out that she'd only brought calamity into her life, she decided now wasn't the time for self-deprecation. While the inevitability of awkward run-ins with her father and his wife sent Violet's nerves into riot mode, she focused on the affection that was flowing over her, slowly mending old wounds.

It was nice to feel like she had a sister, not simply because of shared DNA but by choice. Which made that "half" part of Maisy's title unnecessary.

A sister and a niece, a place to stay, and a bakery to decorate.

The sense of purpose Violet had been missing as of late buoyed her up, giving her a much-needed dose of optimism, no positive spin required. Maybe one day in the not too distant future, she could manage to finally put the past where it belonged.

CHAPTER THREE

Ford rounded Lake Jocassee and stumbled over the tangle of leashes. His father used to say that one dog was a lot of help, two dogs were half as much, and three dogs were nothing but trouble.

Usually he disagreed, but this morning, he could see the tiniest bit what Dad meant.

Of course his father also applied that theory to Ford and his two brothers. Dad would assign them separate chores and turn everything into a competition. Instead of working together, the boys would race to see who'd get Daddy's praise that day.

The past crowded his lungs, leaving his breaths too shallow to counteract his level of exertion.

The whole survival-of-the-fittest outlook had turned their relationships toxic, not pushing him and his brothers to be better but to drag one another down. Which was why Ford refused to use that method.

It didn't help that the puppies' harnesses had twenty-foot lead ropes attached. The first step in search and rescue training required extra length. After getting the fluffballs used to the harnesses, Ford would use a scent pad and reward them until they could scent for long distances without getting distracted.

Pyro glanced at the puppies, his exasperation clear—when it came to work, he had one mode, and that was all-out, same as Ford.

Ford's amusement helped dilute the downer vibes associated with thinking of his family, and he slowed enough to bend and give Pyro's side a quick pat. "They're young yet. Once we get 'em trained, these exercises will go smoother."

Pryo's eyebrows twitched, followed by the doggy version of a sigh.

Affection wound through him, and he cupped his dog's muzzle and locked eyes with him. "You gettin' old and grouchy on me, boy? Soon, you'll be barking at kids to get off our lawn."

In response, Pyro barked and rushed ahead, as if determined to prove his excitement and energy were still well within young and perky range.

The puppies charged after him, attempting to match Pyro's faster, longer stride.

Make that two out of three.

The course fibers of the ropes chafed his palm as they zipped across, and Ford's knees cracked as he straightened and picked up his own pace. While the female of the litter was the most focused, her bigger brother had endurance on his side.

Meanwhile, the puppy with the darkest face and bounciest temperament became distracted by every blade of grass and ripple of water. He'd wandered near the shore, and his paws were a muddy mess.

"Come on," Ford said, a stern note to his voice as he added a gentle tug. His running times were shit this week, thanks to the canine delinquents. *Yeah, that's it. Think tough.*

While he'd deny it, whenever they peered up at him with their big golden eyes, he'd turn into a big ol' sucker. A melty, tender sensation would kick in, and then he'd have to remind himself he had a job to do and couldn't simply play with the frisky puppies.

No eye contact. Must. Remain. Firm.

Eventually he and his entire furry crew hit a decent pace.

But then the ears on the endlessly distracted puppy's head perked up.

"Don't do it," Ford said, in spite of the fact that the dog's snout was already swiveling toward the lake.

The puppy's momentum continued to propel him forward, and he tripped over the branch his brother and sister had easily cleared.

Down he went, skidding through the mud face-first, his hind legs still pedaling.

With a shake of his head, Ford chuckled and righted the puppy. "Dude, you fell. That requires some recalibration—but first you've gotta get your feet back under you. Isn't that better?"

The puppy licked Ford's arm, leaving a sticky trail before rushing after his siblings. His whimpering bark was heavy on the *How dare you guys leave me behind.*

After they made it back to the truck, Ford checked the clock on the dashboard.

Thanks to the fire and the delayed training session, he didn't have time to go shower and change for poker night. Good thing his buddies had to deal with him, clean or not.

It'd also be the perfect opportunity to socialize the puppies with people and Tucker's dog, Flash. Mind made up, Ford drove the short distance to the houseboat and parked next to the row of trucks.

"Are you guys gonna be good?" he asked the puppies.

ADD Puppy immediately bit his sister's ear, so nope. Since the walk onto the houseboat required a wooden plank, he gathered the three furballs and carried them inside, Pyro trotting on after.

Despite there hardly being room for two people and a dog—much less a group of dudes and dogs—the guys greeted them with gusto.

"Hope you don't mind," Ford said, opening the sliding door to the deck and letting his four German shepherds outside. Fortunately, Tucker had already puppy-proofed the railing for his white lab, who was hardly a puppy anymore.

Flash bounded toward the other dogs with an excited bark. In looks and in personality, he and Pyro were polar opposites, but they got along well enough.

Now Pyro will have someone to roll his eyes with.

After making sure there wasn't any aggression with the new puppies in the mix, Ford closed the glass door, save a crack. Then he walked through the narrow alleyway that separated the kitchen and the living area and settled into his usual place at the circular table.

Addie dealt, and after Ford peeked at his cards, he reached over her to grab the bag of Doritos and a bottle of beer.

"Ugh, Ford," Addie said, leaning away from him, "you smell."

He draped his arm over her, yanking her face right to his armpit, the bag of chips *crunch*ing between them. "Maybe you've just been with Crawford too long to remember what a real man smells like."

The slug to his obliques was solid, as Addie's punches often were. "One, a real man showers. And two, thanks to that bet about who could swim the length of the community center's pool the fastest—and how you decided stripping to your skivvies would make you more aerodynamic, even though I still won—I've seen what you've got going on." She shrugged. "Eh. Not impressed."

Oh, she had to go there? "We were ten! That was before puberty kicked in, and trust me, puberty was generous." Ford straightened and began jokingly undoing the knot on the drawstring of his mesh basketball shorts. "Here, I'll show you."

Tucker placed his hand on Ford's forearm. "How about I just prevent a lawsuit before it starts?"

"Like there'd be a lawsuit," Ford muttered. "If I really flashed her, Murph here would bury my body in a backwoods bog, and no one would find me."

"Truth," Easton and Shep said at the same time, and Addie beamed as if it were the best compliment she'd ever received.

"Aww, thanks, guys. I love you, too."

They began their first round of poker, and when Ford took a drink of beer, he twisted his neck and sniffed his armpit. He didn't smell *that* bad. Just used-up deodorant and a healthy dose of smoke.

"Heard there was a fire at Maisy's Bakery today," Shep said, probably getting a whiff of the evidence.

"Oh yeah, how'd that go?" Addie tossed a couple of poker chips in the center of the table. "Rumors ranged between a false call and a blazing inferno where you saved women and children, but the middle ground sounded the most legit."

"It was an easy call. No injuries, and the fire was contained in the oven, so I just unplugged it. Then Darius and I hauled it into the alley to cool down." He matched Addie's bet, and his mind meandered to the intriguing woman responsible for today's emergency call. "I, uh, met Maisy's sister. Anyone know her?"

The game slowed as everyone studied him, eyes narrowing to slits.

"What? I was just curious and thought you guys might've met her before." In high school, Ford hadn't paid much attention to Mayor Hurst and his family, his rebellious nature and infamous family leaving him wary of authority figures.

One by one, Addie placed three cards faceup on the table. "Beats me. I thought Maisy Hurst only had an older brother. Remember Mason? He played running back when we were freshmen, and now he coaches college ball."

That sounded familiar. But Violet definitely wasn't.

"Is that who that woman was?" Poker chips clattered together as Easton tossed two whites and a blue into the pot. "For a second I thought I was seein' double and there were two Maisys. She seemed pretty frazzled when I took the report."

Frazzled. Adorable. A pinch high-strung. "Ah, she just felt bad. She hadn't meant to hit the self-clean mode. Could've happened to anybody, I suppose."

Shep folded, and so did Tucker.

Ford told himself to leave it be, but he recalled those big brown eyes and the way they'd awakened something he thought he'd buried and left for dead. He couldn't help it. He wanted to know more about Violet.

Wanted to know why she'd gotten so worked up when he'd picked up her binder.

Was it wedding plans? Or had he jumped to that conclusion because of the meeting he'd come from?

She had mentioned wanting to lie low. Maybe she was a government spy, sent to infiltrate Uncertainty with a glittery binder. Yeah, that checked out. Most spies struggled with simple electronics.

If she was engaged, it'd be better to find out now so he could put her out of his mind. Not only did he not cross that line, the mere idea of a woman longing to get hitched made him want to run, so…win-win?

Easton nudged him. "Bro. It's your turn."

"I raise." Not the greatest idea, taking into account that Ford had been thinking about Violet instead of paying attention to his friends' faces or calculating probability.

Put her out of your head. It's not like you have extra time right now, anyway. He was neck-deep in training a rambunctious litter, and that'd take him from spring to summer. Which, as a paramedic, was his busy season. People were fishing, hiking, and camping more. Kids rode bikes and jumped on trampolines and found "secret" stashes of fireworks.

While his friends often worried about his inability to relax, his career was what he enjoyed most about his life. No day was ever the same, feeding his appetite for adventure, and in a lot of ways, it was his way to help balance out the universe.

To use the survival skills he'd learned the hard way to help people who *wanted* to return to their families. Just because his story hadn't ended up happy didn't mean others' stories shouldn't.

At the end of the round, the three of them who hadn't folded revealed their cards. Easton won by a mile, earning a curse from Addie. She hated losing.

Usually, Ford did, too. But over the next few rounds, his stack of poker chips dwindled, and he couldn't bring himself to care.

Mostly because Violet's face kept drifting to mind. Maybe it was the hero complex his friends accused him of having, but she had seemed like she needed help. The kind that went beyond putting out the fire in the oven.

You don't have time for unstable and complicated.

Been there, done that, and lost *a T-shirt.*

There was that moment when she'd sagged against him, though. The James Bond joke and the way she'd giggled at Pyro's name. The jolt that'd traveled up his arm after she'd slipped her small hand in his.

"In case you haven't noticed, McGuire," Easton said, "you're losing. So what the hell are you smiling about?"

Ford blinked his way to the present and resisted the urge to stack his chips—an old delay tell he'd learned to suppress. "Can't a guy be happy?"

"No," they all said.

"Not when you're losing," Murph added.

Easton paused his dealing. "It's Maisy's sister, isn't it? Is our boy thinkin' about giving dating another go?"

Tucker put a hand on his chest. "Aww. They grow up so fast."

"What is this, the Craft Cats?" Ford asked, referring to the group of ladies in town who specialized in crafting, meddling, and cat-sweatshirt wearing. "Less gossip, more poker."

Shep reached over Easton to take the Doritos. "Stop acting like you don't eat up the attention and spill the beer."

Now *Shep* was the one with everyone's scrutiny.

"What? I'm around teenagers all day. They have this phrase about spilling the tea, and I thought I'd make it more adult." Since Shep had given plenty of teachers nightmares growing up, they teased him endlessly about becoming a teacher himself. He was on the school board as well, and a few of the older ladies in town volunteered simply because they were sure Will Shepherd still had some ornery in him.

"Whatever," Shep said. "I'm cool, while y'all's slang is becoming irrelevant." He licked orange dust off his fingertips before taking up his cards. "Back to this chick you met at the bakery. She must be hot."

"I didn't say that." Ford loudly raised after the flop, hoping his friends would drop the subject.

"You mentioned her twice already."

"No, I mentioned her once, and you guys assumed I was thinking about her when I smiled. I was thinking of…somethin' else."

The entire gang burst out laughing, and he regretted bringing up Violet.

Evidently there'd been an unspoken agreement that the game couldn't resume until Ford came clean, so he might as well get it over and done with. "Eh. She's cute in a lost, walking-disaster sort of way. But she's also sorta volatile—and I'm sure we all remember why I gave that up. My truck certainly does."

In some states, the amount of love he had for his truck might border on illegal, but the girl had never let him down. The massive grill, roll bar, and lightbar meant she could take on rough terrain, no problem.

Trina, his off-and-on girlfriend through high school and for a misguided year after he'd graduated college, had erratic mood swings. Things would be great, and then suddenly she'd lash out at him.

Not only could he not do anything right, no matter

how hard he tried, their relationship began interfering with emergency calls. Trina would demand he stay and finish whatever argument he'd inevitably lose, even as others' health and occasionally lives hung in the balance.

When Ford finally told her he was done—for good this time—she'd taken a key to the hood of his truck.

"What's an ass cube?" Tucker had asked when they'd come out of the Old Firehouse and spotted Trina's handiwork.

"She must've gotten tired after carving the giant A, S, and S, so she added a circle. Only curved lines are hard to draw with keys, so it looks like a square."

For two whole months, he'd driven around his "ass cube" truck, no money or time to get it fixed. When Dear Old Dad had seen it, he'd guffawed and added insult to injury with his "Told ya, son. They all turn eventually."

"I like my women a little volatile," Easton said, and Ford did his best not to react, in spite of the foreign, toxic churning in his gut. Surely that wasn't jealousy.

It was…indigestion. Yeah. From not eating dinner and then eating chips and drinking a beer. That had to be it.

Easton casually raised, the racket of his chips hitting the table grating Ford's nerves for some odd reason. "She has a nice ass, too."

Ford whipped his head toward him and spoke through a clenched jaw. "That's enough, Reeves."

*Ooh*s went around the table, along with an "I knew it" from Easton.

Okay, so Ford had also checked out her ass in those yoga pants. He'd done his best to refrain, but then she'd bent over the oven, and…well, he could see hearts and a hint of writing through the thin fabric of her pants, and he indulged for a moment before reminding himself to be a gentleman.

"You know, I forget why I hang out with you pricks." It was his turn again, and since he had jack and shit, he folded. "Speaking of women, Shep, yours is scarily organized. Does she plan out your time between the sheets? Do you get spanked when you go off book?"

Shep flipped him off. Then a grin split his face. "Guess what we've had to do as groomsmen so far?" His grin spread to evil-villain range. "Nothing."

"Not a damn thing," Easton echoed.

Addie flinched. "Sorry," she said to Ford. "I didn't think about the planning part when I asked you to be my dude of honor."

"Joke's on them; I like it." He draped his arm over her shoulders, and this time, she didn't shove him away. If she had to endure the planning, he'd be by her side for every overly detailed session.

"Yeah, me, too," Addie said, and Tucker snort laughed.

"Usually your poker face is much better, babe."

She kicked him under the table, a gleam lighting her eyes when Tuck grunted and rubbed his shin. "And guess what we get to do tomorrow? Cake tasting at Maisy's."

The smug expressions faded one by one.

"As groomsmen, we should also attend and make sure you get the right cake and frosting," Shep said.

Addie flipped her ponytail over her shoulder. "Sorry, boys. It's strictly bridesmaids. And my seventy-two-year-old flower girl, since my nonna is impossible to say no to."

And Maisy and her sister, Ford mentally added. When it came to cake, he was all in. If he got to see Violet again because he was part of the bridal party...?

Well, there were worse ways to spend a Saturday morning.

CHAPTER FOUR

A swell of sugary-sweet air greeted Violet as she stepped inside the bakery. She inhaled and held in the aroma, the way a good addict would do. The only way she'd survive getting her feet back underneath her without those feet having to carry around extra pounds was to inhale instead of indulge.

She finished typing her response in the Bridesmaid Crew bubble. Leah and Amanda were most active, but Camille, Alyssa, Morgan, and Christy responded here and there.

Violet: *Surviving small-town life so far. Martin's Trading Post had paint, tools, AND camouflage clothing, if I ever decide to go full country.*

Leah: *If you do, I'm gonna need pictures.*

Amanda: *Same, which we apparently have to say now, since you didn't take pictures of the hot firefighters yesterday! I mean, photos are YOUR THING!*

Correction, they *were* her thing, but her friends had already been so worried when they'd found out about Benjamin's wedding that she didn't want to fess up to that. Not only because they'd stress, but they might think they should confront her ex, and they'd damaged each other enough.

Violet: *Maybe I already sent a picture of the camo but you just can't see it because it's doing its job.*

Violet sniggered at her own joke and withdrew the paint swatches she'd picked up from Martin's Trading Post, along with a pen. She placed the gradient color cards against the formerly white wall of the bakery, checking which shades best fit the lighting and wooden floors.

The clang of pans meant Maisy was already baking, and since Violet had narrowed down the paint options to three, she headed toward the kitchen. "You'll never guess who I saw running in the park with a gaggle of dogs. After yesterday, I'm planning on avoiding him at all costs, so I totally darted into an alleyway like I was running from the paparazzi, but—"

Violet froze in place, her pulse thumping too hard at her temples. *Please,* please *let me be dreaming.*

"But what?" Ford asked from his spot in front of the oven. He wiped an arm across his forehead, and of course the move lifted his T-shirt enough to display a stripe of toned abs and a line of dark hair that led to... well, where hair like that led to. "I'm interested in hearing the rest of that story."

Maisy stood behind him, her cartoonishly wide eyes making it clear that yes, this was as awkward as it felt and fully warranted the flush of heat. "Ford came by early to check on the oven and ensure it was working properly. Isn't that nice?"

Mr. Nice Guy grinned. "Pleased to be of service. Violet, maybe I can help you with whoever you're hiding from. I'm real good at hide and seek."

"Wrong," Violet muttered. "You're not very good at the hiding part. Not only are you a big dude, you're freaking everywhere."

His grin widened.

And like this morning, when Violet had seen his long, muscular legs eating up the distance, his pack of adorable dogs in tow, she decided to pretend Ford wasn't there.

She held the three starred swatches up to Maisy. "I'd like the bakery to be as lovely as your pastries, but I also don't want the colors to overwhelm the desserts." She fanned the cards so the stars lined up and pointed at the varying shades. "This is what I'm thinking of going with for the accent colors."

Maisy slapped flour from her palms. "As you so nicely pointed out, I'm no good at the design thing, so seriously, whatever you think."

"Want my opinion?" a rumbly voice asked from right behind Violet, and she jumped, then gritted her teeth at his low chuckle. Why had she thought about this guy way too many times since yesterday evening?

"Nah." She gave his outfit a pointed look. "Matching isn't your strong suit."

His jaw dropped, but then he laughed, the noise cracking the ice around her heart.

Honestly, his outfit was like him. Sporty. Male. Something she shouldn't be staring at.

The door to the bakery chimed, and Violet couldn't volunteer fast enough to go welcome the first customers of the day.

"What can I help you with?" Violet asked, plunking the paint swatches on the counter and addressing the three women who'd walked inside.

An older lady with gray and white curls stepped forward, a childlike excitement on her face as she surveyed the treats behind the glass. "We are here for cake tasting, but while we wait, I would love some brownie bites."

Violet tried to place the accent. German, maybe? Although that didn't seem quite right.

"Lucia, you're well aware you can't have those," the brunette woman behind her said with a harrumph. "Your blood sugar is going to spike high enough with the cake tasting as it is."

Violet scanned the treats, searching for the label she'd seen on her side of the counter yesterday. "Oh, we have these brownie bites that are—"

"Absolutely delicious." The statement came from the youngest in the group, the one around Violet's age. Her dark ponytail was threaded through a blue and orange AU cap, her face makeup-free and flawless. Hardly fair when Violet needed a half dozen products and palettes to appear that fresh and perky. "But my nonna is cutting her sugar."

She raised her eyebrows, obviously trying to convey something to Violet, but she was lost.

Nonna. That's Italian, right?

Lucia's forehead crinkled as she studied Violet. "Why I don't know you? I know everyone."

"Nonna, that's hardly the way to introduce yourself." The girl in the baseball cap placed a hand on her chest. "Hi, I'm Addie Murphy, the bride-to-be. This is my feisty grandmother, Lucia, and my mother, Priscilla."

"Violet," she said. It seemed like they were waiting for more, but she wasn't planning on spilling her life story simply because they stared at her like they thought she would.

"Okay, Priscilla," Lucia said. "You delivered me and have proof that Addison no let me eat too much sugar. Now, since you not a bridesmaid or a flower girl like I am, shoo."

Flower girl? Violet was overly experienced in all

things wedding-related, so it took her a second to readjust her assumption. And she simply adored the idea of the firecracker of a woman walking down the aisle and tossing petals.

"After I pick up the groceries, I'll swing back by to pick her up."

Lucia linked her elbow with Addie's. "Addison bring me home, won't you, dear?"

"Sure, Nonna. As you've discovered and exploited, I have trouble saying no to you."

Priscilla's steps slowed, and Addie raised her voice.

"Except when it comes to sugar and high-cholesterol foods, because that's for your own dang good."

Seemingly satisfied, Priscilla exited the bakery but paused to hold the door for a blond southern-belle type. Retro and classic with a modern edge and a bright pink lip Violet wished she could pull off. Seriously, was being attractive a town requirement?

The woman breezed inside, her heels clacking against the wooden floor. "Sorry I'm late. My car wouldn't start, so I drove Will's truck and— Oh, shoot. My binder and the magazines were in the trunk of my car."

"Don't worry about it," Addie said before turning to Violet. "This is Lexi, one of my bridesmaids. My sister lives out of state, so we're just waitin' for one more."

Maisy came around the corner, wiping her hands on the apron at her waist. "Actually, your other bridesmaid is already here. He came early to check on my oven."

Great. Violet hadn't even started painting, and her sister was acting like the fumes were getting to her. The *check on my oven* also sounded overtly sexual, especially since Ford had followed her out of the kitchen and was smirking like he'd pulled one over on all of them.

He winked at Violet, and she crossed her arms with a huff. If he thought that was all it took to win her over, he had another think coming.

He strolled past her and rounded the counter to hug Lucia, who greeted him with a smacking kiss on his cheek. He embraced the beautiful blonde next and finished off by fist-bumping the bride-to-be.

"Ah, so you've met my bridesmaid-slash-best-man," Addie said. "Or did we decide to go with bro of honor?" Her head cocked a couple more degrees. "Dude of honor?"

Ford shrugged his big shoulders. "I'm not picky. And while I'm lost with the rest of the wedding-planning stuff, I'm fully qualified for cake tasting." He twisted his wrist and glanced at his watch. "I've only got an hour before I have to be back home, though. No rest for the wicked and all that."

Violet gawked at the scene before her, struggling to process. Every time she visited this town, she discovered a new layer of bizarre. Apparently nontraditional was the new traditional.

Which, honestly, she hadn't expected from a place she'd thought time had forgotten. If she hadn't already made her mind up about Uncertainty, she might even find it refreshing.

"Mind helping me grab the samples?" Maisy asked, nudging Violet's arm.

"As long as you don't need me to bake them," Violet said with a self-deprecating laugh.

Once the various samples were placed in the center of the largest table, Violet moved aside. *Time to finish drawing up plans for these walls.*

Her trusty notebook served as a tiny shield and item to cling to, but the people who filtered in and out of the bakery—and the conversation from the wedding party—kept snagging her curiosity.

If Violet hadn't heard the words "bridesmaid-slash-best-man," she'd assume Addie and Ford were the betrothed couple. They were obviously close, yet there was something lighter than romance. As they *mmm*ed over the samples, they snickered, verbally jabbed, and shoved each other's shoulders, as if they were casual observers instead of choosing one of the mainstays of a wedding.

"Are you two even paying attention?" Lexi asked, and both Ford and Addie shot up in their seats, like two kids who'd gotten in trouble at school. The blonde lowered the notepad she'd pulled from her Louis Vuitton purse and muttered about the almond cake.

Ford glanced over his shoulder in Violet's direction. Too late, she spun to face the wall, fighting the urge to bang her head on it, since he'd caught her staring. It was about the group dynamic, not him.

Not that she hadn't admired the way he kept sliding extra bites toward Lucia, his easy laugh, and his effortless charm. But that just meant he had a conniving side that drew women in so he could later screw them over.

Total player. I can smell it from a mile away.
Now.

Naively, she'd thought the fact that she and Benjamin had been in a committed relationship negated his player qualities. Like how he'd check out women whenever they were out and about. She'd written it off as him being a typical male who couldn't get his ogle under control. Now she realized he'd never stopped searching for someone prettier and better than she was.

Sometimes he'd go a whole week without acknowledging her, besides to criticize her absentmindedness. Eventually, she would get upset, and then he'd apologize and make a grand gesture that lulled her into a false sense of security.

Which is why I'm done with men in general.

No more falling for their tricks. Nope, nope, nope.

Violet busied herself with the multicolored wall stickers she'd discovered on Etsy. She'd originally planned to buy stencils, but she'd found vinyl watercolor dots that were bright, whimsical, and the perfect size.

"Excuse me…" she heard, followed by a gravelly, "Her name's Violet."

"Excuse me, Violet." Out of the corner of her eye, manicured fingernails flashed, signaling it'd come from the blond bridesmaid. "Could I ask your opinion on something?"

Violet slowly pivoted toward the table with the wedding party. Four sets of eyes were on her, but for some reason, her gaze went to the one male pair. In this light, she couldn't tell if they were hazel or green, and why did that matter?

She cleared her throat. "I'm not sure how much help I'll be. Just ask Ford—baking and I don't mix."

Damn it. Why had she set herself up for an embarrassing retelling of yesterday's disaster?

Lexi rose from her chair and grabbed Violet's hand. "Don't worry." She guided her into the seat next to her. Which, as her shoddy luck would have it, was also next to Ford. "I just need another female perspective. While Addie is technically female, she's missing the part of her brain that cares about decorations, dresses, and ensuring the cake is the pièce de résistance it should be."

While this Lexi chick was fancier than Violet ever would be, she agreed on that point. Yes, cake made any celebration better, but a *wedding* cake symbolized a commitment to provide for each other. Cutting from the bottom tier signified longevity.

Addie slumped back in her chair, legs spread wide. "She's not wrong. I've decided on white chocolate with raspberry cream, but as far as style goes, I'm lost. When it comes to cake, my goal is to take a bite ASAP, not note how fancy it is. And big extravagant cakes scare me because I just know I'll bump into the table, knock the whole thing over, and ruin everything."

"In this case, you'll be the bride, so people would forgive you." Lexi shot Addie a semi-stern expression. "Don't you dare knock it over, though—that's not the goal, and I can't believe I have to even say that, but I feel like I do."

"Yeah." Ford flicked Addie on the arm. "Stop trying to sabotage your own wedding. But if you do happen to knock it over, I'll declare a food fight, and we'll turn the party right around. It'll be like sixth grade all over again, when you pelted Derek Wheeler with your apple for saying girls couldn't throw as good as boys."

Addie snorted. "I got in so much trouble, but my detention didn't last nearly as long as his black eye."

The full glare Lexi aimed at the pair made Violet want to slink away but didn't seem to bother Ford in the least.

Addie flashed an apologetic grimace. "Sorry.

Seriously, I couldn't care less about what the cake looks like. I'm sure whatever Maisy makes will be awesome."

"See what I mean about needing another female perspective?"

Violet couldn't help but glance at the grandmother.

"I am also female," Lucia said. "But I say whatever makes cake easiest to sneak underneath my daughter-in-law's nose, and apparently that's no an acceptable answer." The legs of her chair scraped the floor. "Speaking of smuggling, I gonna go get the brownie bites before my parole officer checks in."

For an older lady, she certainly could hustle. She rushed over to the cash register and began pointing at the treats, and Brooke, the nineteen-year-old who worked part-time at the bakery, gathered them into a box.

Lexi sighed. "If Maisy wasn't so busy, I'd ask her for help with my confounded wedding crew. If only I hadn't left my binder in my car, I'd at least have examples. Anyway, could you weigh in? For instance, how many weddings have you been to where the cake hasn't had more than one tier? Addie was like, why not just have a giant flat cake? Like it's a barbecue or someone's retirement party."

Way too aware of the guy on her other side and how heavy his gaze pressed against her, Violet licked her lips. "Admittedly, I've been to a lot of weddings—in fact, I've been a bridesmaid seven times. And every cake has been a tiered work of art. Personally, I love seeing the way a couple expresses themselves in so many different ways, from the cake to the decor to the bridesmaids dresses and tuxes and *gah*, the wedding dress."

Tingles erupted, rushing through her entire body, the overly romantic girl she used to be tiptoeing to the forefront. "There are so many options and variations, and yet, each bride always manages to pick the perfect combination for herself. You can see how amazing she feels, too, not only about the dress and the setting but committing to the one special person who loves her inside and out."

Oops. Violet had gotten caught up in the dozens of ceremonies she'd witnessed in person, through her camera lens, and on the pages of magazines, momentarily forgetting that she was no longer obsessed with planning the perfect wedding.

She'd given that up. Now she was on the aisleless straight and narrow. A single pringle for life.

The string of pink pearls Lexi clutched paired perfectly with her aquamarine dress. "Praise the Lawd, someone who actually gets it. Seriously, I love you…" She scrunched up her eyebrows. "Violet, was it?"

Based on Ford's fidgeting, Violet had scared him with her passionate spiel. Had he scooted away from her, or was that her imagination? Either way, spooking him would only be beneficial when it came to her no-guy decree.

So instead of diminishing what she'd already said, she thought of the four-page spread of wedding cakes in her binder. "Yes, and I think I can help even more." The least she could do was lend a hand, since Lexi was practically planning the event solo. "Do you want the cake to be one texture or different textures for each tier? What about a topper? Lately I've been digging floral bouquets with flowers cascading down to the bottom. What flowers have you chosen?"

Lexi tapped her glittery gold pen to her notebook. "What are you thinking for flowers, Addie?"

"Yes," Addie said. At Lexi and Violet's mutual gaping, she wrinkled her nose. "Is that not the right answer?"

Violet smiled, attempting to undo the shock she'd aimed Addie's way. "Customarily, a bride selects flowers she likes. Or she might choose based on the colors she's decided on."

Addie bit her thumbnail. "Um, I don't have colors picked out, either."

"No worries. What kind of flowers do you like?"

Addie shrugged and looked at Ford, who also shrugged. Watching their interactions from this angle, Violet realized they didn't act like a couple at all. More like siblings—not that she would really know what that entailed.

"Come on," Lexi coaxed, stretching her hand across the table to cover Addie's. "Surely you've spotted flowers somewhere and thought, *I enjoy those*."

"Yellow dandelions make me happy."

"Then they turn white and you can blow them and make wishes and shit," Ford added.

Lexi's eye twitched, but her smile remained plastered on her face. "Those are weeds. Try again."

Addie wound the end of her ponytail around her finger. "Ooh, how about those tiny white ones that open in the morning? They have a hint of pink or purple stripes inside. I accidentally mangled a patch the last time we played Fugitive."

"Are you talking about morning glories? Because those are weeds, too, my dear." Lexi rubbed a couple of fingers across her forehead. "Let me guess, you want a weed bouquet now."

Addie giggled. "Weed. That'll be one way to keep everyone nice and mellow at the ceremony and reception."

"I vote yes," Ford said. "After all the pranks we've pulled on the fine citizens of our town, that's about the only way they'll relax and enjoy themselves during this shindig."

"Excellent point. Though we might have to put a barbwire fence around the cake in case they get the munchies before it's time. What decor is that? Farm chic?"

"Prison-yard love, I think."

"Dude, later we're gonna have to have a talk about what prison-yard love means." Addie patted Ford's knee. "Here's a hint and a tip all in one: don't drop the soap."

The two of them devolved into laughter, flowers no longer on their radar.

Lexi swept her arm toward the duo. "Do you see what I'm dealing with? A bride who doesn't care about decorations or flowers and her man of honor, who is as clueless about wedding stuff as she is."

"I told you to go ahead and choose whatever on my behalf," Addie said, a pinch of offense in the words.

"I thought you'd change your mind once we dove in. The entire un-stoned town is going to be there, and if I'm going to do the majority of the planning, I at least need a sounding board. Asking you two for advice is like talking into a void."

Addie wiped at the tears her laughter had caused. "Sorry, Lexi. You're amazing for taking this on, and I'd be totally lost without you, so please don't let my lack of girliness send you running. I'll do better. I promise."

She nudged Ford with her elbow.

"Yeah, me, too." Ford followed up his statement by nudging Violet.

She twisted his way, her instincts failing to remind her she wasn't going to look directly at him until it was too late. Her mouth went dry—her memory of his face up close didn't do it justice. Unlike a lot of the guys in Pensacola, his beard wasn't perfectly groomed, but untamed, a couple days' growth from out-of-control. One corner of his lips tipped a smidge higher than the other, as if he always had a smile at the ready.

Hello, do not *look at his lips!*

Recalling the nudge that'd made her focus way too much on him, she asked, "What? How can I do better when I barely got here?"

"Where's my nonna? She'd at least have an opinion on flowers—she still sneaks over to the neighbors' yard late at night to water the ones she planted when they were out of town." Addie surveyed the front of the bakery, but Lucia was no longer there. "Oh great, I've lost her. I bet you anything she went to the diner to check if anyone would let her order a burger and fries. My mom is seriously going to kill me."

With everyone distracted, Violet decided to take her leave. "Well, sounds like you're getting it all figured out." She scooted her chair away from the table, already halfway out of it. "I should get back to work. I'm planning out the bakery remodel and—"

"Come on, Violet," Ford said, as though they'd known each other for years instead of hours. He placed his hand over the one she had on the table and her heart *thump, thump, thump*ed. "Help a couple of guys and one desperate wedding planner out."

For a second, she was confused, but then she figured out he was counting Addie as a guy.

"What I should've mentioned is that I'm a *recovering* bridesmaid." Talking wedding options and showing proof of how many she'd gathered were entirely different things, and there was no way in hell she could show Lexi and Addie her binder with Ford there.

More than that, it'd be too painful, and she never should've sat down in the first place.

The alarm in her head wailed, behind as usual.

Recovery was a slippery slope—one she was way too close to sliding down headfirst.

"How's it going over here?" Maisy asked as she approached the table. "I'm so sorry I don't have a look book. I've only done a couple of weddings so far, but if you have a picture, I can make it."

The apologetic note in her sister's voice dug at Violet.

"I feel so unprepared," Lexi said. "Maybe I should drive home and come back."

"No," Addie and Ford both said at the same time, and Addie elaborated with, "I don't want you to go to all that trouble when I should be able to handle something so simple."

Part of Violet wanted to suggest they search up cakes on their phones, but service in town was slow and spotty, and it was hard to make a solid decision on thumbnail images.

The chime over the door sounded again, and Maisy turned to greet her customers. Saturdays were busy, and right now the best way she could help her sister was by doing the last thing she wanted to.

Why me? "Okay, fine. I'll be right back with something that might help."

Bright side spin: if her binder could be used for good, maybe it'd help her let go of everything it stood for.

• • •

Damn, she smells nice.

The scent of Violet's perfume lingered in the air, and Ford *might've* watched her walk out of the bakery a bit too closely.

What on earth had she meant with that *recovering bridesmaid* remark? She'd made it sound as if wearing colorful dresses and holding a bouquet was an addiction she needed to kick. Didn't mean she wasn't engaged, and if she loved weddings as much as her spiel suggested... *Yikes.*

With her gone, it was easier to concentrate, but it wasn't like he suddenly became a wedding-cake expert. Unless being sure he could eat a whole one himself was useful. To further complicate matters, he was growing more and more aware of the time.

Ford needed to get going on his day, but he didn't want to hurt Lexi's or Murph's feelings. Addie would understand that he was on a tight puppy-training schedule, but she was the one who'd always been there for him. The one who listened without judgment when he told her about rough jobs and confessed that, once in a while, they got to him.

It'd taken months to open up to her about the aftermath of the last hurricane and everything that'd happened when he went down to the gulf. Of course Addie had told him he shouldn't blame himself. She'd reassured him that people had to rest now and again and that anyone could've made the same mistake, but he couldn't let himself off that easily.

The chime on the door sounded, and Violet strolled inside.

While yesterday he'd found her disheveled appearance a little too captivating, today she was less harried, her brown hair hanging in loose waves around her shoulders. Her shirt was about as red as her face had been when she'd come into the kitchen talking about hiding from him. He was still a big fan of the yoga pants, but her snug jeans also displayed her figure rather nicely.

As she moved closer, he caught sight of the glittery purple object in her hands. The very same item she'd snatched from him in the alleyway.

She sat between him and Lexi and plopped the binder on the table. Then she moved her fingers along the tabs, mumbling until she reached the middle section. A page slipped free as she opened the book, and she quickly tucked it underneath the back cover. "Here you go. Several cakes to check out."

Ford glanced from her to the page titled MY DREAM WEDDING CAKES. "Wow. That's…intense. Like obsessive-serial-killer level, but for cakes you plan to murder."

"*Ford*. Be nice." Shep's wife placed a hand on Violet's shoulder. "Ignore him. What he meant to say is thank you."

No, what he meant was *holy shit, she has her entire wedding planned out*. And he shouldn't have touched her hand or teased her in the kitchen, and why did he hate the idea of her being already taken so much?

Bracing herself on her forearms, Addie leaned across the table. "Those are gorgeous. I see what you mean about the flowers, although purple isn't really my color." She spun the binder her way. "While I get your aversion to dandelions, Lex, I do like yellow. What about daisies and sunflowers—are they weeds? I realize they're out in the fields, but I want the decorations to match how I feel about marrying Tucker: happy."

Without warning, Lexi launched herself at Violet, arms winding around her neck. The legs of the chair wobbled from the impact, and Ford placed his hand on the chair back so they wouldn't go down. While he wouldn't mind seeing the two women plastered together on the floor, no one was going to get a concussion on his watch.

"Violet, you're a miracle worker," Lexi said, releasing her hold on the woman next to him but not relinquishing her personal space. "She picked a color *and* a flower. Or flowers, as the case may be, but at long last I have something to work with."

Another glossy paper fell from the binder as Addie flipped the page. She excitedly tapped a picture in the middle. "This is the one. A cake like this, but with daisies."

"And a cake." Lexi's voice came out at an octave he'd previously thought only dogs could hear. When she sat back in her own seat, Violet appeared a bit shell-shocked, but a smile slowly spread across her face.

Lexi latched onto Addie's arm and dragged her toward the bakery counter while calling Maisy's name.

A few silent seconds ticked by, and then Violet

haughtily lifted her chin. "See, I'm not obsessed or too intense. I'm a miracle worker."

"My apologies," he deadpanned.

Arms tightly crossed her chest, emphasizing her cleavage. Before he could rein himself in, his fingers twitched with the urge to grab her chair and tug her closer. Ask what was up with that ridiculous binder, and why didn't she have a ring on her finger?

"Why do you sound so sarcastic?" she asked. "Yes, you met me on a super shitty day—"

"The shittiest, I believe you called it. Sounded like it was from more than starting that fire, too." There he went, poking the beast instead of deescalating the situation.

Her nostrils flared. "Right. On both counts, actually, although I'd rather we pretend the fire never happened."

"I'm fine with that. Not sure I can say the same for the oven."

She exhaled as if he'd taken up every ounce of her patience—which, fair. "The point is, I'm not normally like that. All flustered and creating a disaster in my wake. I'd even go so far as to say I'm relatively level-headed, especially considering everything I've been through."

Ford jerked his chin at the binder. "I'm assuming the reason you hid from me this morning and made that *recovering bridesmaid* remark is because you're engaged and get to be the star now?"

Violet's mouth hung open for a beat, and then she blinked and shook her head. "No, nope, and no."

His lungs contracted with an odd amalgamation of relief and apprehension, as if he were facing down a bear and couldn't decide if he should marvel at the sight or slowly back away with his hands up.

Though her answer was far from straightforward— she'd skimmed right past why she'd hid and what her earlier remark had meant. Was she purposely withholding to be infuriating? And why couldn't he stop prying?

"Then why do you have your entire wedding planned?" Call it self-sabotage, but he needed to keep his wits about him. Ever since Violet joined them, his thoughts had been on the scrambled side. He wanted to tempt her closer and push her away all at the same time.

"Oh, don't even start. You sit there all judgy, but I bet you have a stack of wildlife or vehicle magazines— or whatever other country-bumpkin hobby you're into—at your house. It's the same thing; mine's just better organized."

Amusement set in, making it that much harder to disengage. Kitty had claws, and he sort of enjoyed the way she raked them over him. "Sounds like you're fishing for an invite to my house."

"With how big your ego is, I doubt I'd fit inside." Violet began to push away, and he flattened his palm to the thigh of his jeans so he wouldn't reach out, snag her hand, and ask her to stay.

If he did that, he'd also have to apologize for being an asshole about the binder and the jab about starting a fire. Apologizing wasn't one of his many talents, and the faster she fled, the sooner he could scrub her out of his head.

"Thank you for reminding me why I've given up men," Violet muttered, taking a step in the other direction.

The chime that accompanied the opening of the door *ping*ed. With a tiny squeak, Violet abruptly reversed course and dove for the table. She bypassed her chair and dropped to the floor by his mud-coated Adidas. "Shit, shit, shit."

Ford glanced from Mayor Hurst and his wife, Cheryl, to the girl trying to become one with his leg. "Somethin' I can help you with, ma'am?"

"*Shhh.* Just shut up," she hissed.

"Well, if you're going to be mean…" He shifted as if he were going to stand.

"Wait." Violet clamped onto his leg, her fingernails digging into his calf muscles as she held him in place. "I'm sorry, okay? Even though you're a cocky ass, I shouldn't have told you to shut up."

"Anyone ever tell you that your apologies are somewhat lacking?"

The Hursts walked to the cash register, and Violet hunkered down more. She crawled around to his other side on her hands and knees.

A large truck drove down Main Street, its muffler in desperate need of repair, and Mayor Hurst idly glanced out the large bakery window.

Violet wrapped herself around his leg like a koala bear, and her head brushed his inner thigh. If they'd been acquainted for longer and there wasn't a chance of her mistaking a joke for a serious request, he'd make an inappropriate *Hey, while you're down there…* remark.

Not only was he spot-on about her being flighty and temperamental, she had a few loose screws to boot.

Yay for his instincts, but what did he do about the heat stirring in his gut? It wasn't the only part of him slowly waking up, either. It'd been a long time since a woman had been this close to… *Definitely not thinking about that, or the situation's gonna get even bigger.*

"Don't look at me like that," Violet shout-whispered, and he wondered if his pervy thoughts were showing. "I realize this doesn't exactly help the case I was pleading about being levelheaded, but this is an extenuating circumstance."

"My buddy Tucker would approve of your legal jargon—he's a lawyer."

"That's Addie's fiancé, right?"

Ford nodded, stifling the desire to run his fingers through the strands of silky hair draped across his knee. "What's the extenuating circumstance, then, Madam Foreman?"

"Ha-ha." She ducked her head, attempting to peek under his thigh, although he doubted she saw much besides his track pants. "Larry Hurst is my biological father. He only ever acknowledges my existence when he absolutely has to, and the last time I saw Cheryl, she told me I was ruining Maisy's wedding with my dramatics."

"You, dramatic? No." Sarcasm was already their home base, but hurt flickered through her features, and Ford instantly regretted his words. If she wasn't gonna jab back, it sucked out the fun, and he hadn't meant to cross into sore-feelings territory. "You also seem extremely energetic. How would you like to go hang out with some puppies?"

"Trying to lure me into your dark, windowless van?" There was the live wire he wanted to grab on to. Before he could answer, she added, "You know what, I don't even care. Anything to get away from here. Let's go."

CHAPTER FIVE

Ford made a cooing, bird-type sound, and Violet froze in place, afraid to move or blink or even breathe.

That's it. I'm going to have to climb the guy and strangle him.

Sure, she'd blow her cover, but she'd asked him to sneak her out, and instead he was drawing attention.

Addie was the only one who glanced their way, though.

A few hand signals from Ford, and Addie's voice turned boisterous. She began loudly talking about how excited she was for the wedding, and the mayor and his wife would be there, right?

With Larry's and Cheryl's focus on Addie, Ford stood, his back to the counter. Then he pulled Violet to stand in front of him. His warm breath wafted over the shell of her ear, and goose bumps swept across her skin. "Walk with me now…"

He nudged the back of her foot with the toe of his sneakers, and they moved as close to in sync as you could with someone you'd barely met. The stutter step made it clear his legs struggled not to overtake her shorter stride, but in no time, they were out the bakery door.

The loud chime had her striding faster, in the opposite direction of the window that overlooked the sidewalk. "Thanks," she tossed over her shoulder. "You make a pretty good shield."

"Happy to help." Ford's hand moved to her lower

back, his fingertips radiating five spots of heat. He propelled her toward a giant black truck with wheels the size of boulders.

Violet dragged her heels. "Wait, where are we going?"

"To train puppies," he said, reaching around her to open the passenger door. "That was the deal, remember?"

"Deal? I thought it was more like you taking advantage of my desperate situation."

"Why can't it be both? Now, can your teeny legs reach that high, or do you need a boost?"

Despite the *phfft*, *don't-be-absurd* noise she made, she wasn't sure. Using the metal step, she clamped onto the seat. It took nearly doing the splits, but she'd be damned if she was going to ask for help getting into a truck that was clearly overcompensating for something.

The engine also growled as if it had something to prove, and then she was riding down Main Street with a man who was little more than a stranger. How did she always manage to get herself into such bizarre situations?

If it was her gift, she was going to find the receipt, because she totally wanted to return it.

"So, the Hursts are your parents?" he asked.

Violet tilted her head. Was this guy for real? If he was pretending to be unaware of her family's soap-opera history, he shouldn't bother. Every time she'd visited Uncertainty, she'd heard the whispers. Noticed the curious looks.

In this abnormally small town, her notoriety came from being the mistake. The physical reminder of infidelity, which was why she didn't blame Cheryl for not being her biggest fan. "I'm surprised you haven't heard about me."

Ford shifted into a higher gear. "Why? Are you famous?"

"More like infamous. I'm Larry Hurst's bastard. Some people say love child in an attempt to sound less harsh, as if you can put a bow on a bomb to counteract the destruction. But he's made it clear there was no love involved."

Over the years, she'd heard Larry and Cheryl fight several times during the custody agreement visits.

It meant nothing.

I was super drunk, and she happened to be there.

If I could take it back, I would.

Ford squinted across the cab at her. "I don't pay much attention to town gossip."

"Come on. You never heard about me, the daughter who messed up the perfect marriage between the beloved mayor and his beautiful wife?" It didn't help that Mom had kept Violet's existence from him a secret for eight years, until Violet insisted on tracking down her father and meeting him. "Every summer, my visits would stir the pot, and the whispers and stares were unavoidable."

Old news by a long shot, so why did residual hurt rise up? What had started as a daydream about meeting her father ended up a nightmare where lives were ruined in her wake. Mom constantly consoled Violet by insisting her dad loved her and wanted a relationship, thus the visits. Frankly, it was hard to believe whenever Violet was away from her real home and her stepmother glared at her with such disdain.

Violet suspected Dad requested the visits more out

of "doing the right thing" and not so much because he *wanted* a relationship.

Ford turned onto a rutted dirt road. "Now that you mention it, it does sound familiar. One of the many reasons I ignored the gossip stemmed from my family always bein' part of it. The McGuires have been the notorious rotten apples of Uncertainty, goin' on a century now. But what I've discovered through the years is that there aren't any so-called perfect families. Everyone struggles. Some are just better at hiding it than others."

Surprisingly candid. Accurate, too.

The squat white house they pulled up in front of had blue shutters, a porch, and a large yard with a white picket fence. And as promised…

"Puppies!" Violet catapulted out the truck as the pint-size German shepherds congregated by the fence, their dark noses poking through the planks.

Pyro leaped the fence as if it were nothing, and Ford bent at the waist and patted his head. "Hey, boy. How were the pipsqueaks?"

The dog replied with a half whimper, half grumble, like a babysitter who'd been relieved after a rough day.

Ford scratched the thick black hair around the dog's neck until his pink tongue lolled and his complaints turned into pants. "The world needs more amazing search and rescue dogs like you, which means they need us to train them. We can handle that, can't we, boy?"

Pyro pranced around, as if he were now on board and encouraging Ford to hurry it up. For a second, Violet's insides went mushy on her. Since the guy had also saved her from an awkward run-in, she allowed herself to indulge in the mush for another two or three seconds.

Her fingers sought the camera hanging around her neck, only to come up empty.

It was the first time in a long time she'd habitually grabbed for her camera, desperate to capture the moment.

Then it was over—a slice of life she wouldn't get to study and analyze later.

Ford opened the gate for her, and three black-and-brown fluffballs rushed her at once, their ears flopping with every springy movement.

Violet dropped to the ground and let them climb into her lap. One of the puppies took her invitation the extra mile, its paws digging into her right boob as he launched himself higher and licked her chin.

"Thanks for that, buddy. Or girlie. I'm not really sure, and I don't want to embarrass you by lifting your tail in front of everyone."

One of the dogs abandoned getting her attention the conventional way and latched onto her shoelaces. He tugged, gradually dragging Violet's foot out from under her.

A shadow blocked the sun, and she lifted her gaze up, up, up. "They're adorable," she said to Ford.

"They're undisciplined," he replied.

The puppy that apparently loved the taste of her makeup kept licking her face. Violet wrapped her hands around its furry body, right behind the front legs, and lifted it in the air. "Are you undisciplined? Or do you just like to give Ford a hard time?"

The puppy barked.

"I agree," Violet said. "It is super fun. But then he

starts name-calling. Don't tell me he's called you obsessive and overly dramatic, too."

The dog gave another squeaky bark, and she gasped and pointed the puppy's snout toward Ford.

"Say you're sorry," she demanded.

Ford shook his head, but the corners of his mouth quivered with a smile. "Just to clarify, I didn't call you dramatic. I implied it using sarcasm."

"Oh, pardon the hell out of me."

A chuckle escaped as Ford crouched to the puppy's level. He petted her furry head and then his eyes— decidedly more green than hazel, although on the olive side—lifted to Violet's face. "I can see you're all about the fun and games, but the reason I conned you into helping me is for the working part."

"Hmm. You failed to mention that while luring me into your windowless van."

One eyebrow arched, a villainous curve that had her contemplating how to become one of his minions, and evidently her common sense had gone on vacation. "I let you have a window in my big, badass *truck*, but let this be a lesson to ya. This is what happens when you let yourself be baited by puppies."

Violet rotated the puppy and brushed her nose against its wet one. "I guess if this is the way I go, so be it."

The puppy who'd untied her shoelaces had moved on to chasing a grasshopper, and now she felt bad for not snuggling him when she had the chance. "What are their names?"

"They don't have 'em yet," Ford said, still squatting, and she wondered if his thighs hurt. Then she was examining his muscular thighs, and she absolutely shouldn't do that because *dayumn*.

"That's just sad."

"I'll make you a deal—"

Violet sighed, nice and loud. "Oh no, not another deal."

"It's called quid pro quo."

"I really should've asked for the quo—or is it the quid?—before agreeing to the rescue mission."

The third puppy flounced over, and Violet lay back in the grass and reached for him. She placed him on her chest so she had all three doggies crawling over her. Pyro tracked her and the puppies' movements with his eyes, and she patted the spot next to her.

He flopped down at her side so he could get in on the cuddling action, too.

"Trust me," Ford said. "You're gonna want to take this deal."

"I find that any time someone starts a sentence with 'trust me,' it's a good indicator I should run. There's this thing called male-pattern falseness and—"

"My God, woman, do you ever stop prattling on and on?" he asked, pinching the bridge of his nose. If he hadn't cracked open an eye and added a smile to the sentence that came out more on the teasing side, she'd be out of here. But now she wanted to hear the proposal.

Securing the wiggliest puppy to her chest, she sat up and blew her bangs out of her face. "Why don't you give me this offer I can't refuse, and we'll see?" She added an over-the-top zipping motion across her mouth.

"Assist me with an hour of training, and I'll let you help name them."

Violet should pass. Head back to the bakery. But Larry and Cheryl might still be there, if not in near proximity with a high chance of an uncomfortable run-in. She retrieved her phone and sent a text to Maisy explaining why she'd split and informing her that she was with Ford.

She pivoted the screen to him. "There. Now my sister knows I'm with you, so you'd best behave yourself."

Of course she added a quick selfie of her with the puppies to the text, because *puppies*. Bonus, she could send it to the Bridesmaid Crew chat, too. "All right, Mr. Firefighter. You have a deal."

Ford extended his hand, and when she placed her palm in his, her skin hummed. "Deal. But full disclosure? I have no intention of behaving."

• • •

In order to train the puppies to find an object or person by scent, there were these things called scent pads. According to Ford, as the dogs improved and got the hang of tracking, they'd place the pads farther and farther away.

After Ford gave her a rundown of how it worked, they left a pouty Pyro at the house, since he had to stay behind for this mission. They put harnesses and long lead ropes on the puppies and headed behind Ford's house, which backed to a forested area with a path that led to the lake.

"I don't want to confuse the puppies with too many scents, so we should split up." Ford studied the three fur babies. "Although, now I'm wondering which one would be the easiest for you to handle."

Violet scooped up the male puppy that'd undone her shoelaces, and her heart nearly imploded as he cocked his head and studied her. "I want this one."

"Oh, I don't think you can handle him. He has ADD."

"Omigosh, same." Plenty of people joked about ADD, and she'd never minded. Well, up until Benjamin rolled his eyes and asked if she'd taken her meds. At the same time, giving people a heads-up helped her feel less rude when she perpetually lost track of conversations. "It'll be a match made in—*oh look a squirrel*!"

Ford's sputtered laughter startled the two puppies at his feet. They glanced from him to her, tan eyebrows twitching. "I'm not sure two distracteds make a whole."

"Hey, just because someone is easily distracted doesn't mean they can't get shit done." She gathered the puppy closer, and her insides turned squishy on her. The next sentence came out heavy on the baby-animal talk. "We'll show him, won't we?"

Four doggy legs pedaled through the air, as if he were ready to prove Ford wrong, too.

"That settles it. Distracto's with me." Violet lowered him to the ground, rubbed a hand over his soft doggie fur, and grabbed a scent pad. They headed the opposite direction as Ford and the rest of the crew.

Once they'd gotten far enough away that she couldn't see the others, she let the little guy sniff the pad.

She'd only placed it a couple of yards away, exactly like Ford had told her to, but Distracto kept getting... well, distracted. He circled a scrawny tree and peed on it.

A yellow-and-black bird landed on the ground and began hopping around, and Distracto towed Violet *away* from the pad.

His tug jolted her shoulder, and she quickened her pace to keep up with him. "Dude, we're going the wrong way. We've got to head back."

Clearly the puppy understood, because he immediately changed directions.

For two whole seconds.

Then a shrub dared to quiver in the wind. The puppy barked at it, the noise so tiny and high-pitched that Violet released a squeaky sound of her own—he was too freaking adorable for words.

The puppy then attacked the bobbing branch—and lost.

He followed that up by peeing on another stump.

Violet tapped her foot as she waited for him to finish his business, her sense of urgency growing by the second. "What is Ford giving you to drink? I'm not even sure how your tiny bladder could possibly hold that much liquid."

Distracto gave an *arf!*

Violet moved the scent pad in the direction Distracto favored, so naturally he headed in the opposite direction. "No, wait. It's this way."

A bug with a disgusting amount of legs required persecution, and she shuddered as the puppy nudged it with his paw. But who was she to prevent one less bug from crawling into town to find her?

After that, she spotted a carpet of green plants with miniature purple flowers, and then she was the one going in for a closer look.

"No, don't eat them," she said, holding the puppy

back when he tried to chomp on the petals. He nibbled on Violet's finger instead, and she accepted the slobber so the plants didn't have to.

Those would be so cute in a wedding bouquet. Like the purple version of baby's breath.

Not that she needed any more ideas. Much like reaching for her camera, it was second nature. Planning a wedding for a decade did that to you, causing you to catalog each item that might add another touch of perfection.

Over the years, her tastes had changed, but—lucky her—she had more than enough time to update her binder of uselessness.

Enough dwelling on that.

Violet stood and glanced around as Distracto tugged the leash this way and that. "Shoot, where did the pad go?"

It took some zigzagging before they found their target. Since she was afraid Distracto might've forgotten the smell, Violet let him sniff, then gave him one of the doggy treats from her pocket.

"Finding this pad means more treats. Got it?"

She relocated him a few yards away, and they started over.

And by started over, she meant another round with a grasshopper and a blade of grass and a fly.

Finally, Violet knelt on the spongy ground, the knees of her jeans sopping up the moisture. "Listen. If Ford finds out we didn't even make it to the scent pad once, we'll never hear the end of it." She patted the puppy's head, fighting to not let herself be swayed by his big brown eyes. "You like hanging out with me, right?"

Distracto sat on his rump and scratched his chin with his back paw. Once she took over the scratching, he climbed into her lap and nuzzled his nose into the crook of her elbow.

"See, this isn't helping."

Much like her baby talk probably wasn't helping. *Must remain strong.*

Gently, she placed the puppy on the ground. She withdrew one of the bone-shaped doggy treats and waved it in front of him. He pounced for it, and she slowly moved it another foot away. Her thighs burned from being hunched over, but Distracto was heading toward the pad again.

Excitement zoomed through her, overtaking her thoughts about her strained muscles. "Good job, buddy. Now that we've made up the ground we lost, we only have to make it a couple of yards."

Another foot down.

Then a stinking butterfly had to show off, flitting its yellow wings as it flew low.

Distracto charged after it, and Violet gathered the rope and stopped him short.

"You're killin' me, Smalls."

The sad-puppy eyes made her feel like a big jerk.

Violet looked around, and when she didn't see Ford, she picked up Distracto and put him a foot or so past where they'd started. She broke the doggy bone in half and lifted it in front of his face. "If I let you eat this, you've got to promise to make it to the pad. You'll get the rest of the treat when you do. Deal?"

The puppy pawed at her leg, desperately trying to snatch the treat, and she bobbed it up and down. His muzzle mimicked the motion, a coerced head nod that totally counted.

"Good enough." Violet carried him a foot closer to the pad and fed him the first half of the doggy bone.

But before she could get him to keep going—because he certainly wasn't doing it on his own—a loud throat clearing, followed by a deep "What do you think you're doing?" made her jump.

She whirred around to see Ford standing with the other two leashed puppies, his arms crossed. "Hey." Her voice came out way too high, with the guilty edge that accompanied being caught.

Ford cocked his head. "Hey? Seriously?"

"Oh, do you prefer to be more formal? Hello, Ford Whatever-your-last-name-is. It's a pleasure to come across you in the swampy Alabama woods. Tis been such a long time since I had the pleasure of company on my midday stroll."

He pressed his lips into a flat line, refusing to smile, but his eyes crinkled at the corners. "Violet."

Her throat went dry as he strode toward her. "Mm-hmm?"

"I saw you cheating. You can't give him a treat until he reaches the pad."

"We had a deal," she said.

"I know, and you broke it."

"I meant Distracto and me." She turned to the puppy, as if he'd back her up. He, in turn, barked at a bush, lifted his leg, and peed on it. "See, I told him I would give him half the treat now, and he'd get the rest when he reached the pad."

The tips of Ford's shoes hit the toes of hers, and her pulse beat so fast it left her dizzy. "That's not when he gets one. Looks like I'm gonna have to take the treats and give 'em out as *I* see fit."

Violet swung her arm behind her, the remaining two and a half doggy bones clenched in her fist. "He's trying his best."

"No, you're a sucker." Ford extended his open palm and gestured for her to hand over the reward treats.

"No, I'm…okay, maybe a little bit of a sucker, but give me another chance."

His chest bumped hers as he reached around her to pry the treats from her hand, and she stretched the limits of her arm. Fabric rustled, a swirl upended her stomach, and she suppressed a shiver as his callused fingertips grazed her arm.

A shriek escaped as he began prying open her fingers one by one. The puppy at her feet barked and wedged himself between them.

Then Distracto shocked them both with a growl.

She assumed, anyway, since Ford's jaw dropped, too.

He peered down at the fur baby, and Violet winced, afraid Distracto was about to get in trouble.

Instead, pride and a hint of delight shone through Ford's features. "I'll be damned. You must be more motivating than I thought if he's ready to take me on to defend you."

Only with the puppy still growling, his brother and sister came to join the fray. They circled and jumped, barking and carrying on, and, at some point, they began chasing one another instead of defending her honor.

Guess that was the problem with relying on an easily distracted guard dog.

Ford and Violet spun, attempting to get the puppies to calm down, but the lead ropes began winding around their legs, and Violet gripped onto Ford's arms as she was the one suddenly fighting—gravity. "Whoa."

"You guys," Ford started, but the biggest of the puppies took off one way as the female shot in the opposite direction. "Stay! Sit!"

Violet swayed backward, bracing for a fall.

Lightning quick, Ford wrapped his arms around her and pivoted, taking the brunt of the fall. They hit the ground hard, Ford landing on his butt with Violet sprawled on top of him.

A giggle started low in her throat, until she was laughing full-out. "You're right. Your training methods are clearly better than mine."

Ford chuckled, too. "It's a work in progress. One that needs more work."

"Maybe you should try the half-a-treat-up-front, half-once-the-job's-done method. All the gangsters use it, and it works very well for them."

"Oh, and you know a lot of gangsters?"

"What? I don't strike you as the mob-boss type?" she asked as if offended.

"I'm not sayin' that, but I did watch your method fail to yield the desired results."

"That's because you"—she poked a finger to his chest, accidentally noticing how very firm it was—"didn't let me finish."

Distracto chose that moment to charge over and eat the other half of the treat, which had fallen on the ground, along with the two others she'd dropped.

His personal mission accomplished, the puppy bounded away to join his brother and sister. The dogs' movements jerked her and Ford's entwined feet back and forth. She got the giggles again, especially since she kept going to push herself up, only for her legs to be twisted in the other direction.

Ford sat up, bringing their noses mere inches apart.

The shift also had her straddling his hips, and heat she hadn't meant to stoke flared to life. It'd been a long time since she'd been this close to a man, and she'd never been this close to one this…manly.

And big.

Holy shit. If she felt what she thought she might be feeling, there was no overcompensating necessary.

"I…uh…" Her words came out way too breathless.

Ford swallowed, his Adam's apple bobbing up and down. His long fingers wrapped around her hips, and— was he going to kiss her?

More, was she going to let him?

"Sorry, I just need to…" Using his grip, he lifted her up and off him. Then he reached past her for the ropes still secured around their ankles.

This is why I can't be trusted around handsome men. I was sitting there with my head in the clouds, halfway leaning in for a kiss, while he was simply trying to untangle us.

Cheeks aflame, Violet attacked the section of rope around their calves, sliding her legs free the instant she could.

A minute or so later, the lead ropes were separated into three, and the puppies were lying down for a nap, maximum destruction accomplished for the day.

Violet and Ford rallied the pawed troops and walked the way they'd come, the sound of leaves and sticks crunching underneath their feet the only sound. When Distracto refused to keep pace or focus, Violet picked him up and carried him.

Ford didn't comment, so either he was okay with it

or he now believed she was a wishy-washy mess. Honestly, she was beginning to wonder herself.

After her nasty breakup, she'd declared she was done with men. For six months, she'd never once been tempted to cross the line. Then, after a mingy hour with a guy who *wasn't even her type*, she'd almost thrown herself at him.

The guy was dangerous on too many levels, and Violet worked to remain calm while plotting her escape. She still didn't want him to think she was a flighty disaster, so that took away fleeing the scene as a valid option.

Once they returned to Ford's house, Violet plopped Distracto in one of the puppy beds. He tucked his nose into the soft fabric, and his brother and sister joined him. She air kissed them and gave Pyro a last pat, mentally preparing a quick, efficient goodbye.

"So anyway," she started as Ford said, "Well, what do you—" He paused and made a *go ahead* gesture. "Sorry, you go first."

"I was about to say that I should get going." She started for the door. "But thanks for the puppy time and the save in the bakery. I appreciate it."

"What about the other part of our deal?" Ford took a step in her direction, and she took a step backward. The spot between his eyebrows crinkled. He closed the distance she'd created, prompting her to repeat her previous motion. "The part where you help me name the puppies."

"Oh. That. Yeah." Her feet kept propelling her backward, but she rammed her butt into the gold handle. She automatically frowned at it. "Whoa. I just went to first base with your doorknob."

"Lucky doorknob," Ford said, and a flurried pitter-patter tapped its way through her.

"Anyway, so, yeah. Goodbye." She spun and twisted the door handle. Added a wiggle and a yank, but the door didn't budge.

Her heart thrashed as a sense of urgency short-circuited her system. She was alone with a charming guy and his adorable dogs, and if she didn't hurry and get out of here, she might forget she'd sworn off men. She refused to go through the pain again. It hurt too bad. Left her too wrecked.

Violet double-checked the knob wasn't locked, turning it one way and then the other and tugging and tugging.

"Here, let me get it." Ford's voice unbalanced her further, and she forced her gaze to remain on the gold knob. What the hell was wrong with her? Besides the flirty door remark, which seemed more teasing than real, it wasn't like he was hitting on her.

She jerked on the doorknob like she was in a horror movie and the killer was coming for her.

"Violet," Ford said in a calm voice. "I'm trying to help you, but you're in the way. Why are you acting like you're afraid of me? Did I do something that scared you? If so, that wasn't my intention, and the thing about the doorknob was just a jo—"

"I'm not scared of you. I just need to get to the bakery, but the door won't let me go, and I'm worried about how long I've been gone. That's all."

His arm snaked around her, he gripped the knob, and then he pushed instead of pulled.

Like magic—or engineering, as it were—the door opened, letting her out and a fresh breeze of air in.

"Thanks," she called, bolting down the porch stairs. She hit the sidewalk and saw his truck. Her lungs tightened, as did her skin.

With a sheepish grin, she glanced over her shoulder to where Ford took up the entire doorway. He casually leaned a hip on the frame and studied her as if she'd lost her mind.

So much for convincing him she wasn't dramatic or flighty.

"Guessin' you just realized I drove you here," he said.

"Uh. Yeah." She went fishing for the phone in her pocket. "But it's okay. I'll call an Uber and be out of your hair in no time." She tapped the app, which took an eternity and a half to open.

"Hate to break it to you, but we're short on Uber here. Short on taxis. You can order one, but it'll take a good thirty minutes to show. It'll be faster for me to take you into town. Unless you're scared of me. Then I'll find you another ride."

Why did he have to be so nice about it? It only made her feel more absurd. Self-preservation was important, though. Then again, now that she'd calmed down, she could admit that she'd overreacted.

To herself, anyway.

She bounced on the balls of her feet, in severe need of expending the anxious energy coursing through her. "If you wouldn't mind driving me back, I'd appreciate it."

And if she could get her hands on a Time-Turner so she could undo her panicky freak-out, she'd appreciate that even more.

. . .

Ford wasn't sure what to say or do, so he drove Main Street in silence, fighting the urge to look across the cab at Violet.

The mood between them had shifted on a dime. He couldn't help replaying the last twenty minutes in an attempt to figure out what'd inspired the change.

Violet had been laughing when they were tangled up together, her eyes wide, her cheeks pink. She'd felt damn good, too, with her curves pressed against him.

He'd nearly lost control when he'd sat up and their hips bumped together. In another couple of seconds, she would've felt that he was getting turned on, so he'd diverted his attention to untangling the ropes.

Still, she'd been okay until they'd walked inside his place.

"I do think Distracto fits that puppy. But would it be hard to place him as a search and rescue dog with a name like that?"

Ford twisted his head in her direction, one eye still on the road. "My ego wants to claim otherwise, but if I'm being honest, I occasionally come across a dog that's not cut out for search and rescue life. Doesn't mean he'll be ill behaved, but I can't declare a dog ready if he constantly gets distracted, regardless of what his name is."

She nodded. Bit her lower lip.

That lip had been inches from his earlier, which was so something he shouldn't be thinking about. At least she wasn't engaged, although he'd been right about her being high-strung. As someone with plenty of ghosts in his past, he was beginning to think she had a few of her own.

Whether that, or if she was as dramatic as Cheryl Hurst accused her of being, it didn't much matter. Particularly when he factored in the binder that indicated she was obsessed with settling down. He knew better.

One of Dad's pearls of wisdom went along the lines of "Living with a temperamental woman is like inviting a rabid racoon into your house and wondering which day she's gonna bite you."

Dad was the expert, too. With two ex-wives, an ex-fiancée, and a string of tumultuous, short-lived relationships, he had a knack for picking 'em. Same as Ford's brothers, Gunner and Deacon, who had plenty of their own demons to add into the mix.

And himself, until he'd gone and given the hot-and-cold type up for good.

Violet's knee went to bouncing up and down. "What'll happen if Distracto doesn't get placed on a search and rescue team?"

"He'll be put up for adoption and find a good home. No need to worry about him."

Relief smoothed her features for a whole second before she tucked her leg up and turned to face him. "How many jobs do you have, anyway?"

"Depends on the day." Ford slowed for Gordon Johnson, who always drove Main Street at fifteen miles an hour. If he were in a hurry, he'd dart down a side road, but they were almost to the bakery, and a part of him wanted to draw out this ride.

With all the deal breakers stacking up, including the fact that he had no interest in settling down, he couldn't pursue Violet. Which meant this might be one of his last interactions with the intriguing, confusing, beautiful woman.

"Firefighting, training K-9 units…" Violet rolled a finger, signaling she expected him to fill in the blanks.

"I'm on the Talladega Search and Rescue team, too."

"Basically, you're a full-time badass."

Gordon turned into his driveway at a spiffy three miles an hour, and Ford forced himself to speed up so he wouldn't create a traffic jam. "That's what my business cards say, anyway."

She laughed, quieter than earlier in the woods, but it hit him as hard. It'd been a long time since he'd enjoyed himself with anyone besides his closest friends.

But again, he couldn't afford the time, and it wasn't worth the effort if they wanted different things. If she'd only end up hurt.

"Mostly it's a lot of searching for lost hikers and hunters. Occasionally we travel to the coast during hurricane season to help." He angled into a diagonal spot in front of the bakery, irritated at the twinge in his chest. "Which is why I hope if you're in trouble, you won't hesitate to call me. That's not a pickup line, either. I take my job very seriously."

The thought of Violet being in trouble stirred up a foreign sentiment he couldn't name. Maybe he did have the hero complex his friends accused him of. That was it. Nothing more.

"I'm sure you do," Violet said.

Ford dipped his head and squinted through the big window of the bakery, attempting to make out the shapes inside. "Want me to go inside and check if the coast is clear?"

Violet held up her phone. "I already texted Maisy. My father and Cheryl are long gone."

Ford got it—he'd been known to dodge his dad and brothers whenever possible. Both in high school when he used to escape to his cave by the lake for days at a time, and whenever they crawled out of whatever hole they'd been in drinking themselves stupid, all so they could cause trouble and keep on dragging the McGuire name through the mud.

He ran the pads of his fingers over the worn, grooved spots in the steering wheel. "What do you do when you're not painting a bakery for your sister?"

The heavy sigh signaled he'd hit a sore subject. See, the woman was practically a land mine. Why would he keep on dancing around the area, waiting for the step that'd blow his foot off?

"I'm a photographer," she said. "Or I was one. I guess I still am. And, with any luck, will be again, after I finish up here and head home to Florida. Let's just say it's…complicated."

"Complicated" was a good word for Violet. "Trouble" was another.

"Anyway, thanks for the ride." Halfway out the door, she spun around. "What about Trouble?"

Ford froze. Had he called her trouble out loud? How could he explain that he simply wasn't into relationships with women who'd storm into his life and would storm out shortly thereafter, leaving as much destruction as a hurricane?

"For the puppy? Pigeonholes him a bit but doesn't blatantly call him out. I'd be upset if someone nicknamed me ADHD. Trouble, on the other hand…

It's a warning and a threat all in one."

"I like it."

Unfortunately, he'd always struggled with not landing himself in trouble, and if it involved Violet, Ford would probably like it way more than he should.

Which meant he was going to have to actively fight his attraction to the woman.

CHAPTER SIX

The paint fumes in the bakery left her light-headed, so Violet stepped outside for a breath of fresh air, congratulating herself on everything she'd accomplished this past week.

The boring sections of the painting job were done, each wall covered in a shiny coat of eggshell. It'd been a slow process, since Maisy wanted to remain open. The fact that Maisy's Bakery—and most every shop in town—closed on Sunday had given Violet time to finish the first step of the remodel.

Her sister had offered to help, but Violet insisted Maisy go to the park with Isla as planned. Bonus, it allowed Violet to concentrate with less guilt, since Maisy chatted a lot, and Violet often missed blips of what she'd said and botched sections of the wall, too.

Multitasking would never be a talent of hers. However, she'd managed, and through the years she'd gotten proficient at filling in the blanks of conversations she'd missed thanks to her ADHD.

Not only did every wall of the bakery boast a fresh coat of paint, Violet had avoided any run-ins with the Hursts or Ford for a week now.

One of the strings in Violet's heart panged, and she placed her palm over the spot. "Play it cool. It's a good thing, so there's no reason to go doing that to me."

Lottie, the woman who owned the also-closed craft store next door, chose that moment to walk by. She pursed her lips and studied Violet as if she should be wearing an orange jumpsuit—the woman would undoubtedly volunteer to knit her one.

"You're not cooking, are you?" Lottie's glower made it clear she suspected Violet had purposely started the fire. She patted a bag bursting with yarn and knitting needles. "I'm off to a Craft Cats meeting, but if you're cooking, I'd better stick around in case I have to call the fire department."

On top of being insulting, Lottie's call would mean breaking Violet's streak of not seeing Ford. Each day it became more of a struggle to believe it was for the best, which only proved it was. "No need. I'm only painting, and I'm finished for the day."

"I'm relieved to hear it." With that, Lottie continued on her way, and Violet resisted the urge to flip off the woman. For the record, her resentment came from more than treating her like an arsonist. Back in the day, the busybody had been one of the people who'd flapped their gums about Violet's scandalous existence.

After locking up the bakery, Violet jammed the bulky set of keys into the pocket of her paint-splattered jeans and headed toward the center of town to meet Maisy and Isla.

She soon found herself on the sidelines of the field next to the park, where a crowd had gathered to watch a football game. She slowed as she spotted the very guy she'd been congratulating herself on avoiding. There was a difference between not seeing and avoiding.

It wasn't the first time this past week Violet had seen him from a distance.

However, it *was* the first time she hadn't run in the other direction. With him in the middle of a game, it was finally safe for her eyes to look their fill.

He and the other firefighter were working together, Darius blocking as Ford ran the ball downfield.

A smaller guy—no, that wasn't a guy. It was Addie. She came fast, slamming into Ford and then jumping on his back when he barely wobbled. *Pretty sure that's illegal, so they must play with their own set of rules.*

Some dude with copper-colored curls added a hit of his own, and Ford hit the ground just short of the goal.

People around her cheered, and Violet turned to the woman next to her. "What game is this?"

The woman blinked at Violet as if she'd asked if the sun was bright. "It's football, and if you're gonna live in Alabama, you best learn your Ps and Qs when it comes to the gridiron game."

Violet worked to keep her smile in place. "I know what football is. I meant is this a league game, or…?" She couldn't come up with any other options, although she was sure there were plenty. So maybe she didn't know a *ton* about football, and apparently that was considered a crime in Alabama.

"Nah. Just a pickup game. We all like to watch. Reminds us of the glory days when we took state with most of the boys out there. You should've seen 'em." The woman cheered as the football was launched through the air, and the entire crowd roared as Darius caught the pigskin and ran in for a touchdown.

She'd bet her half brother, Mason, used to be in the group. Dad often bragged about his games, and during her summer visits, he spent most of the time at football camp. Currently, he was coaching at the University of Tennessee.

Right as Violet was about to move on, the woman

asked, "War Eagle or Roll Tide?"

Violet shrugged, and the woman clucked her tongue.

"Little tip, sugar. Next time someone asks, you say War Eagle, you hear?"

An arm wound around Violet's shoulders, and Lexi smiled at the woman. "I'll finish schooling our new resident on football, don't you worry."

Lexi walked her a few paces away and whispered, "People round here get beyond passionate about football. I saw the expression on your face, and thanks to wearing it myself way too many times, I thought you might need a rescue."

Violet huffed a laugh. "Bless you."

"Anytime. I haven't seen you around since we picked out a cake. You and Ford disappeared mighty quickly."

Now she needed saving from this subject. "Did you get the cake figured out, then?"

Fortunately, that was the perfect topic to bring up. Lexi informed her that she'd found gorgeous sunflowers to add a touch of earthy nature that perfectly fit Addie and Tucker. She'd also ordered rustic brown ribbon in bulk, and did Violet think that would look okay?

"It sounds lovely," Violet said, and she meant it. At the sound of footsteps, she spun to see Maisy and Isla approach.

Automatically, Violet reached for her fussy niece, maneuvering her out of the carrier strapped to Maisy's chest. She bounced her up and down and placed a kiss on her forehead. "Was the park not all it was cracked up to be?"

"It's nap time, but she refuses to fall asleep. As if

she might miss the party."

In the background, people cheered, and Violet held Isla closer, one hand over her ear to drown out the noise. "Trust me," she told Isla once the crowd had settled. "One day you'll miss nap time."

"Listen to your aunt," a deep voice said. "She might be a little melodramatic, but in this instance, she's not wrong."

Violet's body ignited, a fizzing sparkler that burned head to toe, and she didn't have to look to confirm it was Ford.

Still, she turned, a glutton for handsome punishment. His hair was a mess, his clothes streaked with green. Show-off that he was, he also had on a sleeveless T-shirt that displayed his muscular arms to perfection. "I don't think you have much right to talk. Civil people don't tackle each other for an oblong ball. In fact, I'm pretty sure it's something your *undisciplined* puppies would do."

"One can only hope." Ford nodded at Maisy, and she lifted her hand in a wave. Addie kissed the guy with copper curls, and a guy with shaggy, dirty-blond hair gathered Lexi in his arms and gave her a kiss worthy of a romance movie.

"Violet, hey!" Addie walked over and introduced Tucker.

Violet tried to keep her gaze on them, but it drifted to the guy at her side. He wasn't paying any attention to her, though. For about the hundredth time, she reminded herself that putting space between herself and Ford was for the best.

Obviously, he'd gotten the hint. Or had forgotten about her.

An uncomfortable prickling sensation nettled her—one she did her best to convince herself wasn't hurt feelings. She'd withdrawn to avoid future pain, so her body had better knock it off.

"We're headed to the Old Firehouse for a drink or ten," Addie said. "Y'all wanna come?"

"Oh, I think Isla needs a nap." Violet peered down to see her niece's eyes drifting closed, her chubby cheek smooshed against her shoulder.

"I need a nap, too," Maisy cut in. "I'll take her home so we can both get some sleep, but Violet was just saying she didn't get out much anymore and how she would like to change that."

Violet fired daggers from her pupils, aiming them at her sister.

Maisy gave her a grin that seemed to say *I'm doing this for your own good* as she took Isla from Violet's arms.

In one last-ditch attempt, Violet scratched at a dry glob of paint on her T-shirt. "I'm not dressed for going out."

"Dude," Addie said, drawing out the word. "Look at us. 'Sides Lexi, none of us ever dress up to go to the bar. Trust me, no one will care."

With that, Violet had run out of excuses. Besides, one drink wouldn't kill her. Then she could head home and murder her sister. With love, of course.

Judging by the way Ford bolted for the Old Firehouse, not bothering to check if she was coming, he wouldn't be asking her to stay longer anyway.

• • •

"What crawled up your ass and died?" Easton asked as Ford ordered beer for the table.

Ford picked up a red straw and stuck it between his teeth. "Don't know what you're talkin' about."

Easton leaned an elbow on the polished wooden bar. "I'm talkin' about how I've known you forever, so don't bother bullshitting me. I thought you'd be happy Violet tagged along. You've talked about her enough."

"I mentioned her *once*. And if she doesn't want to even be friends, that's fine. No skin off my nose."

"Aww. Did someone get his giant ego bruised?" Easton punctuated the question with a jab to Ford's shoulder.

"You're about to get your giant mouth bruised, asshole."

"Which is it? Mouth or asshole?" Easton contorted his body, aiming his butt at him as he batted his eyes over his shoulder. "I need to know which one to pucker."

Ford glanced to the heavens. Almost every single one in the group had a big mouth, but he and Easton talked the most shit by far. Usually Ford would give it right back, but seeing Violet again had thrown him off his game. Not football, because he'd dominated on the field. But all week, out and about in town.

He'd caught glimpses of her, mostly when he walked past the bakery and accidentally on purpose peeked inside. He'd thought it would be trickier to avoid her, but evidently she was evading him right back. Possibly even enlisting help, the way she'd done to escape the Hursts, and that chapped his hide.

Maybe even bruised his ego.

If that were all there was to it, he could forget about

the woman easily enough. But calling Trouble's name made him think of Violet every damn time. Of catching her feeding the puppy a treat in spite of never reaching the scent pad—the dog still hadn't, either.

Of the moment she'd fallen on top of him, her amazing laugh, and how she gave as good as she got. For a woman he'd only interacted with a couple of times, she was proving difficult to kick out of his head.

Addie wiggled between him and Easton, calling to the bartender to please add orders of wings and fries. Then she whirled around, her back resting against the bar. "Did I hear correctly? Easton's finally made his intentions clear about kissing your ass?"

"Kicking," Easton corrected.

"In your dreams," Ford said.

Easton grabbed a glass from the tray that'd been placed in front of him and downed a gulp. "Ford got his ego bruised. Now he's all mopey."

"By who?" Addie's eyes widened. "Violet? I thought I was doing you a favor by asking her along. In the bakery the other day, you sounded our escape call and left with her, and today she was makin' eyes at you, so I assumed it went well."

"She helped me with a puppy-training exercise. End of story."

Addie scooted the tray toward Easton, bumping the edge into his arm. "Take those to the table, will ya? Ford and I will wait for the food."

Easton saluted her, bold with the sarcasm—but he took the tray and left him and Addie alone, as requested.

Addie squared off in front of him, and Ford groaned. "Murph, don't say what I think you're gonna say."

"Tough titties, McGuire, it's happening. Ever since that hurricane last fall, you've been off. Hell, you've been *sad*, something you hardly ever are, and that worries me. I get that you went through something big. I understand, too."

Besides a handful of members on the Lower Alabama Search and Rescue team, Addie was the only person who'd heard the whole story. Late one night after the two of them had made their way through a six-pack of beer and a blurry amount of Jack, she pushed.

Out it came, one word at a time.

Addie's fingertips on his arm managed to soothe and goad him at the same time. He'd seen plenty of bad shit go down. Had witnessed death. Wished he'd gotten there sooner. Felt helpless as the life bled out of a person he'd done his utmost to save.

Why did a mission involving a cheery old lady have to be the one that messed with his head?

"You promised Doris you'd live your life to the fullest, but all you do is work and think about work," Addie said. "And you haven't looked at a woman the way you look at Violet in a long time."

Live life to the fullest. The words scraped at him, a reminder of what Doris had told him and how he'd failed her on too many levels.

"I can't get tangled up in a complicated situation— I'm not even sure how long she's staying in Uncertainty." Used to be, he'd take any and every opportunity to chat up a beautiful woman. He'd had a few serious relationships through the years, like his off-and-on thing with Trina and a woman from Opelika who claimed she didn't mind he needed space and wasn't interested in settling down.

Occasionally, when he'd missed plans due to work or extending a camping trip, she'd get pissed. But he'd make it up to her, and things would go back to normal.

Until they hit the one-year mark and she gave him an ultimatum about moving in together.

He'd passed. The next weekend, he came home to find a box of his destroyed belongings. His favorite AU T-shirt and his camo hoodie had been shredded, and the DVDs he'd taken over for various movie nights had been snapped in half.

After that, he'd given up long-term relationships for good. Only on the rarest of occasions did he miss having a special someone.

"Does that silence mean you realized you're not, in fact, living your fullest life?" Murph asked.

Ford arched an eyebrow at her. She raised one right back.

"It means I need to get a new group of friends. All y'all know me way too well."

"Wah-wah-wah. How about you stop being a big ol' baby"—Addie snatched the baskets of food that'd arrived and shoved him in the direction of a certain pretty brunette splattered in paint—"and start living a little, dude? And in case you're wonderin', I'm not takin' no for an answer."

• • •

Surprise pinged through Violet when Ford approached the high-top table and chose the stool next to hers. Another emotion came along for the ride—one best unnamed, since she'd vowed to stay away from guys who wouldn't choose her in the end.

"Here," Ford said, thrusting a basket of fries in her direction.

"Thanks." She snagged a couple and bit into them.

Too hot. She seesawed her breaths in and out, in and out, attempting to cool the food. *See. Things that are too hot are a good way to get burned.*

She grabbed her glass and downed a swig of beer.

Then grimaced.

"Let me guess," Ford said. "Not a beer girl?"

"I try to be."

A contemplative crinkle appeared. "Try to be?"

"It's been implied that not liking beer makes me high-maintenance, which I'm totally not." Funny how Benjamin had given a ten-minute lecture after she'd purchased the wrong IPA—she hadn't paid attention to labels and bought blue instead of black—and then told her *she* was high-maintenance for preferring "froufrou" wine.

Lexi leaned in from the other side. "If preferring wine over yeasty beer makes me high-maintenance, I'll happily own it. You want a rosé? That's what I always get."

"No, that's oka—"

"Will, honey? Can you order Violet a glass of rosé?"

"On it, babe." The guy everyone except Lexi referred to as Shep stood before Violet could insist she was fine.

In some ways, that had been her downfall with Benjamin. In her attempt to tame her anxieties about being too "needy" and her desire to be the perfect future wife, she'd settled for his likes. Let him mow her over in the name of not disagreeing.

It'd been so good in the beginning, though. Back then, they'd done lots of little things to make each other feel cherished instead of nitpicking at each other's flaws.

Always and forever…

Hurt bloomed through her chest, aggravating old hurts that refused to fully heal. Somewhere in the depths of her wedding binder were the vows she'd written. She'd ended them with the phrase she'd repeated to Benjamin upon parting and each night before bed.

I love you. Always and forever.

Always and forever, Benjamin echoed every single time.

Had he ever meant it?

Surrounded by couples, each of them staring at each other with adoration, longing Violet thought she'd ridded herself of tightened her throat.

Addie lifted her head off Tucker's shoulder and nudged Ford's knee. They had some kind of telepathic conversation before Ford turned to Violet. "How's your week been?"

"Productive. I finished the base coat on the walls of the bakery, so now I get to move on to the fun, bright accents part."

Ford tapped his fingers on the table. "Cool."

The rest of the table not-so-surreptitiously watched them, and Violet searched her brain for what to ask in return. "Um, how are the puppies?"

"Good." Ford downed a swig of his beer, and she wondered if he was making a point of proving he found nothing wrong with his drink.

Man, this was painful. What happened to the easy

joking vibe they had the other day?

Maybe it has something to do with you treating him like he'd trapped you in his house.

A glass of pink wine was passed to her, and admittedly it was nice to have a drink she enjoyed instead of tolerated.

Since she'd been working on self-talk and keeping it positive, she reminded herself it was okay to enjoy what she enjoyed. Both while planning the wedding that'd never happened and shopping for items to turn their townhouse into a home, Benjamin had gasped over the cost and remarked on her "expensive tastes."

This from the guy who wore designer clothes and insisted on purchasing a BMW hardtop convertible. He'd claimed his recently-paid-off vehicle was beginning to have problems and of course they should put a down payment on the car *and then* plan their nuptials.

After all, how could he pay for a wedding if he didn't have a reliable way to get to work?

Which was why, after finding him with another woman, fueled by vengeance and more alcohol than she'd ever drunk in her life, Violet had stumbled into the garage of her townhouse, saw the new car and shiny golf clubs, and snapped.

She could still feel the reverberations of the pitching wedge in her hands as she swung and bashed the metal hood and windows. It'd been so satisfying to destroy a thing her ex had loved more than her.

The regret came afterward, when she was dealing with the massive hangover from hell and saw the destruction. When she realized her temper and obsessing over his cheating had gotten the best of her.

It ratcheted up several notches when Benjamin

called the police and she was charged with criminal mischief in the first degree. It'd been the most mortifying incident of her life, but she'd pled guilty and paid her thousand-dollar fine, as well as the sum to fix the car.

Having the guy who promised *always and forever* press charges instead of giving her a break depleted that much more of her passion for photographing happy couples and families.

Another hard pill to swallow…? The realization that she shouldn't have buried her head in her wedding binder like an ostrich in lieu of working on the day-to-day parts of their relationship.

Hindsight wasn't just twenty-twenty; it was an eagle-eyed bitch.

"…bridesmaid update," Lexi said, and Violet was jerked back to the present, where she smoothed her features in hopes her thoughts weren't broadcast upon her face. A slim possibility, yet she could only imagine what this group—what Ford—would think of her lapse in judgment.

He'd probably call her unstable, and during the car-clobbering incident, she had been.

"I got us an appointment on Saturday afternoon at the bridal gown shop in Magnolia where I bought my dress," Lexi continued. "Ford and Addie, I need you there by two thirty. Would you like to carpool with me?"

Ford snorted. "You mean you'd like to carpool so that we'll be on time."

"Fine. I was pretending to give you a choice, so thanks for shattering the illusion."

"Anytime," Ford said with a grin, and Lexi shook

her head but flashed him a smile.

"And before you boys start bragging about how much easier you have it as groom and groomsmen, I also scheduled you an appointment the following Tuesday so the tuxes will match."

"Wait, tuxes?" Tucker asked. "I was thinking of scrapping the penguin suits and going casual for my wedding. Jeans. Or maybe overalls, like the pair Addie's so fond of."

Lexi's smile faded, her expression turning so frigid Violet shivered.

Sputtered laughter broke the silence, and Tucker winked. "Just messin' with you, Lex. I appreciate you making the appointment."

"Tucker Crawford, you're lucky that killing you would completely ruin the wedding, I swear."

They all laughed, good-natured teasing clearly part of their group dynamic. Even as an outsider, she felt the love.

Being around the tight-knit group also made her miss her friends. The chat thread with the "Bridesmaid Crew" kept them in touch, at least, but their different paths left everyone busy and spread across the country. Leah and Amanda were the only two left in Florida, and once they'd moved to the suburbs, it'd been harder to meet up.

Without thinking, Violet's hands searched for the camera around her neck so she could capture the camaraderie—only to remember it wasn't there. Since it was the second time she'd experienced that spark, maybe it was time to start hauling her Canon around again.

"What if you came with us?" Lexi asked, placing a

hand on Violet's shoulder.

"Came with you where?" With her thoughts drifting to how she'd shoot the scene to include the juxtaposition of the rustic local bar in the background, she'd lost track of the conversation.

"To choose the wedding gown. You were so helpful at the cake tasting, and your binder is very impressive. I could use your help reining in these two."

"But remember how I'm a recovering bridesmaid who doesn't do weddings anymore?"

"All I need is your opinion." Lexi brought her hands up in prayer position. "*Pleeease.*"

"We'd love to have you," Addie said, and Violet glanced at Ford. She wanted to gauge what he thought of her involvement.

Hard to do, since Ford was riveted by the widescreen television in the corner.

"McGuire!" Addie smacked his leg.

"What? First game of the official MLB season, and this guy just got an unassisted triple play."

Addie's eyes widened and lifted to the screen. "Seriously? I can't believe I miss—"

"Addison Murphy!" Lexi's voice boomed. "Do I need to draw up some plays? I'm the coach, and I say focus up."

"Wow, have you been giving her lessons, Shep?" Tucker asked. "She's got the tough-coach bit down."

Not only did Lexi manage a seated curtsy, she made it elegant.

Violet smothered a laugh, marveling again at the mixture of personalities.

Then the outsider feeling grew stronger. If she could hide behind her camera lens, she could better filter out the sensation. Without it, the amount of yearning tiptoed into the forlorn range.

Time to gracefully take her leave. "Sounds like you guys have a lot of planning to do, so I'm going to head home." She gripped the edge of the table and began to scoot her stool away. "Thanks for the drink and for—"

"Wait." Ford covered her hand with his. "It's early yet." He paused as if he wasn't sure why he'd stopped her or what to say next. "How 'bout I get you away from the wedding talk and show you the pool table? I've already beat their sorry asses, and I'm lookin' to whip up on someone new."

Lexi gave him a sidelong glance, like she suspected him of attempting to get out of planning, which was probably true. Violet shouldn't take the pity bone she'd been thrown, but Ford stood as if he knew she'd say yes.

With his gaze heavy on her for the first time in a week, pressing against her skin and igniting a whirl of heat, she didn't want to walk away. Wasn't sure she could. Did his magnetism apply to everyone, or was she simply the perfect polarity?

Either way, she decided to give in to its pull and toss her own gauntlet. "Care to make it interesting?"

The red straw in his mouth bobbed with his smile. "Always."

"FYI," Easton, the dark-haired cop, said, "our boy is competitive and acts like a jackass whenever he loses."

Ford flipped him off, and the cop smirked and said, "See?"

"So he needs a lesson in losing gracefully." Violet downed the rest of her wine and set her empty glass on the table. "I'm absolutely up to the task."

With the trash talking done, she followed Ford to

the pool table. He retrieved two sticks and asked if she wanted to break.

Seriously, what had she been thinking, challenging the guy? She was far from a pool shark, but she also hadn't specified what "make it interesting" meant. First, she needed to figure that out for herself.

"You can break," she sweetly said, wrapping a hand over her closed fist. "And then I'll break you." Since she'd never been able to crack her knuckles, she went ahead and added sound effects. "Crack. Pop. Tough noise."

The hypnotic twitching of Ford's arm muscles halted as he went from chalking his pool stick to leveling his green eyes on her. "Did you just *add* knuckle cracking sound effects? I'm not sure you're doing the intimidating thing right."

"That's how I sneak up on people. Plus, even if I could crack my joints, I hate the sound. Gives me goose bumps."

Ford moved closer and, with a grin that bordered on evil, cracked his knuckles without using his mouth.

"I should've seen that coming."

"Lesson number two: never let your opponent know your weaknesses."

Violet plucked the blue square of chalk out of his hand. "Wait. When was lesson number one?"

"When I taught you not to be lured by the promise of puppies."

"Right. How could I forget?"

Ford leaned over the table, an eye squinted. He looked straight out of one of those movies where people go into a bar in the country to get information, usually on the whereabouts of some killer.

This guy? This is the guy who's wearing down my resolve?

His shirt didn't have sleeves. He was chewing on a drink straw, same way he probably chewed on the kind that came from bales of hay.

He was…so frickin' hot.

"Speaking of," she said, right as he hit the cue ball. "Did you ever name the puppies?"

A loud *crack* split the air, and two striped balls dropped into corner pockets.

That cockeyed corner of Ford's mouth twisted higher. "Gonna have to do better than that, Vi. And Trouble, Nitro, and Tank are doin' fine."

"Aww. Nitro and Tank? How cute is that?"

"'Tough'—that's the word you're looking for."

"Mmm, no. Pretty sure I meant cute."

"Since you started with the T and they're destructive little devils, I figured TNT fit nicely. Trouble is what his name claims, Nitro's fast, and Tank crashes on through no matter how much heavy furniture you push across doors to keep him out. Together, they destroy."

Violet stuck out her lower lip. "So, so *cute.*" She pointed at her eye. "Like, I'm getting a tear in the corner from the cuteness."

"Next you'll be sayin' bombs are adorable," Ford muttered. However, the groove in his cheek gave his almost-smile away.

At the drag of his hand across her lower back, every nerve ending in her body stood at the ready. He set up right beside her for his next shot, and her body was ready to spontaneously combust from his nearness.

Suddenly she could relate to those puppies all too well. Search and destroy. Expend and sabotage. Live in the moment, for later you might not be able to pee on every tree in the woods.

In other, more-human terms: carpe this diem and make it your bitch!

Which was why, as Ford retracted his elbow, Violet draped herself across his back and covered his eyes with her hands.

"Resorting to cheating?" His gruff voice traveled down her arms and kicked her heart into motion.

"It's called making it interesting."

Her arms dropped as he pivoted to face her, the shift leaving her plastered against the front of his body.

"Interesting, hmm…?" Ford perched on the edge of the table and maneuvered the pool stick behind him. Gaze locked onto hers, he took his shot.

And the stupid green-striped ball fell in.

Yeah, she was going to lose. But with him staring at her, a cocky smirk on his face, it felt a lot like winning.

CHAPTER SEVEN

While Ford had never held back in a game before, he figured it'd be more fun to watch Violet attempt to catch up than sink the eight ball too early. So he'd purposely botched his last attempt.

The pink tip of her tongue came out as she bent over the table. As she lined up her shot, his pulse thrummed faster and faster.

One tiny bump, and the cue ball knocked into the solid orange ball. It rolled toward the pocket, slowly around the rim…and dropped inside.

Her celebratory booty shake seemed more like a reward than ridicule.

As he leaned against the wall, the exposed brick snagged his shirt and lightly scraped his skin. "Okay, question time."

Violet circled the table and calculated her angles with the pool stick. "I sunk my shot. Why do you get to do the interrogating?"

"So I don't get bored waitin' for my turn." Not that he'd be bored. Watching her overthink each shot was highly entertaining and made it damn near impossible not to notice her lips. Soft and pillowy, and the idea of kissing them buzzed in the background, an incessant mosquito he wasn't sure he wanted to swat away.

Focus, McGuire. Addie would ask if he'd made a genuine attempt with Violet. The classic definition of a "full life" might not be in his wheelhouse, but he supposed it wouldn't kill him to take a stab at a well-rounded one.

"Last week you said you were a photographer but that it was complicated. Explain." Ford didn't want to reveal how often he'd thought about her and that comment, but he'd wondered about it too often to let it go.

Violet wrinkled her nose and ran her fingers along the felt edge of the table. "My muse is proving to be difficult as of late. Spectacular photos involve more than simply pointing and shooting. I used to *feel* when a shot was perfect. That intuition recently disappeared, along with my passion. I came to town to spend time with my sister and niece and to renovate the bakery in hopes I can jumpstart the bitch."

"If you need a jolt, there are electric paddles in the town ambulance, and I happen to have the keys." Ford patted his pocket.

"Oh, I bet you'd love to shock me."

In a different way than she meant, but not altogether untrue. With her so close, he felt as supercharged as a defibrillator himself, and all that crackling energy craved an outlet.

Violet stretched across the table, bestowing him with a glimpse of cleavage. As much as he wanted to linger, he moved aside in an attempt to be respectful—also, if she overshot, the ball would be coming for his crotch.

"Damn it," she said when she scratched.

Planning on giving her shoulder a squeeze while offering a "good try," he rounded the table.

Right as she suddenly spun around.

He dodged, but the tip of her stick skimmed his upper chest and left blue chalk across the front of his shirt.

"Oops." She rubbed at the spot. Every cell in his body pricked up, and his heart went to throwing itself against his rib cage. In order to fully enjoy her touch without having to brace for another hit, he gripped her pool stick. He liked how the top of her head came right to his chin. "At least the blue matches the green grass stains. You might even say I made your shirt look better."

"Where exactly did you go to college? BS University?"

She laughed, and the happy sound kicked him in the gut. "The University of West Florida is where I got my Bachelor of Arts"—her big brown eyes lifted to his face—"but my minor was in BS."

Okay, so maybe Addie had been right. He hadn't had this much fun in a long time. "Explains why you insisted I sink the numbers in order while you can shoot all willy-nilly."

"Geneva Conventions rules—I still can't believe you haven't heard of them before."

A gentle tug freed her stick from her hand. Ford rested it against the wall and then stalked forward. He gripped Violet's hips and hauled her onto the edge of the pool table. "If you bring this up in front of my friends, I'll deny it, but I'm a big fan of the way you play."

The beauty mark on her cheek punctuated the smile she flashed him—another feature he'd foolishly failed to catalogue. She swung her legs through the air, her ankles brushing either side of his knees. "We'll see if that holds true when I beat you."

He peeked over her shoulder so he could line up his shot—thanks to her "rule" about him going in order, he had to aim for the thirteen instead of the easier fifteen.

Since he was a cocky bastard, he pulled back enough to look her in the eye.

Right as he went to take his shot, she slid the toe of her shoe up his inner thigh. His stomach relocated in the vicinity of his throat, and thanks to the involuntary jerk of his arm, he missed the cue ball entirely.

Violet burst into laughter. "Still a fan?"

His mind concocted several ways he'd like to punish her for throwing his concentration. Only he rather liked where it was right now.

If there weren't other people in the Old Firehouse, he'd tackle her. They'd crash onto the table, billiard balls scattering in every direction. Then he'd kiss her until her breaths became his as well.

Heat replaced the blood in his veins, spreading up to his brain and setting fire to the few logical thoughts that were left.

If he followed through, it'd be juicy gossip by morning. He used to be a regular feature in the local grapevine when he and Trina were dating. If they were cuddly, the story morphed into a sordid tale about them practically having sex in public.

During their volatile periods, he'd heard tales of thrown objects and domestic disputes that'd never happened. *He's too much like his dad*, they'd say. Or granddad, depending on the age of the blabbermouth.

After that, he'd tried to keep his dating life out of the public eye. More than that, he had a feeling Violet wouldn't want to be reduced to town gossip, the way she was when she was a kid.

Since they'd caused enough of a scene as it was, he simply loomed over her with a mock stern glare.

"You're so going down for that."

"Big talk for someone who missed his shot. Can't say I wasn't warned you might be a sore loser."

"The word was competitive, and you ain't seen nothin' yet." He bent so that their noses were almost brushing, her lips so intoxicatingly close his entire being became tethered to them. He wrapped his hand around the back of her knee and jerked until she was teetering on the edge of the table, his body the only thing preventing her from falling.

She sucked in a breath but didn't move away. Her fingers clasped his elbows, and her tongue darted out to lick her lips.

His self-control floundered in the exquisite deluge of desire, and the list of reasons he needed to hold back evaporated. Gossip City here he came.

"Excuse me," a shrill voice cut in, popping their intimate bubble, and Ford cursed the interruption that had Violet jumping down and away from him. "Aren't you Larry Hurst's daughter?"

Apprehension bled into Violet's features.

"Wow, it is you," Nellie Mae said. "You look so much like your daddy. Not as much as your siblings, but I could certainly pick you out of a crowd."

Could and had.

"Sorry, how rude of me." The older woman gestured to herself. "My name is Nellie Mae Pruitt, and I work at the town hall with your daddy. I can't believe he didn't mention you were visiting."

"Oh, I haven't been in town long." Violet's words came out rushed and a pinch squeaky, likely due to her loose interpretation of *long*.

Nellie Mae narrowed her eyes on Ford.

Don't get him wrong—there were plenty of incredible, kind-hearted people in town. Even though the woman belonged to the Craft Cats, who were infamous for sticking their noses in others' business, she meant well. For the most part.

She also had the memory of an elephant, and he and his friends had wreaked a lot of havoc. Houses toilet papered; tearing through town on their bikes, focused on winning a race instead of townsfolk on peaceful walks; and leaving open cans of sardines in a locker so an entire wing of the school smelled fishy.

"Ford McGuire. People keep insistin' you've changed since high school, but I didn't just fall off the turnip truck." She scrutinized the minimal distance between him and Violet. "In my experience, people rarely change."

"You must've not noticed I'm taller now. A whole two inches."

After a *harrumph*, Nellie Mae directed her next comment to Violet. "Most folks 'round here are real nice, but you best mind who you spend your time with. You'd hate to sully your reputation.

"Anyway, I'll be sure to tell your father I ran into you when I go into the office tomorrow." The amount of superiority she aimed his way insinuated he'd be mentioned, too. As if drinking a couple of beers and playing pool was the equivalent of planning a bank heist.

If so, most everyone in Uncertainty was guilty.

"Oh. Um," Violet said. "Could you hold off on mentioning it? I haven't caught up with him yet." Nellie Mae frowned, and Violet gnawed on her lower lip. "I've been…busy."

"You haven't told your father hello yet?" She *tsk*ed. "Kids these days. What happened to respecting your elders?"

With that, the woman walked off, muttering about the world going to hell in a handbasket.

Before Ford could attempt to revive the happy mood, Violet said, "It's getting late. I should head out."

She trudged over to where his friends were still shooting the shit, offered to pay for her drink—which was shut down with a chorus that boiled down to *nope*—and told them goodbye.

"I'll walk you," he said.

"I managed to get around Pensacola without an escort. I'm confident I can take on the streets of Uncertainty."

"I'd feel better making sure you get home safely. You never know when another member of the Craft Cats will ambush you, and I've got experience dodging their knitting needles."

Snickers went around the table, and Tucker explained that he, too, had been interrogated by the Craft Cats. "Without representation, I might add."

"I'm all for the independent-woman thing," Murph said, "but McGuire has a hero complex big enough to fill the Mississippi. He'll worry about you the whole time, so it'd be easier for the lot of us if you'd allow the chivalry."

And the award for best wingman went to Addie. Not that she was wrong, although he didn't like the term "hero complex."

"Come on then, Mr. Escort." Violet gave another last wave. "Thanks again. Have a good night."

As they stepped out of the bar, Ford wanted to put

his hand on the small of her back or take her hand in his. Her stiff posture suggested it might not be welcome, though, and he respected people's boundaries. Especially women's.

Should I try to do damage control? Explain what Nellie Mae implied about me?

Not only did he doubt it'd do any good, he couldn't deny what Nellie Mae had implied was somewhat true. He'd never excelled at the boyfriend thing, and there were plenty of locals who might think less of Violet for hanging around a "troublemaking McGuire."

They're all the same, he'd heard about his family, sometimes whispered and other times loud and clear. He'd never liked it much, but he had enough experience arguing with close-minded people to grasp how futile it was.

Still, earlier, when their game had turned flirty, he'd gotten an inkling of what a balanced life might entail. Which made it hard to shrug and say *oh well, guess I already lost my chance with this girl.*

"Now I'm going to have to call my dad," Violet said. "I'd die of shock if he hasn't already heard I'm in town, but he hasn't tried to contact me, so why do *I* have to feel guilty?"

"You don't have to."

"Yet I do." Her shoulders slumped, and she kicked a stray rock off the sidewalk. "It was nice pretending the crappy stuff didn't exist for a while, you know?"

"I can imagine."

The tiniest of smiles touched her lips. "What crappy stuff would you get rid of?"

"Natural disasters, probably. Hurricanes, floods, fires."

"Wow. Way to make my answer sound overly frivolous."

Ford jammed his hands in his pockets. "Sorry. After Nellie Mae called me a derelict, I needed to compensate. Speaking of, have I told you about how I singlehandedly saved every whale in Alabama?"

Violet giggled, and the knot lodged in his chest loosened. "And when will I get to see all these Alabamian whales?"

Keeping up with her wit was a challenge, one that sent a tantalizing zing through his bones. "Hanging out with the Loch Ness Monster in Lake Jocassee, of course. Might ought to mention both creatures are awfully bashful."

"Sounds like your BS degree is more advanced than mine."

His steps slowed as he neared Travis and Maisy's front door. He didn't want his time to be up yet, and he didn't want to wait another week to see her.

Ford braced his hand on the doorjamb, words harder to form with the light from the outside fixture casting her in a golden glow. "Lexi made it clear you'd be a welcome addition to our bridal-shop outing. Honestly, I could use your help there, too. While a guy's opinion can be a real asset—"

"Blech," she said, adding a gagging noise while mimicking sticking a finger down her throat.

Ford chuckled and snatched her wrist out of the air. He lowered their entwined hands and rubbed his thumb over the knuckles she couldn't crack without sound effects, which, how damn cute was that?

As cute as she claimed my puppy's badass names were.

Since he'd been going somewhere with this speech, he reined in his thoughts about Violet's adorableness. "Addie's one of my best friends. You have more experience than I do at the bridesmaid thing, and I don't want to steer her wrong. 'Specially since she's as clueless about dresses as I am."

"Look, I don't believe all that nonsense the lady in the Old Firehouse spouted. In fact, I think you're a great guy—"

Ford groaned. "Great guys never make history."

"Yes, they do. Abraham Lincoln, Martin Luther King Jr., the Dalai Lama."

"Fair enough." He slipped his fingers between hers. "My point is you're not gonna date any of those guys."

"Well, some of them are married or dead. Or married and dead, and—"

"Again. Missin' the point."

"Sorry." Violet slipped her hand from his, leaving it empty and longing to grasp for what it'd lost. "What I'm trying to say is that I've sworn off men. Namely, dating them."

"Good thing I didn't exactly ask you out."

"You didn't exactly not ask me out, either."

Dang Addie, goading him into spending time with Violet so he could go and get his hopes up. This conversation wouldn't have stung his pride if it'd happened *before* the pool game and the almost-kiss. "All right, I hear you. We can just be friends."

Violet sighed. "I don't know if that's a good idea, Ford."

"Fortunately for you, I do know, and it is."

Violet pressed her lips together, fighting that killer smile of hers, and he chucked her on the chin.

The gesture brought out the full smile, along with a shake of her head.

"This is me, asking a friend"—he inclined his head toward her—"that's you, lest you didn't piece that together yet—to help him help his friend pick out a bridal gown."

"Typical dude stuff, then?"

Damn, she was funny, and that only amped up his desire to spend more time with her. "Now you get it."

The reflection of the porch light danced in her eyes as she tipped her face to his. "Then I'll be there. You're lucky I'm such a sucker for wedding dresses."

A thread of panic stitched its way through his chest—jab, tug, jab, tug. Usually talk of wedding anything on a first date would send him running.

But this wasn't a date, and Violet had asserted there wouldn't be any of those.

Disappointment stabbed at him as that realization set in, and he wondered if that made *him* the moody one. This woman was doing a number on his head and his emotions.

He summoned up his most winning grin. "Pick you up Saturday at two. Just know that if we're late, I'm gonna tell Lexi it's your fault."

"Friends all of five seconds and you're already willing to throw me under the bus."

"Absolutely," he said with a laugh.

Then he forced himself to tell her goodbye and beat a retreat. Because friends didn't normally kiss, and if he stood there for much longer, he might go and forget that fact.

CHAPTER EIGHT

It's just my dad. No big deal.

The cat was out of the bag. Bright and early Monday morning, her father had texted, "A little bird told me you're in Uncertainty. We should grab coffee tomorrow afternoon."

Violet wondered if Dad truly hadn't known. Yes, she'd kept a low profile, but she suspected there'd been mention of Maisy's sister. Or, at the very least, a woman helping redecorate the bakery.

Instead of letting that sliver of doubt dig deeper under her skin, she decided to congratulate herself on her ability to lay low.

Thanks to Ford getting her out of the bakery in time.

Conversely, he was also the one who'd challenged her to a game of pool, so those two things might cancel each other out.

"Did you want something to drink yet, ma'am?" a teenage boy in an apron asked.

What she wanted was for him to stop calling her ma'am, but in this part of the south, there was no fighting it. Yay for respect—if only it didn't make her feel so old.

"I'm still waiting." Violet gestured to the empty chair across from her when the kid seemed confused. "Remember how I told you earlier that I was here to meet somebody?"

Kid. Guess I am old.

"Oh. Right." He shook the hair out of his eyes. "It's just been twenty minutes, so…"

Violet worried her brittle smile would shatter and reveal how very aware she was of the time. Her heart twanged with each beat, the pumps sending alternating bursts of doubt and justification.

No wonder she hadn't told Dad she was in town. The guilt she'd pretended not to feel over not visiting since Maisy's wedding dimmed.

Why had Dad asked her to meet him at the coffee shop? To stand her up and remind her how much she embarrassed him? Both by daring to be born and again recently, when felon was added to her rap sheet?

Mason earns heaps of praise for how far he can toss a football, but no one mentions my stellar golf swing. Joking about her life fails helped her cope, but today's feeble attempt wasn't enough to combat the sting.

Her eyes burned, and pressing a fingertip to the corner confirmed that, yep, tears were forming. Violet scooted out her chair, ready to hang her head and take her leave.

Then the door swung open, and there Dad was. Dressed in a suit, dark hair contrasting his ivory skin and combed in the same conservative style as always, though it'd thinned, and strands of gray glimmered under the overhead lights.

He strolled over and plopped in the seat across from her.

Violet waited for a "sorry I'm late" or an explanation of why, but it never came. Instead, he tugged at the lapels of his jacket and studied a menu he must've read a hundred times.

"Hello, Father. Good to see you." At least her

sarcasm was fully intact.

He cast her the briefest glance. "You, too. What would you like to drink?"

The overly formal greeting had gone over his head. If only it'd slammed into his face and shaken loose some emotion. Ugh, why couldn't she stop caring? Why did it hurt every single time he showed how little he cared in return?

"What I'm really hankerin' for is a cupcake," Dad said.

"We should've met at Maisy's, then."

"Nah, Cheryl goes in there too often."

Ouch.

Her face must've dropped, because Dad stretched out his arm and patted her hand. "I didn't mean it that way. You know how Cheryl gets whenever you visit."

"Guess that means you didn't tell her we were meeting up this afternoon."

"I…" Dad pressed his fingertips to his forehead and exhaled. "I'm planning on it. Heaven knows there's no such thing as a secret in this town. She'll likely hear about it before I get home this evening."

And the hits kept coming.

Comprehension spread across his face. "Not that I'm hiding it. Work's been extra busy, so I simply haven't had the chance to mention it."

Sure. Whatever. Admitting hurt feelings hadn't changed anything in the past, so Violet didn't bother.

After a minute chock-full of awkward, Dad asked what she wanted and headed to the counter to order their flavored coffees. He wisely waited for them to be brewed, saving them another few minutes of wrenching silence.

Dad returned, two large mugs in his hands. He set her vanilla latte in front of her, and she smiled at the leaf pattern and well-loved teal mug. Under other circumstances, she'd enjoy the quaint coffee shop. Places like this and Maisy's bakery were upsides to the tiny town where people lived at a slower pace, and she was holding on to those pros for dear life right now.

The wooden chair creaked as Dad settled into his seat. "I heard you were at the Old Firehouse with Ford McGuire."

Violet sipped her latte, biting back a curse at the impatience that'd earned her a burned mouth. She licked at the foam on her upper lip. "I was there, yes. There was a whole group, and Ford was part of it. Why?"

Dad fiddled with his mug. "I realize it's a bit late for me to jump into the protective father role—"

"You're right. It is." She probably should've held her tongue. After he'd breezed in twenty-three minutes late, only to make her feel like a skeleton he wanted to shove back in the closet, she needed to get in a hit. Otherwise she'd leave feeling like a punching bag that'd been worn down and broken, vulnerability seeping from the cracked leather.

Nonetheless, her ire wasn't going to help their strained relationship. *I'll put in my time, and then I'll go back to Maisy's and give her a hug so I can focus on the good that came from being Dad's dirty little not-so-secret.*

His sigh carried his impatience over to her. "All's I'm trying to say is you might want to be careful with that boy. The McGuires don't come from good stock."

"Good stock? Isn't that what you say about cattle and horses?"

Another sigh, but Dad slid aside his mug and charged on. "Funny you mention horses. Back in the day, they used to be horse thieves. They'd come in the middle of the night, steal 'em away, and keep them up in the mountains."

"Did I just step into a wild west soap opera? That had to be, what? A hundred years ago?"

"More like seventy. But the next generation made their own moonshine, and Ford's grandpa frequented the county jail. His father graduated the same year I did. Jimmy's got four kids with three different women."

Anger roiled, heating her blood, and she didn't care if her latte scorched every one of her taste buds. She downed a few gulps, needing the time to gather her thoughts and process instead of reacting in a way that'd cause permanent damage.

One more perfectly warm slug, and Violet slammed down the mug. "Seems hypocritical, coming from a man who also has kids with more than one woman."

Okay, so she couldn't hold it back. But did Dad sincerely not see the connection?

"At least I learn from my mista—"

Dad didn't finish. He didn't have to.

The leg of her chair caught in a groove on the tile floor, and Violet nearly tipped it and herself over. That would've been a more dramatic exit than she intended. "This mistake is done trying. Goodbye, Dad. I think it's best if we keep our distance while I'm in town."

A dejected expression overtook Dad's features as he stood as well. "I get it; I always manage to say the wrong thing. And you don't give me an inch. In fact, every time I try with you, you lash out."

If this was his trying, she might prefer for him to quit. For both of them to accept their relationship was doomed from the start. Maybe then they'd both stop feeling like failures.

Violet's throat tightened, oxygen harder and harder to come by.

"I saw how badly Benjamin hurt you," Dad continued, "and I thought I'd save you from another heartbreak. Ford might be a better man than his father or his grandfather—time'll tell. But besides one on-and-off-again relationship that was tumultuous at best, I've never seen him out with the same woman twice. He's not the settling-down type, honey. Tigers don't change their stripes."

Somebody tell Alanis Morissette I can help her define Ironic, *and it's that statement, coming from Dad's lips.*

A wheeze fell from her lips, and her throat was only growing tighter.

And itchier.

And her tongue didn't seem to fit in her mouth anymore.

She eyed her now-empty mug. "What was in…" Wheeze. "That latte?"

"I ordered what you said. A vanilla latte." He, too, looked at the mug as if it'd hold the answers for why the world wouldn't stay still, the patrons and tables blurring around her.

Then he gasped. "Cheryl and I switched to almond milk, so I told them to go ahead and make both of them with it."

Violet clawed at her throat, desperate to relieve the

itchiness. "I'm allergic to almonds."

She plopped in the chair, unzipped her purse, and riffled through the contents. It'd been ages since she'd had an attack, but somewhere in this mess…

Vaguely she heard the ruckus around her intensifying, the volume and amount of people escalating. She couldn't focus on that, though.

There it is.

It took two tries to remove the cap. Violet gripped the EpiPen tightly, jammed the needle into her thigh, and depressed the syringe.

Her heart was either not beating or beating too fast—her brain wasn't functioning well enough to discern which one.

With the medicine delivered, she stared at the syringe in her leg, waiting for the relief.

Is that a siren?

Why would there be a siren? I must be losing it.

"Over here," Dad yelled, and wow, a ton of people had gathered around her. How embarrassing.

The crowd parted, and a tall, dark, and handsome gentleman appeared.

Hallucination or reality?

"Couldn't wait till Saturday to see me, huh?" Ford asked as he squatted in front of her. Dad was rattling off information about her allergy and the latte with almond milk. Words like "help" and "hurry" were in the mix as well.

Violet's hand drifted up, oddly detached from her body, and she pressed it to the side of Ford's face. Whiskers tickled her palm, and that—combined with the cocky statement—left her sure the man in front of her was 100 percent real.

"I'm fine," she quickly said, another wave of embarrassment crashing over her.

Ford gave a pointed look at her leg.

"That's nothing."

A huffed laugh escaped as he gently removed the syringe.

"See? I'm fine *because* of that." Violet studied Ford as he removed the stethoscope from his neck. Sonnets could be written about his corded arms. There'd unquestionably be a line in there about how his scruff highlighted his lips and that slight upward tick in the right corner.

And the shades of green in his irises—a picture of the Ireland countryside could hardly contain the variety.

Violet scrunched up her forehead. "You never said you were a paramedic."

"How's your breathing?" Ford asked. "Are you getting enough air?"

"Obviously, or I wouldn't have been able to ask you about being a paramedic."

"Technically it was more of a statement." After situating the stethoscope in his ears, he placed the circular end on her chest. "Most firefighters have paramedic training. It's also a necessity when it comes to the search and rescue job."

"I seriously can't keep up with all your jobs, dude."

"Normally I don't have to do so many of them so close together. But you, Miss Overachiever, are keeping me busy." His gaze latched onto hers, steady and fierce, and her heart was definitely beating too fast now. "Ready for another shot?"

He withdrew a tiny vial from his bag and filled a

syringe. "This is diphenhydramine hydrochloride—Benadryl. I'm going to get this into your veins, and then we'll take you to the hospital."

"I don't need to go to the hospital."

Ford hiked up her sleeve, pinched the skin on her shoulder, and jabbed in the needle.

With one eye squeezed closed, Violet focused on his dark head of hair instead of the prick of pain. "For reals. Between the EpiPen and the Benadryl, I'm good to go."

She began to stand, horrified at the idea of Ford driving a screeching ambulance down the streets, announcing to everyone that her own father didn't have a clue about her allergies—or her.

Not that the siren would say that, but Dad had alluded that secrets were unheard of in this town, so it was essentially the same thing.

"You're seeing a doctor," Ford said, pushing on her shoulders until her bum hit the chair.

"I'm not. I don't need one." She spread her arms. "I'm totally fine."

"Oh, really? And have you been trained as a medical professional?"

"I've had an allergy attack before that required the EpiPen, which practically makes me a prof—"

"If you've had medical training, raise your hand." His green eyes challenged her, and she set her jaw, her arm remaining at her side.

Ford did a double take at the grizzled dude a table over with his arm up.

"Taxidermy doesn't count, Bob."

"I took anatomy."

"When one of those animals you've stuffed comes

back to life, we'll talk. Until then, it's my show." Ford grabbed her hand and braced his other palm at her elbow. "Nice and easy."

"I'm neither of those things," Violet muttered as she let him tow her to her feet. She didn't even object to the arm he secured around her waist. But she was going to have to get out of this doctor thing somehow.

"Do you want me to ride in the ambulance with you?" Dad asked. The genuine concern in his voice and on his face was the only reason she bit back her *Won't Cheryl find out?* response.

"There's no call for an ambulance, so no." Arguing with two frustrating males sat low on her things-I'd-like-to-do list, so she figured she'd let Ford escort her outside and then plead her case.

The fresh air made it easier to breathe, and sucking in a lungful cleared her head. She turned to Ford, the guy who was supposedly "bad stock." She couldn't care less about that.

The player thing, on the other hand?

A pinch worrisome, considering she was beginning to like the guy more than she should.

Right now, though, she simply needed to get him on her side.

"So, kinda embarrassing to admit, but my medical insurance lapsed, so I can't afford the ER or even a doctor visit. Going broke won't help my health. Especially when I'm fine." She batted her eyes and added a hair flip for good measure. "Can't you just check me out?"

"Sweetheart, I've been checking you out since the moment you got into town."

The blush couldn't be helped. Wiggle room, on the

other hand, could be exploited, so she ran a fingertip down his arm. "What's it going to take to keep this between you and me?"

Ford loudly exhaled, that crinkle in his forehead showing up as the wheels in his brain turned.

"Another puppy-training session," he finally said. Then he tapped her on the nose. "That way I can watch you closely. Both so you don't cheat and give Trouble undeserved snacks—the rascal still hasn't made it to the pad—and so I can keep an eye on your allergy symptoms and make sure you're as fine as you claim."

"Oh, I am, Ford McGuire." She flashed him a flirty smile. "And you have yourself a deal."

"Oh, and one more condition: you have to bring your camera."

CHAPTER NINE

As soon as they reached the prettiest spot in all of Alabama, Trouble jumped out of the back of the truck. He took a running leap at Violet and gave her the type of greeting Ford would've liked to: a big kiss.

Although he would use less tongue—somebody should teach that pup the art of finesse.

Once Violet admitted to not having insurance, the case he'd planned to launch in favor of the ER fell flat. Growing up, he and his family only went to the doctor if they were on the brink of death.

"If we have to shell out money for a doctor, you'll be complaining about your empty stomachs," Dad would say whenever he or his brothers were sick. "Better do some research and find plants to cure what ails you."

After several iffy remedies, studying proven cures had been a relief. No more chewing on bark, hoping his headache would go away.

He still wasn't sure how the McGuires hadn't ended up with tetanus, lockjaw, or gangrene, considering how much rusted metal they'd played on.

Ford turned to Violet and extended a hand. "Wrist."

"Foot," she said, lifting one and wobbling on the other.

As they'd driven to his place to get the dogs, she'd chatted nonstop, leading him to believe the epinephrine had catapulted her ADD to the next level. Halfway through an observation about the cute shops in town, she'd hit him with: Did you know mustard plants are relatives of broccoli and cauliflower?

"Anyway, mustard shouldn't be a color, and that building over there clashes with the other shops, so I'd repaint it. Actually, mustard yellow is a lie. The yellow comes from turmeric."

Even now, she bounced on her toes as if preparing for a marathon. "Why are you looking at me like that? I thought we were naming body parts."

Stuffing his amusement down deep so he could switch into responsible paramedic mode, Ford stepped closer and grabbed her hand. "No, we're trying to take your pulse—I am, anyway."

He twisted her wrist and pressed his fingertips to her radial artery. At the feel of the steady palpitations under the surface, his breath hitched. Over something he'd done numerous times before.

He'd counted a whole five beats when Violet bent to pick up the whimpering puppy at her feet. Trouble was doing his damnedest to live up to his name, and Ford was beginning to wonder if Violet should come with a warning label herself.

"I swear, woman. Hold still, will ya?"

Violet blinked her big brown eyes at him, not bothering to release the puppy, and his professional medical persona dissolved. So much for being responsible and distancing himself, the way he'd been trained in order to avoid burnout.

A heady sensation inundated his system as he placed his hand on the side of her neck. It was easier to read her pulse there, anyway. Her eyes dilated as he counted the beats of her heart, and then he was the one fighting distraction.

Smooth skin, shimmery lips, silky hair.

She smelled incredible, too, the vanilla note in her perfume tempting him to take a taste.

And time… Her pulse was on the higher side, but that was to be expected.

For a second, he thought she was breathing too hard, but the heavy panting came from the puppy in her arms, and man did Trouble's breath reek.

Yet Ford's hand remained on the side of her neck, the steady beat under his thumb a comfort he hesitated to give up.

"Is your tongue still swollen?" *Would you like me to test it for you?* Ford cleared his throat, cursing his libido and the number this woman was doing on it.

Violet stuck out her tongue, wiggling it side to side. "Nope."

"Any more itchiness?"

She shook her head. Then she wrapped her fingers around his wrist, and his pulse skidded to life, as rapid as hers had been after all the adrenaline hit her. "Hey, you. I appreciate the concern, but I'm fine."

"And you'll tell me if that changes? You swear?"

"Yes, Mr. Paranoid Paramedic. I will."

Unfortunately, paranoia had followed him since his last search and rescue job, and it didn't seem to be going away anytime soon.

It's okay. I've lived a full life.

It's not okay. You're gonna keep on living that full life, you hear me?

A quick grounding exercise blocked the memory before it could take hold and mess with his head all over again.

"Let's get this show on the road." They were on the

far side of Lake Jocassee, about a mile from the cave that used to serve as his second home.

Although he didn't plan on showing Violet that. It was a sacred spot—one he'd never shown anyone.

Noticing one vital item was missing, he opened the passenger door of his truck and gestured to the fancy contraption in the middle of the bench seat. "Don't forget your camera."

Ever the smartass, Violet saluted him. Too bad for her, he wasn't budging. He'd heard the anguish in her voice as she'd discussed losing her passion.

Ordinarily, he kept his nose out of people's business. He struggled to watch talent go to waste, though, and it'd happened too often at his house growing up. If Violet needed a push, he could provide one.

Inspiration, on the other hand, might be harder to come by.

• • •

After an hour of training, Nitro and Tank had found the scent pad countless times, from greater and greater distances.

And her puppy had done a lot of marking his territory.

Violet could tell by the way Ford raked his hand through his hair that he was growing frustrated with Trouble's inability to focus. Which triggered her anxiety and had her heart beating an irregular rhythm. *Pay attention. Try to help…*

"I'm going to the truck to water the dogs. Feel free to take a look around." Ford tapped the Canon 5D Mark IV that hung from her neck. "Maybe use this thing."

Once he and the dogs had disappeared through the trees, Violet forced herself to wrap her fingers around the camera. Being afraid of an inanimate object made no sense.

She wasn't exactly afraid of *it*. She was afraid she'd discover she had lost her touch. Worried she'd take photos, only to look at them later and wonder what'd happened to the woman whose work had been featured in a bridal magazine.

The cover came off the lens with a light *pop*.

Slowly, Violet lifted the camera and peered through the viewfinder.

She swiveled toward the water and messed with the settings until everything sharpened. Sunlight reflected off the rippled surface. Cypress trees stretched toward the sky, their fat, multicolored trunks marking how much the water level rose and dipped.

There was something hauntingly beautiful about the swampy setting.

A crane swooped low, skimming its downy wingtips across the surface of the lake.

Violet depressed the button and waited for the image to show on her viewfinder. Lovely but ordinary. Still, a start.

Around the bend of the lake sat a tree-covered rock formation. Ford had referred to it as chimney rock and said they used to jump off the top and into the lake all the time.

Painted images covered the stacked rocks, dripping colors with faces and peace symbols. Initials with plus signs between them—how had those couples turned out? Did they get their happily ever after?

Click, click, click.

At least the sound of the camera comforted her, making it easier to sink into her first photo session in ages.

Footsteps alerted her to Ford's return, but he didn't approach her. He secured the puppies' ropes around a fat trunk, and then he and Pyro sprinted down the wooden dock. Violet wove around rocks and trees to get a better view.

A bit of zooming, and she had Pyro and Ford in her sights. Ford squatted, placed his hands on either side of his dog's face, and rubbed with enough gusto that Pyro's ears flopped from one side to the other.

I need to get a bit higher…

A fallen tree provided the perfect perch, and, with one hand bracing her climb, Violet managed to boost herself. She zoomed in and changed angles, capturing moments between a man who kept showing up when she needed help and his faithful companion.

The bond between them was palpable, as was the emotion she'd been missing in the scenic shots. Joy pinged through her as Ford tossed a stick and Pyro raced after it. *Click, click, click.*

The puppies whimpered, ready for their turn to play.

Violet continued to move closer.

"…show me you'll listen, I'll let you off the leashes, too."

Ford sat on the grass and gave each of the puppies a rubdown, and Violet snapped more pictures. So much adorableness going on—enough she wasn't sure she could capture it all.

But when she scrolled through the images, warmth flooded her.

She homed in on the puppies' faces and dangling tongues.

Then she gave in to the temptation to zoom in on Ford's face. *Dammit, maybe I do like dark hair and fair skin on a guy.*

When she lowered her camera, Ford asked, "How's it goin' over there?"

"Surprisingly well. You?"

"Doin' just fine." He lifted a bottle of water, the sunlight making it glitter, and then he tossed it her way.

The camera *thunk*ed against her gut as she caught the bottle. Until it hit her palm, she hadn't even realized how thirsty she was.

As soon as Ford slackened the puppies' ropes, Trouble came bounding for her.

Violet crouched to greet him. Affection swirled, the soft hair beneath her fingers sending her worries and cares far, far away.

"I have an idea," Ford said as he, Tank, and Nitro stopped in front of her.

Violet shielded her eyes as she squinted up at him.

"What if *you're* the scent pad?"

Much longer and her burning thighs might give out, so Violet stood, ignoring the joint pops. "I'm not sure how to take that, Mr. McGuire. Are you saying I smell?"

"Not me. Trouble thinks so."

She gaped at the puppy prancing at her feet, ready to go despite being clueless of the destination. "Really? And you decided to tell him instead of me? I thought our bond was stronger than that."

Ford's soft laugh ignited a whirl of desire. "I meant I want *you* to go hide, dragging your scent as you make a trail about ten yards away. I'm hoping that'll get Trouble a first down already."

"Aww. That'd be so cute if he had a doggy football." Violet braced her hands on her knees and addressed Trouble. "Would you like a football? Just bark the word. Or say the bark. Not really sure which one best fits, but—"

"Violet, can you focus for a second so I can try to get Trouble to focus for a few minutes?"

She grimaced and returned to her full height. It hadn't been easy to concentrate with the extra adrenaline and the lake. Plus feeling her camera around her neck, a weight that reminded her she suddenly couldn't do her job anymore.

Ford cupped her cheek and softened his voice. "Please. I forgot to say that part."

His touch danced across her nerve endings, and it took her two tries to force out a reply. "Well, in that case, anything for Trouble."

"Tryin' not to be jealous of my dog now."

Violet flashed him a haughty smile to show him that he should be but that she wasn't mad. She squatted and let Trouble take a big ol' sniff. "Hey, buddy. Ready to play hide and seek?"

Trouble barked and spun in a circle.

Since Ford was watching, she debated whether or not to kiss Trouble's adorable furry face, but she'd resisted for long enough. She lifted him and gave him a loud, smacking kiss on the forehead. "Make sure to find me, okay?"

Trouble whimpered when she handed him off, as if he sensed she was about to leave him behind. An irrational ping of guilt bounced through her because she was.

He'll find me. While dragging her feet, she made a zigzag path. She touched nearby trees and bushes, and once she guesstimated the distance to be about ten yards, she hid behind a boulder.

Before long, she heard the cracking of sticks. She tried to be patient, but an antsy sensation crawled over her skin and had her squirming in place, hope, encouragement, and excitement surging.

She peeked around the boulder.

Right as Trouble rounded it and leaped onto her lap.

Pride sang through her entire body, and she squished his face between her hands. "You found me!"

The puppy licked her chin, and when he rolled over, legs up, she rewarded him with a belly scratch.

"I'll be damned," Ford said.

"I think he's more motivated by affection than by food."

"Afraid I can't relate."

"I can. That's why Trouble and I understand each other so well." Violet extended her hand. "He still deserves a treat, though, and *someone* wouldn't give me any."

Ford relinquished the contraband, which she gave to Trouble while piling on the praise.

A yawn surprised her, her adrenaline quickly fading, and she yawned again.

"We finally did it," Ford said, beaming at her and her puppy and sending her elation to the next level.

"We finally did."

"I meant Trouble and me—we finally managed to

wear you out." Ford flashed her a devastatingly sexy grin. Then he reached down, grabbed her hand, and hauled her to her feet.

And as they walked back to his truck with his brood of dogs, he didn't let go.

CHAPTER TEN

"I think this might be a trap," Ford said as he cautiously walked into the bridal shop.

Lexi had texted the address, along with instructions to turn off his radio, leave his beeper at home, and take the afternoon ALL THE WAY OFF!

Violet stepped onto the thick, creamy carpet he was probably already staining with his worn steel-toe boots. His maternal grandmother used to have a room like this. Look, don't touch.

It'd been a long time since he'd thought of Grandma Cunningham or his mother. Ma was Dad's second wife, and she'd left when Ford was nine. The original story was that she just went to visit Grandma for a while. And Ford had been glad she hadn't taken him along. While his city-slicker cousins managed to remain as mute and immobile as statues, Ford failed with a capital F.

"What?" Violet bumped her shoulder into his. "Afraid some woman is going to leap out and demand you walk down the aisle with her?"

"I am now," he said, having to summon the humor he'd come hardwired with.

A smile curved her peachy-pink lips. They had some kind of glossy stuff on them that glittered in the light beaming from the jeweled chandeliers.

Ford tucked his hands in his pockets, afraid to touch or move or even breathe. One thing was for sure—he didn't belong here.

Violet moved farther into the space, in the direction of the plum-colored couch that faced a three-way mirror. A white pedestal with sparkly high heels sat atop it, and, in addition to curtained dressing rooms, a variety of wedding dresses hung from hangers along the walls. "A bridal shop, huh? I thought putting a jar of jerky in the center of a snare would be the best way to trap you."

He took a reluctant step so she wouldn't leave him in the dust. "Sounds like you nailed me pretty good."

A giggle burst out of her. "There are so many things I could do with that statement, but this is a classy joint."

Shock jolted him, the comment enough to taper his uneasiness. Now he wanted to hear the options, because it sounded like she might have a dirty mind in that pretty little head of hers.

Violet looped her elbow through his and patted his biceps. "Don't worry. If there are any rabid brides who are clueless enough to search for a groom inside a bridal shop, I'll protect you."

"Ha-ha," he said, while a voice in his head whispered *yes, please.*

Sunlight streamed across the carpet as the door swung open and Lexi and Addie walked inside. Lexi shifted her sunglasses to hold her blond curls like a headband. Addie shrunk in on herself a bit. Then she also jammed her hands in her pockets.

"You hearin' Radiohead's 'Creep' in your head?" he asked, and Murph nodded.

"The lyrics 'I don't belong here' are blastin' for sure. Same way they did when I came for the bridesmaids' dress fitting with all of Lexi's fancy-pants friends."

"You two are being silly," Lexi said. Violet simply continued to grin at him.

"What?" he asked her.

"Just recalling how you've used my vulnerable moments against me, coercing me into deals involving puppies and such."

"Hey now," he said, and she laughed, having way too much fun at his expense. "Those deals were mutually beneficial."

A whole heap of mischief shone through her features as she leaned closer. "I'll keep that in mind."

A pint-sized blonde in a frilly black-and-white top and sky-high heels welcomed them in a refined southern accent.

Violet quickly stepped in front of him and threw an arm out as if the woman might attack. "Don't worry," she whispered, casting a wink over her shoulder. "I've got you. I won't let her hurt you."

"Smartass." He flicked Violet's dangly silver earring, enjoying the resulting tinkling noise.

The tiny woman rattled off a stream of facts in a high-pitched voice. Lexi responded in whatever language involved silk and tulle and dress styles.

"Can I get some of that protection?" Addie whispered to his sexy bodyguard.

Violet repositioned herself to cover them both, taking them by the arms and following Lexi as she and the woman headed for the rows of dresses.

Bridal Shop Employee beamed at the three of them before taking Violet's hand. "You must be the bride."

One corner of Violet's mouth twitched, her smile turning superficial. "Actually, this is our bride." She gestured to Addie.

"Oh." The woman eyed her jeans and War Eagle T-shirt. "That's right. A bit of a tomboy, correct?" Without waiting for confirmation, she charged on. "So, what styles and fabrics are you thinking? Tulle? Silk? Organza?"

"Yes?"

"It's fine if you're not sure. We occasionally get a bride like you."

While she presumably didn't mean it that way, the *like you* did come out sounding a pinch condescending. And the way Addie's face fell made it clear she'd taken it as an insult.

Ford nudged her with his elbow. "You know what dress you should get, Murph? That one from the Guns N' Roses 'November Rain' video. All super short in the front."

Addie rolled her eyes. "You guys watched that video way, *way* too many times during our classic rock phase."

"I'm lost," Violet said, and Ford pulled out his phone. He found the image, and she made a sour face. "I guess I see the appeal to dudes—you can see her garter and...*and*."

Ford waggled his eyebrows. "Ah yeah."

Addie's dark ponytail swung as she shook her head, but her cheery demeanor had returned, so mission accomplished. "That short skirt's a hell no from me. And before you ask, that's not going to be our song. The end of that video is devastating, not romantic."

"Is there anything more romantic than a relationship that never got ruined by all the shit life throws at you?"

The raised eyebrow from Lexi conveyed this wasn't

a swearing type of a joint. Which solidified he didn't belong in a place like this. Then she began searching through the sea of cream and white, the *zing* of sliding hangers filling the air.

Addie lifted the dress nearest her. "I like this. Simple yet elegant."

Violet moved closer and flinched—clearly she didn't have a poker face, so playing with her would be highly entertaining. "Um, that's a slip. It goes underneath the gowns."

"Oh," Addie said. Her breaths came faster and faster, and was she… Oh boy, those were tears. Ford had never seen her cry before, and a vise clamped onto his lungs, twisting tighter and tighter. At least he had plenty of experience calming panic attacks.

Typically, he wouldn't be scared that a person's reaction might be to punch him, but he'd take a hit from Murph if it made her feel better. "Hey. It's no big deal."

No move to swing, so he added a back rub to the mix. "This wedding thing's new to me, too. Let's take some deep breaths. In…" He sucked in a lungful with her. "Out."

They blew out uniform breaths.

"If you wanna wear a slip, I'll take out anyone who says you can't."

Addie gave a half-laugh, half-sob. "There'll be talk no matter what I do. I think that's why I'm feeling the pressure, which is stupid. The entire town is just happy I'm gettin' hitched. Forever I was the resident old maid, and everyone feared I'd end up alone."

"If you need me to permanently move to town to fill that position," Violet cut in, "I can."

Lexi rushed over, and she and Ford made a Murph sandwich. "What's wrong? Is it the shop? We can go to another."

"It's not the shop." Addie slapped a hand over her face. "This is so embarrassing. I guess I care more than I realized. I want the wedding to be perfect for Tucker, even though he says it'll be perfect because it's him and me.

"But my mom and my nonna are debating every tiny thing and tugging me in opposite directions, and I'm overwhelmed, which makes no sense because poor Lexi is doing the majority of the planning."

Now Ford was out of his league. Head wound, no problem. Dehydrated hiker, he had the drill down pat. Part of him wondered if an IV would help—not that he had one on him.

The urge to make it better swelled and swelled until his rib cage could hardly contain it.

Violet turned to the bridal shop consultant. "Can you give us a few?"

"Of course. I'll get the champagne." With a nod, the tiny woman on stilts was gone.

Ford followed Violet, guiding Addie to the couch and lowering her onto the velvety cushions.

"Do you want me to call Will?" Lexi asked. "Or Tucker or your mom?"

Addie's eyes went wide, and Ford was about to attempt an "I'm all the man she needs right now" joke when Violet took control. "Can you find her a bottle of water? She's probably dehydrated."

Ford opened his mouth to argue she wasn't showing signs of dehydration—not to mention Addie was a water peddler, constantly demanding her clients, football players, and their group drink more.

Violet caught his eye, though, and he understood there was a method to her madness.

A sense of purpose overtook Lexi's expression. "I'll be right back."

Once Lexi left, the mood lightened, and Violet sat on Addie's other side and patted her knee. "I know this whole thing is overwhelming. You play football, right?"

Addie nodded.

"Okay, so when it comes to the wedding, you're the QB. Yeah, you decide a lot, but Ford, Lexi, and me, we're your..." Violet glanced at him for help.

"I'm your left tackle, Lexi is your tight end, and Violet—"

"Is the coach. I've got a playbook, too." After a reluctant beat, she dug into the bag she'd brought along and withdrew the battered-yet-still-glittery purple binder.

For such a tiny thing, it managed to send his blood pressure through the roof. Yet, he was also kinda turned on by Violet's approach. Smart, breaking it down like that. Grounding Murph in the familiar.

"Remember that you're the bride," Violet continued. "The whole reason we're here. That means you get what you want, and if you don't know what that is, we'll help you figure it out. That's what good teams do. Mind if I...?" Violet motioned to the diamond ring adorning her finger. "Classic band, emerald cut."

"Tucker insisted on getting a bigger diamond." Under other circumstances, he'd mock the way Addie's voice turned dreamy. "He thinks the football players will hit on me, so he wanted to ensure they saw it every time I taped up their knee or ankles or put them through PT exercises."

Violet opened the binder to a page marked bridal gowns. A few of them had star stickers, and if Ford wasn't afraid of the answer, he might ask what that meant. Assumedly, they were her favorites. "These might be more ornate than you'd wear, but if you see anything you like, let me know. Then we'll narrow our options. Of course, you might want to try some other styles, just so you're sure."

"I'm sure that dresses have never been my thing."

"They might have dressy pantsuits if you truly don't want a dress."

"My mom and my nonna might kill me twice if I went that route." Addie turned to Ford, her wide eyes imploring him for advice he hadn't a clue how to give.

"It's your show, Murph." A lightbulb went off. "And don't worry about us mocking you for wearing a dress. We got that out when you were Lexi's bridesmaid."

"I heard that," Lexi called, on her way over with a bottle.

"I wasn't keepin' it a secret," he hollered back. "Truth be told, you make whatever you wear work, whether you're gussied up or kicking ass on the field."

"Aww, thanks, McGuire." Addie turned her smile from him to Lexi as she handed her a bottle of water. "Thanks to Lexi's wedding, I learned that I *can* rock a dress. I want to feel beautiful, and I'd like to stick to the more classic wedding gown thing."

Addie gave the heels on the pedestal a dirty look. "Those torture contraptions, however, are a no go. If I can't wear my comfy sneakers"—she lifted her foot, displaying her gel kicks—"I'd rather go barefoot."

"I bet we can find an option that makes everyone

happy," Violet said. "But in the end, you decide which pass to throw."

Relief and desire made an interesting cocktail, the kind that left him gratified. Not only had they calmed Addie down, Violet had used football analogies that managed to be both useful and superhot.

Ford stretched his arm and grazed Violet's shoulder with the tips of his fingers.

And with Addie's freak-out over, she began pointing at the different gowns, making comments that Violet and Lexi understood and he went along with— yay, teamwork.

The bridal consultant returned, and Violet rattled off terms Ford could hardly follow. Then she, the clerk, and Lexi headed toward the racks of dresses.

Ford resisted the urge to put his feet up on the pristine pedestal.

Addie slumped against the cushions and groaned. "I'm turning into a girl."

"You'll always be a dude in my eyes," he said, hoping he was speaking the truth. While he kept telling himself not much would change, Addie had acted different since she and Tucker had gotten engaged.

"I care about the wedding stuff, though. I'm completely lost, but I want one day of feeling like a superstar. While also being comfy. And nothing too frilly, you know?"

"Totally. In fact, that's what I think every time I open my drawers to get dressed."

She laughed, and he laughed, too.

"The other day I teared up over not knowing which font to put on the invitations. Then I was like, who even am I? So I cried some more." Addie rubbed a hand over her face. "It's a big day, I get that. Since I'm not usually one to stress much, I didn't think I'd get so emotional."

Her spine went stick straight, and she tucked a leg underneath her as she faced him. "The rest of the gang can never know I had this meltdown. If I survive it, I'd die of embarrassment."

"Takin' it to my grave, I swear." He held his hand to the square, like they used to do as kids. "Or may you hogtie me, throw me in a Bama cheerleading outfit, and parade me down Main Street."

Ford placed his hand over hers. "You deserve an amazing wedding, Add." He searched for the right words, ones that would calm her and retrieve the logical girl he'd been friends with forever. "You and Tucker are the real deal. You managed to work things out in spite of the ups and downs, and that's worth celebrating."

"Would you say it's part of a full life, then?"

Ford cast her a sidelong glare. "Really? You're goin' there?"

"Just wondering." She kicked off her sneakers. "Violet's great, yeah?"

As expected, this store *was* full of traps. "Yeah."

"After y'all left the table the other night, we agreed that she seemed funny and nice yet feisty enough to keep you in line."

"I don't need to be kept in line."

"You keep on telling yourself that."

Ford swallowed past a throat that suddenly felt too narrow. "She sure knows a lot about weddings. That's what I'm having a hard time ignoring right now."

"So? I'm fairly certain most women do. Have even

dreamed of their own wedding and all that. Don't make red flags out of molehills or whatever." Addie hit him with her no-nonsense expression. "I just want you to be happy. The other night when you were playing pool, and even today, you're happier than I've seen you in a long time."

"Gear down, big shifter. Violet and I are just friends—and before you go and say so were you and Tucker, it's different."

The way Addie's mouth snapped closed meant he'd been right.

"She's sworn off men," Ford said simply, although his insides rioted at the idea, and what the hell? Was he panicked she'd want to be with him or that she wouldn't?

"Don't tell Nonna Lucia. She'll ask her if she's a lesbian, same way she asked me last year in front of Tucker."

"Sounds like your grandma, always leaping to play matchmaker." Ford exhaled and ran his palms down his jeans. "It's not a good time for me to get serious with someone, anyway. I've got puppies to train, and fire season is coming." Come fall, there was usually a wildfire or two, and he always headed to help.

"That's a cop-out and you know it. No time is ever ideal for a relationship or to fall in love and lose your mind a bit. You think Doris would accept that excuse?"

A band formed around his chest, so tight it hurt to breathe. Why did Addie insist on pushing? "Starting to regret telling you that story."

"If you really never want me to mention it again, I won't, but—"

"Then don't," he snapped. It'd come out harsher

than he meant it to, but he wouldn't take it back.

"*But*," Addie said, her dogged nature showing its head, "it's not doing you any favors, sitting at home every night, waiting for an emergency call to come in. You'll drive yourself mad. Then I bet you feel guilty when one does, because you've been hoping for one, and it means someone's in trouble."

When did his best friend go and become a mind reader? He grunted in response, not wanting to admit she was right.

"I say this out of love, McGuire. Life's too short. The longer you take to start living it, the more regrets you'll end up with. You've never done anything half-assed before. Don't choose now, with Violet, to start."

• • •

Arms loaded with dresses, Violet paused next to one of the fitting rooms, observing the big dude on the couch and the bride-to-be. Both a skosh out of place, but she loved how open they were to this whole adventure.

Admittedly, wedding-dress shopping was akin to pouring lemon juice on an unhealed cut, but helping Addie narrow her options acted as a balm that minimized the sting.

While happy to help, Violet worried that every time she brought out her binder, she was shooting herself in the foot with Ford.

It should provide a sense of comfort and reinforce her willpower. After all, what guy—especially one like Ford—would willingly jump into a relationship with a woman obsessed with getting married?

Not that she was obsessed.

Not anymore, anyway.

Didn't mean she couldn't mourn the loss of the aforementioned dream. In an attempt to avoid letting sorrow take hold, she would concentrate on Addie, try not to concentrate too much on Ford, and no matter what, she would. Not. Cry.

"Time to try on the gowns," the cheery bridal shop consultant said with a clap of her hands.

She, Lexi, and Violet hung the dresses inside the nearest fitting room.

Lexi posted herself next to the curtain in case Addie needed an assist, and with the bridal consultant there as well, Violet decided three was a crowd.

She plunked herself next to Ford to prepare for the montage. He propped his elbow on the back of the couch and settled his palm on the nape of her neck. "You okay?"

The brush of his callused fingertips bulldozed her raw emotions over the subject of matrimony, along with every thought in her head, and how did one go about breathing again? "Just peachy."

"Thanks for your help." He toyed with her hair, and goose bumps prickled her skin. "Told you I was unqualified."

"You grounded her when she was beginning to panic. And honestly, I'd wonder about you if you were an expert on wedding dresses."

As soon as she said the words, she wanted to pluck them out of the air. Maybe it was her paranoia that made her translate his tight smile into *I'm concerned about how much you* do *know*.

Her gut wrenched, her emotional scars nearing the surface once again.

"I'm coming out," Addie called. "And if anyone laughs, they'll get a black eye."

"No one is going to laugh," Lexi said, but she bit at her thumbnail.

The curtains opened with a *whoosh*, and then the swishing of fabric became the soundtrack as Addie exited the fitting room. Her tense shoulders and the stiff way she walked screamed discomfort.

Violet wasn't sure if Addie's unease came from not being used to dresses, disliking this particular gown, or if a stray pin was jabbing her through the yards upon yards of fabric.

"Is that a walk of shame wedding dress?" Ford asked. "Looks like you took off with Tucker's sheets but added a sparkly"—he gestured to the side, where a beaded floral applique held up the skirt—"thingamabob old ladies wear to church."

"Ford," Lexi scolded, which saved Violet from doing so. Perhaps she should provide guidance on helpful feedback versus not-helpful comments.

Addie kicked aside the heels that'd been on the pedestal and took their place. "Broach is the word you're looking for. And you're not wrong. It's basically a fancy toga."

A gasp escaped the poor consultant, along with the designer's name. While Violet never would've made the toga comparison, now she couldn't unsee it.

The next gown consisted of a tight, strapless bodice covered in floral lace and flared to a gauzy skirt. Even if Lexi's face hadn't lit up, Violet would've guessed she picked it out. It would've been a nice fit for the blonde, but Violet didn't think it was Addie's style, regardless of not having a dressy style in general.

"It's beautiful," Lexi said.

Addie hooked her thumbs in the top and hiked it up, but then the waist didn't sit right. "It's too fancy for me. All the flowers, and I"—she repeated the bodice-lifting move—"feel like it's gonna fall. And since I can read your mind, Lex, no, your bridesmaid dress didn't fall off me and had a similar top, but this one is lower-cut and squeezes the girls harder than Tucker does."

Snickers went around the room, save for the consultant, who seemed to be experiencing a bit of shock.

"I want to be comfortable sitting there in front of the town and most of the Auburn coaching staff." Addie twisted the end of her ponytail around her finger. "Is a comfortable wedding dress even a thing?"

Violet stood and circled Addie, studying the dress from every angle. "Would you settle for semi-comfortable? We might even be able to hit mostly comfortable, although you'll still need help to pee."

"Lexi, I'll let you handle those duties," Ford said, and even the consultant smiled at that joke.

The next gown fit Addie like a glove. Also strapless; however, it landed snuggly at her arm pits and covered more cleavage. It nipped in at the waist, showing off Addie's figure.

Ford cocked his head. "Did they forget to iron it? Why's it so wrinkly?"

"It's ruched." Lexi fluffed the billowing silk skirt and let it drop, demonstrating how wide it flared.

Addie lifted the fabric to study it closer, displaying the fact that she still had on her yoga pants. "So, it's the shar-pei of the dress world?"

Lexi sighed. "Seriously, you guys?"

Ford and Addie exchanged a glance, and then Ford said, "Next."

They had that silent conversation thing down pat, and while it caused a pinch of jealousy, Violet's admiration for their friendship overpowered it. She also appreciated that Ford would hop in and be the so-called bad guy when Addie didn't want to hurt Lexi's feelings.

To a certain extent, she had that kind of relationship with the Bridesmaid Crew—especially Leah and Amanda.

Even better, she and Maisy were getting there as well. They'd spent several evenings talking and laughing, and this afternoon, as Violet had been finishing up at the bakery, Maisy had asked, "Would you like me to wish you luck on resisting Ford? Or do you want me to encourage you to go for it?"

Violet had laughed and picked the first one.

With Ford's thigh resting against hers, her resolve cried for help. She considered ignoring it and surrendering to the urge to rest her head on his shoulder.

Then Addie stepped out in a mermaid gown.

While Violet was happy to lend her expertise, she had her limits, so she'd steered clear of that particular style. Addie hadn't mentioned liking them, anyway.

But that dress… Violet was tempted to slap a hand over Ford's mouth before he said anything stupid, because Addie looked stunning. The fabric might be busier than the bride-to-be would've chosen herself, but the gown highlighted every one of her assets.

If you don't stop holding your breath, you're going to pass out.

Addie stepped onto the pedestal and spun, showing

off the ruffles that began mid-thigh and cascaded into a court train.

Lexi once again beamed, and Violet couldn't fault her for picking the dress. It was so close to the triple-starred dresses in her binder. In fact, she suspected it was from the same designer she'd followed for the past five years. She'd almost put a similar dress on hold last year, back when she still believed Benjamin's someday promises.

"Damn, Murph. Who knew you had an ass like that? From a guy's perspective, I approve. Shows off your figure, and I've always been an ass man."

A light blush pinkened Addie's cheeks before she pivoted to face the mirror.

Why did it sting that Ford approved of the dress Violet would've picked for herself?

Being in the bridal shop was messing with her head, fuzzying up her thoughts, and she hated that she couldn't just be happy for Addie.

And she truly was. By *just be happy*, Violet more meant why did complicated emotions like agony and mourning come along for the ride?

It prompted thoughts of what else she'd lost. A future involving vows and babies and the knowledge that, in spite of her faults, someone loved her for her.

Someone *chose* her.

A fissure formed in her heart, as if proving there'd always be a piece missing, and she had to blink triple time to stick to her no-crying decree.

"I do think it's beautiful," Addie said. "But I look in the mirror and see...not me. It's like peering at a stranger with my face, and I'm not sure what that means."

Lexi circled her, cell phone out and snapping pictures. "You don't have to decide right now. Keep it in mind as you try on the rest, and I'll have these photos to help us compare."

The following two gowns were a no go, and then Addie came out in a halter-top dress that made Ford say, "Whoa, Sarah Connor. That one shows how ripped your arms are."

"Does it give off the impression that I'm going to be the one carrying Tucker down the aisle, though?"

They all swore it didn't, and after debating over how lacy the bodice was, she added it to the maybe pile.

Finally, Addie came out with Violet's number-one pick.

The tiniest bit of vertical ruching made up the pure white top. The dress flared around the upper thigh and ended in a puffed skirt that landed at calf height.

Violet wrung her hands, awaiting Ford and Addie's jokes about grabbing the iron again.

Instead, Lexi sucked in a breath and Ford sat forward.

Addie stepped onto the pedestal and grinned at her reflection. Then she turned to face them and ran her hands down the skirt. "Well?"

During the many times Violet had been involved in this part of the process, there was just something different that happened when a bride-to-be put on the right dress. The air changed, as if it and everyone involved had been enchanted, and most of the commentary went silent, when you'd think it'd be the opposite.

"I'm gonna have to kick my own ass later for saying this, but *that's the one*. You look..." Ford's forehead creased as if he were searching the contents of his brain for the right word. "Like you, but pretty."

Violet pinched his arm and widened her eyes at him. His statement about it being the one had caused a fluttery, tingly rush, but then he'd added that last part.

"Not that you're not normally pretty. I just mean... Hell, I said it was the one. What more do you want?"

Addie laughed. "I get you. That's how I feel. It's like an upgraded, fancier version of me."

"And I had this idea that you can take or leave..." Violet kicked off her scuffed purple Vans and placed them at Addie's feet. "You could order yellow Chucks to match your colors. It'd also be super cute if your fiancé and the rest of the wedding party wore them, too. I've shot photos where people did that, and it's insanely cute."

Addie stepped into the Vans, remarking they were the same shoe size. Her grin stretched to a whole new level of joy as she studied her reflection. A euphoric haze filled the room and swelled inside of Violet, and she reached for her camera out of habit before remembering yet again that she no longer carried it everywhere.

Lexi already had her phone out, taking pictures, which would suffice.

After Addie returned to the fitting room to change into her regular clothes, Ford stood. "Ladies, if you'll excuse me, I've gotta take a leak."

Violet began tidying up the dresses that'd been set aside. She paused on the mermaid-style one. Her heart knotted as she traced the intricate design on the bodice, the longing she'd claimed to be rid of rushing forward to out her.

"I can't tell you how much I appreciate your help," Lexi said to Violet once the consultant left to ring up Addie's dress.

"Even though I told her she can wear Converse sneakers?"

"I forced her into heels for my wedding and still haven't heard the end of it, so that's a spot of genius. It fits her. You managed to pinpoint her style in a handful of minutes, which made me realize I've been asking all the wrong questions, thus the nonanswers."

"I've done this seven times. I'm kinda an expert."

Lexi slung one of the other gowns over her arm. "More than just playing bridesmaid or even taking photos. Considering the binder, I'm guessing you've planned a few weddings."

"I did plan one." Violet attempted to exhale her conflicted emotions over the subject and charge on. "Mine. My ex continually assured me we'd get married someday, but he didn't actually mean it. In the end, he played me for the fool I was."

Sympathy softened Lexi's features. "I've been played before. It doesn't mean you're a fool."

"I appreciate that, but I definitely felt like one when I found him with another woman at Maisy's wedding. They tied the knot the same day I started that stupid fire in the bakery."

Lexi put her hand on Violet's shoulder. "I'm so sorry."

Violet separated the mermaid gown from the others. "This was the dress I kept coming back to, no matter how much everything else changed. Over the past six months, I've rehashed our relationship way too many times, trying to find the signs I missed."

Embracing her fanatical, binder-creating side, Violet draped the mermaid gown over herself and glanced in the mirror. Even if she hadn't been indulging in too many sweets at the bakery, she would still require a larger size. "One time, when I goaded Benjamin to set a date so I could book the venue, he told me 'I thought you wanted to lose twenty pounds before the wedding.'"

"That asshole!" Lexi slapped a hand over her mouth. "Oops. While I don't stand by my colorful language, I stand by the sentiment."

"In all fairness, I *had* told him that."

"In all fairness, he's still…" She leaned closer and whispered. "An asshole. One that obviously didn't deserve you."

Violet shrugged, as if it weren't a big deal she'd lost her belief in finding that special someone.

So what are you doing letting yourself get swept up in sweet gestures from Ford?

Ford might be charming, funny, and a hero to boot.

The settling-down type, he was not.

Which was why, no matter how much she enjoyed spending time with Ford, she should raise her shields before she ended up hurt again.

CHAPTER ELEVEN

Ah, shit.

Ford had come back from the bathroom to see Violet in front of the mirror, a wedding dress over her clothes.

A mere moment ago, he'd been ruminating on how much fun he'd had sitting next to her, remarking on gowns of all things. Affection had tightened his chest in a not-altogether-unpleasant way as she'd helped out his best friend, and he'd seriously considered following Addie's advice.

If there were anyone he'd be inclined to attempt a full-blown relationship with, it'd be a woman like Violet.

So why not Violet?

Because she has a fucking wedding dress over her clothes and is after someone to walk her down the aisle.

Dating was one thing. Marriage was a whole different ball game—one he'd determined wasn't for him. Say he *could* open himself to the possibility of more than casual, it'd still be a while before he'd be willing to move past the practice stage.

Along with the nerves gnawing at his insides, his heart thumped a million miles an hour, affirming it agreed.

The only thing keeping him from fleeing the scene—'sides Murph, of course—was the last snippet he'd overheard. *Her ex implied she needed to lose weight before he would marry her?*

Not that Ford was volunteering for a stroll down the

aisle, but what a prick. An ignorant prick at that. How dare someone behold those killer curves and request less of them.

As he'd stated earlier, he'd always been an ass man, and Violet's was perfection.

He cleared his throat as he approached, and Violet quickly shoved the dress at Lexi. Her confusion lasted half a second, and then she placed it with the other dresses.

Violet leaped from the pedestal instead of stepping down, so she must be getting antsy. "You survived your first wedding dress shopping trip. What are you going to do next?"

Run.

Or maybe hop on the dating train and enjoy the ride while it lasts.

Except he didn't want to be another jerk who hurt her, accidental or not. "Get back to work, I guess."

"And here I assumed you were the kind of guy who knows how to celebrate."

"He needs to be retaught," Addie said as she exited the fitting room in her usual clothes. She and their group headed to the front of the store to wrap things up.

The consultant had rung up the dress but suggested other items Addie might want to add: a strapless bra and the slip they'd originally thought was a dress. With each item she rattled off, Ford's skin became itchier and itchier. He scratched at his neck and then headed outside in the name of fresh air.

At long last, the women exited the shop, carrying bags he relieved them of. He placed the bags in the trunk of Lexi's car, and it hit him that he and Violet now had a drive ahead of them.

It'd be easier to evade her gravitational pull if he avoided her.

Not that it was a stellar plan, given how small Uncertainty was, but she'd managed to duck him well enough. If only asking her how wouldn't hurt her feelings.

Violet rocked back on her toes. "I figured I'd ride with Lexi and Addie, since you have to get back to work."

The mutinous bastard in his chest twanged, the reverberations traveling through his entire torso. He swallowed hard, employing the poker face he had down pat, thanks to countless games with the gang. "That'd save me some time. I appreciate it."

Violet wrapped her arms around herself, and he'd swear *she* was offended.

Ma had been hot and cold like that. Tell Dad one thing and be mad whether he agreed or disagreed. As if she were thirsting for a fight. Or an instance to later use against him.

Whether Violet was playing games, testing him, or as sensible as a soup sandwich, he didn't have the time or energy for this.

"See you around," Ford said. But after realizing the only place he and Violet could go was nowhere, he'd do his best to make sure he didn't.

• • •

The scenery morphed from cityscape to green trees that met blue skies.

Violet bounced her knee, her thoughts volleying

between relief and regret. While Addie and Lexi were perfectly nice travel companions, she missed the woodsy scent that filled Ford's truck. His easy jokes. His deep voice…

Staring at his stupidly handsome profile and experiencing butterflies whenever he glanced her way.

"You still alive back there?" Addie peered between the bucket seats.

Violet slid her fingers along her seat belt, the bouncing of her knee creating a rustling noise. Stopping meant her restless energy would have nowhere to go. Then she'd be eyeing the door handle and considering a *Charlie's Angels* roll onto the highway.

And she asked a question. "Sorry. I get lost in my thoughts."

"Let me guess…" Lexi caught her eye in the rearview mirror. "You're wondering if you made a mistake getting in the car with us instead of going in the truck with Ford."

"No. I was hoping to get to know both of you better."

"That explains all the questions you've been asking," Addie teased, light enough Violet couldn't be offended.

"It's just that you and Ford seemed to have a vibe," Lexi said. "And if I'm not mistaken, you told me about your failed nuptials and then ran from him."

"Failed nuptials?" Addie asked, and Lexi winced. "Sorry."

Violet swiped a hand through the air. "It's not a secret. I talked to all my friends about my wedding, we planned several versions, and I ended up holding the short end of the stick. Benjamin didn't even propose, so it's not like I have an epic story about being jilted at the altar."

"Wouldn't that be worse?" Addie asked.

Both Lexi and Violet *hmm*ed.

"Yes and no," Violet said. "While I did foolishly plan an entire wedding, at least I wasn't discarded in front of my family and friends. Fancy dresses and fairy-tale setting aside, the vows are what I truly want, so I guess being stood up day of would've hurt worse."

Like a scab that'd been picked, the wound in her heart throbbed to life once again. Fainter than it used to be but far from fully healed. "But it hurt enough."

"Lexi's better at the pep-talk crap, but I'm sorry, Violet. That guy sounds dumb as a doorknob."

Naturally, her mind flashed to the day she told Ford she'd gotten to first base with his doorknob, and he'd replied, *Lucky doorknob.*

"What Addie means is, I soften it when I call people on their crap," Lexi said with a laugh. "The rest of the group are tactless and blunt. Once I got accustomed to it, it was rather refreshing."

"Wait." Violet ran her fingers through her hair. "Who decided doorknobs are the dumbest of knobs? Are there even other kinds of knobs?"

Both Addie and Lexi opened their mouths, looked at each other, and burst into laughter.

"I like where your head's at," Addie said.

"You mean lost in an earlier subject?" Violet picked at a stray thread on her jeans. "The truth is, after everything happened with Benjamin, I decided to give up men."

"Oh honey, I gave them up for Lent once, and it was the worst forty days of my life." Lexi hit her turning signal. "And that doesn't make me weak. Technically I discovered I *could* live without them, but I'm a fan of sex on the regular and a hot man to cuddle with at night. The experience did give me time to reflect, though…"

After checking her blind spot, Lexi merged onto the smaller, cracked highway that would take them to Uncertainty. "I had this ideal man in my head, but after dating too many self-centered duds, I realized I'd been wasting my time on the wrong guys. That's why, when I met my Will, I gave him a shot, despite my belief that a country-boy schoolteacher—even one hotter than hell and half of Georgia—wouldn't be my type.

"But boy did Will Shepherd prove me wrong." Lexi's voice turned as dreamy as her expression. "And he continues to do so every single day."

The flame that burned inside Violet—the one she couldn't quite snuff out—craved love stories with happy endings and wanted more fuel for the fire. "What about you and Tucker, Addie? How'd you guys meet?"

"I don't even remember my life without him," Addie said. "We grew up together, got into loads of trouble, and earned our reputations as hooligans. I used to get so mad when he treated me like a girl, and then one night, I wished he'd see me as one. After a drunken flirting session where I embarrassed the pants off myself—"

"Literally," Lexi added, "since I'd forced her into a dress."

Their laughter mixed together, and Violet experienced a contact-happy high, same as she'd gotten from their tales of romance. The two of them rehashed memories and explained how they'd become friends.

"Here's what you should take away from those stories, Violet." Lexi slowed as they passed the sign welcoming them to Uncertainty. "One, that I'll force my friendship on you, so do yourself a favor and accept it now."

"Two," Addie cut in. "Her head was obviously full of stump water when she asked me to help plan her wedding."

Lexi raised her voice over Addie's. "Three, when life throws you a curveball, you might want to catch it."

Both of them looked at Violet, so apparently it was her turn to reply. "Oh, I'm not much for catch. Balls just hit me in the face, and two seconds later I try to get my mitt up."

The girls erupted in giggles, and Violet found herself giggling as well.

"How about this, then?" Lexi asked. "*Three*, country boys are sexy, and I think Ford was upset you didn't ride back with him."

Addie nodded. "Yeah, I play poker with him, and that was his fake, it's-all-good face."

A cold lump formed in Violet's belly. "I didn't mean to hurt his feelings, although I'm sure he'll recover in all of two seconds with that ego of his."

"My boys have enormous egos, it's true." Addie lifted her seat belt off her neck and pivoted in her seat. "But they also have their soft sides. Bonus, if you do decide to give McGuire a shot, and he hurts you, I'll kick his ass."

When Addie cracked her knuckles, she didn't have to make the noise with her mouth.

The loud *pop*, *pop* made Violet shudder. "I

appreciate it, but I think I'm better equipped to take over your spinster spot."

"I might not've been forthright enough about what the title entails. For example, it comes with being set up on multiple dates with everybody's single cousin or nephew or grandson. I got nothin' but love for our county, but pickins is slim."

Violet sat back, defeat and exhaustion setting in. "It's okay. I have a way to take care of that. I'll just mention I'm interested in getting married, and they'll trip over their own feet getting away from me."

Lexi shook her head. "I wouldn't count on that. You're a catch. Pretty, smart, funny—"

"You're a hottie with a naughty body," Addie said, flashing her a smile that showed off her pearly whites. "Seriously, maybe a penchant for settling down would scare men in the city, but here, you might end up gettin' hitched before me."

The girl Violet used to be might want that.

"And if Ford was the guy I told that to?"

Lexi and Addie glanced at each other, their wordless exchange saying a lot. Then Addie said, "It doesn't mean he's not a good guy. Tryin' not to cross the line here, but he had a rough family life, and I think he needs someone to show him it doesn't have to be like that. I think even seeing Shep, Tucker, and me settle down will help."

It was what Violet expected. Disappointing yet not surprising. She'd already made the mistake of thinking that if she showed a guy she loved him for him, eventually he'd do the same for her, flaws and all.

As much as she hated labels—and don't get her started on the phrase "daddy issues"—the lack of a father figure had impacted her. After Dad's failure to make an appearance at events like her sixteenth birthday, high school and college graduations, and a dinner where he was supposed to meet Benjamin, she wanted someone who'd show up.

Someone who didn't only spend the required minimum with her out of obligation.

Benjamin had shown up in the beginning. During the past couple years, though, they'd fought over him promising to be at her events and then canceling because he was too tired or too stressed.

She'd settled for his excuses, giving extra weight to the previous times he had managed to show up. Crumbs of affection she'd gobbled up like the starving girl she was.

While Ford seemed like a meat-and-potatoes kind of guy, she worried that in the end, he'd end up only giving her crumbs, too.

CHAPTER TWELVE

"Look at me, beautiful." Violet jiggled the rattle, catching Isla's attention. Despite the size of her cheeks, her niece managed to lift them along with her smile, and Violet raised her camera and depressed the button.

The satisfying *click* filled the air, and Violet snapped a few more. Squeeing over the dimpled cheeks was necessary, as was zooming in on her niece's legs.

"Enjoy this phase of your life, when people adore the rolls on your thighs. No one praises me for my chubbiness anymore."

"That's because you're hardly chubby," Maisy said as she entered the room, her wet hair twisted up in a towel.

"Well, I've got more junk in my trunk after spending so much time at the bakery." Accepting her curves had never been easy, especially when the rest of the Hurst clan were naturally thin. Maisy could eat twice the treats and remain the same size.

While it was easy to tell other women to embrace their bodies as they were, Violet had always struggled to do the same for herself.

"Maybe you can work on making your pastries less delicious?"

"Oh, sure. That'll be great for business." Maisy poured herself a mug of the coffee Violet had brewed. "Thank you for getting Isla. I didn't even hear her wake up, and I feel more rested than I have since before she arrived."

"I hope it's okay that I warmed a bottle from the fridge and used it."

"You could tell me you used my entire reserve of pumped milk and I'd forgive you—sleep makes me nice like that."

Violet laughed. "You're already one of the sweetest people alive, with your 'have a sweet day' and cheery attitude. If you get any nicer, you'll need to apply for sainthood."

"*Pfft.* Hardly."

Maisy reached over the arm of the couch and drifted a knuckle over the cheeks Violet had captured on her memory card.

Isla curled her hand around Maisy's finger, and Violet lifted her camera and documented the quintessential motherhood moment.

"I see you have your camera out," Maisy said.

"My niece is an irresistible subject."

"I agree. But if that picture of me in my robe gets printed, I'm gonna shove your fancy camera where the sun don't shine."

"Taking back that sainthood comment now," Violet teased, and Maisy stuck her tongue out at her. Since she was far from saintly, she took another couple pictures as Maisy headed toward her bedroom.

"The only reason I'm not killing you is because you let me have an extra hour of sleep," Maisy called.

Violet set down her camera and picked up her squirming niece. "Sounds like I'd better get you dressed for daycare to remain in your mommy's good graces. What would you like to wear today?"

Isla babbled, and Violet responded as if she'd picked a particular outfit. "The purple one? I think that's an excellent decision."

As she was maneuvering wiggly baby limbs into a purple floral romper, longing flickered.

As hard as she tried to deny it, she still wanted a baby. The picture on the dresser of Travis, Maisy, and burrito-baby Isla caught her eye.

Snapshots only showed instances in people's lives, a blip of a second. Yet they also told a story about the subjects' past, future, and everything in between.

Maybe she'd been too hasty, giving up men when she hadn't dated more than one in the past decade.

Then again, the only guy who'd tempted her to redact her proclamation hadn't called or texted in five days. She'd taken it to the Bridesmaid Crew chat, asking their advice. Leah said don't go down that road again, and Amanda pointed out that when she met her now-husband, he wasn't looking for anything serious, either, but that quickly changed.

Violet uploaded one of the pictures she'd taken of Ford and Pyro, and suddenly Camille and Alyssa came out of the woodwork to heart-eye the pics and add a GIF of a cartoon character with his eyes bulging out of his head. Not a huge help, considering she was well aware of how hot he was.

Plus, Violet was fairly certain that she and Ford had switched places and *he* was the one avoiding *her*.

• • •

Ford wasn't avoiding Violet. He was just making sure to go to places she wouldn't be.

Which was damn inconvenient, considering he needed to pick up cupcakes for the baseball game.

Like the wuss he'd become, he peeked through the window.

Maisy stood at the cash register, helping out the Garcias.

Violet was nowhere in sight, but that didn't mean she wasn't in a corner he couldn't see. Or the kitchen.

Okay, presumably not the kitchen. Surely Maisy knew better by now.

The instant he stepped inside the bakery, the excessively loud chime announcing his arrival, Maisy gandered in his direction.

And frowned.

Ford lumbered toward the front, waiting for her to curse him out for not calling her sister, even though *she'd* ditched *him* on the ride home and that still stuck in his craw.

"I'm so sorry," Maisy said. "The cupcakes you and Easton ordered for the teams aren't quite ready yet, but I promise, cross my heart, you'll have them by the end of the baseball game."

Since the greeting was different than he'd expected, it took him a moment to decipher what she'd actually said. "No problem. Should I send someone over during the last inning? A parent, maybe?"

"Oh, I wouldn't want anyone to miss any of the game. I'll get them to the field, don't you worry."

"All right. Then I guess…" Ford rocked on his heels and glanced around.

"She's not here."

"Who's not here?" Ford casually glanced at Maisy. "I'm not sure what you're talkin' about."

"Wow. You're not a good liar, Ford McGuire."

Another moment of debating, and he blew the

cover he'd failed to maintain anyway. "How's Violet doing?"

"She's been taking pictures again. I think I have you to thank for that, but since she also keeps checking her phone, waiting for someone to call, I'm gonna keep the thanks to myself."

"I'll take that information and run with it anyway."

"Figured you would. Hope that big head fits out the door. I don't have time to dislodge it. In case you haven't heard, I'm behind."

"I'll get out of your hair, then." Ford left the bakery, unable to conceal his grin. Violet was taking pictures again, and a small part of that was because of him.

And he found that instead of avoiding Violet, all he wanted was to see her face. Hear her laugh.

Ask her *what the hell* and relay how glad he was that she was taking pictures again.

On second thought, maybe he should reverse those two.

On third thought, he should leave it alone. The bakery remodel was coming along, and since Violet had found her muse, that meant she'd most likely be moving on soon.

No point in struggling to buck his nature and form attachments right in time for her to leave.

Ford parked at the baseball field and climbed out of his truck. There was a long rivalry between cops and firefighters, and he and Easton kept that alive and well here in Uncertainty by coaching the two minor league boys' baseball teams.

Dylan, the scrawniest of his players, came running over. "Ford, Ford, guess what, guess what!" He pointed at the gap in his teeth. "Look."

"Uh-oh. Were you not wearing your catcher's mask?" The kid couldn't get over the fear of the ball flying at his face, so his mom bought him a catcher's mask. That he wore in the *outfield*.

Thanks to his protective instinct, Ford almost tried to convince Dylan not to wear it so he wouldn't get made fun of. But the other kids on the team had surprised him in the best possible way. They didn't mock Dylan. They were simply glad he could play.

"Nope. It came out the natural way. And my other front tooth is loose, too." Dylan demonstrated with his tongue. The tooth wobbled, barely hanging on by a thread.

Ford ruffled Dylan's blond hair. "Why don't you use that move to intimidate our opponents?"

"You got it, Coach." Dylan ran to join the rest of the kids for warm-up exercises.

At first, Ford had balked at the idea of being a coach—he didn't think he had the patience. But now he eagerly awaited talking trash with Easton as they encouraged the boys.

The parents always got super into the games, too. Every spring, there'd be a few times when Easton would have to take off his coach hat and put on his officer hat. Then he'd warn the rambunctious crowd members that if they didn't settle down, they'd miss the game due to being hauled down to the station.

A tug on the leg of his jeans snagged his attention. "I don't have anyone to catch with. None of the boys wants to throw with a girl."

Ford squatted so he was eye level with Makayla. "That's their loss. One of my best friends is a girl, and she's got an arm any boy would be jealous of."

Makayla was a new addition. She wanted to play, but not enough of the girls her age did, so she'd joined his team. After growing up with Addie, he recognized how much girls could do on the field.

"I got you." Ford grabbed a mitt and helped Makayla warm up.

As they tossed the ball back and forth, Ford glanced at the stands. Families wore supporting team colors and passed around snacks, preparing to cheer for their kiddos.

"Make sure to follow through," Ford said. "Like this…"

Makayla caught his pass and then launched it back, extra heat on the ball.

"Nice." Ford was fairly certain most men dreamed about playing catch with their son, and as he watched his team, longing he hadn't realized he possessed bobbed its head.

In order to have a kid, he would have to settle down, and that'd never been in his plans. Not after Ma left and he'd watched his dad and his brothers go through too many tempestuous relationships and cutting off a few of those himself.

Do you have a sweetheart? Someone who makes your life worth that much more?

Doris had asked him that question after he'd pulled her out of her flooded car, into a boat, and had performed CPR to get her breathing again.

"I don't," he'd told her, "but if you're offering, I might reconsider."

The click of her tongue echoed in his ear. "Oh, you charmer. My Harold is up in heaven already. He and I had a full life, complete with love and happiness and lots of kids and grandbabies." Doris coughed again, the sound thicker than he would've liked, but his main goal was to get her somewhere safe and dry. "I was hoping to make it to my granddaughter's wedding next month, but since she's also found her soul mate, she'll be okay."

Ford had promised Doris that she'd make it, so she couldn't give up just yet. They'd get her warm and dry and she'd be on her way to her daughter and granddaughter's house in no time.

The feisty woman agreed to fight on one condition—that he would commit to living his own life to the fullest.

There's peace in being fulfilled. In living without regret. And if it's my time to go, I know my Harold will be waiting for me on the other side.

While he'd attempted to watch over Doris that night, he and Pyro had been at it for two days, and exhaustion got the best of him. He should've thought about the possibility of post-immersion syndrome— what people used to call dry drowning.

At some point in the night, Doris stopped breathing, and Ford awoke to find her dead, his promise about her making it to her granddaughter's special event unfulfilled.

Whack. The ball hit the tip of his mitt and bounced by the fence.

Ford mentally shook himself and rushed to retrieve the ball. As he straightened, he caught sight of Violet, dark hair piled in a bun and camera hanging around her neck.

Funny how it took seeing her to feel the hole that'd opened in his chest. It'd bothered him since Saturday, this hollowness he couldn't explain.

When he was training the puppies, he felt it, too. The lack of Violet by his side, giving him hell and making him smile.

The ump called everyone in to start the game. After a bit of friendly trash talk between him and Easton at the pitcher's mound, a coin was flipped. His team—the Mighty Meerkats, as voted by the kids— would bat first.

During his pep talk, Ford's gaze strayed to the bleachers. His eyes met Violet's, and he gave her a small smile and nod.

As she returned the greeting, a warm slushy sensation filled the void in his chest.

Then she lifted her camera and snapped a picture. *Maybe my life* could *be fuller.*

• • •

When Maisy had begged Violet to take cupcakes to the baseball field and deliver them to Ford, she'd asked "Are you serious?"

"Would you rather mix and bake the next batch of cupcakes?"

"Yes," Violet had said, earning a glare. Next thing she knew, her sister had shoved two giant boxes of cupcakes into her hands and practically shoved her out the door.

On the bright side, the game was a good opportunity to practice capturing candid emotional shots, so she lifted her camera and *click, click, click*ed.

Kids with suckers.

Parents leaning in their seats, forward or to the side,

in hopes it'd help their kiddos on the field run farther and faster.

Then there was the other subject she couldn't get enough of: one super-sexy baseball coach who patted kids' heads and dropped to their level to console, compliment, or fire them up.

The commands "retrieve" "sit" and "run" came from Ford's mouth several times, in the exact same tone he used on Pyro and the TNT puppies. Violet sorta expected him to pull candy out of his pocket and toss them at the kids who'd done well.

It dawned on her that in Kid Land, cupcakes were the equivalent of doggie treats, and a grin spread across her face.

Same way it had at Ford's simple smile and nod greeting earlier—so much for the firm front she'd planned on showing him.

"Excuse me," a female voice said, and Violet turned. While most people in Uncertainty seemed vaguely familiar, she would've remembered this woman. She had long aquamarine hair, a septum piercing, and various tattoos. There was something about her that made Violet want to ask for tips on how to be cool. "Do you happen to take pictures professionally?"

Not a particularly difficult question, yet Violet simply blinked.

"I've been fixin' to get family pictures retaken. My oldest was a baby last time we had them taken." The woman pointed at the scrawny kid running in from the outfield. "He's the one in a catcher's mask. Dylan's seven now, and I've had two more kids since."

The woman indicated the three- or four-year-old at

her side and then bounced the blond baby on her knee, who Violet estimated to be around eight months.

"Oh. Yeah. I take photos. Professionally." Talking, on the other hand, was apparently not one of her specialties. Violet introduced herself and exchanged information with Shelby, thinking it'd be smart to book a few jobs here. Family sessions, and maybe eventually she'd be able to dip her toe back into engagement and wedding shoots.

The idea caused a mild twinge instead of completely wrenching her heart.

Violet excused herself and moved closer to the fence for some action shots.

"Good boy," Ford said, high-fiving the kid who'd made a home run.

An unattractive snort-laugh escaped, and Ford glanced back at her. "What?"

"You reward them the same way you do the puppies. Speaking of, I have your cupcakes so you can give them their big treats afterward."

Ford crooked a finger and motioned her closer.

Her heart beat double time as she pressed against the chain links, the light rattling of the fence echoing through her ears. *Don't get carried away. He probably just wants to tell you where to put the cupcakes.*

Ford stuck a finger through a gap and hooked her by the belt loop. Then he gave it a tug, throwing her emotions wholly off-balance. "Hey, you. It's been a while."

Butterflies stirred inside her, stretching their wings and preparing for flight. "I thought maybe I scared you at the bridal shop. I saw the way you looked at me when I was holding up that wedding dress."

"Oh, you did." Ford exhaled, his gaze dropping to the ground, and she kicked herself for bringing it up. Then his green eyes slowly returned to her face. "But I can't stop thinking about you. Even today, when I went into the bakery, I couldn't help searching for you."

Violet's heart went from beating too fast to forgetting how to function.

The crowd behind them grumbled as the ump called the batter's third strike.

"That's okay, kids," Ford pivoted and yelled. "We started strong and put a few points on the board. Let's call the ball while we're in the outfield, and we'll be batting again in no time."

As soon as Ford returned his attention to her, she said, "You didn't mention this job, either."

He shrugged his big shoulders. "This is more like play than work. Easton and I do it for the community. And so we can talk shi—crap later." He checked the vicinity, as if to ensure no one had heard him almost swear.

Shelby's son Dylan stood in right field, wearing his catcher's mask. It wobbled as he bent to pick a dandelion. He tossed it in the air and caught it in his mitt, the ongoing game miles from his radar.

Violet stifled a giggle, already feeling a bond with the kid she'd never met. "I'd better let you get back to coaching. Looks like your right fielder might have about as much focus as Trouble and I do."

The tenderhearted smile Ford gave Dylan melted Violet that much more. She began backing away from the fence, and Ford stepped closer and curled his fingers through the loops. "Hang around after the game for a bit, will ya?"

For a moment, Violet hesitated. She was supposed to be smarter. More careful. And wasn't there something about reinforcing her walls?

But then Ford's eyes met hers, and she found herself saying, "Okay."

CHAPTER THIRTEEN

After making sure the kiddos from both teams had the right cupcakes—they had one allergic to gluten and a diabetic who required low-sugar—Ford sought out Violet.

The sight of her talking to Gunner made his blood run cold. He and his brother weren't exactly estranged, but they weren't close. Nor was Gunner close to his ex-wife and her son from a previous relationship. That was what happened when you picked alcohol over your kin, which was something that ran in their family.

Ford strode over, and at the shameless interest on Gunner's face, jealousy surged to the forefront. He wrapped an arm around Violet's shoulders, securing her to his side. "Sorry that took so long."

Violet's gaze met his, her brow crinkling as she studied him and then smoothing. "No worries."

"Ah," Gunner said. "I see you've already met my brother. He's the good egg. But if you ever want to come to the dark si—"

"I think that's enough." It'd been a while since Ford had been embarrassed of his family. While he wanted to insist it no longer bothered him, an unmistakable burn germinated in his gut.

As the youngest, it'd taken a while for Ford to overtake his brothers during their competitions. By that time, he'd also realized he wanted more out of life than the ability to brag about chopping wood the fastest or downing the most shots. Or whatever other gladiator event Dad created to pit them against one another.

All so they wouldn't gang up on Dad or question his rules. At least Gunner's and Deacon's mothers stuck around to share custody, another splinter that used to dig at Ford and fester resentment.

As he got older, he understood all too well why Ma had jumped at a clean break, although he couldn't quite forgive her for leaving him behind. Eventually Ford had called Grandma Cunningham to ask if Ma was ever coming home. And discovered she'd already moved on with some rich dude.

Just swept him, Dad, and his brothers under the rug like dirt that'd fallen from her shoe.

An ache that had bothered him as a kid stabbed at Ford's chest, the blades too dull now to do much damage anymore. He reckoned he never would've fit in Ma's world anyway, and in the city, he wouldn't have had his sanctuary near the lake.

"That's right. I forgot for a minute that you're better than the rest of us." Gunner's cheek popped out as he switched his wad of chew to the other side. "Thanks for reminding me."

Ford sighed. "I never said that."

Gunner spit tobacco, the brown goop landing inches from Ford's shoe. "You don't have to. It's written across your face."

It wasn't that Ford thought he was better. He'd *worked* to become better. His parents and brothers had been completely unreliable, so he'd decided to do whatever it took to be dependable.

Once Ford was old enough to drive, his friends had

become his support system. His refuge. His family.

His dad and brothers jabbed at him about turning all "responsible citizen," but usually their insults slid off his back. With Violet as a witness, Gunner's words picked at an unhealed scar. One that reminded him where he'd come from and that several people in town still considered him lowbrow.

Easton approached, his posture stiff. "Gunner."

"Deputy Reeves," Gunner sneered. At first the other McGuires had been excited, thinking they'd have a cop on their side. But Easton was more concerned about the welfare of Uncertainty's residents than letting the McGuires drunkenly brawl in the streets. "I ain't done nothing wrong. A guy's allowed to come to his stepson's baseball game."

"Not when your ex-wife has a restraining order against you."

Right as Ford was about to tell Violet he would meet her later—or whatever he could do to get her out of there before Gunner turned unruly—she took his hand.

His eyes met hers, and she laced her fingers through his. Standing her ground. Letting him know she was here.

"She changed her mind about that," Gunner said.

Easton planted his hands on his hips. "Until she tells me that herself, you're required to give her five hundred yards. The station's that far if you'd rather go there."

A storm rolled across Gunner's features, and Ford stepped in front of Violet, just in case things turned ugly.

Easton also closed in, letting Ford know he had his back, too.

Somehow his brothers and father kept finding women willing to marry or shack up with them.

For a while.

Inevitably they couldn't hold back their vile sides, whether thanks to alcohol or lack of self-control. Deacon had a better temperament than Gunner, who was the oldest and meanest, but even he'd had his ups and downs with women and the law. Almost as if eventually the McGuire blood took over no matter what.

Not me, though. I won't let it. If he ever allowed a therapist to psychoanalyze him, they would likely say that was the reason he felt the need to always be busy and ready for an emergency. So he could head toward trouble to help instead of causing it.

Finally, Gunner held up his hands and backed away, spewing profanity as he did so. Heaven forbid he let the town forget that he occasionally came to events just to put a dent in everyone's fun.

Easton clapped Ford on the back. "I'll keep an eye on him. You and Violet get out of here."

"You don't have to do that. It's my respons—"

"This is why we always tell you that you don't have to play hero all the time. Technically, it's *my* job. If there's a fire, I've got your number."

Ford glanced from Easton to Violet and decided to give in. Mostly because he wanted to take the woman holding his hand away from here. Bonus points if he could distract her enough to forget the scene she'd just witnessed. "Thanks, man."

"Anytime." Easton stalked off in the direction Gunner had gone, and Ford guided Violet toward his truck.

His disparaging thoughts ran on a continuous loop: why did his family only ever show up to ruin things? Or when they wanted something? Why couldn't he rid himself of feeling responsible for them?

And then circling back to *why did Violet have to be around for that?*

Ford opened the passenger door and helped Violet inside. A dark cloud hung over him as he rounded the hood and climbed behind the wheel.

"Ford?" Violet said, and he lowered the keys from the ignition and gazed at the woman on the other side of the cab. "You okay?"

"I'm fine. I'm just sorry you had to see that. My family doesn't come into town much, except to replenish their liquor supply and make everyone uncomfortable."

Violet scooted across the bench seat until her thigh rested against his. "I understand complicated family dynamics." She placed her hand on his knee, and every drop of blood in his body rushed to that spot. "If you wanna talk…"

"Not about my family," he said. "But I'd be happy to talk about most anything else."

"Okay, so Sephora—it's this big makeup store. Anyway, they have a new line that's getting a ton of buzz. The high-pigment eyeshadows are so vivid—"

Ford hung his head and began loudly snoring.

"Hey," Violet said with a laugh, shoving his arm. "This is me teaching *you* a lesson about letting me in your truck. You think you're the only one with pearls of wisdom?"

She giggled again, and he twisted his head enough to spot the beauty mark on her cheek. Then he got lost in peering into her brown eyes, the same softening sensation he'd experienced earlier overtaking his entire body.

Violet propped her chin on his shoulder, her nose nearly touching his. "So, Ford McGuire. Where are you going to take me?"

Right here and right now, in the cab of this truck.

While he'd love nothing more, they were in the center of town, and while the families had mostly cleared out, he didn't want to be another McGuire who ruined the ball game. Not to mention his windows weren't tinted enough for everything he wanted to do.

He lifted Violet's hand and kissed her knuckles, sunshine spreading through his chest at the same rate pink spread across her cheeks. An idea popped into his head, one he couldn't decide whether or not to run with. "How do you feel about mud?"

"In general? Or are we talking politically? Because I'm not sure you can run a clean campaign when you start with dirt."

"I meant more in the general way." Ford folded her hand in his and moved his lips next to her ear, his mouth brushing the shell of it. "I just need to know if you're the type of girl who wouldn't mind getting a little bit dirty."

. . .

Charming lines had landed Violet in her fair share of trouble over the years.

Never on a four-wheeler, though. The vinyl seat creaked as she settled in place. Yep, this was what happened when you let a handsome guy whisper words about getting dirty into your ear.

The four-wheeler dipped with Ford's weight as he climbed behind her. He reached around her to turn the key and began explaining the brakes and accelerator over the sound of the idling engine.

Sun streamed across his skin, highlighting the golden-brown hair on his arms. The longer strands of his hair fell forward and brushed his cheeks.

Wow, he smells good. Like lumberjack aftershave, which she imagined involving trimming his whiskers with an ax.

"…the basics. Got it?" Ford asked.

"Um…" Violet tapped her fingernail to her teeth.

"You weren't paying attention, were you?"

"I was paying attention to you," she quickly said. This was something that irked Benjamin, regardless of how many times she explained she didn't purposely drift off. Honestly, it was annoying for her as well, always struggling to fill in blanks. "Just not exactly what you were saying."

That forever-higher right corner of Ford's mouth ticked up, deepening the groove in his scruffy cheek. "In other words, you got distracted by my devilishly good looks?"

"Something like that." Flirting had never been her forte, and being bold left her palms clammy. But after going too many days without seeing the guy, she wanted to spin around, wrap him in her arms, and hold him close.

Almost all of her preconceived notions had been proven wrong the instant Ford had strolled into the bakery with his dog to put out the fire she'd accidentally started. She didn't want to keep running from her feelings, which were intensifying at a rapid pace. While she was at it, she might as well toss aside her misguided stance on what type of guys she preferred and nullify her done-with-men decree.

"Let's try this again." Ford skimmed the pads of his fingers down her arms. A pleasant shiver trickled down her spine, same as when his lips had brushed her ear, and she fought the urge to squirm.

He curled his fingers over hers as she sat, breathless yet revived, and then he lifted her palms and wrapped them around the four-wheeler's handlebars.

His right thumb pressed over hers, and the engine growled, even as they remained in place. "This gets the machine to go." He depressed the metal lever that ran along the left side. "This makes it stop."

Heat pooled low in her gut as his lips skimmed her temple.

"That's essentially all you need to know for now. Any other trouble you get in, I'll get you out of."

Violet squeezed her thighs around the seat, acutely aware of Ford's big body behind her. If she wasn't mistaken, she wasn't the only one getting turned on.

"We'll head to the bog," Ford said. "It's nice and muddy right now."

"And that's a good thing?" she asked.

His husky laugh reverberated through the spot where his torso met her back and knocked more bricks out of the wall she'd built around her heart. "You'll see. I'm glad you've never been mud bogging before. It's gonna make this even more fun."

Violet bit her lip, fighting the impulse to throw herself at the mercy of Ford's mouth. "My mom was always a stickler about staying clean. I think since we were hard up, she didn't want people to think we were poor *and* dirty."

Crap. Why had she told him that? Ordinarily she kept that fact to herself. Not even Benjamin had known the full extent of their financial instability.

That while her siblings and father lived in the biggest house in Uncertainty, she, Mom, and her bubbie could hardly afford their matchbox of an apartment in a not-so-great neighborhood.

It'd taught her a strong work ethic, which was why being unable to do her job, having to pay a giant fine plus the cost to fix Benjamin's car, and losing the townhouse all within a few months had thrown her for such a loop.

"Well, we have that in common," Ford said. "In case you didn't figure it out from meeting my brother."

"I take it you're not close to your family?"

Silence stretched from one second to the next, and she glanced over her shoulder. She didn't want to pressure him. She simply wanted to figure out what made him tick. Plus, it sounded like they had more in common than she'd realized.

Since he didn't fill in the blank, she offered her own backstory. "While I'm fairly close to my mom, I wasn't close to my dad or any of my siblings growing up. Then my mom and I had a bit of a thing over going to art school—she didn't think it was a sound investment and told me I was choosing 'a silly career.'

"Maisy and I only began chatting more after she got married, which has brought us together and shown us how much we were missing."

"When my family talks, it's primarily to argue. And

even if they don't start off that way, it's not long before a fight breaks out. I've tried through the years. I have. But they…" He sighed.

Violet rested her hand on his knee. "Sometimes it's not worth the effort. I get that. I gave my dad one more shot, and he forgot about my almond allergy and poisoned my latte."

"Did he ever leave you in the forest after you broke your ankle while pheasant hunting? Dad did say he was going to get help, but he couldn't remember where he'd left me because he was too drunk. Eventually I found a big stick to use as a crutch and limped my way home."

Her jaw dropped—she couldn't help it. "You win."

A mirthless laugh spilled out. "Oh yeah? What exactly do I win?"

Violet tucked up her leg so she could fully face him. Then she raised onto her knees and kissed his cheek. She pulled back so she could read his expression, and the passion that swam through his eyes sent a shock wave down her core.

One hand gripped her waist. The other tangled in her hair. "A pity kiss?"

"More like half apology you had to go through that, half teaser of what's to come if you play your cards right."

The tip of his nose skimmed across her cheek, and he pressed a featherlight kiss to the sensitive spot under her ear. "I should warn you, I'm real good at cards."

Ford punctuated his warning with a nip to her earlobe, and a shiver had its way with her spine. Her nipples puckered against the fabric of her bra, declaring they were now invested in the outcome of this evening, and the temptation to crawl onto his lap and forget the whole mud-bogging thing inundated her.

She'd managed to deliver a flirty line without making a fool of herself, though, so she stuck with playing coy. "I certainly hope that's not the only thing you're good at."

· · ·

Violet's squeal rent the air as she made a sharp turn. Tires skidded, mud flew. Ford leaned the opposite direction, using his weight to prevent them from tipping into the ankle-height puddle.

Her squeal morphed into a giggle.

"You neglected to tell me you were a speed demon," he said.

"I never have been before, but there's never been mud before, either."

Affection boosted his mood as high as the fluffy white clouds in the sky. At one point in his life, Ford had declared there was nothing better than climbing onto an ATV and getting lost in the wilderness for days.

Violet's happiness, however, had him thinking about empty lives and full ones. It wasn't until this very moment that he realized he had, in fact, been missing something.

"Again?" she asked. "Or do you want a turn to drive?"

"I'll drive us home. You go ahead and play in the mud as long as you'd like."

The girl gunned it, mud splattered his posterior, and then he was hugging her to keep from falling instead of using it as an excuse to hold her.

"Do you see that log sticking out of the water?" he ask-yelled.

"What?" she hollered over the sound of the engine.

Oh shit. Ford lunged to hit the brakes and stop them in time, but his reaction was too slow, the vehicle going too fast.

The four-wheeler hit the log and went vertical, and since he'd let go of Violet to grasp for the controls, the machine bucked him off.

A jolt rocketed his spine and rattled his teeth as he landed on his ass.

Mud squished between his fingers, water seeped into his jeans, and he brought up his forearm and swiped his face. Namely the bit around his eyes.

The engine died, and panic held him captive as he searched for Violet in the mess.

Sucking footsteps came from his other side. Violet lumbered through the puddle and dropped to her knees in front of him. "Are you okay?"

He meant to answer, but then she was running her hands over him, her face crinkled with concern. Finally, he forced his tongue into motion. "I'm fine. You?"

Relief smoothed her features and loosened her shoulders. She swept mud-speckled strands of hair away from her pretty face. "Yeah. The four-wheeler did a total parkour move off that log, but I felt you fall, so I killed the engine and came running."

Violet wobbled to her feet and extended a hand. He gripped hold of it, the mud slimy yet gritty between their palms. The current between them snapped and sparked, igniting his libido, along with his mischievous side. She heaved, and rather than helping, he gave a sharp tug, throwing her off-balance.

She fell on top of him, their wet skin and clothes slipping against each other as he braced her hips. His evil laugh sounded similar to the cackling noise she'd made every time she'd taken a turn that left him significantly dirtier.

Ford rolled so she was the one lying in the goop. "Like a hog to mud…"

She scowled, the mostly unsullied skin around her eyes emphasizing her fiery side. "Comparing me to a hog isn't as charming as you think it is, Ford McGuire."

"If you're a hog, I'm a hog, too. Does that make it better?"

"No," she said as she propped herself up on her elbows, but she giggled and slapped murky water at him.

They splashed and batted water at each other until they were both soaked.

As their rapid breaths slowed, the ripples stilled, and their gazes latched on to each other. The air shifted, and damn she was beautiful.

Ford braced his palms on either side of her hips and crawled over her until his body hovered over hers. "Violet?"

A shaky breath filled the space between them. "Yeah?"

"I'm going to kiss you now."

Her pink tongue flicked out to wet her lips, enticing him closer, and he stifled a groan. It'd been a long time since he'd wanted to kiss a woman this badly, yet he hesitated.

Once their mouths met, their carefree puppy-training and wedding-planning sessions would come with extra baggage. There'd be expectations and feelings and a whole mess of other stuff he still wasn't sure he was ready for.

She angled her head, drawing his attention to the column of her neck and lower… Thanks to the water, her shirt was plastered against her chest. Hypnotized, he watched it rise and fall. Rise and fall.

Going back was for suckers anyway.

Ford brushed his lips over hers, a quick taste that had him wanting a whole lot more. A quick readjust so that his forearms were in the mud, and he sank into her curves as he molded his mouth to hers.

Violet parted her lips, inviting him deeper, and he swept his tongue inside to tangle with hers. Her moan spurred him on, and he slid his hand underneath the hem of her shirt. He stroked her soft skin, sucking her upper lip into his mouth as he put more of his weight on his left side. His erection strained against his zipper—a deluge of pleasure and a zing of pain.

Ford skirted his fingers along the underside of Violet's bra, and when she linked her arms around his neck and lifted her knee so their hips fully met, he grunted. Dark spots danced across his vision as he palmed her breast over her bra, finding her nipple hard and straining against the lace.

He gave the needy nub a flick, and Violet arched underneath him, her hips knocking into his and ripping a growl from his throat.

Afraid he'd lose control and inadvertently crush

her, Ford sat back on his heels, pulling her up with
him.

"What're y—? Oh," she said as she settled on his
lap, his pulsing erection notched against her center.
"Yeah, this was a good idea."

Violet dipped her head and kissed him again,
sucking and licking until the world spun off its axis.
Ford wrapped his hand around the nape of her neck
and held her in place as he devoured her mouth.

He wasn't sure if it was his gasp or hers that cut
through the silence. Right now, all that mattered was
they were both writhing and breathless, and why the
hell had he taken so long to kiss this woman?

She tugged at the bottom of his shirt, and he gladly
shed it. "Whoa," she said, tracing the muscles in his
chest and abdomen with her fingers.

Before she returned to his lap, he wanted to rid
her of her shirt as well. He yanked it up and off and
tossed it aside.

The last rays of the day danced across her skin,
casting a soft glow that accented every salacious
inch. She wrapped her arms around herself, half
hiding, half emphasizing, and his breath lodged in his
throat.

"Damn, Vi. You're… I… *Fuck, you're beautiful.*"

A shy smile spread across her face and her arms
slowly fell away. Her brazen side reemerged, dangerous and intoxicating and… *Mine.*

Ford lifted a muddy finger and painted a line
between her breasts, her belly button, the waist of her
filthy jeans. He swiped back and forth, and Violet
gripped his shoulders, her nails biting into his skin.

She nipped at his lower lip, her breath soft and

sweet. "Not that I'm not enjoying our fancy spa mud bath, but..." She shivered and snuggled closer. "The wet-and-cold thing is starting to kick in."

He wrapped his arms around her, giving her as much of his body heat as he could. "We're closer to my house than where we parked, so we can head there to dry off and warm up, and I'll get my truck later."

They stood and, after they grabbed shirts that were too caked in mud to wear, slipped and slopped their way over to the four-wheeler.

Violet danced around as he fired up the engine. "What are the odds we can make it to your place without someone seeing us? I've been the topic of gossip in Uncertainty before, and I was really trying to stay out of the spotlight. Shirtless and coated in mud will undoubtedly land me on the radar."

"Who cares what people say? Just ignore 'em. Sooner or later, those biddies'll find something new to gossip about."

"I wish I didn't care. Every time I visited this place growing up, I tried to convince myself I didn't. But I never could pull it off." She climbed on behind him and hooked her arms around his middle. "You'll have to teach me your ways."

"Easy. Step one: stop giving a shit."

"Yeah, but how?"

Ford shrugged. "You just stop."

"Is that how you train your dogs? Tell them to do something and they magically comply?"

"You want a motivational treat? I might have a few doggie bones on me."

They both glanced at the pocket of his jeans, which was beyond crusted shut.

"Pass," she said, and another shiver racked her body.

"How about a shower and dinner? I have both those things at my place."

The way she tightened her arms and rested her head between his shoulder blades made him feel ten feet tall. "Sold."

CHAPTER FOURTEEN

The ride over had dried parts of them, save Violet's front and Ford's back, since they'd been mashed together. Once they'd peeled themselves apart, Ford told Violet the door was unlocked and that he'd be right behind her.

She did the sort of sprint-waddle a penguin might while running from a hungry polar bear. With warmth one twist away, she paused, her hand on the doorknob. Then she looked down at least three layers of mud and sludge.

And smiled.

Never before had she been so filthy. While crusty and moderately uncomfortable, it made her oddly happy.

Free.

Usually she held closer to societal constructs. Always had to focus on focusing. She didn't rock the boat while also craving attention, which never had gone very well together. Often it felt like she worked her butt off to be a casual observer of her own life.

Today she'd grabbed an amazing moment by the horns, wrestled it to the muddy ground, and experienced sensations she hadn't even realized she'd been missing.

A shirtless Ford ambled up the sidewalk, speckled in much the same way she was after a day of painting, and it was as if her blurry life twisted into focus. Happy, tingly emotions crystallized, and she *click, click*ed a button in her brain so she could always remember this perfect moment.

"Evidently mud makes me sappy," she said. "I'm about to start waxing poetic."

Amusement danced along the crooked slant of Ford's smile. "Spout some poetry for me, Shakespeare."

"Wasn't Shakespeare more of a playwright?"

"Ooh yeah. Those are the sexy words I was hoping for."

Violet gave his chest a light shove. "Ha-ha. What I'm trying to say is this afternoon was the most fun I've had in a long time. I was completely in the moment."

Ford wrapped an arm around her waist and drew her close. "I rather enjoyed several of those moments myself." He kissed her hard on the lips and reached around her to open the door. "Finally, I can show this doorknob who's boss. He's been bragging for weeks about how he got further with you than I did."

The guy was such a ham, a joke always at the ready, a smile a second away. She'd never been with anyone like Ford.

Not that she'd been with him.

Was she going to be tonight?

If the way he kissed was any indicator, they could have a whole lot of unbridled fun together. He saw her, too—the real, unfiltered version. Scattered brain, bursts of energy, and previously buried passion for photography, which he'd encouraged her to rediscover.

Unlike her ex, Ford didn't attempt to calm the mayhem inside her brain—he rolled with it and patiently repeated himself. He made every minute an adventure.

The way he'd looked at her as he'd told her she was beautiful, as if he'd been in the middle of the desert for days and had just spotted water…

Her stomach whirled as she tipped onto her toes and initiated another kiss.

A tug-of-war began between her heart and her brain.

Sex without commitment often ended in tears and asking yourself what you did wrong.

Then again, so did sex *with* commitment.

More than physical attraction crackled between them, and she could feel their connection in her very soul. A sort of kindred recognition.

Their entwined bodies knocked into the front door, nudging it open, and barks erupted. The *clickety clack* of paws filled the air as the dynamite trio came running.

"Sit," Ford firmly said, and all but Trouble obeyed. He bounded over to Violet, and she hinged at her waist to pet him. Only a strong hand grasped her upper arm and hauled her upright. "You can't reward him unless he obeys."

Violet grumbled, and Ford arched an eyebrow.

"I want to see if your method works. And it's not fair to the dogs being obedient if Trouble gets rewarded for disobeying."

Turned out Ford was a stickler in one area, and since it was his job to train dogs that'd be in charge of people's lives, she supposed that was fair.

"Sit," she told Trouble. He whimpered and pawed at her muddy pants legs, and as hard as it was to ignore the twinge in her chest, she remained steadfast. "Sit."

Trouble's furry butt hit the floor.

"Good boy!" Violet squatted and showered him with affection. "Who's a good boy? That's you, isn't it?" She patted the other puppies, and Pyro glanced at Ford.

At Ford's nod, Pyro rushed over for the snuggle party.

With all the puppies wagging their tails, Violet declared her mission accomplished. The crusted mud that fell from her jeans reminded her how filthy she was. "I'm going to leave a trail from here to the bathroom."

"We can shed our shoes and jeans here in the tiled entryway."

While she'd been halfway naked in front of him only ten or so minutes ago, her adrenaline had ebbed, and it was brighter in here. Suddenly she was calculating how long it'd been since she'd shaved her legs.

Of course she hadn't worn her fancy underwear—she'd never dreamed anyone but her would be seeing them.

"I can't speak for the puppies, but don't worry, I'll be a gentleman and turn around." Ford pivoted toward the wall, and she caught his arm.

"What if I...?" The fervor that'd assailed her body earlier pulsed to life, beseeching her to carry on with living in the moment. "What if I don't want you to be a gentleman?"

A harsh breath whooshed from his lips—one that broadcast his desire for her. And that made it a lot easier to be bold.

She unbuttoned her jeans and began shimmying out of them. The gritty silt made feeling sexy more of a challenge, but she peeled the denim past her thighs and puddled her jeans on the floor.

Ford's Adam's apple bobbed, and her blood turned molten.

With his eyes glued to hers, he unbuttoned and

unzipped his own jeans. He shucked them off and kicked them next to hers.

A giggle arose as she glanced at their captive K-9 audience. "I think they're waiting for our next trick."

"I can conjure one or two." Ford scooped her up, his arms binding her upper thighs, and a squeak escaped her as he strode in the direction of the hall.

Thinking of something clever to say with his whiskers lightly abrading the tops of her breasts and his bare skin heating hers proved impossible. All pesky thoughts had been removed to make way for the lust coursing through her.

Violet combed her fingers through his hair, shaking loose some of the crusted mud on the ends.

A door opened to their left, and after Ford had carried her inside, he kicked it closed behind them.

The bathroom ceiling was lower than the hallway's, and the top of her head skimmed the light fixture. Ford loosened his grip, and she slid down his hard body, her pulse leaping as he groaned.

He swept aside the shower curtain and fumbled with the handles.

Once he'd gotten the water flowing, he spun and cupped her face in his hands. She nearly purred as his thumb dragged across her jaw. "Believe me, sweetheart, I'm aching to get under that hot water with you. But I'm also willing to walk out that door and give you privacy. I don't want you to feel pressured or for you to do anything you might later regret."

He was usually so cocky—now, his sincere words and the hint of vulnerability in his voice made her freeze in place.

One beat...

Two…

With deliberate casualness, Violet slipped one bra strap off her shoulder. Then the other.

She reached behind her.

The usual pinching motion didn't dislodge her bra, so she added her other hand to aid her efforts. "Dammit. I was trying to be all sexy, and this just shows why I can't pull it off."

"I'm happy to help." Ford placed his hands on her hips, twisted her to face the mirror above the sink, and fiddled with the clasp. "The mud's acting like cement, but don't you worry, I'll win this fight."

The bra came loose and fell to the floor.

Ford placed a hand on the center of her stomach and tugged her against him. His erection pressed into the crease of her butt, and he caught her eye in the mirror. "Look at you. Feel what you're doing to me. How can you say you're not sexy?"

The woman peering back at her was a mess. Disheveled hair, dirt-streaked, and carrying a few extra pounds.

But as she bypassed features she'd always considered flaws and concentrated on the way they fit together, she did feel sexy. Desire left her skin flushed and dewy, and Ford's massive body and the large hand splayed on her abdomen made her feel tiny.

His other hand came up to fondle her breast as the one on her stomach drifted downward. He dipped a couple of fingertips into the waistband of her simple cotton panties, and she melted into his embrace.

It'd been so long since she'd been touched. Her knees threatened to give out as his fingertips moved lower.

And lower.

She curled her hand around the nape of Ford's neck, using it as an anchor and arching against his chiseled torso. Electricity jolted her core as the tip of his index finger found the bundle of nerves pulsing to life, the live-wire reaction a spectacular mix of frenzy and ecstasy.

The mirror steamed over, blurring the two nude figures writhing against each other.

Ford kissed her temple and maneuvered her toward the shower. "I think it's time to get underneath the warm water."

"Sure, yep, whatever," Violet said on a breath as he jerked her panties down and off. She was far too desperate for more of Ford's touch to concern herself over where it happened.

The when, though—that needed to be *now*.

Water sluiced over Violet as she stepped into the shower, heating her skin to the same blazing temperature as the rest of her.

Ford shed his boxer briefs and climbed in after her. She grabbed the bar of soap and lathered up. When he held out his palm, she knocked it aside. "I'd better help. You're adept at getting filthy, but I'm not sure you're experienced enough in good clean fun."

The crooked smile appeared. "Do your worst, gorgeous. Or should I say do your best?"

Foamy bubbles clung to his dark chest hair as she rubbed the bar over his body. She tipped onto her toes, both of them letting out throaty noises as their skin slipped together.

Focusing on getting the mud off instead of the way his shoulders rounded and his pec muscles twitched...

Where was I again?

Labored breaths echoed around them as she scrubbed his abdomen, ensuring every dip and groove was covered.

For a moment she watched in awe, mesmerized as the stream sent water down his body, his massive thighs. His arousal.

She teased him with the bar, circling his dick but never quite touching. A growl came out as her pinkie skimmed the impressive length of his shaft. Needless to say, the overcompensating question had been cleared up and then some.

Violet's throat went dry. This guy? She was going to have sex with *him*? What even was her life right now?

Callused fingers brushed damp strands of hair off her face. "How you doin'?"

"A bit frustrated, if I'm being honest. Some guy got me all turned on, and then he just stopped."

"Inexcusable."

Violet set the soap aside. "Right?"

"Some girl did the same thing to me," he said, and his husky voice cranked her desire up to the irrepressible range. "But you're in luck. I have just the thing to help us both."

Ford wrapped his hand around the base of his arousal and walked forward until the head of his penis hit the apex between her thighs. He rubbed it over her slick, ready center, the friction sending frissons of pleasure down her legs and up her core.

A carnal expression overtook Ford's features before he crashed his mouth to hers. The kiss was beautifully brutal, teeth and lips and a lashing tongue.

Another step had her pinned against the shower

wall, his erection pressing into her stomach. Ford reached between them and renewed the circling of his fingertips, delving and stroking until she whimpered, "Don't stop, don't stop."

Every muscle in her body clenched, and she gripped onto Ford's biceps so she could lose herself to the euphoric sensations rendering her legs useless.

Another stroke and she shattered apart, his name spilling from her lips.

The world spun, water and tile walls and an exquisite specimen of a man flickering in and out of her vision. She might've even blacked out for a second or two.

But when she opened her eyes, Ford was watching her. The amount of satisfaction in his features suggested it was as good for him as it was for her, although that couldn't be true. Clearly he'd derived pleasure from hers, though, and that left her unbalanced in the best sort of way.

He lowered his forehead to hers. "Better?"

"Much." She flattened her palms to his chest and ran them down his abdomen. She traced the line of obliques with her fingertips and then hovered her hand over his bobbing shaft. "You?"

A grunt was her only answer.

"Sounds like I'd better get the soap again. I'd hate to miss any part of—"

Ford fell forward, palms braced on the wall on either side of her head, the line of his jaw razor tight. "Violet." Her name was half command, half plea.

She closed the miniscule gap between her hand and his dick, gripping the base and squeezing as she stroked his hard length. A gruff curse escaped as he fell to his forearms, every muscle taut and vibrating with tension.

Violet stroked him again and again, basking in her power to control this big, tough country boy, if only for a little while.

"If you want this to be over"—he groaned—"keep doing that. But if you want me to grab a condom—"

His eyes rolled back in his head, his words an undecipherable gravelly jumble. The idea of watching him lose control while buried deep inside her made an ache form between her thighs.

One finger at a time, she released him. Then she kissed his jaw. The spot where it met his neck. "Get the condom."

"Yes, ma'am," he said.

After a moment of rummaging around in what she assumed was the medicine cabinet, Ford returned with the requisite foil square.

The spray of water cooled a few degrees, signaling they'd almost used all the hot water.

And she could hardly wait to use up the guy in front of her as well.

• • •

Ford about dropped the condom as he reentered the shower. He'd spent the last several minutes staring at the naked creature in front of him, yet her beauty struck him again.

Yes, Violet was curvy and beautiful, and he could write a dozen poems about her exquisite dimpled ass. But it was more than that. The way she'd gone from mud-coated cutie to siren. How she'd meant to do a striptease but needed help.

And lathering him up…? The teasing had effectively driven him out of his mind, but he'd never experienced the tender, doting manner Violet had employed.

More than that, he loved that she didn't hesitate to tell him she was frustrated, her enthusiasm—and how whenever he was with her, he experienced a soothing sensation that also managed to rev him up.

It made no sense.

Hell, half the time *she* made no sense.

Yet everything about here and now felt right in a way nothing else had.

Admittedly, a lot of his experience with women began with sex, and if that went well, they might attempt the relationship thing. Now he saw what he'd been missing, but he didn't think it would've come along with anyone but Violet. There was just something about her.

"Oh. Do you need help, like I did with my bra?" Completely sincere, and she was already reaching for the wrapper.

A condom he could manage and then some, but who was he to refuse? He handed it over and watched as she struggled with the wrapper.

At long last, she ripped the gold foil with her teeth and proudly held up the condom.

Heated blood sang through his veins as she began to roll it on, and how could his restraint be so shaky already?

Ford covered her hand with his. "Full disclosure, I didn't need help. But now I'd better do it, or this might be shorter than both of us want. I'd hate for you to tell me I got you all hot and bothered only to leave you frustrated again."

"No one wants that," she said, giving him a shy smile. Unbelievable how she could go from vixen to bashful and everything in between, and each was a win.

After securing the condom in place, he slanted his mouth over hers, savoring the way her entire body responded. Melting and tugging and stroking her tongue over his until he couldn't tell her breaths from his.

Ford pushed inside her, swallowing her gasp, and *holy shit* she felt good.

Ever so slowly, he pumped his hips. He guided her back against the wall so he could get better leverage. Then he thrust inside her again and again, gathering speed and depth while clinging to his self-control. It'd been a long time, and she fit him so perfectly, and he had to stop dwelling on that or he'd do the opposite of what he was going for.

"Not quite the right angle," she muttered, so he gripped her knee and hooked it up and over his hip.

In addition to the resulting keening noise, the move opened her up to him, allowing him to thrust deeper. They both moaned as they found the ideal rhythm. Their rapid breaths mingled with the water pouring over their bodies, taking him higher and higher as she clenched tighter around him.

"Ford. I'm about to—"

"Go ahead and let go, sweetheart. I've got you."

Her eyes locked on to his, and then her walls were sucking him harder as her orgasm rocketed through her body. He eked out every last drop of her pleasure, and then he followed her over the edge with a roar.

Seconds passed or maybe an eternity, but eventually

he forced his jelly limbs into motion. He grabbed a towel, wrapped it around Violet, and then reached for his own.

For a handful of seconds, they just grinned at each other, as if congratulating themselves on having such a phenomenal time.

"If you follow me," Ford said, "I can lend you some of my clothes. Then I'll get to work on that dinner I promised."

"You were serious about that? I sorta thought it was a line."

"One thing you should know about me: I never joke about food." He skimmed his fingertips down her silky-smooth arm and laced his fingers with hers. He might be the obsessed one now, because he couldn't get enough of touching her and staring at her and he'd done gone and lost his head.

They managed to make it to his bedroom before the dogs could catch them, but as they dressed, the puppies pawed and whimpered at the door.

Once the drawstring on his shorts was secured, Ford checked on Violet. He'd given her a pair of boxers she'd had to roll to get to stay in place, but thanks to the fact that his large T-shirt hit her thighs, he couldn't even see the boxers.

The collar slipped off her shoulder, and she pulled it up, only for the other side to fall.

"You look perfect," he said.

She bit her kiss-reddened lower lip. "Thank you."

He leaned in and sniffed her neck. "You smell nice, too."

"I smell like you."

"Like I said: you smell nice."

Violet shook her head and headed for the door. "Cocky bastard. I can't believe I slept with you."

Honestly, he could hardly believe it, either.

Ford led her to the couch, and the dogs barraged her with sloppy kisses. "I've seen what you do to kitchens," he said, "so you make yourself at home while I go start dinner."

Thanks to his lightning-fast reflexes, he dodged the pillow she launched at his head.

So that's why Lexi brought them over to "spruce up the place."

He'd thought she'd been implying his decor was lacking, but he bet his buddy's wife had planned to toss them at him during planning sessions.

Sessions that'd become more fun as of late, on account of the woman reclining on his couch, her bare legs stretched across the cushions. Trouble snuggled up on her lap, and Violet idly ran her fingers through his hair, leaving Ford a pinch jealous of a puppy.

Shit. Speaking of… "I meant to warn you earlier not to get too attached."

Her mouth dropped, hurt streaking across her features as tension crept into her neck and shoulders. "Oh. I'm not making assumptions just because we had sex. I realize that—"

"I meant to the puppies," Ford quickly said, kicking himself for not realizing how it'd sound. Not only was he rusty in the relationship department, he'd never been the best at communicating in the first place.

He gestured to Trouble. "When it comes to training a new litter, I always remind myself the dogs are only mine for a short while. I just don't want you to get too attached and end up hurt. That's all."

A hint of anguish radiated from Violet as she fondly scratched between Trouble's ears. "I'll do my best."

An argument about doing better than that was on the tip of his tongue, but she'd promised to do her best, and that was all anyone could ask anyone.

At the archway that led from the living room into the kitchen, Ford paused and took in the scene again.

Violet relaxing on the couch, Trouble curled up in her lap while Tank warmed her feet.

Pyro on the floor next to the couch as Nitro used him as her own personal climbing course.

Well, his living room certainly looked fuller with Violet in it. Suddenly he was beginning to see what all the hype was about.

Do you have a sweetheart? Someone who makes your life worth that much more?

Maybe someday in the future, when life's not so hectic and I have time for that kind of thing, he told himself before he got carried away. *Violet's only here temporarily, anyway.*

Which was why, as he pulled ingredients out of his fridge, he thought he should point that warning about not getting too attached right back at himself.

CHAPTER FIFTEEN

"Somebody's awfully happy for six thirty in the morning," Maisy said as Violet skipped into the bakery, humming a song that'd include cartoon birds if her life were a Disney movie. "Especially since that same someone got home super late last night."

Violet propped her forearms on the counter opposite her sister. "I didn't wake you, did I? I tried so hard to be quiet."

"No, I slept like a rock—Isla didn't even get up once. But you weren't home when I went to bed, so I sleuthed my way to the getting-home-late conclusion." Maisy tapped her temple. "Elementary, my dear Watson."

"I've been framed," Violet said, throwing her arms up in a surrender stance. "It wasn't me. It was…Professor Firefighter, in the shower, with a…very large candlestick."

Maisy scrunched up her face, but the *beep beep* of a timer sounded. She straightened and headed around the wall that separated the storefront from the kitchen, gesturing for Violet to follow. "I assume you were with Ford?"

All the smiling began to hurt Violet's cheeks, but it was an ache she'd gladly endure. "Mm-hmm. He took me mud bogging. Have you ever been?"

"Does Dolly Parton sleep on her back?"

Violet blinked. Then the lightbulb snapped on and she laughed.

"Oops, that sort of popped right out." The sweet scent of muffins filled the air as Maisy opened her slightly-worse-for-wear oven. "Thanks to Mama, I've had all the proper debutante training and etiquette lessons. But you don't live in the sticks without picking up what Mama would deem inappropriate language or getting your feet dirty."

Maisy snagged the knitted pink oven mitt off the wall, and Violet flinched as her sister retrieved the muffin tin, afraid she'd get burned through the holes. When she'd asked about the yarn mitten the other day, Maisy informed her the Craft Cats had gifted it upon the reopening of the bakery, along with hand towels, dishcloths, and the tea cozy that transformed the kettle into a big cupcake.

Who in town even drank tea, except the iced, overly sweet kind? They'd never brought out that costumed kettle, not once.

Maybe I should start. Violet had read green tea was one of the healthiest beverages on the planet. Lots of antioxidants, lowered your risk of cancer, along with a myriad of other benefits. "Do you have any green tea?"

The muffin tin hit the counter with a *clink* as Maisy tilted her head. "Are you avoiding the subject on purpose?"

What subject? "No?"

The fist went to her hip, which meant Maisy was about to whip out the thick southern accent—she tended to save it for when she was short on patience. "I need me some deets. Yesterday you wouldn't stop caterwaulin' about delivering the cupcakes to the ball game because you didn't want to see Ford. Then I find out you went mud boggin' with the guy."

Maisy tossed aside the mitt. "I'm guessin' *something* happened between Points A and B." Suddenly her spine went stick straight. "Shower. Very large candlestick." Her eyes flew so wide, Violet feared they'd pop right out of her head. "You had sex with Ford McGuire."

Even though no one else was there, Violet glanced around before excitedly nodding. "We fell in the mud, and then we kissed a little—more like a lot. Naturally we needed to clean ourselves off. One thing led to another…"

"And you had sex," Maisy said, her voice pitching at the end.

A flutter careened through Violet, swelling into a torrid wave as their shared shower replayed in her mind. "*Supah-hot* sex." Violet closed the distance and grabbed her sister's shoulders. "We're talking the kind where I left my body for a minute and I was, like, looking down at us having sex as the water poured over us. Then I thought *wow, that's so freakin' hot. I should jump back in my body to finish.* And I did. Twice."

Maisy's mouth formed a meticulous O, the red lipstick she'd put on today accenting her shock, and Violet feared she'd overshared.

Then Maisy threw a hand to her chest and said, "Praise the Lawd. I was worried you'd never have sex again, and, bless Benjamin's heart, I could just somehow tell he was not good at it."

Violet almost defended him, the way she'd mentally done whenever their time between the sheets fell on the lackluster side. He was busy. Stressed. It was her fault for not reminding him the position he preferred didn't work for her. For her mind drifting to her to-do list and if she should paint the walls a different color and which photo shoot had she scheduled for the next day?

It hit her how many excuses she'd made on his behalf over the years. Not only for the someday wedding thing but in several aspects of their relationship. "In the beginning he made an effort, but this past year, he more went through the mediocre motions. Ford, on the other hand…" Violet fanned her face. "Oh my."

Maisy gave a diminutive clap before she threw her arms around Violet's neck. "I'm so happy for you. And I'm not tempted at all to point out that he has dark hair and fair skin."

The eye roll Maisy couldn't possibly see was no match for the wattage on Violet's smile anyway. "I'm tryin' not to get ahead of myself."

Huh. If she wasn't mistaken, there'd been a bit of southern twang in that statement. Being in Uncertainty was rubbing off on her.

A handful of years ago, that'd send her running, but now…? Violet squeezed her sister. It didn't seem so bad.

When they broke apart, Violet noticed the massive number of cupcakes on the counter. "Whoa."

"Yeah. Remember how the Craft Cats' quilting bazaar is tonight? The one that funds the historical society, so that whenever a building requires renovating or repairs, they have the money."

Violet searched her gray matter but came up blank. "I'm so sorry, but I don't remember." Either she hadn't been paying attention or her brain had shoved it aside for new information.

"No big deal," Maisy said. "You did warn me that

while you were painting and decorating, your ADHD kicks in hard. I guess I figured you were exaggerating."

"I wish," Violet said. Irritation came along with her struggle to focus—not just for whoever she'd accidentally ignored but for herself. She constantly lost her keys, purse, sunglasses, et cetera. Her muscles tensed, steeling herself for Maisy's exasperation.

"Seriously, Vi, don't worry about it. I kind of wish I could forget about the bazaar—I can't seem to catch up. I was behind yesterday but thought I'd have extra time during my usual lull. I forgot that it was bingo day and the seniors stayed until close, and then it was time to get Isla, and"—Maisy pressed her fingers to her temples and rubbed circles there—"between all the diaper changes and pumping and feeding sessions, I seem to have misplaced my brain, along with my ability to multitask."

"Hey," Violet said, adopting a pragmatic pose. "You're still a new mom, and not getting enough sleep would wear on anyone. You're brilliant and beautiful and kind and…"

Violet hesitated, not because she didn't mean the words that'd snagged on the tip of her tongue but because emotion clotted her throat.

"I love you. I don't know what I would've done without you these past several months. I'm so lucky to have you for a sister."

Tears gathered in Maisy's eyes. "I love you, too. This morning I panicked at how close you are to being done with the remodel. I don't want you to leave."

"Well, I still plan on painting your tables and chairs to match the accents on the walls. And I'm barely getting my photography feet underneath me, so I haven't so much as contemplated my next step. But I'll be staying put for at least another two or three weeks."

"Or—hear me out—you could stay forever. Plenty of people around the county could use an award-winning photographer."

Violet wasn't quite sure what to say, since she hadn't considered the possibility of staying in Uncertainly indefinitely.

"Isla adores you," Maisy continued. "She could use a fun auntie as her grandma puts her through those stuffy lessons I had to endure—it's the Hurst way, goin' back generations. And Travis keeps talking about how happy I sound, and it's because of you."

Warmth flooded Violet, and she opened her mouth to respond, but Maisy wasn't done.

"I'm willing to exchange baked goods and room and board for biannual pictures of my family, which, trust me, is an unbelievable deal. If you're having out-of-body sex with Ford, that's a bonus."

"Oh, so now you're offering me a bonus in the form of sex?" Violet added a dramatic gasp. "What would human resources say?"

Humor and exasperation battled it out in Maisy's features, her lips remaining pursed through both.

"I'm not even sure what Ford would say about that," Violet said.

"Sex on the regular with a beautiful woman with curves I can't help but envy…? I *guarantee* he'd be beyond fine with it."

Violet leaned her hip against the counter, careful not to disrupt the cooling cupcakes. The idea that Maisy envied anything of hers while she'd often wished for her sister's metabolism and cute nose struck her as

funny. Guess everyone wanted whatever they didn't
have. "From the sound of it, you've given this a lot of
thought. You're not going to unveil a presentation with
bullet points, are you?"

The endearment Maisy packed into her words as
she said, "I'll create one if that's what it takes" caused
Violet to blink back tears of her own, so much warmth
radiating through her, she fretted she might start
another fire.

This one she'd let consume her, though.

All her life, she'd sought this type of unconditional
love from men. First her father, then her boyfriends,
and particularly with Benjamin—probably because
he'd come the closest. Maybe even because she thought
he was the closest a person as scattered as herself could
get.

With Maisy, Violet wouldn't ever have to worry
their relationship was one-sided, which made it that
much easier to say, "No need. I'll think about it."

CHAPTER SIXTEEN

So far, the table where kids could decorate their own cupcakes had been a smashing success. A messy one, and now several children were sugared up and running around like overgrown hummingbirds, but a win—and a nice moneymaker—nonetheless.

"I still can't believe you got Lottie to agree to this," Maisy said, slinging an arm around Violet's shoulders. "It was such a relief not to have to decorate them all."

After watching Maisy stress all morning, Violet had suggested that instead of a cakewalk, they should let people frost and decorate themselves. Maisy replied that it was a genius plan, one that would make her life easier, but that Lottie would never go for it.

So Violet had trudged over to the craft store to convince the woman.

"That's what sisters are for. Scaring old ladies into agreeing with them."

"It's like you took on the witch from Hansel and Gretel and won. Seriously, you need to teach me your secrets."

Funny enough, Violet had learned quite a bit about Lottie. For one, she'd never cared much for Mayor Hurst's policies or his "holier-than-thou attitude." This came out after Violet informed her that while the mayor was her father, she was an Abrams. It was the first time she'd felt like not being an official Hurst in Uncertainty had helped instead of weighed her down.

Nevertheless, when she'd told Lottie "We've

decided to forgo the cakewalk in favor of having kids decorate their own cupcakes," fire had flared in the depths of the woman's eyes.

Old Violet might've backed down. The new version was working on Ford's who-cares-what-others-think method.

"We already have the cakewalk circle of chairs set up. Tell Maisy to have the prizes there by five. Doors open at six."

"Here's the thing…" Violet worked to remain firm as her insides trembled. "I'm not asking. Having the kids decorate will keep them occupied, and they'll still walk away with a treat. I'll drag a table in myself if I have to. Maisy is a new mom, and she's running a business by herself. I'm not going to add more stress to her plate, and neither will you."

The way Lottie's jaw hit the floor made Violet think no one had ever challenged her before. At long last, the woman had nodded and snatched the cup of coffee and bag with the bear claw from Violet's grasp.

Now, out of the corner of her eye, Violet caught sight of Ford. When she'd texted earlier to ask if she'd see him at the bazaar, he'd claimed it wasn't really his scene, so she hadn't expected him to show. Thanks to the arduous day, it seemed like eons instead of hours since she'd seen him last.

He looked damn good, too, all big and burly, and that freaking swagger…

Desire heated her veins, catapulting her pulse to a primitive rhythm, and she barely refrained from sprinting over, throwing her arms around him, and claiming him as hers in front of everyone.

It's only been one night.

One amazing night. Plus the other times they'd hung out, but she wasn't sure those counted, since they'd been more friendly with flirting than flirting with intent.

What if he wants to keep us on the down low? Her stomach wrenched at the idea, the assertiveness she'd gleaned earlier today wavering.

His eyes locked onto hers, and time lost all meaning…

A slow smile spread across his face, and he changed directions on a dime, heading her way. Butterflies overtook Violet's internal organs, their flailing wings stirring up hope and returning her courage.

"Well, what do we have here?" Ford asked once he reached the table.

"We've been busy decorating." Violet gestured to the cupcakes in front of her. "Want one?"

"Does anyone ever actually say no to that?"

"Can't say I've run across anyone yet."

His gaze remained on hers as he leaned closer. "Gimme some sugar."

Violet met him halfway, but instead of kissing him, she picked up a chocolate cupcake and jammed it into his mouth. Too late, she realized it was similar to a cake cutting at a wedding.

While her brain fretted over that, Ford grabbed a vanilla cupcake and shoved it in the vicinity of her mouth.

They swiped at each other, squealing and giggling and painting buttercream and chocolate frosting over each other's faces.

After an opposite tug-of-war, Ford hauled her upper body over a relatively empty part of the table and planted his lips on hers.

What started as a game morphed into the tastiest greeting in history. The exquisite stroke of his tongue had her curling a hand in his T-shirt and relinquishing control. A protest drifted up as his mouth released hers.

Then Ford cupped her chin, twisted her head to the side, and gave her cheek a languid lick. Violet attempted a swallow and failed.

"Y'all are gonna need to get a room," Maisy said. "Don't get me wrong, I'm missing my husband even more after that display, but this table hosts mostly children."

Violet managed to straighten despite her quaking legs. She'd been so caught up in the kiss, she'd forgotten people might be watching. More than that, with her lips still tingling from the kiss, she found she didn't care. "Sorry," she said to Maisy. "Kinda."

Her sister made a shooing motion. "You've helped me enough today. Go enjoy the bazaar."

"Yes, ma'am." Violet rushed around the table, and once she and Ford reached the pathway where people were strolling around, he grabbed her hand and laced his fingers with hers.

As Violet walked past the rows of quilts on display, she slowed. They hung from a clothesline, numbered squares of paper pinned to the fabric. Each one boasted bright colors, intricate designs, and beautiful patterns. Hours of work that led to artwork blankets that could keep you warm, not only because of the fabric and batting but because you could see the amount of love that'd gone into every stitch.

For years, she'd thought of Uncertainty as the small town where everyone was all up in one another's business, but tonight she felt the strong sense of community. Most of Uncertainty's residents had shown up to support and raise money for the historical society so they could preserve their forefathers' legacy.

The fact that surrounding towns pitched in caused Violet to see the place in a whole new light.

Ford tugged her to the left, toward a kids' plastic swimming pool filled with toy fish. "Time to show off my impressive fishin' skills."

"I'm pretty sure this is a kids' game," she said, and he placed a finger on her lips and shushed her.

"Don't scare 'em away." For some reason, he'd taken on an Australian accent. "Crikey, you'd think this was your first time."

"It is my first time fishing."

"Fishin'," Ford corrected with a smirk that had her rolling her eyes and giggling.

Ford greeted a woman with salt-and-pepper hair that had been twisted up in an intricate bun. He placed a couple dollar bills on the table. "Tell her how it's done, Misaki."

"Oh, I only agreed to run this booth so I could watch the excited faces of the kids. I don't do the fishing," she said with a laugh as she handed over the fishing pole. "I am much better at crochet."

"See those stuffed animals?" Ford asked. Crocheted bunnies, pigs, dogs, cats, and other animals of every size and color covered two of the three tables surrounding her. "Misaki makes them herself."

"It is called amigurumi. A Japanese art my grandmother taught me when I was a young girl."

"They're so cute," Violet said, picking up the purple pig that caught her eye. "If I tried to make something like this, I'd end up with a ball of tangled yarn."

Misaki laughed, the sound happy and full. "I will teach you someday if you want to learn."

Violet's heart turned sappy on her. This woman had met her two seconds ago, and she was offering crochet lessons? How sweet was that?

Add the crowd of people milling about, laughing and enjoying the event, and Maisy's suggestion to stay in Uncertainty permanently held more and more of an appeal.

"...medication, right?" Ford asked, and Violet jerked her attention to the conversation going on in front of her.

"I promise. I bought one of those pill boxes with the days of the week, just like you told me to," Misaki said, and Violet filled in the blank—Ford had asked if the woman was taking her meds. Just in time, too, because Misaki looked at her. "One day this past winter, I couldn't remember if I had taken my medicine or not, so I took my pill. Only I *had* taken it, and doubling up made me so dizzy I passed out. My daughter found me and called 911."

Okay, so she was slightly off but close. "Let me guess. Ford showed up."

Misaki nodded. "Yes, thank goodness. He took good care of me. Now he always asks if I'm being careful with my medication."

Ford rubbed at his neck, bashful on the one point he could be arrogant about. "Yeah, so anyway..." He lifted the fishing pole. "Shall we get started?"

The magnet hit the water with a *kerplunk*, and Ford dragged it around in search of a fish. A blue-and-green fin snagged the end, and Ford jerked the pole. "Whoa, it's a big one." He hooked his hand on Violet's hip and navigated her in front of him. "I'm gonna need help reeling it in."

Indulging him in the game—mostly because it meant having his strong arms caging her in—Violet took the offered fishing pole. As he instructed her to go slow and steady so she wouldn't lose the fish, he wrapped his hands around hers, as if she needed the support.

Considering the way her heart skipped a few beats, it might be hampering her skills, but it'd be a chilly day in hell before she asked him to let go.

Out came the fish, droplets of water flicking them as Ford grabbed the string and swung him closer.

Misaki clapped, as if they'd accomplished a great feat. Then she took the pole and toy fish and pointed at the carnival prizes. "You can choose any one of these."

A boy with ebony curls and tawny skin toddled by, and Ford greeted his parents—Darius the firefighter and a woman with ivory skin and fiery red hair—and asked if Trevon wanted to pick a prize.

Ford placed his hand on her shoulder. "Remember Violet? Maisy's sister?"

Darius stretched out his hand, and as Violet took hold, she said, "Ford's being nice, leaving out the part about the fire at the bakery."

Darius chuckled and introduced his wife, Willow, and his son. Then Ford lifted Trevon so he could choose a prize. The toddler settled on a toy truck, and Ford set him down and ruffled his hair.

Before she could remind herself not to get carried away, the strings that made up Violet's heart gave a sharp tug. How was she supposed to avoid falling for a guy who had a giant heart that he inexplicably tried to keep hidden?

Not that he was very successful—the secret was definitely out.

After waving goodbye to Darius and his darling family, Ford leaned in and whispered something to Misaki. Her face lit up as she took the twenty-dollar bill from Ford and tucked it in her cash box.

Ford placed his hand on the small of Violet's back. "The toys are for the kids, but Misaki is also selling her... Oh, I'm gonna butcher it, but here it goes anyway. Her amigomi."

"Amigurumi," Misaki kindly corrected with a titter.

"Yeah, that." Ford's thumb slipped under the hem of Violet's shirt, a quick brush that left her dizzy. "So, go ahead and pick one."

As a teenager, she'd daydreamed a date that went this way—and standing next to Ford, his thumb hypnotizing her more with each swipe, she felt like that overly romantic girl she used to be once again.

Violet scanned the crocheted animals, pausing on the purple pig she'd picked up earlier. But then the white-and-black-speckled dog caught her gaze, and everything in her shouted *that one*. "Can I please have the dalmatian?"

Misaki handed it over, and Violet hugged it to her chest. "I love him already. I'm gonna name him... McGuire."

One of Ford's dark eyebrows arched.

"Get it? Because he's a firefighter dog and you're a firefighter?"

"But I train German shepherds."

"Well if you're so picky, McGuire," she said,

addressing the stuffed puppy instead of the guy at her side, "I'll have to get you a German shepherd to play with someday."

Ford shook his head, but that sexy indent popped in his cheek.

They thanked Misaki and told her goodbye, and once they were a few steps away, Violet curled in close for a kiss. As she moved her lips against Ford's, she took a second to inhale his cologne and soak in the way he towed her closer and nipped at her lower lip.

If she got any happier, she might float right up to the ceiling next to the helium-filled balloon some kid was probably regretting letting go of.

"What next?" Ford asked.

"I need to thank Lottie before I forget." She took a step, but Ford went full statue, his feet cemented to the floor.

"Sweetheart, I would do most anything you asked. But that woman and I have a long history, and I'd only be a detriment."

"Oh, come on." A tug, and he reluctantly began to move again. "She's not that scary."

"Hell yes she is. You haven't seen her after a puppy's dug up her flowerbed—not one of mine, for the record. Tucker's old dog, Casper, got into her yard one day while we were…doing kid stuff, and she came charging after us. Regardless of not knowing why, we were all terrified."

"Describe this kid stuff," Violet said.

"We *might've* been changing the marquee at the school from 'Due to the championship football game, no class on Friday' to 'no ass on Friday.'"

Violet giggled. She could totally see him and his

friends doing that back in the day.

"Then there was the time we moved the soda machine into the school elevator. It was Addie's idea, and she was the smallest, so she pulled while we pushed. Then—since there was hardly an inch of room to spare, save the top—she climbed up and over to sneak back out.

"Lottie was at the school that day for some reason. I think she was picking up her daughter." Ford secured Violet to his side as they skirted past the ring toss booth. "A few of the teachers thought it was funny, but not Lottie. She pointed at me, Shep, Addie, and Tucker and said, 'I guarantee those are your culprits right there.'"

"In her defense, she wasn't wrong."

His sigh held mock disappointment. "You must've been one of those goody-goody kids."

Violet gasped, even though he wasn't exactly wrong. "Well, in *my* defense, the school I went to wouldn't have found it funny or even referred to it as a prank. I would've been suspended at the least, and I was all too aware that I needed perfect grades and a spotless record in order to get a scholarship if I wanted to go to college."

Ford dodged a family of five with a double stroller. "I reckon I would've ended up in juvie if I'd grown up in a city instead of this small town." He jerked his chin toward the table just down the way.

Lottie sat behind a row of clipboards, chatting with Nellie Mae, who'd approached her in the Old Firehouse a couple weekends ago and outed her presence to Dad. The tablecloth had a sign over the front, identifying them as the "Craft Cats," a ball of yarn speared through with knitting needles on one side and a cat on the other.

"Is this where we deliver the catnip?" Violet asked, and the two women furrowed their brows as the guy at her side snorted a laugh.

Tough crowd. Violet cleared her throat and tried again. "Lottie, I just wanted to thank you for switching up the layout for Maisy. I super appreciate it, and she does, too. Everyone's loving decorating the cupcakes themselves."

Lottie crossed her arms over her ample bosom. "I hope you're not spreading that news around. If I make an exception for you, people will be clamoring for me to do the same for them."

"Um, okay. Anyway, thanks again."

Lottie's gaze lifted to Ford. "Mr. McGuire. Good to see you out supporting our community. Although I seem to remember you tellin' me that you'd be too busy tonight to be our auctioneer."

"My, uh, schedule freed up. A bit. Not enough to be here for the whole auction, but enough to—"

"Accompany Miss Abrams. Yes, I see that. Shame, though. You're so good at running your mouth."

Shock left Violet blinking at the older woman. Residual nervousness rose up, as in she now realized how scared she *should've* been to ask for the switch-up.

That was some brutal honesty, which Violet had always considered someone justifying being rude before running their mouth. Despite what those type claimed, there was a way to be honest *without* the brutality.

Angry heat flared, setting fire to every other emotion. "As the biggest busybody in town, you could surely give him a run for his money." Violet hooked her

hand in the crook of Ford's elbow. "Now, if you'll excuse us, my escort and I need to go find a corner to
make out in."

Seriously, if she hadn't had the positive interactions
with Misaki and so many of the other townsfolk earlier,
Violet would be tempted to storm all the way out of
the building.

As soon as they'd stepped away, Ford said, "You
didn't have to do that. I can handle it."

"Well, I can't. I swear half this town is blind." It
seemed to be the wealthier, older half, too. Or maybe
that was her biases rising up.

"It's the yin and yang of small towns. Sometimes
you can't outgrow your reputation. Or your father's or
grandfather's. Particularly with the older generation."
Ford shrugged. "Several have come around, though.
And when it comes to Lottie, it's personal. One of her
daughters married and then divorced my brother, and
her other daughter just got divorced as well, so I think
she's bitter at men in general."

"She shouldn't take that out on you." Hypocritical,
perhaps, since she'd sworn off men herself. Not that
she'd lasted long.

"I'd rather her aim it at me than someone else. Like
I said, I can handle it." Ford banded his arm around her
shoulders and nuzzled her neck. "But I appreciate that
you worry about me."

Would he appreciate that she more-than-worried?

Evidently her give-a-damn was broken tonight, so
she ran with it. "I get that reputations can be hard to
overcome, but to blame you for something your father
or your brother did…?"

Thanks to her past, she was extra passionate about

the subject. It just took seeing people judging Ford for her to get pissed enough to say something about it.

"That sucks, and people should get over it. Seriously, if you weren't around, who would put out the town's fires? Who'd show up for medical emergencies and find their lost loved ones in the wilds of Alabama?"

Ford hung his head, his skin reddening slightly. "You're making me sound much cooler and more important than I am."

"Is that…?" Violet reached up as if to wipe something off his face. "You got a little humility right—" She smudged her thumb across the corner of his mouth. "There. I think I got it all."

His eyes locked onto hers, amusement twinkling in the green depths. "Oh, good. I'd hate for anyone else to see that. It'd be so embarrassing."

"Does that mean you kinda sorta care what they think once in a while?" Violet leaned in conspiratorially and whispered, "Don't worry, I won't tell anyone."

He lowered his head so that his forehead touched hers. "I care about what one person in here thinks." He used his thumbs to tip up her chin and close the scant distance between their mouths.

While it was one of the more chaste kisses they'd shared and lasted only a second or so, it felt more intimate. Like wrapping yourself in a fleece blanket and sinking onto the couch at the end of the day next to someone you loved.

It was the type of desire she'd tried to snuff out six months ago. One that had her picturing a picket fence and a couple of kids running around the grassy yard as she and her husband sat on a porch swing, watching on and sipping their lemonade.

Because of this particular guy, Pyro and Trouble jumped into the mix as well. Even though, like with the man, she wasn't supposed to go getting attached.

Uneasiness bobbed its head, even as Violet assured herself it wasn't a big deal. As long as she kept the longing off her face. The last thing she wanted was to scare Ford off.

Then again, maybe she should find out now if he'd run from commitment.

She wasn't asking for forever. Just that one day he might be open to more than…whatever they were.

"What would you say if I told you I was considering staying in Uncertainty for good?" The question burst out of her, and Violet held her breath, scrutinizing his features as she awaited his answer.

"If you want to stay, you should. Even as biased as Lottie is, I guarantee if you or I or anyone else in town needed help, she'd show up. And while it was hard growing up with the McGuire reputation looming over me, plenty of others have shown me kindness and made me who I am today.

"I worked a summer at Martin's Trading Post, and when it came time to pay for college, my boss gave me a loan, no interest. One he refused to let me pay back after I graduated."

That was it. No more, no less. Not particularly what she'd hoped for, yet if he told her she *should* move here, she might balk at that, too.

Still, was he trying to talk her into it? Or out of it?

"Hello, Violet." The voice made her freeze in place—not because it'd been cold. No, Cheryl Hurst had the kind of voice that'd persuade you to thank her for driving an ice pick into your eye.

CHAPTER SEVENTEEN

While Violet had loved feeling like a teenager at the fishing booth, she wasn't so much for it right now.

Slowly, she pivoted and summoned up a smile. "Cheryl. Hello."

"I was wondering when I'd run into you."

Me, too. Except replace it with wondering how to avoid running into you. "Here I am."

Cheryl's glacial blue eyes homed in on how close Violet and Ford were standing. As usual, her auburn hair was styled in a less-poofy version of the news anchor bob. Pearl earrings and a matching necklace accented her dress suit, and every inch of her dripped style and class.

In other words, the opposite of Violet.

Awkwardness crowded the air, and then Cheryl aimed a tight smile at Ford. "Would you excuse us for a moment?"

Obviously not an actual request, but instead of immediately agreeing with Cheryl Hurst like most people did, Ford looked at Violet.

"It's okay," she said, hesitantly loosening her grip on him. "I'll find you afterward."

"Pro tip: check the food area."

A simple tilt of head implied Cheryl wanted to take their conversation to one of the empty, darker corners of the community center.

It took Violet back even further, to her elementary years, when she dragged her feet as her mom forced her into the car before school.

Steeling herself for their interaction, Violet lifted her chin and followed. Cheryl nodded to people as they passed, radiating amiability, and Violet wanted to believe she'd get the same treatment. During those few weeks she'd spent in Uncertainty every summer, evasion had been both of their coping mechanisms, for the most part.

Once they were away from prying eyes and ears, Cheryl said, "I hear you've run into a rough spot with your career."

Violet attempted to swallow. "I'm getting back on my feet."

"Happy to hear it." Cheryl lifted her purse and withdrew a checkbook and a pen. "How much would it take to finish the job?"

Offense socked Violet in the gut as she gaped at the woman. Surely she'd misunderstood. Getting financial support from the Hursts had always been a struggle. Dad claimed it started too many fights with Cheryl, and the only time Mom had swallowed her pride and demanded help was for college tuition.

Considering the scholarships Violet had earned, she'd covered everything besides books and housing. "Excuse me?"

"You and I have never had a heart to heart, so I'm sure you think I don't like you. The truth is, I don't *dislike* you."

Okay, that was sort of like telling someone you were fine with them continuing to breathe, as long as they didn't do it around you.

"There's forgiving and there's forgetting," Cheryl continued, "and anytime you're in Uncertainty, it makes it extra hard to forget. When it was for a week or two at a time, I dealt with it, but people are starting to talk about you more and more.

"It's 'have you seen what Violet's done with the bakery?' 'Did you hear that Mayor Hurst's daughter has been helping Addison Murphy with her wedding?'"

Cheryl uncapped the pen and swung it around. "And on and on it goes… As if that wasn't difficult enough to ignore, now you're cozying up with a McGuire." Her nose wrinkled as she spat his surname.

Deep breaths, Violet told herself, struggling not to lose her temper for the second time tonight. "Ford's a good man. I'm so sick of how many people in town don't see that."

"Given his family, he's come a long way. But the McGuires don't settle down—not for long, anyway." Cheryl fiddled with the pearls around her neck. "Between Ford's father and his brothers, they have four divorces and several children with various women. They're always looking for the greener grass." A muscle twitched in her jaw. "Unfortunately, I know all too well how that feels."

For the first time ever, Violet saw a crack in Cheryl's perfect facade. Hurt shone through, creasing a forehead she'd previously believed was uncreasable, thanks to Botox.

As hard as Violet attempted to bat away the doubts tickling her mind, they increased, breeding like bunnies that spread unease far and wide.

"Whatever you think you have, it won't last." Chery's voice cracked, and she lifted her chin, much the same way Violet had done to prepare for this very conversation. "There will always be someone younger and prettier. Someone who doesn't nag or expect anything of him."

A lump took up residence in Violet's throat, and her nose and eyes burned with the urge to cry. She wanted to insist Cheryl was wrong. That she had no idea what she was talking about. It'd be easier to write this off as her being severe and selfish—and dead wrong—if anguish didn't hang so heavy in her features.

"As strained as our relationship has been," Cheryl said, placing a hand on Violet's shoulder, "I'd never want you to go through that. Especially after witnessing the fallout from your last relationship."

You mean when you told me I was being overly dramatic and ruining Maisy's wedding?

Cheryl hadn't seemed very concerned at the time. More like the woman thought it karmic balance, as if Violet were somehow responsible for her father's actions before she even existed.

Another memory possibly tainted by how very raw Violet's emotions had been after discovering Benjamin with another woman.

"I also feel bad that we didn't give you more support. Your father and I are gifting Maisy a new sign for the bakery, so look at it as us helping you with your business as well. It's the least we can do." Cheryl looked at her, as if she honestly thought Violet would give her the sum it'd take to make her go away.

Violet's pulse pounded in her ears, drowning out the noise from the bazaar. Then she heard a *rip*, followed by a rectangle of paper—a blank check— being placed in her hands.

Everything inside her wanted to insist Cheryl was wrong about Ford.

With memories of her past relationship flooding in and reminding her how very wrong *she'd* been before, though, words refused to form.

• • •

Ford had just taken a giant bite of a hot dog when he spotted Violet. Something was off, the happy, easygoing woman he'd been with fifteen minutes ago gone.

He washed down his food with a swig of fresh-squeezed lemonade and crossed the steady stream of people to reach her. "What's wrong?"

Violet rubbed a couple fingers across her forehead. "Every time I deal with Cheryl or my dad…" She shook her head as if she were attempting to dislodge the memory—maybe more than one. "You want to get out of here? Maybe go to your place for a while?"

His phone vibrated in his pocket, and he wiped his hand on his jeans before digging it out and reading the text from Shep. "Uh, there's a porcupine in the school, so my night is suddenly booked."

She shuttered her eyes, despair flickering so quickly he'd barely caught it. "Seriously?" She crossed her arms. "You don't have to make up some lame excuse. If you're starting to feel crowded or like we're spending too much time togeth—"

"Violet, it's not that."

The skeptical set of her lips remained.

"I'm not clever enough to come up with an excuse involvin' a fake porcupine."

Nope, still not getting through to her. How did one convince a city girl that there were plenty of times when his job or life or whatever you wanted to call it included tasks that sounded completely bananas?

Finally, he realized there was only one surefire way. In addition to proving he wasn't lying, it'd be a handy way to see if she could handle these types of small-town situations and the fact that they were part of his job.

It took a bit of work to pry her hand free of its rigid position. "Come on, and I'll show you."

CHAPTER EIGHTEEN

Ford had just opened the passenger door for Violet and called for Pyro to jump out of the truck bed when Shep approached.

"A raccoon, bunnies, and now a fuckin' porcupine."

"Sounds like the start of a bad joke. Lemme guess, they all walk into the school." The tailgate screeched as Ford lowered it and began snapping leashes on puppies. "What's the punch line?"

"Me, I guess. I bet a bunch of kids think they're awfully damn funny right now, tryin' to turn the school into a petting zoo." Shep seemed to register Violet's presence, and, as usual, his poker face was shit. He conveyed, loud and clear, his surprise over her tagging along. "Violet. Hey."

She waved. "Hi, Will. Nice to see you again."

"Violet's lookin' for a slice of country life," Ford said, giving her a wink as he handed her Trouble's leash. "We're gonna play this like a training drill—only with a short leash instead of a long lead rope. Keep a tight hold of him, otherwise Trouble might get too close to the porcupine and end up with a snout full of quills."

Violet hoisted Trouble into her arms and rubbed the underside of his chin. "We don't want that, do we? That's why we're just going to sniff out the creature and…" She glanced to Ford to fill in the rest of the plan.

"Herd him outside so he can hightail it back to where he belongs."

"Or her," Violet added, as if she were a pro at animal rights.

"How presumptuous of me," Ford said. "Don't wanna be sexist and call the prickly vermin a dude if it's a chick."

"Exactly." Violet lowered Trouble to the ground. "You ready to put your skills to good use? Afterward there will be treats, and even better, so, *so* much cuddling."

Hopefully, that reward would extend to Ford as well. It'd been too long since he'd gotten his arms around her without an audience.

Ford handed Tank's and Nitro's leashes to Shep. "Same speech I gave her. The puppies'll track the porcupine, but let Pyro and me take lead." He squatted and patted his canine companion's side as he hooked a rope onto the red collar. "I know, I don't usually bother with a leash with you, but it's for your own good. Ready to get to work?"

Pyro gave an enthusiastic bark that the puppies echoed, and they were on their way, a ragtag group of marshals on the hunt for a fugitive.

"You both are acting like this is so normal," Violet said. "*Is* this normal?"

Shep headed up the ramp to the double-door entrance of the school. "Not sure normal applies in Uncertainty. Kids have been pullin' pranks for generations. Hell, it's something Ford, Tucker, Easton, Murph, and I would've done back in the day."

"Only we wouldn't get caught," Ford added. "Well, we got away with fifty, sixty percent at least."

Violet tucked a stray strand of hair behind her ear. "So you know who did this?"

"Not yet," he and Shep said at the same time. Then Shep took over the explaining. "After we get the animals out of the building, we'll review the video footage. It's always blurry and dim, so it's a bit like lookin' for smoke in a cloud of fog, but we can often make out hoodies or hats or whatnot. The kids wear 'em to school 'cause they haven't got a lick of sense.

"After the last few pranks—three bunnies numbered one, two, and four, as if we hadn't already pulled that trick of making the admin think there was one missing—and a few weeks later a racoon in the cafeteria that scared the bejeebies out of the lunch ladies. Anyway, we upgraded to high-res cameras, including one aimed right at the parking lot."

A light tug slowed Pyro's eager pace. "We used to wait till the next school day to hear how our pranks went over. Kids these days can't help but drive by several times to catch a peek at their handiwork."

The giant retractable key ring on Shep's belt *zing*ed as he used one of his many keys to unlock the doors. "The porcupine was just yonder, at the far end of the lobby. I spotted a moving blob and shined my flashlight inside. I caught sight of quills, but by the time I got the doors open, it'd melted into the darkness. Figured I could either go pokin' around for the rest of the evening and end up with an ass full of quills, or I could call for backup."

As soon as they stepped inside the building, the dogs went wild sniffing the ground. Ford lowered his voice into authoritative mode. "Seek."

Pyro nearly jerked Ford's arm out of the socket as he headed across the lobby, nose to the ground. It'd been years since Ford had used a leash on him, and unlike the puppies, he didn't do anything slow.

"He's got a bead on it," Ford said as Pyro charged down the hallway to the right, and then he picked up his own pace and rushed on after him.

• • •

Where even was she right now? In the middle of an odd dream—one she'd later wake up from and think, *How didn't I realize I was asleep? The situation was way too bizarre to be real.*

Trouble tugged on his leash, headed in the same direction Ford had gone, and Violet had to half-run to keep up.

Lights flicked on, bathing the hallway in light, and she skidded to a stop a handful of yards short of Ford and a growling Pyro. "Holy shit. That's a porcupine. I've never seen one in real life before."

The creature had been up on its haunches, scratching its side, an oddly human gesture. It turned, its stumpy face and beady black eyes staring out from the type of hairdo Violet ended up with whenever she went to bed with wet locks.

"Aww, it's so cute." In fact, Violet experienced the same syrupy phenomenon as whenever she saw Trouble. "I kinda want to pet it."

Ford gave her a *don't you dare* glare. "Trust me, you don't. That goes for you, too, Pyro."

As if Trouble had only now realized there was a foreign animal, he began barking like mad, which set off a chain reaction with his siblings. TNT, on the case and just as explosive.

The porcupine's quills flared, going from bedhead to

static electricity.

Violet's blood pressure spiked, and she backped-aled, dragging a stubborn Trouble with her. Elongated teeth clattered together as the animal became agitated. It lumbered around, displaying its raised, extra-spiked backside, and Ford and Pyro gave it extra space as well.

A series of squeaky grunting noises came from the creature, as if it were swearing at them for interrupting what'd been a nice, leisurely stroll through the school halls. With its teeth out and the quills in ready-to-fire position, the urge to pet it waned, and its agitation set the dogs off again.

"Hold the puppies back," Ford said, throwing out an arm. "Just a second, Pyro. Let's come up with a plan." He glanced around and then indicated a door to Violet's right. "Is that still a janitor's closet?"

"Yep," Will said from her other side. "Doubt it's changed much since you and Trina turned it into your own personal make-out room. We keep it locked now, of course. I don't want any teen pregnancies on my watch."

A heavy exhale came out as Ford ran a hand through his hair. "Gee, thanks for that."

Will looked from him to Violet, somewhat cha-grined. The toxic flare in her gut made it hard to pretend she didn't want to hunt down this Trina chick and strangle her.

Fortunately, they had their hands full with other things. Country things, apparently. Even with the creature in view and prattling on and on, she could hardly believe this was real life. And people said Florida had all the perplexing news stories.

Tank and Nitro continued to sniff the ground. Then

they went to barking, towing Will in the direction of the lobby they'd come from. "Uh-oh. What if there's more than one?"

Will unhooked the key ring from his belt. "I'm going to go check the other hallway." He tossed the keys to Violet. They clanged together as they fell through her hands and onto the floor—sports had never been her jam.

Luckily, Will was already off and running, and Ford had his eyes on the porcupine and Pyro as they egged each other on.

Trouble, on the other hand, circled the keys and growled, absolutely on top of the mission.

"Good job, buddy. We need those, so thanks so much for helping me find them." Violet retrieved the key ring. Thanks to the extra adrenaline and slight tremble in her hand, it took two tries to unlock the closet.

"Is there a big push broom in there?" Ford asked, and she scanned the area. Roomy enough for a make-out session for sure, if you didn't mind the overwhelming scent of three to five types of cleaner.

Paper towels, spray bottles, a mop and bucket, and…

"Found the broom." She grabbed the wooden handle, fighting the wide bottom as it snagged on the bucket and then the doorjamb. Didn't help that she was trying to prevent Trouble from taking a drink from the murky contents of the bucket. "No. I'll get you clean water later."

As soon as she finagled the push broom free, relief filled her.

For two whole seconds, before Ford extended his palm for it. So much for her short-lived celebration.

She rocked into motion again, rushing the broom over to him.

The porcupine spun and snapped its teeth at her, and a squeal escaped as her heartbeat tripled. Trouble decided to defend her honor, and her pulse skyrocketed into the danger zone as she used her foot to nudge him away from a snout-full of pain.

Violet retreated, keeping Trouble close to her side.

"Now I need you to backtrack the way we came and prop open the doors," Ford said, his voice low and placid. Did he truly feel that nonchalant, or did he simply have years of practice pretending to be while in tense situations? "Then give us a wide berth so Pyro and I can get our boy—*or girl*—pointed in the right direction and nudge it on out the door."

The squawky grunts grew in intensity, leading Violet to believe the porcupine was either on board with or opposed to the plan.

"Oh, and in case there is another one, watch for it," Ford called after her as she ran down the hallway, as if she had any idea what that meant.

Like give a shout if she saw the porcupine's significant other? Try to catch it? Assure it they were going to get them out of here in one piece?

Let Trouble handle it?

Since the puppy in question began sniffing every single locker before finding a pencil to gnaw on, she scooped him up and ran. "Buddy, I hope you're more qualified for this than I am. I needed an escape from life, and suddenly I'm breaking animals out of high school."

Once Violet had propped open the doors and ensured the kickstand thingies could hold them, she rushed across the lobby.

Ford and Pyro had managed to get their porcupine turned around and halfway down the hall, Pyro barking and growling at it to stay the course while Ford wielded the broom like a hockey stick.

Holding Trouble firmly, Violet darted into the other hallway lined with lockers. Hopefully she and her fierce hound would be enough of a deterrent for the porcupine to head outside instead of in their direction.

"We've got to look scary, 'kay?"

Trouble licked her chin, causing an undercurrent of adoration that made her mostly okay with his total lack of obedience.

In the distance, Nitro and Tank barked out a cacophonous racket. One that was growing louder and louder…

They rounded the corner of the hallway at a full sprint, Will hot on their heels.

Trouble jumped out of her arms and rushed toward his siblings, leaving Violet to race after the end of his leash.

Last second, she completed a home-plate slide and snagged it, her knees and palms burning as she hit the floor.

Wait, is that a mouse?

The rodent apparently decided her prone form was less threatening than her pursuers and skittered over the top of her.

"Ew, ew, ew." Violet swatted at her head, failing to repress a shudder.

Nitro and Tank charged right on after the mouse, using Violet's back and butt as a launchpad.

Will yanked on the leashes, forcing the puppies to

stop in their tracks, and squatted to check on her. "Sorry," he said through labored breaths. "I didn't see you in time. You okay?"

Her hip bones throbbed, her hands and knees stung, and a mouse had crawled over the top of her. And yet, as she rolled onto her side, a laugh came out instead of the assurance she'd most likely survive.

The dogs were still barking up a storm at the mouse, who'd paused in the hallway, a foot or so from the lobby, as if it weren't going to bother to flee if the puppies didn't give chase.

Then it must've caught sight of the porcupine, Pyro, and Ford and his broom, because it skidded across the tile and rushed out the open door.

"Pull back, pull back," Ford yelled as he and Pyro rounded the corner. The push broom had quills sticking out from its bristles, so the makeshift puck had put up quite a fight. Sure enough, its grunted complaints echoed through the lobby. "Dude, it's for your own good."

Will clutched the two leashes in his fist and reeled Tank and Nitro away from the mouth of the lobby. They fought their restraints, desperate to go help Pyro as he barked and urged the porcupine toward the door.

Violet reinforced her own grip on Trouble's leash, but he'd turned his attention to her shoelaces and was ever-so-helpfully biting at the ends and untying them for her.

Once the porcupine spotted freedom, the prickly beast followed its smaller mouse cousin outside, and Ford quickly kicked up the stands and yanked the doors closed behind them.

Violet returned her head to the cool tile floor,

wondering if it'd be odd to take a quick nap.

Then again, when in Alabama… Odd seemed to have a new meaning here, as in there might be a variety of woodland creatures roaming the hallways of the school. *Speaking of…*

"Did you find another porcupine?" she asked Will.

"Nah," he said. "Just a pile of porcupine shit. Right as I was about to turn the dogs around, they unearthed that mouse. Figured it'd be a good training exercise for 'em."

Right. Training. Not odd at all.

Next thing she knew, Ford and Pyro were looming over her.

She smiled up at Ford's sexy, rugged face. "So? Did Trouble and I do a good job?"

Ford glanced at her puppy, who'd moved from untying her shoelaces to attacking a stray gum wrapper. "I mean, he's not entirely focused, and you're takin' a nap, but hiccups are common during first jobs. I'd give you guys a C. Maybe even a C plus."

"Did you hear that, buddy? We passed." Violet pushed herself to a seated position and held her hand up for Trouble to smack it—not that she'd taught him that trick.

The traitor ignored it and leaped on top of his sister, choosing to bite her ear and start a fight instead of celebrating.

Pyro nudged her side, so she turned to shower him with affection. "You got an A plus, *plus*, didn't you? You're such a brave dog."

Ford crouched down on Violet's other side, forearms braced on his knees. One corner of his mouth kicked up while two creases appeared between his eyebrows, as if he couldn't settle on concerned or amused. "Bet you'll rethink coming along the next time I get a strange emergency call."

"Are you kidding me? That was such a rush! Save mud bogging and…"

Will's focus was on untangling the leashes, and naturally the dogs had decided to help by climbing on and licking him.

Violet lowered her voice to a whisper. "Afterward in the shower…" Yep, her cheeks were turning red; she could tell by the heat that accompanied her bold declaration. Lingering on it would only make her trip over her words, so she charged on, her voice returning to a normal decibel.

"This is the most adventurous date I've ever been on. Most guys go for the typical dinner and a movie." She patted the side of Ford's face and left her palm against his stubbled skin. "But you, you pull out all the stops."

"Anything for my girl." He slid his hand behind her neck as he guided her mouth to his. He began to pull away and then dove back in, capturing her lower lip between his teeth and topping the kiss off with a sensual nip. "Shep, we might need those keys to the janitor's closet. You go on ahead, and we'll lock up in a few."

Violet smacked his arm and did her best to hold a dirty look. "Nice try. One, a *few* minutes? Seriously? You think that's motivating? And two, I don't want some hussy's leftover make-out spot."

Obviously she didn't mean the hussy part.

Well, she did her best not to, even as the envy coating her insides thickened. There'd been times in the past she'd caught women flirting with Benjamin, but she'd never felt jealous. Partially because she thought the two of them were unshakable.

But even when she'd caught him at Maisy's wedding, this desperate sort of need to claim him as hers hadn't come along for the ride.

"Sounds like I'd better find us a nicer spot, then." Ford grabbed her hand and helped her to her feet.

"I'd suggest you do," Violet said, and then they grinned at each other and all the world was right.

Which was wild, considering she'd just survived her first bazaar, a run-in with Cheryl, and a porcupine hunt in one hectic night.

CHAPTER NINETEEN

It'd been ages since Ford brought a girl with him to Tucker's houseboat. And by ages he meant since high school, when they used to have the occasional party. One that would generally get a few of them grounded.

Never him, though.

For that, Dad would have to give a shit where he was. A lot of nights, Ford had ended up sleeping on the couch, and more than a few times, the floor. That was the beauty of being young and recovering in hours instead of days.

Before he'd picked up Violet, he'd sent Tucker a text telling him they were on their way to the houseboat that moonlighted as Tucker's law office. Ever since he moved back to Uncertainty last fall, Friday nights were once again reserved for poker.

Ford assisted his beautiful date out of the truck, taking a moment to admire the woman he'd spent a few nights with this past week. So far, Violet had handled most everything the country had thrown at her like a champ. The confrontation he'd had with his brother at the baseball field, mud bogging, stirring up rumors at the bazaar, and even a porcupine chase with a mouse using her as a springboard.

Unease churned in his gut, although he couldn't pinpoint why. Possibly because every aspect of his life that he pulled her into was another string that could trip or entangle.

"You're quiet." Violet wrapped him in a side hug,

linking her fingers above his hip. "You're never quiet."

"Not never. Once in a blue moon I get all thought-ful-like."

She snuggled closer. "Sounds dangerous."

"Oh, it is," he said, brushing his lips across hers, and there was the serenity he'd been missing. "Primarily for you. Most of my thoughtfulness involves getting you naked."

Even in the dim light, he could see the blush, and he savored the fact that it hadn't dimmed in spite of how many times they'd had sex this past week.

Muted laughter drifted toward them as they crossed the wooden walkway. Light spilled from the windows, the glow yellow and happy.

Various greetings met them as they stepped inside. Ford guided Violet through the narrow alleyway between the kitchen and living room area.

"It's so good to see you," Lexi said, leaning across the table to hug Violet. "One might even say you're looking rather *succulent*."

Violet giggled, and Ford shared a glance with Addie, since the two of them were the butt of the joke.

Night before last, they'd gone to a floral shop to finalize bouquets and arrangements.

"What about succulents?" Violet had asked Lexi when she suggested they add a bit of greenery to the white and yellow daisy and sunflower bouquets.

"Succulents?" Addie bounded closer to the counter. "Are those flowers you can eat?"

Since Ford could get on board with that, he'd peeked over the top of the women's heads. He and Addie had exchanged a WTH expression when they saw the plant the florist had placed on the glass countertop. "Isn't that a cactus?"

Addie touched the end of one of the fat leaves and jerked back her finger. "Ouch, it's pokey. What, you guys don't think wearing a dress will be uncomfortable enough? Like hey, let's add stabby plants to the mix?"

"Oh, come on," Violet had said. "They're cute."

"Putting a bow on a turd doesn't make it a present," Ford countered.

Lexi carefully lifted the plant by the tiny stem. "It's like a lovely reminder to nurture your relationship."

"But cacti don't need nurturing. That's the beauty of them."

Simultaneous sighs had come from Lexi and Violet, and eventually the hoity-toity cacti were vetoed in favor of seeded eucalyptus, which was apparently different from regular kind. What he and Addie had agreed on was that it smelled good and looked nice, and Violet and Lexi were so thrilled they'd agreed on anything that they ran with it.

"Very funny," Ford said now, adding waggling eyebrows as he looked Violet up and down. "Although not untrue. You're absolutely succulent tonight."

"Are you saying I'm only a little prickly?" The pinch Violet gave his side was more affectionate than prickly.

Easton paused his shuffling, half the deck in each of his hands. "I feel like I'm missing something."

"Bro, you're missing a lot of things," Ford teased, adding a smirk. "But this particular thing's a brides-maid thing."

Ford turned to Violet and placed his hand on her lower back. "You know how to play Texas hold 'em?"

"In theory," she said. "In reality, it's been a while."

"We can be a team if you'd like." He settled into his

usual chair and pulled her onto his lap.

"Good idea. Ford needs all the help he can get," Easton said, and Ford shot him the bird.

It took a few rounds, but Violet caught on to the game and the house rules. Right as Ford was about to bet, she twisted her head, her lips brushing his ear as she whispered, "Addie didn't get the card she was hoping for. Raise twice your usual amount and see what she does."

Without thinking, he almost looked at Addie. But that would give him away.

Still, she was the hardest one of them to read, so he struggled to believe Violet already had her pegged.

Pegged. Now that's something I'd like her to do to me.

Ford shifted in his seat, but Violet's sharp intake of breath made him think she felt his reaction, and that certainly wasn't helping matters.

Since talking quietly had never been one of Ford's special skills, he held his phone under the table and sent a text to Violet.

Ford: *How do you know Addie doesn't have it? None of us can ever read her, even Tucker.*

Seconds later, his phone vibrated in his hand.

Violet: *Remember how many times I've been a bridesmaid? It means I'm a pro at reading brides. I saw her reactions to dresses and cakes and flowers. There's a sparkle in her eye when she sees what she likes, and it's not there.*

Sink or swim time, and was he honest-to-God going to rely on an eye sparkle? Or lack thereof?

No, he was relying on Violet, and that made it a lot easier to go all in. His heart quickened at the idea, because now he was thinking about more than his stack of chips.

All in, all in, all in… Violet hadn't pushed or asked him again what he thought about her staying in Uncertainty for good. The question had gobsmacked him at the time, and he'd responded in the most neutral, up-to-you way he could muster.

Once in a while, he felt it hanging in the air between them, this unspoken question that he suspected she wanted a solid answer to. Or maybe that was his paranoia. Add in the fear that he'd ask her to stay, only to feel suffocated and realize he wasn't ready for more of a commitment, and *shit* his lungs were doing that deflating thing again.

"McGuire? You're looking a little pale," Addie said. "Is someone thinking they bet off more than they could chew?" She slapped her knee. "Get it? Bet off?"

The rest of the guys groaned as if they hadn't come up with jokes just as cheesy before. It provided what Ford needed, though. The opportunity to pull himself together and focus on the cards—much easier to read.

One by one, everyone folded except him and Addie. She was taking forever to decide whether or not to match or fold like everyone else. That wouldn't do. He needed to know if Violet had been right.

"Come on, Murph. Last month you told me you've seen the size of my balls and made it sound like yours were bigger. Are you really gonna back down now?"

"Wait, what?" Violet said, spinning on his lap and making his dick lose focus on the game.

"Don't worry," Lexi said, swiping a hand through the air. "They talk like this all the time. It's all balls and boobs and trash talk."

Shep wrapped an arm around his wife. "I'd like to talk to you about my balls and your boobs."

Easton reached into the bag of Doritos, adding another layer of orange dust to his fingertips. "I thought they'd be less lovey-dovey after half a year of marriage."

Goofball that he was, Shep leaned in and placed a loud smacking kiss on Lexi's lips. He added a boob grab that made Lexi cluck her tongue and say, "*William Irving Shepherd!*"

But then she grinned and kissed him back, climbing on his lap to do so.

Ford squeezed Violet's thigh, hoping this wasn't making her uncomfortable.

When she glanced over her shoulder at him, though, she was grinning.

Now he was the one leaning in for a smacking kiss. With his erection testing the bounds of his zipper, he was about to fold and carry her out of the boathouse and into his truck, where he could worship her body in private.

Well, he might have to drive a mile or so into the boonies for privacy, but he'd never make it home.

"Babe, it looks like we're about to lose everyone," Addie said. "And speaking of boobs and balls..." She and Tucker shared a kiss of their own.

A groan came from Ford's right, and Easton shook his head. "Great. Now I'm surrounded by couples. Let's see the cards before this shindig turns into an orgy and I get to be the loser guy standing in the corner alone, holding his dick."

Chuckles went around the table, but the word "couple" spun through Ford's head on a steady loop.

He was part of a couple.

It should freak him out—it had mere moments ago. But it felt damn good, having Violet on his lap, his friends surrounding him.

This is what Doris meant when she called her life full. Contentment filled him head to toe, as if every part of his life was precisely as it should be.

The arch of Addie's eyebrow conveyed she could read his thoughts and agreed. She always did like to say "I told you so."

Time to end this game and bask in how okay I suddenly am with all this.

Ford flipped his cards, pumping his fist when his two pair beat Addie's jack and shit—literally. A jack and a lot of diamonds, save one.

"Ready to get out of here?" he whispered in Violet's ear, and she melted against him and pressed her lips to his jaw.

"As ready as you feel," she said with a siren smile that made him even harder. Having her sit on his lap might've been the wrong call, yet he wasn't willing to let go.

Ford cleared his throat. "Thanks for the game, y'all. Violet and I are gonna go get a room."

"I wasn't going to be that TMI about it, since I'm a lady, but I'll echo his thanks." She scooted out from the table, and he had to think about anatomy terms in order to compose himself.

Still sporting a halfski, he stood, winding his arms around Violet's waist to keep her close and himself concealed.

Just like that, the situation in his pants returned full force. When he was two steps from the door, though,

Lexi jumped up. "Ford, wait. Um, Addie and I need to talk to you really quickly."

Confusion wrinkled Addie's brow, her bafflement clear. "We do?"

Lexi widened her eyes at Addie. "Yes. Remember?"

"Please don't say it's about the weddin'," Addie all but begged. "We talked about makeup and hairstyle options all day, and I'm certain you were speakin' French for all I understood. You're welcome for the lack of phone call, McGuire."

His gratitude made it hard to refuse, even as his libido revolted at the idea of walking away from the beautiful temptress in front of him. "Give me a minute?"

Violet nodded, and as he started away from her, she smacked him on the ass. "Go get 'em, tiger."

Since there wasn't anywhere to go in the boathouse where everyone wouldn't overhear, they ended up outside on the deck.

Once the sliding glass door *snick*ed closed behind them, Ford turned to Addie and Lexi. "What's up?"

• • •

"Is this where y'all tell me I'd better take care of your friend or else?" Violet asked, a nervous laugh coming along for the ride. And dang it, she was picking up more southern slang by the day.

Then again, if she were "fixin' to" stay in Uncertainty, perhaps she should give in. *Not that Ford's been exactly forthcoming on how he feels about that subject.*

A tiny, persistent voice in her head—one she had too much pride to voice—constantly begged *Want me.*

Choose me.

"Nah." Tucker procured a beer from the fridge, removed the cap, and extended it to her. "In case the meeting goes longer than expected. Lexi's a talker."

"It transfers to the bedroom, if you know what I mean." A smug, smitten grin spread across Will's face. "For as proper as she is, things get real dirty real quick in there."

Violet gripped the cold beer bottle, taking a generous pull in hopes it'd calm the anxiety rising up and wheedling her to fidget.

"How long are you stickin' around town?" Easton asked, sitting on the edge of the table, where several stacks of chips and cards remained.

"I'm not sure," Violet said. "There are a lot of variables up in the air right now." One of them being the guy outside, in addition to Maisy and Isla.

Cheryl had also inserted herself into the equation last weekend, leaving Violet agonizing over the best way to solve it. While the allure to stay in Uncertainty was strong, impulsivity had bit her in the ass before. As had factoring in a man who didn't want her the same way she'd wanted him.

The police officer nodded, not giving her much to go on.

Another sip of beer decided like the best course of action. "You guys have been friends for a long time, right?"

Tucker, Easton, and Will gave uniform nods.

"This is me trying to make conversation," Violet said. "Help a girl out, will ya?"

The heaviness crowding the air dissipated. "Guess we're not used to Ford bringing a girl along," Tucker said, huffing a laugh. "Apparently we've forgotten how to act."

Was that good? Bad? She wanted to feel special because he'd brought her, but what if that meant Cheryl's warning was warranted? That Ford McGuire bounced from female to female, always looking for greener pastures?

And how much longer could she delay making a decision before she fell back into old patterns and made too many excuses for a guy who didn't bother making any of his own?

• • •

"Are you and Violet an official thing now?" Lexi asked, fists on hips, as if it were a reason to scold him instead of to celebrate.

While he'd grown accustomed to Lexi's fancy manners and boundless enthusiasm and appreciated how quickly she'd embraced small-town life, Ford felt like he'd never quite gotten on the right footing with her.

Too backwoods, he supposed, although she'd accepted that side of Shep.

He glanced at Murph, who shrugged. "Lexi said jump, and I just asked how high."

Lexi lowered her eyebrows and turned to Addie. "You honestly don't know why I'm asking?"

Addie grimaced. "Not a clue."

At least the exasperated sigh seemed to apply to both of them. "Okay, let me go old-school on you, then. Ford, what are your intentions with Violet?"

He intended to take her home and give her as many

orgasms as possible. Never let it be said he didn't learn anything, though, because instinct and experience told him that wasn't the answer Lexi was searching for.

"Relax. She and I are just getting acquainted." Ford nudged Addie. "In the biblical sense, if you know what I mean."

Addie rolled her eyes. "I always know what you mean."

Another sigh from Lexi. "That's what I was worried about. Are you just having fun, or is there more to it?"

In spite of landing plenty of inches below his throat, Ford tugged at the collar of his T-shirt in an attempt to get more air. "We haven't bothered labeling it."

"Do you know anything about women?" Lexi asked as she paced the deck, and while he assumed the question was meant for him, Addie shrugged. "You're thinking it's all fun and games and whatever happens, happens. Meanwhile, she's thinking you're connecting and on your way to something real."

Lexi stopped her pacing directly in front of him. "And if you're willing to put in the effort, I'm all for it. But Violet's been hurt before. If you're only playing with her heart—"

"I'm not that cruel," he said, offense churning in his gut. "It's not like I go out with women planning on playing them." In the past, he hadn't thought a whole lot about their feelings, but he'd always been up-front about not getting too serious.

"I'd never call you cruel. But sometimes things end up broken, even when you don't *plan* to break them."

That statement hit him in the solar plexus. "So, what? You're telling me to leave Violet alone?"

Another hit, harder, leaving him short of breath.

"Wait," Addie said. "Violet's good for him—I see a difference. And I can tell Ford likes her. He and I have talked about him getting serious and settling down."

"Whoa, whoa, whoa," Ford said, throwing up his hands. "I never said I was ready to settle down. More like I'd think about it."

Now Addie took up the stern expression, crossing her arms for emphasis. "Seriously? Can you honestly say your life doesn't feel fuller lately? Like a piece that you didn't realize was missing has suddenly clicked into place?"

He couldn't deny either of those things. "I care about her, yes. Violet's funny. Smart. Sexy. She's got this energy… And other times she's calming. Plus, I never know what's going to pop out of her mouth."

His burgeoning feelings for her scared him, frankly, but he wasn't going to own up to that.

Besides, it was akin to the fear he felt after cliff diving or rappelling. Adrenaline-fueled with a promise of adventure. "I just… I like her."

"I like her, too," Lexi said, loud enough the words echoed across the lake. "That's why I'm telling you that if you're not serious about her…" She took a breath. "Ford, she thought she was going to get married, and the guy ended up destroying her heart and doing a real number on her self-esteem. At one point, she'd given up on men, and I'm afraid next time she won't change her mind. Do you want to be responsible for that?"

If it was other men besides him, then yes, yes he did. "Why does everything have to be ride or die? Why can't we have fun and see where it leads? I can tell you I'm more serious about her than I've ever been with anyone else."

"That's good." Lexi softened her voice and patted his shoulder. "I don't mean to come across so harsh. While you and I may not always understand each other, I know you'd do anything for your family and friends. You're a great guy, and the matchmaker in me wants you and Violet to see how perfect you are for each other."

Lexi's gaze clamped on to his, steady and inescapable and stirring up a whole tornado of emotions. "All I'm saying is that she's had enough of false promises. So, until you're sure you're ready to follow through… Just be careful. For both your sakes."

Ford glanced at Addie, waiting for her to chime in with her two cents. Needing it, really.

"You deserve to be happy and to experience life," Addie said. "Decide what you want, and then go after it. That's my advice."

What he wanted…?

He'd always had a long list growing up. Each item involved adventure and adrenaline because they overpowered his worries and kept bad memories shoved to the background.

Eventually he'd realized he could use his adventurous nature to help people. To rush toward danger. To help instead of run away. To prove to himself that he could be good and create a different life, no matter where he came from.

And that had become all he wanted. Adventure, training dogs, and a life without complications. Particularly a life without screaming matches where people spewed hateful words and walked away after destroying each other.

At some point between seeing Violet in that

kitchen, smoke barreling from the oven, and now, she'd moved to the top of the list of things he wanted.

But if even his close friends thought he was going to hurt her... What if they were right?

And what if he went all in and ended up losing everything?

CHAPTER TWENTY

The bottle of beer Violet downed while talking to Tucker, Will, and Easton wasn't enough to prevent her anxiety from spiraling out of control.

What had Lexi and Addie talked to Ford about?

He'd shrugged it off with a mutter about wedding stuff, but the mood had drastically shifted, the easygoing guy from earlier replaced with a stoic version. Still handsome and rugged and able to set her afire with one simple glance, but he felt far away.

Why does everything feel off?

Is he going to dump me? Why would he take me to meet his friends and then dump me?

Unless they didn't like me. But they were so nice, not to mention straightforward enough that surely I'd notice.

After she sorted her fears and concentrated on Ford, though, the repeated raking of his fingers through his hair and gripping the steering wheel seemed more like stress.

While Violet couldn't do much about the emotional distance, she could eradicate the physical space. Her heart beat at a hammering, punishing pace at the idea of putting herself out there.

Either she could drive herself mad or attempt to provide an anchor for whatever storm was raging inside Ford's head.

The unclicking of her seat belt sounded loud in the quiet. She slid across the cab of the truck, watching Ford's profile.

A muscle in his jaw ticked.

And Violet kept on scooting until she was plastered against his side. "There," she said. "That's better."

Give me a sign. Something to go on. Anything…

Ford wrapped his hand around her thigh. The muscles in his shoulders and neck loosened as he slowed for a stop sign. Then he planted a quick kiss on her temple. "So much better."

Violet clamped on to the bone he'd thrown her as ferociously as Trouble would. Speaking of, she missed the furball who loved her exactly as she was.

Headlights flashed behind them, and Ford glanced in the rearview mirror. "Want me to take you home? I'm working through some shit in my head right now, and it's making me grumpy. I don't want you to catch the brunt of it."

"What if I'm willing to catch it? Or…" she said, afraid she was being too bold but not wanting to wonder *what if.* "We can head to your place and see if I can make the grumpy go away…"

Violet could do without the raw sensation overtaking her chest, but she told herself giving love a shot was worth it. While hoping she wasn't repeating past mistakes. "Besides, I miss my puppy. Each day I go without a slobbery greeting, this little hollow spot forms in my chest."

"You're getting too attached to a puppy that's not yours. It's not even mine."

"Don't act like you're surprised. We both knew it was going to happen. And he's attached to me, too."

"He has been a right pain in my ass the past two days. I think he misses you." Ford stopped at another intersection—the one where he'd turn right to take her to Maisy's or left toward his house. His grip on her thigh tightened as he coasted his lips over hers. "I've missed you being there, too."

There they were—the words that filtered into her soul and mended her broken pieces.

The instant she opened for him, Ford swept his tongue inside and stroked it over hers. "Actually, I have a different idea," he said, his voice gruff. "Feel like another adventure?"

"Hmm." Violet acted as if she had to mull it over as everything inside her shouted *yes*. "Will there be rodents or vermin involved? Thanks to last weekend, that's a question I now feel I have to ask."

He huffed a laugh and shook his head. "No vermin. Well, we might come across some out in the wild, but no herding will be required."

Speaking of wild, her body was short-circuiting, and thank goodness no one had pulled up behind them. She pressed her lips to his, basking in the way they automatically moved against his and said, "Kiss me like that again, and I'll go just about anywhere with you."

• • •

Ford's antagonistic thoughts had almost ruined the evening.

Instead of getting upset or letting him hold her at a distance, Violet had reached out and reminded him how incredible she was.

Maybe he didn't have all the answers, but the woman showed him how it felt to be genuinely happy. He thought he'd experienced joy before, but these past couple weeks had shown him an entirely new level.

On top of all her other amazing qualities, she'd helped him train the puppies and become a better bridesdude. She'd even defended his honor to the scariest woman—nay, person—in town. Not to mention how well she'd fit in with his friends. Truth be told, since the moment they'd met, she'd just *fit* in general.

What was he doing, allowing his issues and fears to get the best of him? Especially when every other part of him screamed that he'd be an idiot to let Violet go?

High risk, high reward was his home base, and it was time to take a risk already.

After a quick stop for supplies and to grab Violet's camera, Ford drove to the hillier side of Lake Jocassee. He parked his truck at the trailhead, and then he was out and rounding the cab. He opened the passenger door, gripped Violet around the waist, and lowered her to her feet.

The moonlight lit up her bewitching features, and his doubts melted away. They had an undeniable connection, and they owed it to themselves to see how far it could go.

He slung on his backpack and then linked his fingers with hers. "Ready for a short hike?"

"What's a short hike in Ford McGuire speak?"

"A mile or so."

"Is that how long we have to go to find a spot where you haven't made out with another woman?" she asked, the words on the teasing side, although a hint of curiosity underlay the question as well.

"Shep and his big mouth," Ford murmured with a shake of his head.

Violet craned her neck and peered at the dirt trail

that led to chimney rock. "I suppose a mile is surviv-able, even for someone as out of shape as I am."

"Sweetheart, I like your shape just fine." Evidently, thinking about going all in had him going to the cheesy extreme, but the happiness singing through him and leaving his steps lighter made it impossible to give a damn.

Halfway up the trail, Violet accused his "or so" of meaning five miles. But she continued to climb at his side, her labored breaths giving him flashbacks of their sessions between the sheets.

His heart beat a heady, carnal rhythm that awak-ened his inner caveman.

If this night went as planned, he'd have her in that position again soon—he had a quilt in his bag, just in case. As the saying goes, better to be prepared than end up with pine needles poking your ass.

Finally, they reached the top of chimney rock. From this bird's-eye vantage point, you could overlook the entire lake. The way Violet's jaw dropped as she took in their surroundings affirmed he'd made the right choice in bringing her here.

She clasped a hand to her chest, awe softening her features. "It's beautiful."

"So are you." Right as he was about to kick his own ass for being so sappy, a slow smile spread across her face.

Violet shot pictures while Ford spread the quilt under a nearby tree. He knelt on the fabric and poured wine into two scorch-marked camping mugs that had only ever held coffee before.

When Violet approached, he stood and exchanged one of the mugs for her camera.

The thing was heavier than it looked. He deposited his mug on a flat rock and held on to the camera extra tight, aware of how important it was to her. "Do I just point and shoot?"

"Hold the button halfway down to focus, and press it the rest of the way to take the photo, but there's a lot more to it than just poin—"

Ford snapped a picture of her, and she cocked her head.

"I wasn't even ready, and you didn't let me fini—"

Click, click. That last one captured a blurry palm and not much else.

"Would you say your muse is back, then?" he asked as he surrendered the camera.

"Mostly," she said.

A thread of worry stitched its way through his chest, the needle jab, jab, jabbing. Did that mean she might leave town soon? For some reason, he thought they'd have more time to figure everything out. "It's because of me, right? I'm so inspiring and shit."

"Yes. You and your handsome face"—she placed her hand on his cheek and a kiss on his lips—"and your fancy vocabulary."

"Big talk for someone who didn't know Shakespeare was a poet, too." In addition to googling it, he'd memorized a line from one of the sonnets. "Shall I compare thee to a summer's day? Thou art more lovely and more temperate."

Violet laughed, and it bounced across the area, from rock to tree, and hit him square in the chest. Her eyes shone, and there was the goddess he'd unleashed the day in the mud. "That's the bard? Well, don't I feel sheepish. And honestly, most anyone's more temperate than the Alabama sun."

After downing the contents of her mug, Violet set it and her camera next to his backpack. Then she straightened and shook her hair out of her face. "As for my muse, I haven't put her to the real test. So far I've only taken pictures for fun, not work." She closed the distance and snaked her arms around his waist. "That'll be the real deciding factor, and I have a couple of sessions booked—including one with Shelby and her family—so we'll see.

"But let's not talk about work right now." Violet slipped her hands in the pockets of his jeans. "I'm assuming that's not why you brought me all the way up here to enjoy this amazing view."

She squeezed his butt, which had him hardening against her, and he could scarcely remember what they'd been talking about.

"I might've had ulterior motives." He swept her hair behind her shoulder and lowered his lips to the base of her neck. As he licked and sucked that delicious spot of skin, he backed her against the tree.

With one hand braced against the trunk, he slipped the other underneath her shirt. Her soft skin contrasted the rough bark underneath his palm, and he stroked the line of her spine with his thumb as he kissed his way across her jaw.

His lips found hers in the dark, and then he was devouring her mouth between peeling her shirt up and off her. As soon as it hit the ground, he yanked her back to him, needing her skin on his once again.

He unhooked her bra and gave it a yank, exposing her to the cool night air and his heated gaze. "Damn. I keep thinking the next time I see you naked it won't knock me on my ass, but every time it hits me just as strong."

Pink flushed her skin.

His heart thundered.

Off in the distance, a whip-poor-will sang its song.

Ford took a moment to soak in the vision before him and revel in how lucky he was to touch this woman. To kiss her and hold her and *fuck*, if he let go, he could very well lose his mind over Violet Abrams.

Time slowed to a crawl as he unbuttoned and unzipped her jeans.

Violet moved to pull off his shirt as he went to tug down her pants, and they crashed in the middle. Giggles burst out of both of them, and she wobbled, her bound legs leaving her gripping him for support.

At the bite of her fingernails into his skin, his arousal pummeled the zipper of his jeans like a battering ram with one thing on its mind.

Once he freed her legs of the denim, he pulled his shirt over his head and tossed it aside. Violet reached around his back, her hands exploring and massaging as she kissed the line of his jaw.

Ford skirted a knuckle along the undersides of her breasts and down the center of her stomach. Her muscles contracted under his touch, and as he neared the waistband of her panties, he lingered there, torturing the both of them.

As soon as he dipped his fingers lower, Violet arched against him, searching for his touch.

A strangled groan rasped free at how wet and ready she was for him, and she shuddered as he found the sweet spot. Their moans filled the air, desperate and needy, and relief barreled through him as Violet undid his jeans.

Now his ankles were the ones bound in denim. He guided her backward, over to the blanket. They went down in a tangle of limbs, and he crashed his mouth to hers. Using his toes, he pushed at the fabric restraining his legs.

The shift pressed his throbbing erection up against her center, and her cry of pleasure matched his growl as the friction from trying to free himself drove them both higher.

At long last, he was free, and not a second too soon. He could feel her damp heat through her underwear, and being out in the woods with patchy-at-best cover ended up being even hotter than he'd imagined.

As Violet shimmied out of her panties, his fingers groped the backpack in search of a condom.

Ford held it up like a trophy.

"Hurry," Violet said, tugging down his boxer briefs. "I need you inside of me *right. Now.*"

"Your wish is my command." He rolled on the condom and poised himself at her entrance. He dragged his swollen head over her slick flesh, teasing her and testing his willpower.

"Ford," she whimpered.

"What?" he asked innocently.

With a snarl of frustration, she raised her hips to meet his, and he lost the ability to speak. In fact, he wasn't sure his arms were going to be able to hold him up anymore.

Fortunately, Violet took care of that, hooking her ankles around his waist and then yanking him down so that his body covered hers, shoulder to thigh.

After a quick second to center himself, he took

control. He twined his fingers through hers and brought her hands up above her head so he could revel in every inch of naked skin.

Then he plunged into her, hard and deep. His lips covered hers, swallowing her gasps as he thrust over and over.

Sweat slicked their skin, and Ford reached between them and sought the bundle of nerves that would make her squirm with pleasure.

The instant he found it, her walls sucked him deeper. He circled faster and faster, the ecstasy overtaking her features echoing through him.

Her eyes locked onto his and then went hazy as her orgasm took her.

Not only was it the hottest fucking thing he'd ever seen, a sensation he didn't quite recognize washed through him, laying waste to every thought besides this woman and this moment.

The final thread on his control snapped, and his own release rocketed through him. He fell to the side of Violet and drew her against his chest, breathing in and out against her skin.

And as he held on to her, he had the thought that he never, ever wanted to let go.

CHAPTER TWENTY-ONE

Once she'd caught her breath, Violet ran a finger down the slope of Ford's nose and tapped the center of his mouth.

He kissed her fingertip, eliciting more goose bumps than the cool air.

"Cold?" he asked, cocooning her in his arms and shifting so he could pull the blanket up and over them. With the heat of his body soaking into hers, she didn't bother mentioning he'd been the main reason for the shiver.

While she'd been harsh on herself for those twenty pounds she never managed to lose, the way Ford worshiped her body made her grateful for every extra inch. Add in the passion that'd swum in his eyes as he did so, and it was easier to be kind to herself. Whenever she was with him, she felt beautiful and sexy and—best of all—desired.

Sure, it was something she should've been capable of herself, but after the number Benjamin had done to her self-esteem, the boost was much appreciated.

A soft glow caught her eye, a fleck of yellow between dark pine needles. Another spark and another. "Lightning bugs," she whispered as the insects lit up the dark, adding an enchanted-forest effect.

Her skin hummed as Ford's soft lips and scruff skimmed the line of her shoulder. "Yeah, I asked them to put on a show just for you."

"Oh, did you now?"

A grin spread across his face as he nodded, all false innocence and mischief.

"Well, it's insanely romantic."

"Before you showed up, I'd never call myself a romantic. Thanks to you, Violet Abrams, I might be changing my stance."

Another string looped around her heart, tethering her to this man, this night, and this place.

Dangerously close to falling had come and gone. Affection had been replaced by a stronger emotion—one she dared not name.

Violet's defenses sounded the alarm, a belated warning to reinforce her walls. It had a Trojan War vibe: letting the enemy in and then closing the drawbridge so they were stuck inside to battle it out, no escape in sight.

Now her only option was a white flag, one she hoped not to have to wave, but she clenched it in her fist just in case.

"I haven't had a girlfriend in years, and the few I've had…"

Violet froze, afraid to move or breathe.

"What I'm trying to say is that I don't bring girls here. I don't do this." He gestured between him and her, and everything inside her began to crack. "But I want to do it with you."

One by one, she peeled her fingers off the metaphorical white flag so she could hold on to Ford instead. She placed her palm over the center of his heart, feeling the *thump, thump, thump* in response.

When she glanced up through her lashes, he was peering deep into her soul, imprinting himself upon it, and she knew she'd never be the same.

And for the first time, instead of scaring her, it comforted her.

"Thank you," she whispered.

"For what?"

For making me feel witty, cared for, understood, and *beautiful. For showing me a different side of Uncertainty and another side of yourself. Pushing me to pick up my camera. Bringing me here.*

Getting me to believe in love again.

The words lodged in her constricting throat, and she wasn't sure which ones to choose, anyway, so she kept it simple. "For everything."

Strong fingers wrapped around her hip, and then he rolled her so their hearts lined up and beat against each other. He splayed his fingers on her lower back as he sealed the perfect night with the perfect kiss.

Lost as she was in a sea of euphoric happiness, his words sounded far away when he said, "Get dressed. I wanna show you one last thing before we go home."

• • •

Between cutting off Violet's circulation and a possible fall off the rocky path, Ford decided to err on the side of holding her hand too tight.

Gravel skidded underneath their feet, and he made sure she was steady before stepping on the next large boulder. Finally, his feet hit a familiar flat landing. "See that alcove there?"

Violet peeked around him. "Yeah."

"I spent countless nights there in high school. My dad would go on these binges, and that'd rile up my brothers. Or one of his new girlfriends would be around, and they'd be loudly fighting or fu—" Ford rubbed at his neck, wishing he'd cut himself off earlier. "Anyway, whenever it got to be too much, I'd head here with my pack, sleeping bag, and fishing pole."

"For how many nights at a time?" she asked.

He shrugged. "Eh. Anywhere from two to five."

"Your dad didn't send the search and rescue team after you? Or was that what inspired your career path?"

Although it wasn't exactly funny, he chuckled at the thought of Jimmy McGuire admitting he might need help of any kind. "That'd require him realizing I was missing. He did teach us wilderness survival skills, so I guess I have him to thank for that. My ability to rough it allowed me to find peace out here, even at the most contentious times."

Violet lowered her eyebrows. "I... I don't know what to say." She hugged him around his middle. "It sounds rough. But I'm also glad you had those skills, and admittedly I do find your badass side super sexy. I just wish you didn't have to run away to find peace."

A band formed around his chest, one that contracted with each inhale and exhale. The fact of the matter was, he'd often been jealous of his friends' parents and home life. They'd complain here and there, and he'd pretend he was glad he had so much freedom.

When in truth it was indifference.

Now he got a bit more than that—mostly whenever his dad or brothers wanted something. They jabbed at him about being the reliable McGuire, until they were the ones who relied on him.

Since he didn't want to get into that, he focused on Violet's other question. "As for my career, we had a drought one year, and there was a big fire."

Ford spun Violet around in his arms so that her back met his chest and pointed across the lake. "Over in that ridge. Fall of my junior year. The fire crews worked endlessly to put it out. I thought 'now that's a badass job, running toward the flames instead of away from them.' Before that, I'd been set on becoming a stuntman." He rested his chin on the top of Violet's head. "I talked to a few of the firefighters when they came into Martin's Trading Post, and one of them told me I should become a paramedic, since it'd open up my options. When I looked into certification, I stewed over whether I was smart enough to learn all that medical mumbo jumbo. But you might have noticed I'm a tad competitive—"

"Just a tad?" Violet teased, and he gave her ass a light smack that only made her giggle.

"Addie needed to take anatomy as well and bet me she could get a better grade, and it was on after that."

Violet relaxed against him, her fingers drifting across his forearm and soothing his inner turmoil about spilling so many personal details. "When did the search and rescue and dog training enter the picture?"

"Sorta stumbled into them. There was a lost hunter, and I'm familiar with the area, so I helped out. The Talladega Search and Rescue asked if I'd be interested in joining the team, and it was nice for people to want me around instead of waiting for me to leave so they could whisper about my family."

Violet gazed up at him, adoration gleaming in her eyes. He wasn't sure he deserved all that, but his heart swelled that she obviously did.

"The guy who trained me also trained canine units,

and he was about to retire. When he asked if I wanted the job, I about gave him a heart attack with my enthusiastic yes."

Man, he was in deep now. While the gang accused him of being the loudmouth, mostly he blew hot air and talked shit. Flavored the conversation with jokes. When it came to real talk, he'd only ever gotten this intense with Addie.

For a moment, he second-guessed taking Violet into the alcove.

But then she twisted to face him, the smile on her face turning her from gorgeous to woman-of-his-dreams material. She kissed him softly and rested her head against his chest. "I love everything about what you told me. Are you ready to concede that you're, indeed, a good guy?"

"Don't know that I'd go that far," he said, and she tipped her head up enough that he could see her roll her eyes.

That cemented his decision. If nothing else, he wanted to sear this memory into his brain. That way, no matter what happened later, he could recall the night nothing existed besides him and the woman making a mess of his insides. "We'd better get on with what we came here to do—besides sex, of course."

"Of course," she said, her husky voice suggesting she was reliving their session underneath the big Alabama sky.

Linking his fingers with hers, he led her into the alcove.

A pile of ash from fires past sat in the pit where he'd cook any fish he'd caught.

Ford turned on his flashlight and ran the beam over

the walls. "The outer rocks have all those different names and colors and flags painted, and I was thinking…" He dug through his bag until he came up with the spray paint. "We should make our mark here, where only we can find it."

Shit. With that out in the air, he wished for the ability to undo, undo. It was such an absurd idea. "Or is that stupid?"

"Not stupid," Violet said, hijacking the purple paint. "I'm going to get to work, because otherwise I might cry over such a perfect gesture"—sure enough, her words came out clipped—"and then you'll go calling me overly dramatic."

The peck she bestowed on his cheek set off fireworks in his chest. "If it makes you feel better, I'm fairly certain I'm the one obsessed now."

"Not sure you'll agree once you see how old-school I'm about to go on you—don't make fun." The can rattled as she shook it, and then she wrote her initials. She added a plus sign underneath, and next came his initials. "Do I add the TLF?"

"I don't follow," Ford said.

"True love forever, duh."

Was she asking…? Even scarier, did he…?

Relax. It's initials, not a proposal.

His heart palpitated and expanded, and it hit him that he might just be developing L-word feelings for this woman. "Do it," he said.

Violet connected the L and used the bottom part as the middle of the F, and he did recall seeing that in high school. After she'd completed the F, she drew a big heart around the entire thing.

Using the white can in his hands, Ford painted the

petals of a flower. He exchanged the white paint for the purple and outlined the image. "There you go. It's a violet."

"Aww." She pressed her lips together, one hand going to her heart. Then she lifted the white can, the tip aimed at a blank spot of rock. "I have to add one more thing."

Blocking the section where she was making her mark, she sprayed, shook, and sprayed again. With a flourish, she stepped back. "Ta-da!"

The symbol for Ford trucks stood out against the dark rock.

"Get it?" Happiness shone through her features, and right then and there, he didn't have to wonder anymore. No might or maybe about it.

Falling in love with Violet had snuck up on him. He wasn't sure what to do about it, and the idea of telling her caused pressure to cumulate beneath his ribs.

Instead, he decided to show her. He drew her to him and planted a kiss on her still-smiling lips. He meant to just take a taste, but all it did was whet his appetite and awaken his carnal side.

Breaths sawed in and out of their mouths.

Hers...

His...

Theirs.

And before he could analyze and stifle the words, he said, "I want you to stay."

CHAPTER TWENTY-TWO

It took Violet a handful of seconds to figure out where she was.

Different ceiling than at Maisy's, and then there were the warm bodies. A large male with dark disheveled hair, strong arms, and massive legs rested against her right side. She was tempted to drag her toes up his calf, but the canine curled on top of her feet prevented it.

Both she and Trouble had been told there were no dogs on the bed, but evidently Trouble had conveniently forgotten.

As if her German shepherd puppy sensed she'd awoken, he perked up his head. One of his brown-and-black ears flopped over in that ridiculously adorable way that it did, and Violet patted her stomach and whispered, "Come here, buddy."

Pyro also lifted his head from his doggy bed on the floor.

Violet wondered how much trouble she'd get in if she told Pyro he could join them.

Before she could deliberate the pros and cons, Trouble bounded onto her chest and went to licking her face.

Ford grumbled as he cracked open an eye. "Pretty sure I told you two that there were no dogs allowed on the bed. You baby him too much."

"That makes sense, since he is a baby. Aren't you?" Violet scratched all the way down her puppy's back, ears to haunches. "You're my baby, but don't tell Ford, okay? He thinks I shouldn't get attached, but it's too late for that, isn't it?"

"I can see that. He's also doin' the kissing that *I* should be doing."

"Yeah, I've been meaning to talk to both of you about the amount of tongue you use."

"That's it." Ford rolled on top of her, pinning her body to the mattress. "Not so funny now, are we?"

Trouble had abandoned her, running off to join Pyro in his bed—or possibly to try to kick him out, since he didn't seem to understand he was much smaller than the big black dog.

Thanks to Ford's large frame squishing the air out of her, Violet's giggle came out low and strangled. Yet she craved him pushing her deeper into the softness. To use that tongue she'd teased him about.

She wound her arms around Ford's neck and basked in the weight of him. The coarse hair and protruding veins and the musky scent that made thoughts hard to keep hold of. "I was going to say that I like it very much. I mean, I'm glad that you don't lick my chin like Trouble, but—"

The tip of Ford's tongue hit the base of her neck. He flattened it and dragged it up to the sensitive spot under her ear, one long, wet lick that had her clenching her thighs.

"Never mind," she breathed. "Obviously you already know what I like."

Ford devoured her mouth, delving and exploring, tasting and taking. He was so responsive toward every moan, and before long, they were tangled up in round two of sexy sleepover fun.

By the time they fell back to the mattress to catch their breath, the dogs—two of whom had been kicked out when heated kisses turned into lovemaking—began pawing at the door. Ready for food and attention, no doubt. At least they had the doggy door so they could use the bathroom as the urge hit them.

Ford climbed out of bed, opened the drawer to his dresser, and grabbed a pair of boxer briefs.

As she was pulling on her panties, he stared and made a *mmm, mmm, mmm* sound. "A guy could get used to this view."

With a quick jerk, Ford yanked on his jeans and stalked toward her. Shirtless, the top button of his pants undone. When he reached her, instead of putting on his T-shirt, he slipped it over her head. Then he pressed his lips to hers.

"Hungry?"

"Starving. All that hiking and hot sex really works up an appetite."

"Damn straight," he said, taking her by the hand and leading her into the living room.

Since Violet was more qualified to prepare dog food than eggs, she fed them and then headed into the kitchen to watch Ford move from the fridge to the stove.

Sunlight streamed in from the window over the sink, highlighting every muscle and groove in his naked torso. He placed a plate of eggs and bacon in front of her and then circled the counter and sat beside her with his own plate.

Violet swallowed a bite of food as she gathered enough courage to ask the question she'd yet to ask. If she was going to truly consider staying in Uncertainty, she needed to know that meant commitment. Slowly integrating their lives by doing typical couple activities.

Not that she wanted to test Ford, but she also didn't want to make the same mistakes she'd made before. Ever since the run-in with Cheryl at the bazaar, she'd had a hard time not fretting over the bakery's grand reopening.

"Do you have plans on Thursday evening? Full disclosure: I kinda have a favor to ask."

Ford twisted on the stool, his knee bumping into hers. "Well, you're not wearing pants, so the odds are in your favor."

Okay, big breath in, big breath out… "So you know how my father and I have a strained relationship?" Completely rhetorical, since she'd made it clear, so she kept on spilling her guts. "And in case you didn't notice after the bazaar, that goes double for Cheryl. She seriously tried to bribe me to leave town."

Ford clenched his jaw. "Typical Hurst move. Throw money at their problems to make them go away." His fork hit his empty plate. "Sorry. I shouldn't have said that."

His clear and present anger turned her into a boneless pile of a girl. "It's okay. I appreciate it, actually."

Time to ask him her question and see if he was the type of guy who'd show up.

"Anyway, Maisy's having this sign-hanging and reopening event for the bakery at four o'clock. It was Cheryl's idea, and my dad will be there to perform his mayoral role of cutting the ribbon, and to support Maisy, of course. I could use a hand to hold." Violet gnawed on her lower lip. "Would you go with me? It'll be easier to deal with everything with you there, and that way I don't have to take on my dad and Cheryl alone."

"I'll be there," he said.

Violet almost let the rest of what she wanted to say slide. But that stupid "shame on me" phrase bounced through her head, reminding her that she had to learn from past mistakes.

"While I'm sure this will shock you, I have some issues…" Violet arched an eyebrow, warning him not to comment. "Trust issues, mainly." Her anxiety left her internal organs in tatters, targeting the air in her lungs until it'd eaten away the last of her reserves. "While I'd love to say everything was all Benjamin's fault and he's the only reason we fell apart, I didn't always tell him what I needed. I made my fair share of mistakes, too…"

Like bashing in his car. A subject for another time, because her point was heavy enough without that fun tidbit in the mix.

"My dad's also broken promises, and it's made me realize how badly I need a guy who shows up." She fiddled with the hem of the oversize T-shirt Ford had put on her, restless energy getting the best of her.

Ford grabbed her hand and folded it into his. "Hey. It's my job to show up."

"Yes, but I need you to show up not only because it's your job but because you do what you say. Because you want to be there for me."

Ford lifted her knuckles and placed a featherlight kiss atop them. "For you, Vi, I'll always show up. I promise."

Oxygen gradually returned to her lungs, and right as she opened her mouth in an attempt to find the words to express how much that meant to her, the dogs went wild barking.

Then a loud knock split the air.

• • •

Ford answered the door and immediately wished he hadn't when he saw his father on the other side. The happiness that'd been on full blast since last night evaporated, his worries rising up and poking holes in it.

A visit meant Dad wanted something, and Violet was here, and the pedestal she'd put him on—while it felt damn nice—was about to get kicked out from underneath him.

"What do you want?" Ford asked.

"Is that any way to greet your dear old dad?"

Ford glanced over his shoulder, which was a mistake. Not only did it provide the opportunity for Dad to charge inside, it implied he wasn't alone.

"You got company?" Dad asked, confirming Ford had been busted.

"Yeah. Take a seat and give me a second."

Ford padded into the kitchen, but all he found were empty plates. He hustled down the hall to his bedroom, where Violet was pulling on her jeans.

"I'm sorry about this," Ford said.

"About what?"

"You're about to meet my dad. I wish I could better prepare you, but…" He sighed. "I'm not even sure that's possible."

Angel that she was, Violet wrapped her arms around his waist. "I can handle it. Especially now that I have pants on."

"Shame, that. But if it'll help…" He kissed her forehead, soaking in her scent and the way her embrace soothed his rankled nerves.

While he could linger forever, it'd be better to get this whole awkward meeting over with. He took her hand and led her to the living room.

Under other circumstances, the shock on his father's face might be comical.

Ford cleared his throat. "Dad, this is Violet. Violet, my father, Jimmy McGuire."

"Nice to meet you," she said, smoothing a hand down her sleep-tangled hair.

After a beat, Dad found his manners, stood, and extended a hand. "Uh, you, too. You look familiar. You're a Hurst, aren't you?"

"I go by Abrams, but Mayor Hurst is my biological father."

Dad nodded. His eyes narrowed as he studied the two of them, and Ford wrapped a protective arm around Violet's shoulders.

"Looks like I interrupted somethin', so I'll get right to it. Gunner and I are headed to the hills and need to borrow your four-wheeler. Mine's still having clutch issues."

"Sure," Ford said.

"Might need some help loading it."

"I should head to the bakery anyway," Violet said. "I warned Maisy that I'd be late, but I don't want to leave her hanging." She gave Ford a quick peck. "Oh, and don't forget the planning meeting tonight at six."

"Shit, I totally spaced on that. Lexi would've killed me."

"In other words, *I'm* saving *you* now."

In more than one way.

Violet patted his chest. "Can you pick up a bottle of rosé on your way over? That way Lexi feels appreciated. Plus, Priscilla and Lucia probably don't drink beer or whiskey, and as you already know, I'm in that same boat, too.

"Pratsch or Château La Cardonne—Endless Crush by Inman is my favorite. Not sure they'd have that in this tiny town, since it's on the pricey end and only a limited number of bottles were made." Violet tapped a finger to her lips. "I'm sure you won't remember those off the top of your head anyway, so I'll text you."

Reluctantly, Ford escorted her to the door.

As soon as she'd left, Dad said, "Mayor Hurst's daughter? Really? You sure can pick 'em." Bitterness pinched his features. "And did I hear the word *wedding*? I taught you better than to get caught up in one of those."

"Addie and Tucker's wedding. It's weekend after next." If Dad thought he was going to discuss Violet or dive into the subject of love, he was sorely mistaken. "Come on. That four-wheeler isn't going to load itself."

The dogs thought he meant them, and all four made a mad dash for the door. Ford went ahead and opened it, letting them out and waiting for Dad to hop to.

Dad lumbered on over, but instead of heading outside, he paused at the threshold. "You're not gettin' serious with that girl, are ya?"

Ford hesitated a beat too long.

"Not a good idea, son. For one, that family ain't never gonna accept you."

The urge to correct the double negative flickered—not like it'd make any difference. When it came to tirades against relationships, Dad could go on all day. "Violet's not even close to her family, save Maisy. And I'm a big believer that a person is more than who they're related to."

Dad guffawed. "Just because you run around playing hero doesn't mean people forget who you are. You think you're so much better than me and your brothers, but you can't even learn from our mistakes."

Years of history choked the air. Sure, he wished his family the best. That didn't mean he was going to get sucked into the toxic dick-measuring environment he'd grown up in. Who was stronger? Faster?

Sometimes it seemed like they competed for whose life was the best, and other times whose was worst.

Finally, Dad stepped onto the porch, and Ford resisted the urge to shove him on down the sidewalk so this would be over already.

"I couldn't help but notice she gave you a honey-do list," Dad said. "That's what women call 'em, but really they're marchin' orders. Today she's ordering you around, demanding fancy wines while implying you're a dumb redneck who won't remember the right brand. Next thing you know, it'll be new furniture and remodeling the kitchen…

"Your ma was that way. When we got hitched, she claimed all she needed was love. Less than a year in and it was 'when are we gonna get a bigger, nicer house?' and 'I need to go into the city and buy new clothes' and on and on until we were broker than we started out. And still nothin' made her happy."

Ford's sigh failed to carry away his frustration over this line of conversation. That type of fights made up the majority of his memories from when he was

younger. His parents arguing about who worked the
hardest, each attempting to win, when, truth be told,
everyone involved lost.

Including him and his brothers, who bore the brunt
of the anger from whomever hadn't stormed out first.

"Violet's not like that," Ford said. "You don't even
know her."

"All women are like that. In the beginning they put
their best foot forward, all sugar and spice, showcasing
their best behavior. Basically they're a shiny lure, and
once you commit and take a big ol' bite, you discover
the hook hidden in the bling.

"That's when they flip that crazy switch and it's nag,
nag, nag. Pick a fight over any and everything. Tell you
that you need to change. It's taken me two failed
marriages" — Dad held up his fingers as if otherwise
Ford would be lost — "and one broken engagement to
learn that."

Luckily, they'd reached the four-wheeler ramp. Ford
maneuvered it onto the open tailgate of Dad's truck.
He fired up the four-wheeler, lined up the tires, and
rode into the bed.

From there, Ford shoved the ramps on either side so
Dad could get the vehicle in and out himself. "There
you go. Just drop it off whenever you're done."

Dad placed a hand on Ford's shoulder, and when
Dad's eyes met his, at least they were more white than
bloodshot today. Which inconveniently fractured the
assertion his old man's words were nothing but hot air.
"I'm all for enjoying that beginning, fun part of
relationships — hell, I'm addicted to the rush myself.
But as soon as she mentions weddings and babies, it's
time to cut and run. Serious relationships always bring

about fights, and once kids get thrown in the mix, forget it. Soon it gets messier and messier, until neither of you recognize who you've become."

Dad fell silent, the twitch of his lips signaling he was fighting his emotions, something Ford had witnessed all of once before.

The day Ford informed Dad that he'd talked to Grandma Cunningham and not only was Ma never coming home, she was engaged to some rich dude.

For years, he'd attempted to stay out of the middle of his parents' fights, and the one time he actually wanted to rant about Ma, Dad had fallen apart.

And now he was thinking of Doris's words in a different way. She'd mentioned missing her husband for the past ten years and how hard life was without him. How she wanted to go be with him, since she was sure he was waiting.

What if the real risk with love was that you eventually ended up losing yourself? Feeling like half a person? Ford's breaths came fast and shallow, dizziness setting in as he struggled to maintain control of his lungs.

"You've made a good life for yourself," Dad gruffly said. "One where you get to enjoy havin' your adventures. Girls like Violet, they expect the finer things in life. Sooner or later, it'll become an issue. Just…be careful."

Ironic that Dad chose the word *careful* now, instead of during Ford's younger years when Dad let him and his brothers run wild in the woods.

"As for me…" Dad clapped him on the back, his features free of emotions once again. "I've decided when it comes to my addictions, between women and alcohol, booze is the safer bet."

With that lovely sentiment hanging in the air, Dad climbed into his truck and took off, and Ford stood there telling himself that he was just a cynical old man.

Even as he started to wonder if he truly knew what he'd gone and gotten himself into.

CHAPTER TWENTY-THREE

"Did you get the rosé?" Violet asked as soon as he met her in front of the bakery.

Ford lifted the bottle, doing his best to not let Dad's "she thinks you're a dumb redneck" jab get to him. During his perusal of the liquor store shelves, he'd almost chosen a cheaper brand to test Violet's reaction.

Especially since the reason she'd suggested he bring a bottle was to keep him in Lexi's good graces.

Then again, why did *he* need to put in effort for that? Wasn't being part of the wedding party and supporting Addie enough?

Violet let out a tiny squeal. "They had Endless Crush? That's going on the pro side of staying in Uncertainty for sure!"

Her excitement lifted his mood while punching him in the gut. If good wine was all it took to make her so happy, it didn't matter if it cost twice as much. He easily spent that on drinks at the Old Firehouse. If it tipped the scales in favor of her staying, even better.

"Earlier, when Lexi was in the bakery and we were discussing place settings, she mentioned wine, and I was hoping you'd remember. She'll love the hint of watermelon—it's my favorite, and she and I have a lot of the same tastes."

His stomach bottomed out again, his erratic swings grating at him. Since Dad's visit, everything felt off.

None of the puppies had paid a damn bit of attention when he'd run drills this afternoon. Even

Pyro had looked at him as if he'd lost his touch.

Irritation surfaced again as they began the short walk to Addie's house, not due to the location but the topic that'd be discussed ad nauseum. "I can't wait till this wedding is over and we can all move on with our lives."

Violet *tsk*ed. "It's not that bad."

"It is. This will be my first *and last* time playing bridesmaid."

"Never say never."

"I'm saying it. Never *ever*."

Violet hooked her hand in his elbow. "What if I asked?"

"Then I'd say no." Ford went to take another step, but Violet jerked him to a stop, her mouth hanging open. "What? That means you'd be marrying someone else, and I could never watch you do that."

Delight replaced her offense, and perhaps he shouldn't have stated that so boldly, true or not.

"What's the deal with this house?" Violet asked, indicating the yellow Victorian on Main Street with the big for sale sign.

"It's for sale and has been for about a year."

"It's beautiful."

"It's expensive."

"Guess I'd better get my photography business going ASAP, then."

Was she saying…? The only house in town bigger than the old Victorian was her father's house.

Girls like Violet, they expect the finer things.

Ford studied Violet's clothes. Problem was, he didn't know enough about fashion to determine if they were the fancy kind. That and his attention snagged on the way her jeans hugged her ass, and then his mind was headed down a completely different avenue—one called Hard-On Lane.

Dammit, he'd been fine before that visit. Plus, Dad was extremely biased about women. It was always how difficult *they* were, as if Dad were a walk in the park to live with, overindulgence in alcohol and withholding affection and all.

With Addie's house mere steps away, Ford reminded himself he had a female best friend, and she happened to be one of the most logical people he knew.

Knocking was more a warning than asking to be let in, so after a couple of raps, Ford stepped on into Addie's place.

And nearly backed out, sure he'd come through the wrong door.

But there was Addie's signed jersey and the couch he'd helped her move. Although it was covered in sunflowers and yellow ribbon and a myriad of other craft items.

The instant Lexi looked their way, his flight instinct kicked in—unfortunately, Violet was holding him in place. "Oh good," Lexi said. "Y'all are here so we can get going."

Like the gentleman he'd been told to be, he handed over the wine, which Lexi fawned over and went to grab glasses for.

Meanwhile, Lucia Murphy rose from the loveseat and greeted him and Violet with cheek kisses.

Addie and her mom were in the middle of a conversation about her sister, Alexandria. Something about her being sick with what her husband thought was a tummy bug. Maybe even a late case of the flu.

Murph glanced up, bleary-eyed, from the seating chart on her lap. "She'll be okay in time for the wedding, right?"

Of all the ways Ford had expected her to respond to that news, that wasn't one of them.

"I mean, I hope she feels better soon, of course," Addie said with a shake of her head, as if she'd realized how calloused that'd sounded. "I'm just stressed because I thought she'd be here in time for the bachelorette party next weekend. She still hasn't tried on her bridesmaid's dress, and I was hoping she and I could catch up before I left for my honeymoon."

"Don't worry. She's going to the doctor today, and I'm sure she'll be up and running soon." Priscilla pursed her lips and studied him. Decades of experience forewarned that the next words out of her mouth wouldn't bode well for him. "Addison?"

Or maybe he was losing his touch.

"Have you talked to Ford about his hair? He needs a trim. Think of the pictures and the fact that you'll have them hanging on the wall forever."

At his side, Violet turned her laugh into a cough. She ran her fingertips up the center of his back and toyed with the ends of his hair, making him want to go Samson on everyone and declare he'd never cut it.

"Actually," Addie said, "it's long enough that I was thinking he could pull it into a man bun and match Lexi's and Alexandria's updos."

This time Violet failed to hold back her laugh. It came out with a snort at the end, and then he was laughing, too.

He leaned over and whispered, "Do you think she realizes I'm right here?"

"Of course I do," Priscilla said—he'd forgotten about the woman's bat hearing. "But if I tell you what to do, you'll do the opposite just for the sake of bein' difficult."

Addie's mom strode over and jabbed a finger at him, and he regretted putting more distance between himself and the exit. "But you listen to me, Ford McGuire. I'll be watching you like a hawk. There's a time and a place for pranks, but a wedding isn't one of them."

The woman retreated to the couch, still shaking her head. "First, Addie goes and plays groomsman, and now she puts a man in her wedding party. Why are kids these days so set on bucking tradition? If you ask me, there's nothing wrong with a little tradition."

The way Addie pinched the bridge of her nose suggested she'd been dealing with this all day. "There's also nothing wrong with making new traditions, Mom."

"I'd hoped getting engaged might help you grow up. Become a lady."

"Nope and nope, but thanks for your concern. Now, remember how much you love to decorate?" Murph lifted a disturbingly familiar purple wedding binder. "And how I gave you and Lexi free rein as long as you respected my other choices for the ceremony? I.e., my dude of honor, no rehearsal dinner, and absolutely no dancing to be done by me."

"But I found the perfect song and—"

Addie raised an eyebrow.

Priscilla harrumphed and then took the binder. "Violet, you said that you've seen this done before with roses, right?"

Violet slipped her hand out of Ford's and moved to

study the picture. "Yep. Lexi and I were talking earlier, and we can fill the fishbowls with water and tea lights and put daisies in place of the roses. It's going to be stunning. Like I said, I'd planned to do that same thing for my wedding, but with violets."

Lead filled Ford's veins, and his feet cemented themselves to the floor. *My wedding* flashed across his vision like one of those red emergency news tickers, over and over, raising his blood pressure.

"You're sure you have enough?" Priscilla asked.

"Positive." Violet settled next to Addie's mom on the couch. "I have these same fishbowls in storage—I bought several at a craft store on clearance. Plus, every time I was a bridesmaid, people handed me a box and told me I could use them at my wedding."

There it was again. *My wedding, my wedding, my wedding.*

"Which clearly didn't happen," Violet continued, "but I'd feel better about buying and storing them these past few years if they went to a cause as amazing as Addie's wedding."

Priscilla scribbled something on a Post-it note and stuck it to the plastic cover. "And you'll get them from your storage unit in Florida next week?"

"That's the plan. My car doesn't have a ton of room, and it's about a three-and-a-half-hour drive, so I was sorta hoping…" Violet's gaze lifted to him, and he did his best to stifle the panic ravaging his insides. "I thought we could go on a mini road trip to pick them up if you have time. Maybe meet my mom for a late lunch before heading back?"

A road trip. To pick up wedding supplies. Meeting her mom…

The walls seemed to be closing in around him, his lungs only allowing shallow, fruitless breaths in and out.

"Perfect," Priscilla said, not waiting for an answer—although what was he going to say? No? After promising Violet he'd always show up.

Would she give him an ultimatum, the way his exes had done? Now she was planning road trips, assuming he'd go along.

As soon as she mentions weddings and babies, it's time to cut and run. Dad's words rang in his head, slightly unfair when it came to the W word, because planning Addie's nuptials were why they'd come over tonight.

"...totally help you throw them together." Violet turned to Lexi, excitement and a whole heap of longing radiating from her. Then they were talking a hundred miles an hour, and he was telling himself not to freak out, not to freak out, not to freak out.

Meanwhile, his throat ignored his mind's advice and continued to grow tighter and tighter.

Until he was the lone dude standing in a room, slowly suffocating from all the talk of matrimony.

CHAPTER TWENTY-FOUR

"Maisy."

Bowl after bowl hit the counter as Maisy went berserk on her kitchen. Violet readjusted her grip on Isla, who'd been thrust into her hands about two minutes previously. Right after Maisy looked at the giant table packed with refreshments and declared, "I'm not sure that's going to be enough."

Violet placed herself and Isla between Maisy and the ingredients she'd begun pulling off the shelf. "Slow down for a second."

"Can't slow down. If everyone chooses chocolate cupcakes, there won't be enough to go around. Or do you think everyone will want vanilla today? Strawberry sells well in the summer, which is just around the corner—why didn't I whip up some of those?"

Violet gripped Maisy's shoulder with her free hand. "If anyone complains about free cupcakes to celebrate *your* grand reopening, I'll tell them to shove their comments where the sun don't shine."

While blocking Maisy with her entire body had been only partially successful, that remark landed. "You can't tell people that."

"Or what? They'll go to the other bakery in town?" Violet ran her hand up and down Maisy's arm, switching from stopping her movements to attempting to reassure her. "The people of Uncertainty love you and your treats, and we have more than enough to go around. Now, step away from the mixer, or I'll start pushing buttons on your oven."

Maisy gasped. "You wouldn't dare."

Violet shuffled toward the oven, one finger extended. "Which one should we push, Isla?"

"Hello?" The deep voice coming from the front of the bakery kickstarted Violet's heart in a different way than Maisy's jitters had done.

"Ooh, Ford's here. Let's go say hi." Violet readjusted her grip on Isla's chubby thigh and herded Maisy out of the kitchen. "He brought a ladder so we can hang the banner without standing on the freshly painted tables and breaking our necks. See? It'll all be okay."

They'd been prepping since sunrise, the bakery closed for its first weekday in forever. Since Maisy wanted Isla at the opening, she'd picked her up early from daycare while Violet placed cupcakes on tables and arranged the DIY reupholstered chairs.

The bakery looked amazing, all colorful and delicious. Not to toot her own horn, but the touches she'd added had completely transformed the place.

"Hey, Mr. Hot Handyman," Violet said, leaning in for a quick kiss on Ford's lips. While her nerves had taken a backseat to Maisy's, they'd still been unraveling bit by bit. With Ford here to help her survive being in the same room as Dad, Cheryl, and the rest of the town, the decibel level on her anxiety lowered to a whisper.

As Ford climbed the ladder to hang the grand opening sign, Violet sashayed over to her water bottle, humming to Isla about how the party was going to be a huge success. Over this past month, she'd gotten rather good at optimism. It helped that she didn't have to work as hard to find silver linings or redirect negative thoughts.

Thanks to the guy currently lifting and lowering the sign 0.2 inches to fit Maisy's instructions, the bright side surrounded her. She had an incredible boyfriend, an amazing sister, and thanks to a photo session with Shelby, Dylan, and the rest of their charming family yesterday, confirmation that her muse was back.

Out of the corner of her eye, Violet caught a flash of Maisy's yellow floral shirt—she was headed to the kitchen.

Seriously? I'm going to have to duct tape the woman to one of the colorful chairs.

Ford stepped off the ladder and turned. "Anything else?"

"Here," she said, handing Isla to him. "Hold her for a quick minute while I go tackle my sister."

"Oh, I—"

"Her pacifier is pinned to her outfit," Violet called over her shoulder as she raced toward the kitchen, "so if it falls out and she cries, just pop it back in."

• • •

Ford peered at the baby in his arms. Once again, he was in a position where he couldn't help thinking of all the other things he'd rather tackle.

Torrential winds. Wading through neck-deep water to reach cars and houses as Pyro swam by his side. Rappelling down a sheer cliff.

Playing hopscotch on the back of hungry alligators.

"I don't know what your aunt was thinking," Ford said as the baby blinklessly stared up at him. "I've never held a baby before."

Two dimples formed in Isla's chubby cheeks as she grinned, causing the pacifier to fall out of her mouth.

"You think that's funny? As the baby I'm talking about, I'm not sure you should."

Another grin, accompanied by a loud squeak, as if she were still figuring out how her voice worked. Which, come to think of it, she likely was.

When he'd seen Violet holding a baby in her arms, his blood pressure about shot through the roof. It reminded him of watching her secure that wedding dress over her clothes.

During the past couple weeks, he'd managed to bury the incident in the shop and the binder filled with wedding plans.

Until their last meeting at Addie's house. Then he couldn't stop chewing over the fact that Violet had planned a whole wedding. Bought decorations. She'd almost gotten *married*. She undisputedly wanted to, and given the awe and longing on her face as she'd danced her niece around the bakery, babies were part of her long-term plan as well.

Which, yeah, lots of women craved those things. Settling down. Stability. A family.

Serious relationships always bring about fights, and once kids get thrown in the mix, forget it. Soon it gets messier and messier, until neither of you recognize who you've become.

How attraction and affection turned to dynamite and destruction so easily, he had no idea. He'd seen it happen time and time again, though.

Now he was agonizing over the idea of spewing loathsome words at Violet. Of ruining everything they once had, including the tenderness she'd shown him and amount of faith she'd placed in him. She insisted on calling him a hero, but presently, "coward" would be more accurate.

Ford eyed the exit that would soon open up to an influx of people, including Violet's father and Cheryl and the Craft Cats. If his skin could, it'd crawl right off his body and leave without him.

But he needed to stay. Not only had he promised Violet, he was also holding a baby. Which left his internal temperature flaring and his muscles aching from not moving because what if he moved wrong?

She is pretty cute. Like a furless puppy.

Isla's round face scrunched up, jarring his already rapid pulse into the fever zone, and Ford boosted her higher in his arms. "Don't cry, okay? Because I like your aunt, and she thinks I'm a big strong bada— dude—and I don't want her to change her mind when she sees I'm scared of a baby."

Five tiny fingers wrapped around one of his big ones, and a mushy sensation he hadn't felt before twisted through him.

"Confession time," he heard, and turned to see Violet rounding the bakery counter. "I don't think you're a big strong dude."

Ford frowned, going over-the-top with his *blasphemy* face.

Violet walked up and placed her hand on his arm. "I know you are." She squeezed his biceps, and his insides turned liquid on him. Apprehension and anticipation made a strange yet strong cocktail, and his gut didn't know how to process them at the same time.

Isla's scrunched face returned, flushing red, and she

squirmed and let out a wail.

Violet reached over and popped the pacifier in her niece's mouth. "Were you playing with Ford while I calmed down your mommy?"

A crinkle formed between Isla's eyebrows, and the pacifier fell out as she began "talking" to Violet.

"At first I thought he was a bit cocky, too. He is, too, but you get used to it. More than that, he's a fireman-slash-paramedic-slash-search-and-rescue-guy who also trains cute puppies and coaches baseball, so he can totally back up his giant ego."

"And then some," Ford added, shooting a grin at the woman at his side. To Isla, he whispered, "For the record, I thought your aunt might be a little off at first, and she's shown me she can back that up as well."

Violet went to smack his arm but seemed to realize he was holding a baby. Between her teeth she said, "I'll get him back for that later. Yes, I will."

Isla beamed at Violet the same way Ford couldn't help doing whenever he was around her.

Okay, maybe he could do this. He just had to focus on Violet. On how he felt about her.

Vaguely, he heard the chime over the door, followed by, "Aww, how precious."

Lucia Murphy strolled farther into the store. "I come early to sneak a cupcake before Priscilla gets here, but this is another sweet treat I no expect." She added a chef's kiss noise. "*Bellissimo.* It so nice seeing you two happy and together, like a picture-perfect family. Now you can settle down and have your own adorable *bambini*."

What started as a nervous laugh came out as more of a hacking sound, and Ford quickly handed Isla to

Violet. "I'd, uh, better go see if Maisy needs any help."

"Do you have a tranquilizer in your paramedic bag?" Violet asked. "Because I think that'd be the most effective method to subdue her."

"I heard that," Maisy called. "And FYI, Dad and Mama are on the way, so steel yourself."

Violet cast Lucia a sidelong glance, assumedly because she didn't want people knowing she had to prepare herself to deal with them. Which was why she needed *him* here, so he'd better get his head straight.

Lucia lifted a finger to her lips. "Do not worry. It will be our secret." She brushed her hand over Isla's hair and flashed Violet a smile. "As long as you hook me up with extra brownie bites."

"You're incorrigible."

Ford tried to smile but wasn't sure he pulled it off. The words "picture-perfect family" ran through his head until it throbbed from them.

He wasn't ready for a family.

Didn't even know if he wanted kids.

Babies were cute—that wasn't exactly a news flash. Didn't mean he was ready to give up his adventurous lifestyle for a routine that included diapers and feedings while the prime of his life passed him by.

What about poker nights? Training dogs? Being able to take off to the mountains on a whim for several days at a time. People with kids didn't do that. Hell, married dudes didn't get to do that.

I could use a strong bottle of whiskey about now.

Great. Now you're dealing with things the way the rest of the McGuires do.

"Hey." Violet nudged his arm with her elbow, and he feared his panic was written across his face. It felt like he was in uncharted territory without a map, the sky dark and the stars obscured, with nothing to help him regain his sense of direction. "You okay?"

"Yeah." The vise on his too-tight lungs cranked another turn as he realized how much of a hold this woman had on him. She was turning him into the type of guy who showed up for town functions on the regular. Volunteering him for a road trip to pick up wedding decorations and to meet her mom without talking to him first.

What else was she going to plan and inform him of afterward? A wedding, like she'd done with her ex?

He'd decided to step down this path of coupledom, but he'd underestimated the twists and turns. Now he was glancing at the trailhead, debating turning back.

"I'm gonna go get some air real quick," he said.

"Oh. Of course. You'll be back soon, though?" She leaned closer, and her voice trembled slightly, her happy facade cracking and letting the worry shine through. "Because my dad and Cheryl are on their way, and I'm trying not to be a wimp, but—"

"Just a quick stroll around the block." His brain and lungs needed to get their acts together—and if they'd get on the same team, even better.

Violet's eyes met his, and he wasn't sure what she was waiting for. Did she think she could guilt trip him into changing his mind? If he didn't clear it of his thoughts, it was likely to explode.

One slow inch at a time, she tipped onto her toes and kissed his cheek. "See you soon, then."

Ford twisted his neck and gave Violet a proper kiss that Isla seemed to take offense to. This time, he did the honors of popping the pacifier in the baby's mouth.

Then he rushed out of the bakery, gasping for air.

Getting away from the hubbub was supposed to help, but Ford couldn't walk fast enough. Far enough.

Without realizing he was heading there, he ended up in front of Murph's. Not that he usually believed in signs, but this seemed like one. After all, it was Addie who'd pushed him to give Violet a shot, and now he needed her advice on how to keep from losing his mind *and* Violet.

Footsteps alerted him to the fact he was no longer alone, and a glance over his shoulder revealed Lexi hustling up the sidewalk in heels.

"Whoa, where's the fire?" Ford patted the pocket that held his phone. "I didn't get a call."

"You're not here for the emergency?"

Evidently, his heart *could* pound harder and faster. "What's wrong? Is Addie hurt?"

Lexi darted around him and reached for the doorknob. "I was on my way to the grand reopening for the bakery, and Addie called me crying. I couldn't make out what she was saying, so that's all I know." She pushed open the door, and Ford followed on her heels.

Addie sat on the couch, a box of tissue at her side and a blanket wrapped around her as if it weren't eighty degrees outside. She loudly blew her nose and then lifted her red-rimmed eyes. "Sorry I made y'all waste so much of your time planning, because right now, I'm not even sure there's gonna be a weddin' anymore."

With that declaration, she burst into tears.

CHAPTER TWENTY-FIVE

Tears were one thing; tears falling down *Addie's* cheeks were another. If he comforted her, she might punch him, and if he didn't, she might punch him.

Lexi rushed across the room and crouched in front of Addie. "Honey, what happened?"

"Nothing. I just…" A sob racked her chest. "I found out I'm engaged to a misogynistic jerk."

"What did he do?" Ford asked, curling his hands into fists. "Just say the word, and I'll dump his body in the swamp where no one will ever find him."

Addie dropped her head into her hands.

The knock on the door made them all jump, although Ford would deny it.

"Addison." Tucker's muffled voice carried through the wood. "Come on. It didn't come out right. Please let me in so we can talk about this."

"I have a better idea," she shouted back. "Go call the boys so you can play ball without me. And FYI, you'll be playing with all types of balls by yourself from *now on*."

Ford paced the length of the couch, the hostility in the air magnifying the five-alarm fire currently laying waste to his sanity. "Murph, what do you want me to do?"

"Just…tell Tucker I'll call him once I'm not so mad that I want to strangle him. Whether that'll be tonight or tomorrow or never, I'm not sure."

Always fun to be the bearer of bad news.

Ford stepped outside and used his body to block the doorway as he delivered Addie's declaration.

Tucker threw back his head and sighed. "Dude, every little thing turns into a huge fucking mountain lately. Half the time she's the girl I grew up with, and half the time I sit there wondering what the hell just happened and why."

"I get it. But like the first time the two of you had a big fight, I made a promise to Addie that I'd protect her, even from you. It's a promise I intend to keep."

"And like that night at Lexi and Shep's rehearsal dinner, I appreciate that. I feel better knowing she has you." Tucker ploughed his fingers through his hair, sending the waves off in different directions. "Tell her that whenever she calms down, I'm ready to come over on hands and knees and beg her to forgive me. Even if I'm still unsure what for."

Murph rarely got mad without a reason. As he'd thought countless times through the years, she was one of the most logical people he knew, hands down. While she had been less so this past month, Ford still put his money on Tucker having said or done something stupid.

It was sorta their group's specialty.

Before the two of them began dating, things were so blissfully uncomplicated. At the same time, Ford had never seen either one of them so happy.

Save this afternoon.

After promising Tucker he'd see what he could find out, Ford fortified himself the best he could to deal with all the emotions. Then he headed back inside to check on Addie.

The instant he stepped into the room, both women

looked up at him, eyes narrowed, as if they suspected he might've turned redcoat.

"Is he gone?" Addie asked.

"Yeah," Ford said. "But he wants you to call him after you calm down."

Fire flared through her eyes, and her voice came out at the same pitch as his dog whistle. "*Calm down?* Like I'm just overreacting?"

Ford held up his hands. "Don't shoot the messenger." He sat on the arm of the couch, since Lexi was seated on Addie's other side. "Maybe let him in on what's going on, though."

More tears welled in her eyes. "Tucker and I were talking about our future—about plans for the house we're building and our yard—and then he says he's always wanted a *son* to play catch with."

Lexi frowned while Ford racked his brain for what the hell was wrong with that. He'd thought the very same thing when he'd been at the baseball field with Dylan.

"So I said, 'what if we have a daughter? You can play catch with a girl, too.' And he…" Addie sniffed. "He said it's not the same. Can you believe that?"

Ford brought up his shoulders in case he needed to block one of Murph's jabs. "Um, don't kill me, but I'm lost. I think every guy dreams of playing catch with his son."

Despite his request that she not kill him, Addie glared like she was considering how to tear him limb from limb. "Seriously? You both grew up playing catch with me. Are you sayin' it wasn't fun enough? That I can't throw as far and hard as either of you?"

Ah, hell. Because Addie was a girl. Sometimes he…

well, not exactly forgot. Just didn't take her gender into consideration. "No. Which is why every time I was team captain for our football matches, I picked you first. Not only can you throw, you're fast as shit."

"Oh, don't patronize me, McGuire."

Now he was regretting not fleeing the scene with Tucker. What had happened to his best friend, and who was this irrational woman in her place? "I'm not. I wouldn't dare."

"You say that, but once we reached junior high, you were protective of me. Not as bad as Tucker, but sometimes you left your route to block for me."

"Did I tell a few guys that if they hurt you, I'd put my foot so far up their ass they'd taste the gator shit on my shoe? Sure. Never had to follow through. Mostly because of the speed I mentioned."

"Then, wouldn't it be only natural to assume that my daughter would be equally as good? At catching and running and doing everything my son could do?"

"Yeah, to a point," Ford said. "Once people get to a certain age, the muscle mass and weight class—"

Both women glared, so he switched tactics.

"Would you be disappointed if you had a daughter who hated playing ball? A daughter who wore frilly dresses and threw tea parties?"

Addie fiddled with the diamond ring on her finger, spinning it round and round, and he fought back a wheeze as the last of his breath left his lungs. *No thinking about marriage or how much Violet wants it— gotta focus on one disaster at a time.*

"No. I mean, I might be sad I can't share football with her, but…" Her frown deepened. "That's not the point."

What is *the point?* he wanted to ask but knew better. "All's I'm saying is that Tucker adores you. You're arguing over a what-if. Aren't there enough things to argue about in the present?"

"Yeah, like how he told his mom we could add a few dances because she insisted on a mother-son dance, even though I made it clear I didn't want to dance at my wedding." Addie's mouth pulled to one side as she glanced at Lexi. "No offense, Lex."

"None taken." Lexi twisted in her seat and smoothed her hands down her skirt. She was a girly girl, and if the tension in the air wasn't so thick and perplexing, he might point out that Addie got on great with her, fancy clothes and total lack of throwing skills notwithstanding.

"Look, I've been in your shoes." Lexi's gaze dipped to Murph's sneakers. "Well, in your place, since you and I have very different footwear preferences and that's okay." She patted Addie's thigh. "Differences are what keeps the world from being one big snoozefest. Planning a wedding is stressful. Both families are tugging at you, and that leads to everyone feeling overwhelmed. Which means small fights blow up into big ones.

"Tell you what…" Lexi popped to her high-heeled feet. "I'm going to grab the carton of ice cream I stashed in your freezer, along with your bottle of Jack. Then we'll banish all talk of weddings and unwind. Things will be right as rain come tomorrow morning—that or we'll be too hungover to care."

Addie's snort-laugh was capped off with a sob. "I used to brag about how cool I was under pressure and how I rarely got emotional. I don't even know who I am anymore."

Ford slipped into the spot Lexi had abandoned and slung his arm around Addie. "You're the girl with a killer right hook; the girl who pranked teachers and outswam me. The girl in just about every single one of my memories."

And the girl who had changed the instant she'd gotten engaged.

The thought hit him, and regardless of his resolve to lock it away in his brain and never dare utter the words, it didn't change the facts.

With two of his closest friends hurting, Dad's warning about relationships—and how they always brought on fights—drifted up to haunt him.

Or perhaps to taunt him.

It was hard to tell, but either way, warning bells began trilling, growing louder by the second.

His phone vibrated in his pocket, and when Easton's name flashed on-screen, he excused himself and walked into the kitchen to take it.

"You're at the reopening, right?" Easton asked.

"Murph's, actually. I should probably head to the bakery, though." Ford glanced at the time. Violet's father had undoubtedly arrived by now, and he wondered how much trouble he was in for not being there.

With things between Addie and Tucker all messed up and his train-wreck thoughts, it was the *last* place he wanted to go.

"Okay, well don't worry about the flat tire call that came in from dispatch. I'm on my way, and it sounds like Darius is ahead of me."

This was what happened when Ford ignored his radio and didn't pay attention to alerts. He hadn't even heard about the flat tire. The excuse called to him like a life saver in the lake of confliction he was about to drown in. "Where is it? I'll meet you there."

"Are you deaf? The entire reason I called was to tell you we have it handled. Go to the bakery and do your thing. Then maybe later, you and I can grab a beer at the Old Firehouse. I have something I need to talk to you about."

• • •

So far, Violet had avoided Dad and Cheryl, who were getting the big sign reveal ready. Sure, she'd strapped her niece into a carrier and used her as an excuse to walk around and evade an awkward encounter of the parental kind, but Isla was having a great time.

Since Violet had seen Ford run before, she knew he could move quickly and was flummoxed he wasn't back yet.

"Do you see him, Isla?" Violet tipped onto her toes. Every dark head of hair had her heart quickening, but then they'd turn, and it wouldn't be him, and she'd experience a twinge of disappointment.

Her phone vibrated in her pocket. She considered ignoring it, figuring it was a message in the Bridesmaid Chat she could read after the mini ceremony, but curiosity got the best of her.

Ford: *I know I promised to be there, and I'm so sorry, but I'm not going to make it. I got an emergency call I have to take care of.*

Violet's stomach bottomed all the way out, splatting against the hard ground. *He's not coming. I'm on my own.*

He can't help when there's an emergency. While I feel like I'm in the middle of one, I'm not bleeding out.

Ever since he walked out the bakery door, she'd been replaying their last few minutes. Catching him talking to Isla. Seeing her tiny hand wrapped around one of his fingers.

Her ovaries had stood at attention, kickstarting her biological clock. She felt the residual ping, as if they wanted to say they hadn't given up.

Violet patted her lower stomach and muttered, "You need to calm down, baby box. Ford and I barely started this relationship, and that's the kind of thing that'd freak him out."

Isla tipped up her chin and blinked at Violet, tiny eyebrows puckered.

Violet kissed her cheek and whispered, "I guess Ford was right about me being a little off. But just wait until you have to deal with boys. They're confusing and amazing and frustrating and fascinating. One day they'll be amazing and the next they'll act all cagey."

The way Ford had been there at the end.

The longer he'd taken to show, the more she'd worried he'd noticed the visions of babies dancing in her head. Long term, of course. After dismissing the notion as futile, it was simply nice to daydream about the possibility again.

Violet readjusted the pink sock that'd slid halfway down Isla's foot. "Unless what you decide you want is a girlfriend. Honestly, I'd go that route if I could choose, but attraction is a powerful thing. Although drama comes along with every relationship, I suppose, so—"

"Are you talking to me?" the woman next to her asked, and Violet gave her a sheepish smile.

Oops.

Dad began his mayoral speech, Maisy at his side as he discussed how proud he was of his daughter, and Cheryl on his other side, nodding her agreement. With them occupied, Violet moved closer.

She swung her camera from where it'd awkwardly hung at her back to avoid bouncing against Isla, lifted it, and snapped several photos.

"...proud of both my daughters." Dad's gaze pinned Violet in place. "As most of you probably know, Violet's done the majority of the repainting and decorating."

Violet glanced around, as if she expected another Violet who happened to have her same biological father to step forward.

"Can you come up?" Dad motioned Violet forward, and a light drumming began beating at her temples.

Slowly, she made her way to the podium. She made a fist and then released it—opened, closed, opened, closed. Ford was supposed to be here to hold her hand. To provide support.

What if I make a fool of myself in front of the entire town?

Is Dad extending an olive branch? Or is he about to pull the rug out from underneath me?

I really wish Ford was here.

I'm about to pass out anyway, so maybe someone will call 911, and he can resuscitate me after he fixes whoever he's helping now.

Maisy stretched out her hand, offering a much-needed anchor in the storm, and Violet took hold. Just like that, her inner turmoil calmed. "I want to thank the entire community for their patience as we were remodeling and for coming here today to celebrate. I couldn't have done any of this without my sister." Maisy gave her a quick squeeze, and a boulder-sized lump formed in Violet's throat. "And now, without any further ado…"

Maisy gripped hold of the string affixed to the canvas fabric hiding the new sign. She tugged, and the fabric slipped free to reveal a cupcake-shaped sign with the words Maisy's Bakery.

Everyone cheered, and people rushed forward to congratulate Maisy and head inside. Violet hung back, lifted her phone, and composed a reply to Ford. Yes, she'd been dismayed upon receiving his apology text, but the important thing was, he'd choose to be here with her if he could. *That* was what mattered.

Violet: *No worries. I have Isla to protect me. I'll make sure to save you a cupcake and check in later. XOXO*

She snapped a quick selfie of herself and her niece and sent it along, too.

"Hello there, little angel."

Everything inside of Violet froze, much the same way it'd done at the bazaar when she'd heard Cheryl's voice.

Violet plastered on a smile and held on to it for dear life as she pivoted toward her dad's wife. *Oh, holy crap. Dad just publicly acknowledged me in front of most of the town.*

With too many emotions firing through Violet at once, she still hadn't sorted out exactly how she felt about it, but she worried Cheryl would be more upset than usual and searched for a way to placate her. "Did you want to hold Isla?"

"Always."

It took a bit of finagling, but Violet managed to get Isla out of her carrier and handed her to her grandmother.

"Guess I'll head inside and—" Violet was moving past Cheryl as she spoke, but she stopped her with a hand on her arm.

Dad walked over, too, going against the flow of traffic, and Violet's heart attempted to beat out of her chest. *Never mind*, she wanted to text Ford. *Whatever emergency you're taking care of, mine is bigger, so get over here!*

So what if she was being as melodramatic as Ford once teased her of being?

"I wanted to apologize," Cheryl said, the words clipped. "I haven't treated you fairly. Not only the other night at the bazaar but since the beginning."

Dad took the last few steps, closing the distance between them. "I also want to apologize for not being there for you more through the years." He struggled to meet Violet's gaze. He cleared his throat, and she realized he was attempting to rein in his emotions. A soft smile curved his mouth as he grabbed Isla's hand.

It was weird, thinking they were grandparents to the baby she'd spent so much time with.

"Maisy's been so happy this past month, and I thought, 'oh good, she's finally through the baby blues.'" Cheryl brought a trembling hand up to her mouth. "But whenever we talk, she mentions you, and today it hit me that it's mostly thanks to you."

Violet tucked her hair behind both ears. "Oh, I wouldn't say that. All I did was help her decorate and provide a little company."

Dad's hand came down on her shoulder. "We haven't given you nearly enough praise through the years. Let us tell you how wonderful we think you are. Please."

A floaty, surreal-yet-happy sensation brewed underneath her sternum, slowly spreading to other parts of her body.

The next half hour was filled with apologies, tears, and cupcakes.

While it stung to be snubbed for simply existing, the fact of the matter was, Violet understood how hard it must've been for Cheryl to accept her. Being cheated on hurt you right down to the core of who you were. It made you doubt yourself and your worth and was hell on the self-esteem.

Every time Violet had seen or heard mention of the woman Benjamin had cheated on her with, it opened up old wounds and formed a deeper scar.

Now that she had Ford and realized how much better he was for her in every possible way, it wouldn't send her to her knees anymore. Still, she'd done insane things in the name of retribution, and even after damaging Benjamin's stuff, she'd wanted more justice, even as she'd felt instant regret.

The smile that spread across her face as she watched Dad and Cheryl laugh and hug was blessedly genuine.

She couldn't imagine ever forgiving Benjamin, the way Cheryl had forgiven Dad. And it must've been hard for her to apologize. Violet wasn't sure her relationship with Dad or her stepmom would ever be a super close one, but for the first time in a long time, she believed they had a shot at being...well, more than acquaintances.

After cleaning up the party, when Violet and Maisy had flopped on the couch, too sore to move, Violet informed her sister that she'd made a decision.

She was going to stay in Uncertainty.

CHAPTER TWENTY-SIX

Violet had only been to the Old Firehouse a couple of times, including the night she and Ford played pool, but she was certain it'd never looked like this before.

Pink balloons that said YAY! SAME PENIS FOREVER! floated in clumps around the room, glittery streamers stood out against the exposed redbrick walls, and bouquets of blush-colored roses adorned tables, along with shaft-shaped silver confetti. It was very Cinderella meets Passion Party Barbie, where you were just as likely to find a glass slipper as a glass dildo.

So far, every dude who'd walked inside the sports bar promptly backed out.

Lexi fluffed her platinum curls. "I put a sign on the door warning them the place had been reserved for a bachelorette party—as if everyone in town doesn't already know—but that people over twenty-one can enter at their own risk."

Fuchsia lips that perfectly matched the decor curved into a pixyish grin. "I think the men of Uncertainty are curious until they see the intimidatingly large four-foot inflatable penis."

Violet snorted. Earlier, as she and Lexi had taken turns blowing up the thing for the ring toss game, the male bartender kept eyeing them. He'd run into tables and stools and spilled countless drinks as the novelty item grew bigger and bigger with all the, um, blowing.

Poor guy would need to be gratuitously tipped for volunteering to work this party. Then again, he was about to get an education on women for free, and wasn't that—as the commercials say—priceless?

Lucia Murphy, on the other hand, had her fists on her hips as she studied the peachy pink atrocity. "It's been so long, I almost forgot what they look like. Either my memory no what it used to be, or they change in the past decade. And why is it smiling at me?"

The cartoon face with its creeptastically large grin didn't fall into the realistic category, but again, neither did the size. "Dicks are always more than happy to smile at a beautiful woman."

Lucia giggled like a teenager. "Oh, you." She bussed Violet on the cheek before pulling out a chair and taking a seat. "I like you. You decided to stay in our little town, yes?"

"Yes." Excitement swirled through her belly. After the grand opening, she'd almost texted Ford the good news, but she thought it'd be more fun to deliver in person. Waiting hadn't been easy, considering he'd been fishing with Easton all day yesterday. "I'm moving to Uncertainty."

"That make me happy. Ford is such a good boy. I knew someday a woman would come along who could put up with him."

Violet had learned Lucia Murphy thought everyone was a good boy or girl. While in the next breath she'd mention how they were a real son of a gun, or had a few screws loose, et cetera.

Since discussing the guy she was beyond happy to put up with would result in squeeing and celebratory dancing, she tabled it for later. She'd volunteered to be the photographer tonight, and her trigger finger was itching to start documenting the evening.

The bride-to-be was going to die twice when she saw the decorations. Addie had said all she wanted was a memorable night at the Old Firehouse, but she had no clue how very "memorable" it'd be.

The bar door opened, and Lottie and several of the other Craft Cats walked in.

Violet had asked Lexi if she worried the group would be offended by the phallic paraphernalia. Lexi then told her that she'd visited their quilting circle to learn the skill herself, and what else she'd discovered along the way was that the ladies were a lot raunchier than expected.

For years the ladies had been passing around a dog-eared copy of the *Kama Sutra* and starring their favorite positions. Apparently, the "Be Louder In Bed" section was a club favorite.

With the Craft Cats approaching, Violet did her best to scrub that information from her brain. Still, the fleeting image of Lottie in a pleather dominatrix outfit, whip in hand, had Violet yearning for a nice, strong drink.

A stripe of sunlight preceded Maisy's entrance to the bar, and Violet rushed over to help with the dessert trays. The technique her sister had shown her at the bakery this morning was called flooding, a smooth frosting that made each sugar cookie a work of art.

Pink hearts with the phrase "Bride to Be" and diamond rings with the wedding date adorned the silver trays, along with corsets that'd been a pain in the butt to decorate but turned out super cute.

While Violet's art classes had helped in the remodeling department, cookie decorating tapped into a completely different skill set. One she didn't have.

"Wow, this place looks awesome," Maisy said as they placed the cookies on the table with the rest of the hors d'oeuvres. "Is it wrong that I'm most excited to see how Ford handles the party?"

"If it is, I don't want to be right. He's a good sport, though, and one of the things I love about him is that he'd do anything for Addie and the rest of his friends."

"One thing you *love* about him? Does that mean you…" Maisy glanced around, evidently concluded there were too many ears close by, and propelled Violet toward the empty hallway with the restrooms and stack of extra stools. "Do you love him?"

As if it meant to answer on her behalf, Violet's heart pumped affection throughout her entire body, head to toe. "I…haven't told him yet. But yes."

A high-pitched squeal came from Maisy. "I knew it. And you said he wasn't your type."

"Are you ever going to let me live that down?"

"Nope," Maisy said with way too much glee. "I figured he factored into your decision to stay in town. I could tell he was smitten with you from the beginning—I've never seen him look at anyone the way he looks at you."

Maisy sighed and took both of Violet's hands in hers. "You deserve this, Vi. After everything, you deserve a happily ever after more than anyone."

Part of her wanted to object—not to having a happily ever after but discussing one so soon. Surrounded by decorations celebrating love, though, Violet went ahead and let herself believe her story might end with wedding bells of her own.

"They're coming!" Lexi yelled.

"Things they say on their honeymoon," someone yelled, and everyone cackled as they rushed into place.

An orchestra of party horns greeted Ford and Addie as they walked inside, along with whoops and hollers and a whistle loud enough to break glass. Lexi grabbed the personalized "Future Mrs. Crawford" veil and jabbed the comb in front of Addie's ponytail.

As she took in the decorations, Addie burst into laughter.

Meanwhile, Ford's eyes bulged like they might pop out of his head, the urge to flee written across his rugged features.

Violet lifted her camera and caught it all.

As the bride-to-be began hugging people, the sense of community filled Violet, mixing in with everything she felt for the guy by Addie's side. It was like Ford said—the citizens showed up for one another. They cared, and she could feel the compassion hanging in the air.

As soon as she'd snapped pictures of everyone, she zoomed in on the dude of honor, who still had a deer-in-headlights expression.

Then she decided to go rescue him for a change.

She practically skipped, her head in the infatuation-laced clouds.

A clump of balloons drifted in front of Ford, and he batted them away. One of them must've been extra staticky, because it floated back to his arm and bopped, bopped, bopped, as if it had something to tell him.

Dark eyebrows arched as Ford read the words printed across the pink latex. With a shake of his head, he knocked it away from him again and muttered, "What the hell have I gotten myself into?"

"It's probably best if you don't know and just let it happen," Violet said as she closed the last foot of distance between them.

He ran his fingers along his jaw. "I'm a little scared."

"You should be a lot scared." Violet placed her hand on his chest, and he flinched. "Are you sore or something?"

"Nah. Just…" He shook his head again, his gaze moving to the rest of the decorations. "Whoa."

"Don't worry. I'll protect you. You might be the expert when it comes to porcupines and racoons and gators, but me? I know cocks."

She expected a laugh, but her joke failed to land. Or maybe it wasn't as funny as she thought it'd be.

Before she could ask about his fishing trip, people swarmed the area, so many conversations going on at once that her head began to swim.

Lexi tapped Violet on the shoulder and asked if she wanted to be in charge of the ring toss or prosecco pong.

Then the party was officially off and running, the crowd pulling Violet and the man she planned on confessing her love to off in different directions.

· · ·

Over the course of the last thirty minutes, Ford had heard a lot of talk about having sex with one person for the rest of your life.

He'd also heard way more about the Craft Cat members' sex life than he'd ever, *ever* wanted to. Oh, and the jokes about tucking saggy boobs into their pants?

Well, he wasn't sure he'd ever have a boner again.

Normally he could shake it off. Maybe make jokes or tell the guys he was getting behind-the-scenes info on women.

But his thoughts kept circling back to one woman.

Violet had been running the table with prosecco pong for the past forty-five minutes. While Ford used to rule at beer pong, he hadn't tried the girly variation, and it had nothing to do with him not being much of a sparkling wine drinker.

"I've been going back and forth on whether or not to tell you something," Easton had said as they'd been fishing at the crack of dawn.

"Now you have to tell me," Ford had responded, no clue what would come out of his buddy's mouth next.

Or how it would fray that last thread he'd been holding on to when it came to his relationship with Violet.

One minute he'd look across the bar and think he was a lucky bastard that a woman like Violet would consider hitching her wagon to his star. Then, the matchmaking women of Uncertainty would comment that he'd be next down the aisle, and he'd fight the urge to sprint through the wall like the Kool-Aid Man.

Ford had always been the type of guy to make his decisions and stick to them, and he hated that he kept volleying. The other fun thing his brain had opted to do was replay fights he'd overheard. Between his parents. Couples in town. The arguments he and Trina had, and boy were there a lot of those.

The fist that'd first gripped his throat the night Addie freaked out about Tucker's dream of playing catch with his son squeezed tighter.

Fortunately, it seemed everything had been forgiven and forgotten on that front. The wedding was back on, and they were happy. But that also reminded him how Addie and Lexi had warned him not to hurt Violet.

It was the last thing he wanted.

Unfortunately, he wasn't sure if not hurting her was an option.

And after what Easton had told him, he wasn't sure he'd be safe from harm, either.

Ford could feel the rocking of the boat earlier, smell the water, and feel the bait between his fingers as he put it on his hook.

"You know how I run background checks on everyone who visits town for more than a week or so?" Easton had asked as he'd taken the PowerBait from him.

The hair on Ford's neck had pricked up, his instincts shouting he wasn't going to like what came next.

"I ran one on Violet," Easton continued. "If you want me to stop, just say so."

Ford cast and slowly let out the slack on his line. His doubts had already been gnawing at his insides, so he wanted to tell Easton he'd rather not hear it. While scolding himself for not using his common sense and digging into her past *before* getting attached.

Easton's hook made a light *plop* as it hit the water. "Did you know she was charged with first-degree criminal mischief?"

The tension claiming Ford's body eased up, his buddy's words so far from what he'd expected they felt like a relief. "No. But that doesn't sound so bad."

Silence stretched as Easton's gaze lowered to the floor of the boat, and what little remained of Ford's hope divebombed into the murky water.

"She took a golf club to her ex-boyfriend's car," Easton said. "We're talking broken windows and dents so big, it looked like it'd hailed bowling balls."

Inch by inch, ice crept through Ford until his limbs grew heavy and burdensome. "What type of car?" He wasn't sure what that had to do with anything besides delaying a conclusion he didn't want to come to.

"A brand-new BMW three series hard-top convertible."

Ford made a sour face. "That's the kind of car rich pricks flock to so they can brag about driving around their Beamer and how amazing the wind feels in their hair."

"All while sipping some fruity-ass drink." Easton began reeling in his lifeless line. "You're not wrong. It's a stupid car for a guy to drive."

"But taking a golf club to it…" Ford dragged his fingers across his jaw, the fishy scent of the PowerBait making him drop his hand to his lap. "That's something a crazy person would do."

"Crazy. Angry. Or crazy angry." The chair squeaked as Easton propped his forearms on his thighs. "I just thought you should know. Maybe err on the cautious side and take your time. I know how paranoid you are about relationships."

"*Pfft.* Not paranoid," Ford had said. "Skeptical, maybe." He punched Easton's shoulder. "Like you're one to talk."

Easton had tossed a beer to Ford and popped open a can for himself. "I'm not the one getting serious, though."

Those words played through Ford's head all day, a

stuck record that wouldn't be fixed by any amount of head shaking.

A tipsy Lucia danced past him, paused, and flung the hot pink feather boa around her neck over her shoulder. "See this? I win it at ring toss. Don't I look fabulous?"

"You always look fabulous. But the hot pink feathers suit you."

Lucia laughed and patted his cheek. "Speaking of beautiful, you and Violet are going to make beautiful *bambini*. And I get to be their nonna, too. Because knowing Addison, she will drag out making me a *bisnonna*—that's a great grandma."

Humming and swaying, Lucia lifted the glass in her hand. She sipped at it, slurping loudly from the phallic-shaped straw. "I all out. Better get more."

Continuing to hum, she shimmied over to the drink table.

That damn fist that'd seized his throat tightened, the room growing fuzzy as he struggled for air.

The bump to his shoulder allowed a sip of oxygen through.

The sidelong glance that revealed Violet had sunk onto the stool next to him took it away.

"I've been relieved of duty." She slid a red drink in front of him. "Don't worry; it's whiskey. Mixed with cherry juice and almond amaretto. Lucia made them so Addie would have her whiskey but they'd also match the decor. Cool, huh?"

Violet wrapped her lips around her straw—something he was working very hard not to pay close attention to—and sipped at the drink in her hand.

Figuring he could use fortification, Ford lifted his

glass and slurped from the ridiculous straw. *Damn, that is good.*

Focus, McGuire. The longer you go without addressing the issue, the more hurt both of you are gonna end up.

When it came down to it, they didn't want the same things. She wanted to settle down and have babies, and he was an adventure seeker. One who craved freedom, dangerous jobs, and the ability to head into the mountains for days at a time.

That "full life" stuff was all well and good for other people, but wasn't for him. Not when his contentedness required adventure and independence.

Ford cleared his throat—not that it helped. Maybe if they just slowed down the runaway dating train, they could find a happy medium. Or was that drawing it out for more future pain?

Either way, he couldn't hold it in anymore. "I feel like things are gettin' too serious."

"Dude, I'm drinking from a dick-shaped straw—as are you. I don't think we're anywhere near serious."

"I meant with us."

Her face crinkled—and then crumpled—as the words hung in the air. In the background, women continued to laugh and scream and celebrate.

"I was hoping we could pump the brakes a little. Take things slow."

Violet lifted her gaze from the spot on the bar she'd fixated on. The lights reflected off her glistening eyes, tears an inevitability, and he cursed himself for not waiting until after the party.

In his defense, drawing it out any longer would be akin to torture. Wouldn't it make him more of an asshole to pretend things were dandy?

The muscles in her jaw clenched, and her words came out strangled with emotion. "Too serious? Are you for real right now? What? Did you just realize you've only had sex with one person the last two weeks? Better pump the brakes and start banging other women ASAP."

"It's not that." Truth could be a burden, and he desperately needed to unload before it crushed him. "It's the marriage talk, and people mentioning kids, and I can feel the shackles getting tighter."

Violet winced as if he'd slapped her. "Shackles? In this scenario of yours, am *I* the shackles? Or did I slap 'em on like a prison warden and drag you around behind me? Because I seem to remember you asking me to stay. And I was so excited to tell you tonight that I'd decided to."

He exhaled a shallow breath.

"Hey! It's our local hero!" Noah, the bartender who occasionally joined them for pickup games, chose the *worst time ever* to pass by and clap Ford on the back.

Ford spun on his stool, opening his mouth to ask for a few minutes of privacy.

"Future generations will be telling the tale of how you, Easton, Darius, and sixty-year-old Mrs. Reynolds saved Mr. Garcia from a flat tire one mile from the tire shop."

"You never mentioned anything about a...." An oddly calm mask descended upon Violet's features, and, judging from the static electricity that buzzed through Ford, the storm was on its way. "What day was that?"

Ford raised his voice, desperate to stop a disaster

already in motion. "Listen, Vi—"

"Thursday evening," Noah said. "People have been making 'how many people does it take to change one tire' jokes ever since." He added a snort. "Anyway, this is some party, huh, Ford? I'm glad you showed and relieved me of being the only dude here."

The murderous glare that'd filtered in with Violet's forming tears suggested that soon enough, Noah would be the only male once again.

"Can you excuse us for a minute?" Ford asked, although what he wanted to do was bark at Noah to leave, rewind time, and do the opposite of everything he'd done since taking that emergency call that ended up being anything but.

"You..." Violet struggled to swallow, and darkness crept through him, robbing him of every ounce of happiness he'd ever felt. "Did you know when you took the emergency call that other people would be there?"

Ford opened his mouth, came up with a whole lot of nothing, and hung his head.

More tears filled her eyes, one blink away from overflowing. "I told you that I needed you. I faced my dad and Cheryl alone. And while it went better than expected, that's not the point. You promised me you'd do what you say. That you'd be there for me. I told you it was the one thing I needed, and it didn't matter."

Violet tipped back her drink, a strangled choking sound coming out as she slammed the glass down on the bar. "I'm not the one who keeps bringing up marriage—you're in a fucking wedding. If you'll remember, I told you I'd given up weddings and men. You asked for my help being a good bridesmaid, and what's worse is you led me to believe you were different from the rest.

"And hello, people talk about kids—I suppose I do, too, since I have an adorable niece, who I love to pieces. Those are *your* issues, not mine."

"Oh, so you *don't* want to get married?" His voice came out louder than he'd meant for it to, and he readjusted the volume. "You're telling me that binder you carry around isn't filled with the dream wedding you can't wait to throw?"

Her hand clutched her chest as her shoulders curled in on themselves, but his tongue was still off and running.

"And you wanna talk about issues? Like how you were arrested for beating the shit out of your ex's car? Something you failed to mention, by the way."

Her eyelashes fluttered, and salt water spilled streams onto her cheeks. In spite of everything, Ford had the strongest urge to use his thumb to wipe her tears away.

"Silly me, not confessing one of the most embarrassing experiences of my entire life up-front." Violet sniffed. "My ex cheated on me, and yeah, I got super drunk and made a bad decision. Not only do I regret it, but it's in the past, so I don't see how it's relevant to you and me."

"Sure, until I piss you off and you take a bat to *my* truck. I saw the warning signs that you were unstable and obsessed with getting hitched, and that's on me for ignoring them."

Violet nodded over and over. "And I saw the signs you were a player. Heard all about how you weren't the settling-down type. How stupid am I for falling under your spell anyway? For thinking that with me, you'd be different."

Dammit. The reality of the situation caught up to him and his big mouth. His heart and lungs turned into shriveled organs that might never work again. Heaviness pressed against his chest with an ache he'd never experienced before.

This wasn't what he wanted.

"Look," he said, backtracking as quickly as possible. "This conversation's getting out of control, and that's not what I meant to happen. The last thing I wanted was for us to tear each other apart. I just thought we should pump the brakes. Slow things down." He grabbed her hand and curled it into his. "Maybe someday—"

She jerked free of his grasp, and as frustrated as he was, he immediately missed having her hand in his. "Let me guess. You want to stick to being sex buddies. Perhaps go on a date now and then, and maybe someday, you'll magically be ready to get serious."

Ford blinked. The woman had taken the words right out of his mouth, save the *magically*. "What's so bad about that? I mean, I wanna be more than sex buddies. It's about preserving my freedom, not about dating other women. I just thought we could keep on doing what we've been doing and get to know each other. Take it a step at a time."

A terrifying, mirthless laugh spilled from her lips. "You guys are all the same. I might've fallen for that once, but I've already been with a someday guy. Thank goodness I don't move as fast as you accuse me of, or I would've planned another dream wedding to a total asshole."

Violet scooted the stool away from the bar so violently, it tipped over, the clatter drawing the attention of everyone in the near vicinity. "This time, I choose me."

The disappointment and hurt that flooded her expression unleashed a swell of vitriol within his chest. A different sort of panic—one he didn't totally understand—dug claws into what remained of his lungs.

"Goodbye, Ford McGuire." Violet tossed the napkin crumpled in her fist on top of the bar. The YAY! SAME PENIS FOREVER! seemed to taunt him. "Thanks for reminding me why I gave up men in the first place."

CHAPTER TWENTY-SEVEN

To say the past several days had sucked was a major understatement. Over and over, Ford tried to convince himself he'd done the right thing. That even though he hadn't wanted it to end the way it did, it was better to find out they weren't compatible in the long run than drag it out.

He fully understood he had no right to see Violet. To stop by the bakery and ask how she was. Didn't stop him from wanting to.

Lexi was pissed upon learning he and Violet had broken up, and when he'd asked *her* how Violet was, she'd reminded him of the one thing she'd instructed him not to do: hurt Violet, because she'd been hurt already.

To top off her rant, Lexi told him that if he wanted to know, he should grow some balls and ask Violet himself.

It was the first time he'd ever heard her say something less than debutante-ish.

While he'd originally been excited about Addie and Tucker's wedding—and about it being over and done with, to be honest—he wasn't looking forward to tomorrow.

For all his insistence that he didn't care what the townsfolk thought, it wasn't going to be easy to ignore them, Violet, Maisy, and whoever else decided to glare daggers—that he totally deserved—at him.

Not that anyone could say anything worse than

what he'd been telling himself. He'd done far too good a job of searing his and Violet's night at chimney rock into his memory. If he dropped his defenses for even a second, he'd be under the tree with her.

Worshiping her naked body as they lay on the blanket.

Picturing the symbols they'd sprayed in a place that used to belong to only him.

Trouble padded over to the front door, stared at it, and whimpered.

"I know, buddy." A lump formed in Ford's throat, and he rubbed his gritty eyes. "She's not coming back."

The whimpers grew louder as Trouble pawed at the wood, and Ford didn't have the heart to scold him.

Not when he wanted to flop on the floor next to the puppy and cry himself.

Ford eyed the stack of empty beer cans on the coffee table from last night's pity session. It'd started at the bachelor party, which had been a low-key celebration that'd included poker and rehashing old memories.

After losing his stack of chips in record time, he'd come home and continued to drink and drink until there wasn't another drop of alcohol in the house. All those months of his friends insisting he turn off the scanner and be present, and he couldn't. Until last night, when he'd clicked off the damn machine and hurled it across the room.

Between the empties and the disheveled state of his place, he felt more like his father than he ever had before, and that chapped his lazy ass.

Insult to injury seemed to be the theme lately. Like when Tucker and Shep were baffled he and Violet hadn't worked out. Easton relayed the news about her record in an attempt to stand up for Ford's choice to cut things off, and the two whipped guys of the bunch had looked at him as if *he* was the unstable one.

"Guess I'd better shower and clean up this place," Ford said to his canine audience. His joints creaked as he retrieved the scanner. He clicked it on, glad it didn't seem any worse for wear, and set it on the mantel. "Then we should continue our training. I've been slacking lately, and we'll never reach the six-hundred-hour mark if we sit around and sulk."

Pyro's eyebrows twitched, his unspoken *you're the one who's been moping* coming across loud and clear.

"That's what I'm saying. That I'm done whining about it. Yeah, I liked Violet. For as squirrely as she was, she also had a calming presence about her. Not to mention that killer sense of humor." A smile trembled across his mouth, even as his heart jackknifed in his chest. "Then there was the way she'd get all distracted and off in her own world…"

Well, that wasn't helping, and Ford buried the mushy sensations attempting to overtake him under images of that ridiculous wedding planning binder. "But I'm not ready to settle down. In the end, we wanted different things. Life is supposed to be an adventure, not an institution."

With a huff, Pyro flopped onto his bed, and then it felt like the entire world was disappointed in him.

"Great. I lost the girl, and now I'm sitting around talking to dogs, one more loss away from becoming a country song." Factor in the fact that he smelled like a brewery and he might already be there.

Ford gathered as many beer cans as he could into his arms and walked them to the trash can. Thanks to his lack of desire to do a damn thing, it was overflowing, so he had to compact the garbage before he could remove the bag and take it outside.

All four dogs were barking when he reentered through the back door.

His heart leaped in his chest, a foolish thought accompanied by an even more preposterous amount of hope.

Maybe Violet's here.

As awful as the ending had been, they'd had a lot of great moments. With her moving to Uncertainty for good, would he have to relive them again and again?

Worse, would he watch her date some perfect schmuck who was ready for marriage and babies?

Staticky words filtered in from the scanner, bringing him back to reality—a harsh place where Violet Abrams would never speak to him again.

"…injured hiker… The storm coming…"

A renewed sense of purpose found its way to the surface, and Ford hurried over to the mantel and cranked up the scanner. Then he called in and talked to dispatch.

See, this was what his life was all about. Heading into an oncoming storm to find a lost hiker. Adventure. No one to answer to, his life free of drama and completely his own.

"Who's ready for a mission?" Ford asked his dogs, and Pyro pranced around in circles, eager to get going.

Now to figure out which other dog he should let tag along.

Trouble was biting Tank's tail, and while Violet might get the distracted mutt to be halfway useful, Ford didn't have time to deal with the puppy's lack of focus.

Nitro could scent the farthest, and she followed commands the fastest and most accurately.

After grabbing his gear, Ford let Pyro and Nitro into the cab of the truck—they'd have to deal with the cold plenty tonight. Then he raced to the police station, where the family members of the lost hiker were waiting.

Twenty minutes later, Ford was speeding north on a rutted dirt road. Mr. Wagner had called his family and left a patchy message. They were able to make out the words "left the trail" and "lost," and when his family tracked the phone, it said it was offline.

Luckily, they were able to narrow in on the coordinates from before he lost signal, which gave them a place to start.

Unfortunately, most people continued to move when they should stay put.

A red truck sat at the top of the trailhead, and a quick glance at the make, model, and license plate confirmed it belonged to Mr. Wagner. Ford climbed out of his truck to peek inside the vehicle, but it was empty.

His GPS indicated they were about two miles from where the man made his last call. "Looks like we're gonna have to hike the rest," he said to Pyro and Nitro as he opened the passenger door for them.

Not a big deal if they weren't running out of time.

Heavy gray clouds obscured the sky, and the scent of rain and pine hung in the air. Storms in the forest were a beast of another kind. One minute it could be sunny and cloudless, and before you noticed the change, torrential rain would be upon you, soaking you to the bone.

Ford radioed in to the crew from the town over and

informed them he'd be coming from the southeast.
They were going to start on the northwest part of the
trail, and they'd make wide passes till they met in the
middle.

So he wouldn't end up wet and suffering hypother-
mia, Ford slipped into his neon orange waterproof
jacket with the words SEARCH AND RESCUE emblazoned
on the back. Then he pulled his lightweight nylon pants
over his jeans and slung on his search and rescue pack.

Since the last thing Ford wanted to do was lose
Nitro on her first trip out, he snapped on the longest
lead rope he owned.

Then he walked over to Mr. Wagner's truck, offered
a prayer to the karma gods, and yanked on the door.

The door was unlocked, and while the dogs could
still scent near the truck, inside of it would be more
effective.

Pyro put his paws up on the seat and sniffed,
already on task, and Ford instructed Nitro to "Scent."

She padded the length of the bench seat a couple
times, her nose against the frayed fabric.

"Now seek," Ford said in a firm voice.

Both dogs put their noses to the ground, and after a
couple seconds, Pyro took off at a full sprint.

Nitro barreled after, although neither she nor Ford
would be able to keep pace.

The other thing about following dogs—they didn't
choose the easiest path for someone six foot three who
walked on two legs instead of four.

Speed was most important, though, so Ford
hunched under bushes, launched himself over fallen
logs, and rushed as fast as he could without injuring
himself.

"Hold tight, Mr. Wagner," he muttered.

A fat droplet splattered his nose, his cheek, the forearm of his jacket...

And then time was up when it came to getting in and out before the storm.

• • •

"Are you sure?" Maisy asked, sitting next to the piles of clothes on Violet's bed. She laid Isla on her back, and the cutie clamped onto her toes, her eyes widening as she studied them.

In her excitement, Isla kicked and lost her grip. Her face wrinkled up and pinkened, displaying her devastation at losing her new toy, in spite of also being responsible.

Maisy stuck a pacifier in Isla's mouth, and she concluded it was roughly as cool as her toes.

If Violet didn't force herself to look away from her niece's chubby cheeks, she wasn't sure she'd follow through with the decision she'd made.

She unzipped her suitcase and began transferring the piles of clothes. "One thing I've learned this past year is that being *sure* isn't as reliable as I used to think. I promise I'll visit more, but I'm sure that I need time and space."

"Just keep avoiding Ford, and you can get those things here."

Violet cocked her head. "You and I both know that in Uncertainty, avoidance is futile. Every single place reminds me of him, and I saw him running three out of the past six mornings. Each time, it felt like someone had sliced me right open again."

Simply speaking the words jabbed at the gaping wound in her chest, each of their shared memories another gush of stinging lemon juice.

Stop or you'll cry. And you don't have time to cry. Not to mention she'd shed enough tears.

"My muse has returned, the bakery looks amazing, and I have a new job all lined up, so mission complete." Violet debated whether or not to pack or leave out her beloved worn yoga pants. "I can stay with my mom for a month or two while I find an apartment, and then I'll be back on my feet, too."

"You should take my mom up on the offer she originally tried to bribe you with. She and Dad owe you, after all. They loaned me money for my bakery, so it's only fair."

When she'd spoken to Dad during the lunch they'd met up for this afternoon, he'd also offered to help her financially.

Still, Violet shook her head. "Stubborn pride or not, I don't want to glance around and think that I only have what I have because of them. That's how I felt after Benjamin, and it sucked. Then it sucked even more as one by one those things were taken away."

The cute underwear she'd worn to the bachelorette party—when she'd been foolish enough to think she should tell Ford that she was going to stay because she was in love with him—seemed to taunt her. She'd idealized the moment, imagining telling him and then stripping, and…

Violet shoved the panties under a stack of T-shirts. "Fiercely independent is my new motto. I don't need anyone else."

Maisy's lower lip stuck out. "No one?"

The pile of jeans protruded a couple of inches, and Violet shoved them level with the suitcase so she could fasten the thin divider. Then she reached out and took her sister's hand. "Except you and Isla, of course. You can visit me anytime, and I hope you will. We can take Isla to the beach and cruise the bay."

Maisy lifted the one pair of heels Violet had brought—strappy and silver, with a purple bow on the toe. "I meant to borrow these before you left."

"You can borrow them when you come to visit me." Violet plucked them out of her sister's hands and shoved them in the other side of her suitcase.

"Commercial photography is far from your dream job," Maisy said.

"Don't start," Violet warned.

"Too late. You say your muse is back, but you like taking emotional shots. Not pictures of other people's yachts for a magazine."

"Don't forget fishing boats."

Isla began fussing, and Violet scooted her suitcase aside, hovered her face over her niece's, and toyed with a curl on the top of her head. "Hey, pretty girl."

Isla grinned, and she happily kicked her feet.

"Can you tell your mommy to not make this harder than it already is? And remind her I can take on side jobs?" Violet skimmed her fingers down Isla's torso and then grabbed her toes and wiggled her foot. "Maybe add in that your daddy will be home in less than a month, and he's not going to want to share a house with his mopey sister-in-law?"

Isla pushed out a squeaky noise that Violet took to mean she'd do what she could.

Maisy's sigh made it clear she wasn't convinced. She

opened her mouth, but the doorbell rang, and she mumbled they weren't done discussing this yet.

Since Violet had everything packed except the items she needed for tomorrow—the plan was to head out after the wedding—she picked up Isla. She cuddled her close, adding a dozen kisses to her epic cheeks.

"You're going to grow so much before I see you again, and that makes me super sad, but I have to attempt to be a grown-up with a life of her own." It'd be her very own, too, because she was never going to pull someone else into it ever again.

Not only was she completely giving up on men—for really reals this time—she was considering getting a puppy.

Only she wanted *her* puppy that wasn't actually hers. She might need time to mourn losing Trouble as much as she was grieving over the breakup with Ford.

How could I have been so blind?

More like how could she have let her eyes and her heart do the decision-making when she knew better?

They were questions she'd already asked the Bridesmaid Crew chat, after telling them that she and Ford were no longer, and instructed the girls to please smack her upside the head if she ever started talking about a tempting hot guy again.

They replied with a mixture of validating her feelings, consoling comments, and threats to Ford's person. All of which she appreciated, and it made her love her group of friends even more.

I can't wait to get back to them, she thought, but it didn't quite ring true. Yes, she wanted to see them, but they'd still have their lives, and she'd have… Well, she'd figure it out along the way as she put herself back together once more.

Addie and Tucker's wedding was going to be painful, but Violet wanted to be there for them and for Lexi. She'd stick near the exit and congratulate the happy couple when they stepped away from the dude of honor. She'd survive.

Somehow.

"Violet," Maisy called. "It's for you."

For a second, the world ground to a halt.

Ford? Her traitorous heart fluttered, its short-term memory ready to make a fool of her. She'd overrule it and use her brain this time. As she walked toward the living room with Isla in her arms, though, her throat went bone dry.

Instead of Ford, Lexi and Addie stood in the living room.

Violet told herself she was relieved, even though her stomach bottomed out and called her a liar. "Hey, ladies. How's it going?"

"Horrible," Lexi said. "The wedding is falling apart, and we have a giant favor to ask." She glanced at Addie and motioned between them, muttering something about should she do it or did Addie want to?

Foreboding pricked her skin—and where was her glass of water, because she might die of thirst in the next minute or so if she didn't rehydrate.

"Well, you know how my sister was supposed to be one of the bridesmaids?" Addie asked. "She didn't have a tummy bug. Turns out she's pregnant—the ultrasound estimated she's already three months along. She's been super nauseous but was still planning on being in the wedding.

"Only when she arrived yesterday, she started

bleeding and ended up in the hospital. The doctor prescribed bedrest. She can come to the ceremony, but not the reception, and she can't do anything but sit and watch. The doctor told us, like, a hundred times. And he added a threatening reminder that he'd be attending, too."

While Violet was upset on Addie's behalf, she wasn't sure why they'd come to her with the news. "I'm so sorry. I wish I could do something to help."

"Funny you say that," Lexi said. "Because you and Alexandria are about the same size. And you already know everything about the wedding, so…"

"Would you be my fill-in bridesmaid?" Addie asked, hope shining in her features. "I get that it's complicated, thanks to my dude of honor being a huge jerk—something he and I are gonna have some words over, trust me."

"And we'll make sure you don't have to walk down the aisle with him," Lexi said. "You literally just have to stand there in the dress and occasionally help straighten Addie's gown. Maybe hold an extra bouquet and make small talk with townsfolk. Stuff like that."

"Otherwise, Lexi will be the only female besides me." Addie twisted the end of her ponytail around her finger. "And after decades, I finally got the town to realize I am, in fact, a girl. So even though part of me wants to say who cares what they say, I do, to a certain extent. Especially when it comes to my wedding."

A pit opened up in Violet's gut as her brain screeched into overdrive. She'd given up playing bridesmaid and everything wedding-related because it hurt too bad. Given up men.

Given up most everything.

Lexi lightly touched the forearm Violet had wrapped around Isla's middle. "We realize we're asking for a huge favor and that it's totally last minute."

"I just want tomorrow to be perfect, and you've done the bridesmaid thing before, and…" Addie's breaths came faster and faster. "I'm trying not to panic, but the bridal rollercoaster is throwing me for a loop. And when I was lost on decorations and cake and a dozen different things, you stepped in and calmed me down, lickety split."

Addie stepped closer and squeezed Violet's shoulder. "I've even thought that if I'd met you earlier, you would've been in the wedding party. Now we have the opportunity to fix that. And no pressure or anything, but I won't be able to sleep until I know this is taken care of."

Both she and Lexi brought their hands up in prayer position and, as if they'd practiced it a hundred times, added, "*Please*."

CHAPTER TWENTY-EIGHT

Rain poured in a steady stream—enough that Ford had pulled the hood of his jacket over his baseball cap. The bill kept his face fairly dry, and he was grateful for the waterproof duds. Rivulets formed on the hillside, and mud caked the soles of his boots, adding an inch or two to his height.

Slowed him down some, too.

It also left Nitro struggling and unsure. While the rain wouldn't erase Mr. Wagner's scent, it could muddle it by carrying it into formed puddles that confused the dogs. Particularly inexperienced ones.

Pyro will find him. He's the best of the best.

It'd been a while since Ford had seen his trusty black German shepherd, but he wasn't worried. Even with the flooding down south, Pyro understood his limits. He'd find the hiker, and if Ford didn't respond to his barked alert, Pyro would find him and lead him back to Mr. Wagner.

Nitro sniffed the ground and yipped.

"You pick it up again, girl?"

She took a sharp right, one that led them up the side of a hill. Ford scraped off what mud he could on a rock so he could get better traction for the climb.

A howl cut through the air.

Pyro had found Mr. Wagner.

Better yet, Nitro was headed in the right direction.

Ford shined his flashlight around until he spotted Pyro up on an enormous boulder. Nitro scrambled up the rock as well and began howling along.

After slipping and slopping a couple of times, Ford reached the top.

Unfortunately, Pyro and Nitro both had their noses pointed down.

Lashing rain muffled a shout, and Ford glanced over the edge of the boulder, into the crevice. There at the bottom was Mr. Wagner.

Ford introduced himself and asked for a quick recap.

Mr. Wagner had been hiking and wanted to see the view from the top. He'd lost his footing and fell. The narrow, stony outcropping he'd landed on was lucky in a lot of ways. If it hadn't "caught" him, he would've plummeted six or seven stories, and Ford would've been retrieving a body instead.

"I'm going to secure a rope," Ford called to the man. "Do you think you can climb?"

"Not sure. My ankle might be broken. It swelled up enough I had to take off my shoe."

Shit. The last thing you were supposed to do was remove the shoe—it gave the ankle too much room to swell. "Hold tight. I'll be down shortly."

Ford radioed in his location and asked for backup. Then he searched for the best spot to set up a single point anchor.

The nearest pine was dead and thus a no go. After assessing the trunks of the other nearby trees and the length of rope needed, Ford got to work.

A quick water knot, two strands of tight webbing, and he clipped in the carabiner.

With that rig set up, Ford put on his harness, secured everything, and headed to the edge of the rock so he could rappel down. He glanced at the dogs. "Sit. Stay."

Their furry butts hit the ground, but Pyro whimpered, his attention on the hiker.

"I'm gonna get him. You two stay and wait for backup." Slowly, Ford hung over the edge. As sure as he was in his anchor, this moment always tested his nerves, an intoxicating mix of trepidation and thrill.

One foot at a time, he began the descent.

Halfway to the outcropping, Ford's foot slipped out from under him, the moss, rain, and mud caking his boots a dangerous combo.

The rope zinged, and pain shot up his calf. For a breathless beat, he was free-falling, the miles and miles underneath him coming fast.

His harness jerked, and he slammed into the rocky cliffside. *Ow.*

On autopilot, his feet and fingers searched for and found purchase.

Each thump of his heart was a punishing relief, the beats frenzied but life-affirming.

The clouds parted, revealing a full moon, and the world lightened a shade. Enough to see the distance between him and going splat.

Just like that, his life flashed before his eyes, along with his regrets.

Namely, one.

She had dark hair, brown eyes, and the kind of smile that lit a fire inside him and obliterated his troubles. Violet made him feel strong, assured, and more important than anyone else ever had.

She made him better, not only because he'd worked to rise above his past but because her faith in him made him want to be his best version.

"You okay?" Mr. Wagner asked, their roles momentarily reversed.

"Yeah. Happens all the time in the rain," Ford answered. The latter was true. The former, a bald-faced lie.

Do you have a sweetheart? Doris's words echoed through his mind. *Someone who makes your life worth that much more?*

There's peace in being fulfilled. In living without regret. And if it's my time to go, I know my Harold will be waiting for me on the other side.

The past several days had forced a magnifying glass to his life. He'd stubbornly denied what his brain had whispered since Violet walked away from him last Saturday night.

With his adrenaline taking over, his mental shield was down, and he saw his life for what it was.

Incomplete.

At night, as he tossed and turned, he felt around for the woman who should be next to him, only to come up empty. No one called him on his shit. The absence of laughter rang through his house, the silence so loud he could hardly stand it.

Hell, even the dogs noticed the void.

If he plummeted to his death right now, his life wouldn't be worth anywhere near what it could've been with Violet by his side.

For all his talk about adventures, he'd been too scared to take a real risk. Love was the biggest adventure of all, and he'd tucked his tail between his legs and pushed away the woman he'd fallen for.

No one would ever compare; he knew that much. He'd made a horrible, awful decision. Chalk it up to lapse in judgment or good old-fashioned fear—it didn't matter. What mattered was he loved Violet, and he'd been an idiot to let her go.

I miss her. My life isn't full. It's so empty I can hardly stand being around myself.

Ford gripped the rope as resolve seized his body.

He wasn't going to fall, because as soon as Mr. Wagner was on his way to the hospital, Ford was going to get his own act together and come up with a plan to fix what he'd carelessly broken.

A quick recalibration, and Ford lowered himself onto the outcropping.

After checking Mr. Wagner's vitals, he assessed the ankle.

Definitely broken, and Ford reached into his bag and fashioned a splint.

Barks shattered the silence, and a couple of minutes after that, two beams of light cut through the dark. Backup had arrived.

Ford patted Mr. Wagner on the shoulder. "Hear that? That means you just have to hang on a little longer. We'll have you out of here and on your way to the hospital in no time."

"They'll call my wife so she's waiting when we get there, right? I need to see her."

Ford's heart expanded, flooding with images of the woman he hankered to see. He cleared his throat and nodded. "She'll be there."

Meanwhile, his house would be empty, save dogs who'd be happier to see Violet.

I'm gonna fix it. There's gotta be a way to fix it.

Fingers crossed he wasn't too late.

CHAPTER TWENTY-NINE

Violet's feet dragged as she followed Lexi out of the dressing area, Addie right on their heels.

While she could only imagine how much Tucker and Addie were waiting for this moment, it was the one Violet had dreaded since agreeing to fill in as bridesmaid.

But the day wasn't about her, and as she glanced over her shoulder, the nerves that'd been using her stomach as a trampoline settled.

Addie reached up as if to twist the end of her ponytail around her finger before seeming to remember her hair had been weaved into a romantic updo. Her makeup was on the natural side, and her white gown fit her impeccably. She swiveled the toe of her bright yellow Converse sneaker as she fiddled with the engagement ring on her finger.

"You look beautiful," Violet said, and tears rose, threatening to test the bounds of her waterproof mascara.

This was how she'd get through the day—by focusing on Addie's happily ever after.

Lexi pivoted and grasped Addie's hand. She grabbed one of Violet's as well. "In all the madness, I'm not sure I told you two how much I've enjoyed planning this wedding. I can get a smidge uptight when it comes to being prepared—"

"No," Addie teased, and the three of them giggled.

"I hide it well, I know," Lexi said, eliciting more

laughter. "But you two made it fun."

Addie's eyebrows arched. "Aversion to everything girly and all?"

"Yes. Mostly because Violet had my back with that." Lexi gave Violet's hand an affectionate squeeze.

Now Violet truly *was* going to cry. She dabbed a fingertip to the corners of her eyes, and Lexi waved a hand in front of her face as she demanded they cry on the inside.

While Violet knew it was time for her to return to her real life, in her heartbreak, she'd underestimated how much these women had come to mean to her. They'd instantly accepted her and made her feel welcome in a town she used to view as an adversary.

Then there was her reconciliation with Dad and Cheryl—and *gah*, Maisy and Isla—and if she thought about that now, no amount of blinking would prevent her from turning into a sobbing mess.

Footsteps broke through, a stride Violet somehow recognized, even as she told herself that was silly. It was simply because she couldn't help thinking of Ford.

Not to mention it was time for him to join the bridal party.

He cleared his throat, and Violet told herself to think of him as the sun and avoid looking directly at him.

While her brain was on board, her eyes went rogue.

For all of Ford's jokes about wearing a bridesmaid dress, the way he rocked a yellow bow tie, daisy boutonniere, and golden suspenders was unfair. His gray slacks hugged thighs she absolutely wasn't going to think about. His jaw-length hair had been cut to right above his ears and was lightly gelled, and misery pumped in and out of Violet's heart until her entire body ached with it.

Seeing him was harder than she imagined it'd be—and she'd imagined it plenty.

More than that, she'd hoped she'd feel differently now. But the mangled heart thudding away in her chest whispered that somehow, she still loved him.

As she sorted through the tornado of emotions, she snatched the furl of anger and clung on to it.

"Violet," he said, and the blood in her body turned icy and sharp.

Lexi stepped forward and hissed at him, the words inaudible but the warning clear.

Will and Easton rounded the corner, dressed identically to Ford.

Lexi and Will did the telepathic-couple thing, and he pulled Ford aside while Lexi reached for the bouquets she'd kept in a cooler by the door.

The golden sunflowers, white daisies, and seeded eucalyptus contrasted the chiffon fabric of the yellow bridesmaid's dresses. The ruched tops were practically identical to Addie's strapless, sweetheart neckline, and the flirty skirts flared at the knees.

Addie's father and grandmother arrived, and while seeing Ford had sucked every ounce of joy out of the air for Violet, Lucia managed to bring the happy vibes.

The older woman completed a twirl. The yellow tulle of her ankle-length skirt flared to reveal her pair of matching Converse sneakers. A sunflower adorned the white lace top, and the sunflower crown on her head contrasted her white curls. "Where is my basket? I ready to throw petals at everybody!"

"On the aisle, you mean," Lexi said.

Lucia snatched the basket of petals, and Violet bit the inside of her cheek to keep from laughing at how adeptly she'd avoided agreeing.

The woman did whatever she wanted, and Violet respected her spirit. When they'd discussed her outfit, Lucia insisted on a flower girl dress, scoffing at the conservative styles her daughter-in-law had shown her. In the end, they'd asked Lottie to tailor one.

Considering the way Lucia beamed and twirled, Violet was of the opinion more people should wear whatever they wanted. Who'd decided only little girls could enjoy tulle skirts and flower crowns?

Violet's gaze snagged on Ford's, and anguish sledgehammered her chest.

Another hit like that and she feared her heart might cease beating altogether.

"It's time." Lexi shooed Lucia to the front and then hooked her arm through Will's. Violet settled her hand in the crook of Easton's elbow, thankful Ford had moved behind her, where her eyes couldn't as easily stray.

Mr. Murphy stepped up to the bride-to-be's other side, he and Ford each taking one of her arms.

This setup had been settled on to counteract the uneven numbers, even before Violet had taken Alexandria's place.

Still, the idea of being on the same aisle as Ford was excruciating.

Since her brain hated her, it drifted to the night when Ford had said he'd never play bridesmaid again, and she'd teasingly inquired *What if I asked?*

And he'd told her no, because it would mean she'd be marrying someone else and he could never watch her do that.

Stupid charming jerk, and even stupider me for thinking it was romantic at the time. Her idealized hopes and dreams had been exposed and on display, like the fool for love she'd always been.

In order to survive the rest of the evening, the walls around her heart needed to be reinforced. As in extra bricks, a layer of steel spikes, and a moat with a giant, man-eating alligator.

Think porcupine. Prickly, and if Ford dares to get close, I'll make sure he ends up with a face full of quills.

In a non-dramatic way, of course, since I refuse to be accused of ruining another person's wedding with my relationship fails.

I can do this, I can do this, I can do this…

Summoning every last drop of her willpower, Violet plastered on a crowd-pleasing smile and began her very last march down an aisle.

• • •

Razor-edged desperation seized Ford as he watched Violet head away from him on one of his best friend's arms.

While he had no one but himself to blame, it felt as though Easton had ripped her away, and the farther and farther she got, the stronger his sense of urgency became.

She was slipping through his fingers, and not just physically. He'd seen the hurt in her eyes, quickly replaced by scorn.

Last night, by the time they'd gotten Mr. Wagner settled at the hospital in Alexander City, it'd been nearly eleven. Then a nurse insisted Ford get the scrapes and cuts on his leg tended to, ignoring his many attempts at insisting he was fine.

By the time all was said and done, he got home at one thirty in the morning. Exhausted, he fell into bed without setting an alarm and woke late. After walking the dogs, he raced to Maisy's house to try to make things right.

Only Maisy had informed him Violet wasn't there and refused to tell him where he could find her. While he was sure he'd see her at the wedding, he'd wanted to fix things before the ceremony.

Her phone had gone straight to voicemail, though, and now he realized she'd been with Murph and Lexi, getting ready.

"You could've warned me about Violet being a bridesmaid," he whispered to Addie.

"I'm trying to avoid drama and not have a panic attack, okay? It was stressful enough that Alexandria ended up on bedrest, and I had to scramble to ensure everything went smoothly while worrying about her.

"But it's my wedding, and I don't have to explain anything to you. And trust me, this is the least violent of the options I considered after finding out you dumped Violet. How big of an idiot do you have to be to let someone like that get away?" Addie fired a stern expression his way. "And I say that with love."

He'd hate to hear it *without* the love part. "I know I fucked up."

"Damn right, you did."

Mr. Murphy peeked around from Addie's other side, his eyes wide. "Not to sound like my wife, but you two do realize we're a handful of minutes away from standin' in front of the preacher."

"I'm painfully aware," Addie said. Then she turned to Ford, her hand dropping from his arm to her hip. "Look, after this shindig, I'll have some more words for you. Right now, I'm fixin' to get hitched to my sexy best friend."

That was the reality check Ford needed to pull his head out of his ass. "And I'm doin' a shi—crappy job of being your dude of honor. I'm sorry. I'll shut up." He straightened and settled her hand in the crook of his elbow once again.

With everyone else in place at the front, Lucia was off and on her way.

She grabbed a handful of sunflower petals and flung them in a wide arch, one that unmistakably hit people on the edges of the walkway. She spun and flung and spread smiles to everyone around her, and Ford forced himself to focus on the wedding. On making sure Addie got every single thing she wanted today.

But then he had a thought, one that aroused his curiosity yet again, and he'd never been good at keeping his trap shut. "Here's another thing I probably shouldn't be asking about right now, but how'd you and Tuck smooth over your fight? The one about playing catch with your son?"

"Totally wrong moment, but I reckon we have another thirty seconds to kill. After I cooled down, Tucker came over and apologized. He told me that when he gave more thought to the idea of having kids, he realized our superior athletic genes would be passed on whether we have a son or a daughter."

The smile that curved her lips spoke volumes about how much she loved Tucker and the idea of having a family with him. "Then he added that when it came down to it, the only thing that mattered to him was that regardless of what our future held, the most important thing was we would be going through it together."

Addie leaned her head on Ford's shoulder. "I get to spend my life with Tucker Crawford. Once you find the right person, the other things you thought were so important fade away."

"Hear, hear," Mr. Murphy added from her other side, pride beaming from the man as he grinned at his daughter.

The music switched, signaling it was time to get this show on the road.

As promised, Ford did a quick check to ensure Addie's dress and hair were perfect, and then he started down the aisle. *Right foot, left foot*, Ford repeated in his head, forcing himself to walk slower than usual.

As they neared the end, he couldn't help himself anymore. Thanks to the lightbulb moment he'd had last night, he'd already been sure he was in love with Violet and didn't want to live without her.

As he gazed at her, the music, the decorations, everything but her faded into the background.

Throughout the ceremony, he couldn't help glancing at her here and there.

When Tucker and Addie read their vows, a glowing, raptured expression befell Violet's features, her watery smile stirring up emotions he didn't realize he had: joy, empathy, and so much adoration he thought he might drown in it.

Addie promised to give Tucker the benefit of the doubt; to wear his "ratty Saints cap" on the rare occasion; and to accompany him fishing on his hand-crafted boats.

Tucker vowed to only protect Addie when she asked, which he knew would be never because she was too stubborn. Then he told her she could protect him anytime.

"For a long time, the future scared me," Tucker said. "But then I returned to Uncertainty and became certain that as long as you, Addison Diana Murphy, were in my life, it'd be full of joy, love, and happiness."

As much as Ford hated to admit it, he'd gotten scared. He'd let other people—and his past—mess with his head.

Violet Abrams was his future, though. And as soon as the ceremony was over, he was going to do whatever it took to win her back.

CHAPTER THIRTY

The photographer had an older camera, a giant contraption that must've taken weight training prep to lug around. And although Violet wanted to make suggestions, she worked on being a good subject.

Taking pictures wasn't her job today.

Being the perfect bridesmaid was.

So she lifted her chin and stuck it out a few inches, shifted her weight onto her back leg, and popped her hip.

Not that it mattered, but Ford would see these pictures, so she'd put her best foot forward. Literally, since the photographer had them lift their skirts an inch or so as they stuck their sneakers together.

The dude of honor was on Addie's other side, and he lifted his pants leg as well, his much-larger sneaker joining theirs. While she'd been sad about the idea of Ford cutting his hair, it made his jawline stand out and highlighted lips she'd dreamed about too often to scrub them from her mind. Short hair, long hair, beard, or trimmed scruff—like he had now—he was illegal amounts of sexy.

"Perfect," the photographer said. "Now, let's get the entire wedding party."

They lined up, Lexi and Will next to Violet and Easton.

The photographer backpedaled, lowered her camera, and frowned, and Violet's instincts went on high alert for reasons she couldn't understand.

"Lexi and Will, you switch to the other side of the bride. Ford, you stand by…" The photographer pointed at Violet. "What was your name, sugar?"

In a trance, Violet stood helpless as she was sandwiched between Ford and Easton.

As soon as the flash went off, Ford placed a hand on her lower back. Sweet torture. Her skin hummed to life under his touch, and did he have to smell so incredible?

"I need to talk to you," he whispered.

Violet held the tenuous grip on her smile and spoke through her teeth. "If you make drama or force me to cause a scene at this wedding, I'll have to kill you. Then Lexi will kill you, and then Addie will revive you so she can kill you."

"I'm not tryin' to cause a scene. But I—"

"Just shut up and smile so we can get this over with."

"Eyes on me, everyone," the photographer chirped. *Click, click, click.*

Shift positions, pose, and do it again.

The photographer announced they were nearly done, and Violet gave a longing glance at the tables filling the reception area.

During most weddings, it was her feet begging her to take her seat. Thanks to the Chucks, her feet were sublimely comfortable, but if she didn't get a break from being plastered against Ford's side, she was going to have a mental breakdown.

With the last staged photo snapped, Violet strode toward the tables, but large fingers wrapped around her wrist.

"Ford, I swear," she said as she spun to face him.

She had half a mind to slug him in his devastatingly handsome face.

"Just promise that after the reception, we can talk."

"Do you promise not to say anything else to me until then?"

Hurt flickered across his face, and a pang struck her chest. How unfair was it that she couldn't stop caring?

"If that's what you want," Ford said, and she told him it was. His grip loosened, and she renewed her clipped pace, eyes on the chair Lexi had set up for her—as far away as possible from Ford.

A compromise had been struck over the dancing. Ford and Addie had their first slow dance as a couple, swaying in the center of the area for less than a minute before the DJ asked everyone to join them.

Easton glanced at Ford, and Violet's muscles tensed. "Don't you dare."

With a sigh, the cop escorted her onto the dance floor. His hand left her lower back to rub at his forehead. "It's just... I feel responsible. I'm the one who told Ford about your record."

She'd wondered how he'd found out, but when it came down to it, she couldn't arouse any anger for the conflicted dude in front of her. "It's okay. It happened, and I paid my dues. Ford's the one who decided it was worth dumping me."

"Yeah, but he's dealt with a lot of volatile women. And I guess I sorta thought you might be one of them. But then I talked to Addie and Lexi, and I judged you wrongly. Now I feel like I need to make it right."

"I'm leaving town tonight. There's nothing to be done. Please just let it go."

Easton didn't appear happy about it but dropped the subject.

After the dance with the parents, there were toasts and cake cutting and more photos and a myriad of greetings and well-wishes.

As the reception wound down, Violet sought out Addie and Lexi. "Congratulations again," she said as she hugged Addie.

"Thank you so much for stepping in. For everything."

Lexi came over and turned their embrace into a group hug. "Are you heading out?"

Violet nodded, her throat too tight to speak.

They said their last rounds of goodbyes, and then Violet snuck away from the bustling town center. She'd have felt guiltier about breaking her promise to Ford if he hadn't broken her heart.

She just couldn't say goodbye to him. It was better to make a clean break, although she doubted that was a thing that even existed.

Tears filled her eyes as she changed clothes and packed the last of her stuff. So silly, crying over leaving Uncertainty, Alabama, when having to visit used to move her to tears.

• • •

Ford searched the crowd as people lined up to wish Addie and Tucker goodbye. Where was Violet? It shouldn't be so hard to find a bright yellow dress.

After passing twice through the farewell line that'd formed, he darted inside the building. The rest of the gang was there, gathered in the lobby, but Violet was nowhere to be seen.

"Where's Violet?" he asked, and Addie—now dressed in her typical T-shirt and jeans—and Lexi glanced at each other. "What?"

"She's leaving town," Easton said. "Tonight."

"*Dude.* And you decided to wait to tell me why?"

"She seemed determined. I tried to take the blame, but she said there was nothing to be done and asked me to let it go."

"I don't accept that." The panic Ford felt before he'd gone full dumbass and ruined things with Violet paled in comparison to the hysteria suffocating his body now. "I love her."

Shock transferred from face to face.

"Tell me what to do. I'm throwing myself on your mercy, begging you to tell me what to do." His gaze homed in on the bags in Tucker and Addie's hands. "Shit. Here I am, ruining your day again. You guys go. These guys got me." Ford turned to Lexi, Shep, and Easton. "You guys got me, right?"

"We've got him," Lexi said.

Ford gave Tucker a quick bro hug, then pulled Addie into his arms and squeezed her tight. "Enjoy your honeymoon. Love you."

It wasn't something he normally said, but he'd decided to learn from his mistakes.

"We don't fly out until tomorrow morning, so send me a text letting me know how it goes with Violet." Addie pressed a quick kiss to his cheek. "I believe in you, McGuire. Always have, always will."

A lump took up residence in his throat, and he managed to choke out a mangled goodbye.

Hand in hand, Tucker and Addie rushed out the

door and down the pathway the townsfolk had formed.

As soon as they'd climbed into Tucker's decorated truck, Ford turned to the rest of his friends. "I've got an idea, but I need help, and we've got to work fast."

CHAPTER THIRTY-ONE

Hug number three was too short, so Violet went in for hug number four, embracing Maisy once more.

Violet gave Isla's cheek one last kiss, and then she forced herself to climb into her car and fire up the engine.

While she'd already been crying, the instant she turned onto Main Street, the tears flowed. Part of her heart would always remain in Uncertainty with Maisy, Isla, the friends she'd made, and the rest of the ragtag mix of people who made up the small town.

And okay, a piece would always belong to Ford McGuire.

Even though things didn't work out, she wished him well as she reached the bend that would take her away from him forever.

Red and blue lights flashed behind her, and she swore. Then she checked her speedometer and discovered she was well within range.

Do I have a taillight out?

If so, she would promise to fix it, and that'd be that. To keep her in town for a few extra minutes over something so trivial seemed cruel.

However, she wasn't the deviant her record made her seem, so she pulled to the side of the road and reached into her glovebox for her insurance and registration.

Muggy night air filtered into her car as she rolled down her window. Once she got a look at the cop, though, her irritation intensified. "Are you serious?"

Easton folded his arms across the open window. The suspenders were gone, as was the tie, leaving him in a plain white shirt, the top couple of buttons undone, and his gray slacks. "Afraid I can't let you leave town, ma'am. I need you to step out of the car and come with me."

"You're not even wearing your police uniform."

"I've still got my badge." He held it up as if that changed everything. Then he opened the door and gestured for her to climb out of the car. "I've been ordered to bring you to the town center."

Instead of following his instructions, she crossed her arms. "No."

"What are you gonna do? Call a lawyer?"

"Maybe."

"That'd require you having one, and I know you don't."

"Yes I do," she said, narrowing her eyes. "It's… Tucker."

Easton rolled his lips until his mouth formed a tight line. "You want me to call the man twenty minutes into his honeymoon?"

Everything inside of Violet deflated. "No."

"That's what I thought. Now if you'll please come with me, we'll have this matter resolved shortly."

With a growl, Violet unbuckled her seat belt, grabbed her purse and phone, and stepped onto the road. "I hate this town."

"Noted," Easton said, his calm demeanor tempting her to add smacking a police officer to her record. She stomp-walked to the cruiser. He nudged her around the hood and opened the passenger door instead of having her sit in the back, as if that'd lessen her brewing anger.

Violet recrossed her arms as Easton settled behind the wheel of the cruiser. "This is an egregious use of your power."

"Egregious. Gonna add that to my vocabulary." Easton spun the car around and headed into the heart of town. "It's not that I disagree, but you did make a promise to talk to my boy that you didn't keep."

Steam practically poured from her ears, and she gave up talking, since nothing about this situation involved logic.

Within a handful of minutes, Violet was right back in the middle of town. Most of the wedding decorations were being put away, but there was still one bright spot.

The gazebo.

Only purple lights had been strung along with the white lights.

And was that Ford standing in the middle?

Easton parked as close to the gazebo as the street allowed, then rounded the hood and opened her door.

The turmoil churning through her left her body frozen in place, unsure if she could handle whatever this was. She'd been strong all day. She was supposed to be alone in her car right now, crying over what could've been, and curse Ford and Easton for not letting it be.

"If after he says his piece, you decide to still leave town," Easton said, "I'll get you out of here in record time."

"Fine." Violet climbed out of the car. Each step required three times as much effort as usual. Her feet grew even heavier when she noticed the purple bouquets placed around the gazebo.

So much purple it almost looked like... Well, like

it'd been pulled from the pages of her sparkly binder.

A bark cut through the silence, and Trouble rushed toward her as fast as his doggy feet could take him. A giant purple ribbon and bow circled his neck, and in spite of her trepidation, Violet squatted and petted her puppy.

She scooped him up and buried her nose in his fur, and her heart didn't know whether to expand or knot, and she loved him so much her body could hardly contain it. "Using Trouble against me?" she said in Ford's direction, unable to fully look at him. "That's a new low, even for you."

"I deserve that." Ford took a step toward her—was he limping? "I'm not using him against you, though. He's a gift. If you want him."

Her tears blurred Ford's features—not enough to weaken the effect they had on her, unfortunately. "Of course I want him."

"And me?" Ford asked. The question came out gravelly and raw, and the strings inside her heart tugged and tugged until all that was left was an unraveled clump.

Tears slipped down her cheeks in warm trails, and Ford closed the distance between them.

"Violet, I screwed up. You were right when you told me that the marriage and kid talk were my issues, not yours."

She opened her mouth, and he pressed his finger to her lips.

"I've been rehearsing while scrambling to pull this whole thing together, and I know it's not as fancy as the pictures in your binder, but with you leaving, I couldn't risk spending any more time on it. I did convince Nellie

Mae to open the flower shop and cleared her out of every single purple flower she had."

Ford plucked a purple anemone out of the vase nearest him and slid it behind her ear.

Violet held tight to Trouble, who launched himself off her boob and attacked the flower.

"Thanks for that, buddy," Ford said with a laugh. "I've realized a lot of things this past week. For instance"—his green eyes locked onto hers as he took her hand—"even though I like to play hero, I'm a coward. You're the heroic one, putting yourself out there and not making excuses about who you are or what you want. I let my fears get the best of me, and in the process, I lost you.

"For some reason, I thought if I settled down, my adventures would come to an end. But last night, as I was rappelling down to an injured hiker—"

"Is that why you're limping? Are you hurt?" Violet set Trouble on the bench and squatted to peek at Ford's leg. She lifted the slacks and gasped at the giant scrape crisscrossing his shin.

Ford crouched as well, placing his fingers under her chin and gently tipping her face to his. "There's my distracted angel," he said with a smile. "The cuts and bruises I can handle. But losing you..." Ford's voice turned husky, and his thumb brushed her jaw. "That's an injury I'll never recover from. It took me way too long to realize it, but if you give me another chance, I'll spend the rest of my life making it up to you."

Violet's heartbeats tripped over each other, and her breath lodged in her throat. "The rest of your life? You know what that phrase means, right? That it could be decades?"

One corner of his mouth kicked up in that way that she adored. "It doesn't scare me anymore. I *want* to be with you, Violet."

Ford dropped fully onto his knees. "I'm down here *begging* you to give me another chance. I want all my adventures to include you. Because I've fallen completely in love with you."

Her eyes widened, and her mouth fell open. Did he just…?

"That's right." He took both of her hands in his. "I love you, Violet Abrams. I don't want to move too fast and ruin everything or scare you, but if you take my sorry ass back, I promise you that I'll be in this for the long haul. That I choose you, and I'll show up, and I'll continue to choose you forever.

"And not someday—*but one day*—I wanna marry you and have kids with you. It doesn't scare me anymore. The only thing that scares me is losing you."

Another wave of tears hit her, and she couldn't withhold the sniff.

Trouble jumped onto her lap and licked at the saltwater trails, a whimper coming out.

"I'm okay," she whispered to the puppy. Then she glanced around the gazebo at all the work Ford had done in such a short time.

The flowers and the lights and Ford down on his knees, his declaration about loving her hanging in the air. It was a dream she'd given up on, and yet here it was, coming true. "You realize I'd have to be a fool to accept this apology and stay in town, right?"

Ford swallowed thickly, the hope shining in his features fading as he hung his head. "I know. But I had to try."

Violet placed her hand on the side of his face, studying the man she loved with her entire heart and soul. "Lucky for you—and as you've implied several times since we met that day over a fiery oven—I happen to be a bit bonkers, especially when it comes to you."

His head jerked up, the happiness flooding the curve of his smile transferring joy to her, too. "Are you saying…?"

"I love you, too."

Ford crashed his lips to hers. He hauled her onto his lap, hugging her to his chest as if he were afraid she'd float away if he let go. "I need you to say it. Tell me that you'll stay."

"I'll stay," she said.

A laugh spilled out, and he peppered her cheeks and mouth with kisses before grinning at her. "And I promise I'll never be an idiot again."

Violet arched a dubious eyebrow.

"About us, anyway," he added with a low laugh.

This time, she initiated the kiss, flinging her arms around his neck and moving her mouth against his.

At the sound of cheers and whistles, Ford stood, hauling Violet to her feet with him. Easton, Will, and Lexi came out of the shadows, and Violet laughed again.

She buried her head in Ford's chest, too blissfully happy to care about the embarrassment heating her cheeks.

"Real quick, we have to take a picture and let Addie and Tucker know we're back together." Ford extended his phone for a selfie, and Violet pressed her lips to his as he snapped the picture.

"Better loop Maisy in, too," Violet said, rattling off her sister's phone number.

Later, there'd be details to iron out and calls to make. But for now, she basked in the fact that right when she'd given up on love, it'd decided not to give up on her.

EPILOGUE

Violet: *Hey, would any of you gals happen to be available for bridesmaid duty? Like possibly May or June?*

    Leah: *Wait. Are you saying?*

    Amanda: *Ford popped the question?!!!!! Girl, I need details!*

    Camilla: *That sucker didn't stand a chance once he met you.*

    Alyssa: *Congrats! I'm so happy for you!*

    Morgan: *OMG!!! I'm sure you're all shocked I'm responding—lol. But since the triplets, Mark and I are outnumbered. I almost had a breakdown today, so he sent me for a pedicure, and with this news, it's the best day ever! So happy for you, Vi.*

    Leah: *And you know that we'll be there for you, the same way you were there for us.*

    Amanda: *But remember that one of us—cough, me— just had my second baby and will need a flattering dress to hold everything in place.*

    Alyssa: *LOL! And you keep asking why I haven't had another yet. Between you and Morgan, I'm scared. Although Jeff is definitely team procreate more. I think that's mostly because it involves sex, though.*

Violet grinned, signed off, and slipped her phone into her pocket. She tucked ketchup under one armpit, mustard under the other, and then scooped up the potato chips and bags of buns. Ever so carefully, she balanced everything and headed out the back door.

There was her sexy fiancé, swinging her niece

through the air. Isla giggled and clapped, already eager to go "again," which was her favorite word besides "no." The scent of roasting hot dogs and burgers filled the air, and Maisy stepped up to relieve Violet of the condiments.

They set the items on the picnic table Violet bought for Ford's backyard—well, hers, too. She'd moved in early last week, and they were celebrating with a barbecue with their family and friends.

The entire gang was here, and while Violet had considered them Ford's friends in the beginning, they were hers now as well. Everyone was spread around the grass on camping chairs, and she soaked in the happy vibes, excitement tickling her stomach as she prepared for her and Ford's big announcement.

She walked over to Ford and Isla and tickled her niece's neck. Isla giggled and dropped her head on Ford's shoulder as if she expected him to save her.

Which he would. Same way he'd saved a lot of people in town, including her.

Violet thought her ovaries had caused a ruckus the first time she'd seen Ford holding Isla, but it was nothing compared to watching him play with her. Half the time when they visited Maisy and Travis, Ford would forget to say hi to them because he rushed to pick up Isla.

Trouble bounced around Violet's ankles, and Isla insisted she be put down. She crawled after his doggy tail while he chased her bare feet, and round and round in a circle they went.

Travis recorded the adorableness on his phone, and Maisy looked on, a giant grin on her face. While Violet would miss what'd seemed like a six-month sleepover at Maisy's, it was time for a new phase.

With Travis home, her sister had the support she needed. It also helped that Isla had begun sleeping through the night.

Ford wrapped his arms around Violet's middle and pulled her back against his chest. As she basked in the chatter and laughter of their closest loved ones, all felt right with the world.

"FYI, I might never let you go." Ford kissed her neck, sending goose bumps across her skin. Every tiny gesture, every day, every *everything* was better with Ford in her world. Not only had he kept his word to always show up and be there for her, last night he'd fulfilled another one of his promises.

One day…

Violet had been snuggling with Trouble and felt something whack her chest. When she'd spotted the diamond ring hanging from his collar, her heart had stopped.

Then she'd turned to see Ford on one knee, Pyro at his side, and that kicked her heart back into motion. Occasionally she still felt the lack of Nitro and Tank, but in a few months they'd have another litter to train. The teams the dogs had gone to also sent updates, which helped her feel like their little family was off to a strong, happy start.

Ford cleared his throat and raised his voice. "Violet and I would like to welcome y'all to our home."

Violet let the phrase "our home" wash over her.

"We do have another announcement," he said, and then he glanced at her.

The diamond on her finger twinkled as she lifted it in the air to show it off. "We're getting married!"

Everyone shouted their congratulations. There

were hugs and jokes, and then they settled in their chairs to eat, because food went hand in hand with celebration.

As they finished up the meal, Ford nudged Easton with his elbow. "So, I was hoping you'd be my best man."

"Dude, I'm starting to think we throw weddings as often as we play poker. My boys are dropping like flies." Easton winked at Violet and then punched Ford's shoulder. "I'd be honored."

Lexi shifted in her seat, leaning so she could peer around Will at them. "Have you started planning the wedding yet?"

"I'm pretty sure Violet has like a…binder, wasn't it? A super-organized, serial-killer-type one, but for weddings? Isn't that right, sweetheart?"

Violet cocked her head at her fiancé. Yeah, she was going to be using that term a lot.

"Only kidding." Ford wrapped his hand around her thigh and leaned in for a kiss. "You know I love your binder almost as much as you. And not just because it means less work for me this go around."

"Dream. On." Violet spun in her seat to address Lexi. "While I do have certain aspects planned, I'd love your help."

Lexi clapped and bounced in her seat. "Ooh, I love weddings."

Everyone began laughing and talking again, and when they needed more beer, Violet headed to the kitchen to grab some.

Apparently, Easton was way ahead of her. He stood in front of the fridge, six-pack in hand, but his focus was on the wedding invitation she'd hung in place with a magnet.

"When did you get this?" Easton asked, gesturing toward the invite.

"I just hung it up this morning. It was in the mail, and I figured it was one of Ford's friends. Since the sure way to get him to see something is to put it on the fridge…" She laughed, but the tension in Easton's posture remained.

She'd never seen him so broody before.

"Vi? You get lost on the way to the fridge?" Ford's heavy footsteps came on the heels of the question. "Don't worry, your big strong badass is here to save you."

As soon as Ford stepped into the kitchen, Easton yanked off the invitation and showed it to Ford. "Did you know about this?"

Ford squinted at it, two creases forming between his eyebrows, and then his features smoothed as he studied the pictures. "No. Bro, I'm so sorry."

"Whatever. I… I'm going to go." Easton handed the six-pack to Ford, crumpled the invitation, and tossed it on the counter. Then he stormed out of the house, the screen door slamming in his wake.

"What was that all about?" Violet asked, debating whether or not to follow the guy, although she hadn't the faintest idea what to say.

"This woman." Ford tapped the crinkled picture, and Violet studied the beautiful couple. He wound an arm around her, his large hand splaying on her stomach and making her think of the day that'd come when he was feeling their little one growing inside of her, and he said, "As far as Easton's concerned, she's the one who got away."

ACKNOWLEDGMENTS

Usually I end up thanking my family near the bottom, but after one of the hardest years we've ever had, I need to tell them how much I love and appreciate them. They make me laugh, they boost me up, and everyone pitches in when I get down to the deadline wire. They are the reason I get out of bed every day. (Well, them and the cats, who follow up their cuddles with demands for food.)

At this point, I don't even have words for the amount of love I have for Rebecca Yarros and Gina L. Maxwell. From our daily running chats to our writing sprints to our late-night phone calls and everything in between. #UHT4EVER.

Thanks to Stacy Abrams, Liz Pelletier, and the entire team at Entangled. Again, this year was extremely difficult for me, and I know that things came down to the wire, so thank you for having my back when I needed to take care of my family and myself. Thanks to Riki Cleveland, the marketing team, Jessica Turner, Katie Clapsadl, Heather Riccio, and everyone else who helps my book get into readers' hands.

Did I mention it's been a year? Well, thank goodness I had my rock-star agent, Nicole Resciniti, by my side to help me maneuver the twists of not only this industry but my life. Thank you for the phone calls and the assurances and for the emotional support. I can't thank you enough for all you've done for me.

Miranda Grissom, I was drowning in to-do list items, and you swooped in and took several of them off my plate. Big hugs!

Huge thanks to my readers for supporting my books and sending me messages that keep me going. And thank YOU, dear reader! Whether this is the first book of mine you've read or if you've read several, I appreciate every time a reader gives one of my novels a chance. And of course I'm extra grateful for repeat offenders. XOXO

Smoke jumpers and a steamy romance collide in this new romantic comedy series from USA TODAY *bestselling author Tawna Fenske.*

the two-date rule

Willa Frank has one simple rule: never go on a date with anyone more than twice. Now that her business is providing the stability she's always needed, she can't afford distractions. Her two-date rule will protect her just fine…until she meets smokejumper Grady Billman.

After one date—one amazing, unforgettable date—Grady isn't ready to call it quits, despite his own no-attachments policy, and he's found a sneaky way around both their rules.

Throwing gutter balls with pitchers of beer? Not a real date. Everyone knows bowling doesn't count.

Watching a band play at a local show? They just happen to have the same great taste in music. Definitely not a date.

Hiking? Nope. How can exercise be considered a date?

With every "non-date" Grady suggests, his reasoning gets more ridiculous, and Willa must admit she's having fun playing along. But when their time together costs Willa two critical clients, it's clear she needs to focus on the only thing that matters—her future. And really, he should do the same.

But what is she supposed to do with a future that looks gray without Grady in it?

Fans of Debbie Macomber and Robyn Carr will fall for this sweet, heartfelt novel that celebrates family in all its forms.

Accidentally Family
SASHA SUMMERS

Life for Felicity, and her teen children, is finally back on track. After her divorce, she wasn't sure if her sweet family would ever be the same. But things are good—right up until her ex's spirited toddler lands on Felicity's doorstep. If the universe is going to throw lemons at her, thank God she has her best friend, Graham, to help her make lemonade out of them. How did she never notice how kind and sexy he is?

Graham is still recovering from his wife's death years ago and trying to help his teen daughter get her life together. Who is he kidding? His daughter hates him. Forget lemons—he's got the entire lemon tree. So when Felicity suggests they join forces and help each other, he's all in. And suddenly he can't stop thinking about her as more than just friends. Too bad their timing couldn't be worse…

Because life rarely goes as planned. Luckily there are many different kinds of family to hold you together and lift you up…plus maybe even a little love between friends.

When a shy woman inherits a ranch, she'll have to find an inner strength to succeed—and open herself up to love—in this heartwarming novel from New York Times *bestselling author Victoria James.*

Cowboy for Hire

Sarah Turner has led a very sheltered life. So when her parents pass away tragically, suddenly she's left in charge of the family ranch with little know-how but plenty of will to keep it afloat. Determined not to lose her parents' legacy or her newfound independence, she needs a hero fast—not to save her, but to show her how to save herself. But she's unprepared for the ruggedly handsome cowboy who answers her ad.

"Cowboy for Hire," the ad said, and Cade Walker is quick to respond. Betrayed as ranch manager by his former boss, he's looking for a new place to put down roots—without the pressure to prove himself again. Except when he meets his new boss, it's clear he's not only there to run a ranch but to also teach Miss Independent how to run it. But as they struggle to make the ranch flourish, they'll both need courage if they hope to find a family...together.

AMARA

an imprint of Entangled Publishing LLC